(3)

Vacation of a Lifetime

a novel by

Brenda Sue

Vacation of a Lifetime
Copyright ©2015 Brenda Sue

ISBN 978-1622-877-99-7 HC
ISBN 978-1622-877-98-0 PRINT
ISBN 978-1622-877-97-3 EBOOK

LCCN 2014959068

May 2015

Published and Distributed by
First Edition Design Publishing, Inc.
P.O. Box 20217, Sarasota, FL 34276-3217
www.firsteditiondesignpublishing.com

A special thank you to my special friend and editor, Jeannie Collins, thank you! Without your guidance and help I know that "Vacation of a Lifetime" wouldn't be as good as it is.

This book is dedicated to my first cousin, Wendy, who gave me the inspiration to openly talk about Lung Cancer and her battle with this terrible disease.

To Harvey: You are my inspiration and I know that I can always count on you to help me in every way possible.

A special thank you to David Wang and his team from Tepson Translation. You helped me in understanding many Chinese names and the meaning of each.

Sean Bogaard was instrumental in helping me with the nautical terms and the layout of the sailing ship. THANKS!

Other fiction books by Brenda Sue

Web of Deceit

Beyond Murder

Vacation of a Lifetime

Non-fiction book

Jack and Jill, not an easy climb!!!

I am in the midst of doing research for my next novel, (Murder at Millers' River) which will be about murder and re-incarnation. I know that you'll enjoy this new book and will love some of the new people that will join the cast of characters that keep coming back into your lives.

CHAPTER ONE

Do not think you are obliged to repent only for transgressions involving acts, such as stealing, robbing, and sexual immorality. Just as we must repent such acts, so must we examine our evil feelings and repent our anger, our jealousy, our mocking thoughts, our excessive ambition and greed. We must repent all these. Therefore it is written: "Let the wicked forsake their ways, the unrighteous their thoughts (Isaiah 55.7)

Maimonides, 12th Century

Suzanne and Nancy were blindfolded, their hands cuffed behind their backs, as they heard yelling, screaming and fighting above them. They were surprised by four pirates invading their boat. They didn't know who fired the guns, and they heard something being thrown overboard. Suddenly they were hoisted from the crew's bunks to their feet and their blindfolds removed.

The bearded, filthy and gruff men slapped them with open palms on their newly re-constructed faces. The leader of the group put a knife to Nancy's throat. "The other members of your party are upstairs. They're not in good shape." His cohorts chuckled at his remark. "The captain and crew are overboard, being fed to the sharks." The laughter of the leader's men seemed to fill the entire lower deck. "If you don't want the same happening to you, tell us where your money is and we'll let you go peacefully."

"We already collected your friends' money. Where is your stash hidden?" Suzanne read many brochures and magazines on the subject of new age pirates and didn't want any more harm done to herself or Nancy. Leading the bandits to their suite they showed them where the money was located. After greedily taking their vacation funds the men ran up the stairs. Suzanne heard additional firing of semi-automatic guns and glass shattering. The men ran down to their small ladder that they used to board the sailboat.

They heard the engine of the skiff turn around, their motor driving these men away from the crippled yacht. Running up the stairs the first thing they saw was that all the windows were shot out, the communications equipment broken and unusable to radio for help. They ran to the other passengers who had become dear friends. The women were crying and the men trying to comfort them. Someone cried, "They took our motor, valuable electronic equipment and all the essential apparatus that we needed to get us to safety."

Suzanne felt herself thrashing, her bed covers thrown onto the floor. She envisioned herself wet with seawater. Perspiration was running down her entire body. She suddenly sat up realizing that this was a nightmare. She didn't know why she dreamt that horrible dream. She realized that she often had a sixth sense but knew she would never find herself on a sailboat, ever!

MASSACHUSETTS

Suzanne and Nancy were finally on the mend from the terrible ordeal they had in Japan. It had taken a while for their many operations and the physical therapy sessions to work. Through diligence and determination they started seeing a definite improvement in their bodies. The pain (usually lived with day by day) started decreasing. During the day it was easier for Suzanne to perform her work on clients. She found it easy to accomplish regular tasks around the house, the laundry, cooking and straightening up her home. She was happy to see the therapy sessions end. The idea of working out appealed to her. Suzanne signed both herself and Nancy up at a local gym in Boston to work out on a regular basis.

At first Nancy balked at the idea but after Suzanne enlightened Nancy on the merits of physical fitness, Nancy decided to give it a try. They made a definite time to meet (four days a week) at the fitness center in downtown Boston. It was easier for Suzanne to work out before starting her busy schedule. In that way she could shower at the facility rather than do it at home before leaving for work. At the gym, they talked her into hiring a personal trainer for her and Nancy. At first she resisted the idea but, after thinking it over, realized it would be beneficial to them both.

Nancy found having a definite schedule easier for her during the day. If she started out on an upbeat note, it was uncomplicated to follow through on any agenda she wished. The partners found that they liked the physical challenge presented to them.

Suzanne's children teased their mother endlessly about her new regime. It was so unlike Suzanne to be so organized. Sometimes, during their workout sessions, Nancy and Suzanne felt the pain that they endured during their confinement in the hospital. The many injuries they sustained (courtesy of the Yakuza in the last mission) were the closest encounter to death the two women had experienced.

Their triumph for justice against the evil ways of people and deliberate criminal aspects sometimes erupted with definite sore and aching muscles. The multiple wounds were healed, at least on the outside. In their hearts and souls it was difficult for the two women to go along with their everyday, mundane assignments when they knew that evil was still lurking all around them.

As hard as they tried to ignore the call for justice, some days it was difficult to ignore life as it really was. Although many people thought that the world was fine, Suzanne and Nancy realized that most people were delusional. They didn't discuss their feelings openly to each other or to others or admitted their inner feelings to themselves. The concern and empathy for people or circumstances just stayed inside their hearts.

Suzanne's daughters, Hope, Melanie and Taylor were glad to have Suzanne and Nancy out of the hospital; home once again and on the mend. They came very close to losing their mother and never wanted to experience anything like that again. It was a traumatic experience for all. Nancy, who was like a beloved aunt to them, almost died in the mayhem and they wanted to show their admiration for the two wonderful, courageous women in their lives. If they didn't show their appreciation for how hard Suzanne worked when they were youngsters in order to give them a beautiful home, they wanted to show it now. They realized how dedicated a mother she was. She never wanted them to suffer because she was a divorced woman bringing up her children by herself. Yes, it was easier once Mrs. Walsh entered their lives, but Suzanne was the breadwinner.

The girls made a date to get together to discuss the events that occurred. They didn't want to include other members of the family, just themselves. They all had a lovely dinner at Hope's house and after the dishes were put away, they made themselves drinks and sat around the comfortable yet lavish furniture in Hope's new living room. Taylor, sitting Indian Style on the silk, blue, flowered sofa made Hope's skin crawl. She didn't want to come across as a bitch, but was furious that Taylor had no regard for her interior-designed living room set. Clearing her throat, she asked Taylor nicely to kindly uncross her legs and sit down like a lady. Taylor was offended by her sister's rude remark and reluctantly uncrossed her legs.

"Okay, let's get down to business! I don't mean the family business. I want to suggest something totally out of character for us and Mom. Of course, anything that we do for Mom must include Nancy. We know Mom wouldn't want it any other way. We all realize what they went through this past year. They went through Hell and back. Yes, we realize that, in a way, their situation was one that they created themselves. We have to forget what happened, and be thankful that

they're alive, well, and, at times, can be a pain in the ass to each and every one of us." They lifted their glasses at the same time and said: "Cheers to that!!"

"Okay, what did that mean and why did we have to get together tonight for this sentimentality?" Taylor asked. "Well, speaking for myself," Melanie piped in, "I felt we should do something to show our appreciation for our mother and, of course, Nancy."

"How do you, or should I say we, intend to do that?" Hope inquired. "We all know that Mom and Nancy are on a new kick, physical fitness. Now that's all well and good, but knowing Mom as well as we do, and I'm sure that you feel the same," she addressed her sisters, "I think we should show our appreciation that's a little above and beyond the realm for the two of them," Melanie stated.

"So just exactly what do you think we should do, Mel?" Hope asked. "I've been thinking and thinking what is different that they haven't done. Let's not forget they have enough money to do anything they want to do. But wouldn't it be nice to do something totally different that they'd never think of doing for themselves?" Melanie looked at her sisters, waiting for an answer.

The girls sat in their chairs, looked at each other, not saying a word, thought to them-selves and came up empty; they all looked to Melanie for a suggestion. "Okay, I see that no one has any ideas on the matter at hand. I've been racking my brains out and I have an idea that I'd like you to consider." She looked at her sisters and took a deep breath. "Go on Mel, what's your bright idea?" Taylor inquired.

"Well, we know that Mom and Nancy don't swim. For some crazy reason they never seemed to get the hang of it or just didn't care enough about it." Melanie stated. "Duh, no kidding Dick Tracy," Hope sarcastically voiced her frustration. "So what does that have to do with the vacation?" Hope asked. With a smile from ear to ear as she thought of the idea Melanie blurted: "Let's have them go on a special vacation on a large private sailboat. I've looked into it and researched this idea for over a month. The sailboat I'm thinking of is approximately 108' or a little more and carries about five to six couples, plus crew. It usually goes out for a four-week cruise."

The sisters were dumbfounded. They all took a large swallow of their drinks and with mouths wide open, looked from one to the other, shaking their heads. "I don't believe what I just heard come out of your mouth, Mel," Hope spoke. "Of all the crazy ideas, I think this one takes the cake." Melanie, taken aback by her sister's reply, looked at Taylor for some support. Clearing her throat, Taylor piped in: "If you ask me, Hope, I think that Mel has come up with an ingenious idea. What else could they do that they haven't done before? As far as I'm concerned, I'd love to find out more about this sailing adventure and find some research that I could look at for myself."

"If you look on the web sites of sailing vessels and vacations, you'll find lots of different schooners that do this type of vacation all the time. They have gourmet cooks and crewmembers on board who man the vessel. Of course all the people on board have to have lessons about sailing and what to do in case of an emergency but believe me, there usually aren't accidents aboard these sailboats. It's just a precautionary measure," Melanie affirmed.

"Okay," declared Taylor, "that will be my assignment for our next meeting, if that's all right with you Hope?"

"I really don't have much of a choice. I'll let the two of you do all the research and I'll go along with anything you say. But have you even thought about if our mother and Nancy will go along with this crazy idea? I'm sure Spencer won't mind pitching in money; he really likes Mom. So let's pick a date and time and I'll make sure that Spencer joins us. Is that all right with the two of you?"

"You don't even have to ask such an absurd question. When you married Spencer he automatically became our brother." The girls decided that they'd meet in three weeks. "Before we leave, try to think where we should send them on this vacation," Taylor interjected.

Melanie piped in, "Don't forget that we have to find out if Nancy and Rich have made plans for an upcoming wedding. We don't want this vacation interfering with any up-coming nuptials they might be making. As far as Mom is concerned, we know that her love life is as crazy as ever. Between Stephen and Lawrence, we're never aware of her arrangements. We'll let her figure out what to do once a definite date is made." The girls nodded their heads in agreement.

CHICAGO, ILLINOIS

As always, it was a windy evening in the big city of Chicago. The branches of the trees were bending and the leaves were dropping onto the ground as Sandy and Arthur Swartz's children were meeting for dinner at The Grill on the Alley, a fine dining restaurant at The Weston on Michigan Ave. As each couple entered the spacious lobby of the hotel, they were overcome by the soothing music and the magnificent scents from white tea to the visual beauty of the floral arrangements and botanicals by Jane Packer's vivid imagination. The eldest of the five siblings, Veronica and her husband, Tim Owens, were the first to arrive. They gave their name to the Maître' D and were seated at the large round table reserved for ten. After giving their order for the drinks of their preference, they waited anxiously for the other guests to arrive.

The conversation was strained but amicable as they drank their favorite wine when it was presented to them. Veronica and Tim's eldest son was presently in a rehabilitation center for drug abuse. It was a difficult decision for them to make, but they were forced to by Jason's actions over the past two years. It was a tough day when they drove Jason to the center. After years of being enablers, they came to the hard conclusion that there was nothing else that they could do. After many late hour discussions, they finally called the New Beginning Clinic in the outskirts of Chicago. It was a sad, but hopeful day when they signed the papers of consent for Jason to be a patient for at least a period of three months.

After a few sips of wine they looked into each other's moist eyes. Their inner thoughts had nothing to do with the subject of tonight's meeting. "It doesn't seem possible that our life is in the turmoil it's in. Who would have thought that Jason's life could be so screwed up as many other children's around the country? We are good parents; we've done our best for Jason and Courtney since they were born. You've come far and are respected in your job and now you're a Manager for the lumber departments at Home Depot; I'm the assistant to the vice president of Secor Inc. We've come a long way since the young kids of 18 who had to get married in our first year of college." Laughing, Veronica continued, "So we're college drop outs. I think we've done pretty well for ourselves." Tim smiled at his beautiful wife who he still adored. "Things will turn out fine, I'm sure of it. Jason is young, and I think that's a plus for him. We're caring parents who want the best for our children," Tim voiced his opinion to Veronica.

"I still try to analyze how Jason got mixed up with these kids who are into the drug scene. I always thought I knew who his best friends were and where he was at all times. We should have seen the obvious signs that he was acting differently. Don't you think I blame myself for not noticing his changing personality?" Shaking her head, she put her elbows on the table and put her head between her hands. "I love you so much, you have no idea." She told Tim as he looked lovingly yet confused on what there was to be said. "I don't know; I'm just as baffled as you are." He put out his hand and Veronica put her delicate one into his. "I don't want you to blame yourself for this nightmare. I should have done or seen something out of the norm. We could have gone to his school and found out why his grades went down from A's to C and C-s to failing in his classes. We blamed it on the sports he was involved in. When it was too late, we realized that he hadn't attended many of his team sessions." They sat there, with not another word spoken. As they were sitting, disoriented thoughts between them, Veronica spotted her sister Victoria and her husband Mike approaching the table.

"Hi, glad to see you're almost on time," Veronica jokingly said as Victoria and Mike sat down. "I just spoke to Vinny and he said that everyone else should be here momentarily," Victoria announced to her sister and brother-in-law. Looking for a waiter, and spotting one, Mike ordered drinks for himself and Victoria. Talking amongst themselves, they kept the conversation light. Victoria knew of her sister's situation at home and didn't want to bring up unpleasant dialogue. The two couples spotted the rest of the clan and were glad that everyone was punctual.

After looking over the wine list, a few bottles of wine were ordered for the table. They talked about the menu and what everyone was ordering. The family kept the chatter light, and Glen, Violet's husband, told some funny jokes to the immediate family of Sandy and Arthur Swartz. After enjoying the excellent meal and desserts, the family talked about the reason for the gathering. "As the eldest of our group I think I should tell you what my idea is for Mom and Dad's fiftieth anniversary present. Now this suggestion isn't written in gold, so I want all of your input and plans that you can come up with for their special occasion."

"Excuse me," interrupted Veronica, "but am I a nut or have I lost five years in the making. It's their forty-fifth wedding anniversary coming up. But that's not the point; let's pretend it's their fiftieth."

"I don't want to mention that these last two years have been Hell for all of us, most of all for our parents," Violet softly added.

The assemblage was at a loss for words. They kept looking at one another, and then Vinny spoke. "I don't know about the rest of you, but isn't it traditional to throw them a huge party with all the relatives and friends? They can redo their marriage vows and everyone will have a great time." In unison they all shook their heads in agreement. "I came up with an unusual and terrific idea. I mean, everyone expects a party for their big anniversary. Do you think that Mom and Dad will be surprised? No," Veronica continued, "they'd expect us to throw them this large, elaborate party. That's a great idea, but let's give them something that they wouldn't do for themselves. They've been great parents and have never been on a real vacation, just the two of them. With all the bills they had from giving us lessons, orthodontic work, everyday expenses and then the big one, college educations, it was impossible to do or go anywhere that they'd like. Don't forget that Mom and Dad gave us money for our wedding plus paid for Vinny and Gloria's honeymoon." Everyone was quiet, except for the conversations from the other patrons in the restaurant. "Okay, what is your suggestion?" Violet piped in.

"Well, a friend of mine in the office told me about this wonderful experience she'd had. She came back and didn't stop talking about this sailing voyage that

she and her husband took. As she put it: *'it was a special event that they'll always treasure.'* Now something like that is a memorable experience." They all sat there with their mouths open. The wine was consumed and they were speechless. "Would they enjoy something like that?" Vinny asked. Vivian, who'd been quiet through the evening, gave her opinion. "To me, that seems to be a perfect gift. It will be like giving them the Honeymoon that they didn't have." All the children thought about what she'd voiced and begrudgingly, admitted that it sounded good.

"Okay," Violet chimed in, "who's going to do the dirty work and find out all about what this vacation entails?"

"I'll be glad to find out the details since Tim and I came up with the idea. I wouldn't expect to put the burden on any of you."

"When you put it that way, Richard and I could do a little exploration and see what we come up with," Vivian volunteered. "Hey, how did I get mixed up in this?" Rich teased his wife. "It's part of a married man's duty to help his wife, isn't that true, kid's?" They all agreed. "Okay, okay, I'll go on the net and find some information about this so called, sailing adventure."

"Now remember, the one that my friend went on was a very large sailboat. It took 5 couples and a crew and captain. Oh, and did I mention a gourmet chef as well?" Her siblings and their significant others seemed impressed.

"I'll go on the internet. At least I have some parameters to go by. I'll do my homework, and report back to you within a couple of weeks. Does that sound all right with you?" Rich asked. After dividing and paying the bill the sisters and brother gave the mandatory hugs and kisses to each other and went their separate ways. In the lobby Victoria jokingly said to her husband; loud enough for her siblings to hear: "I'm glad that Mom and Dad had as many kids as they did. It won't cost as much with all of us pitching in." Mike rubbed her hair, shrugged his shoulders and nodded his head while looking at his relatives.

ST. PAUL, MINNESOTA

Tracy Razzaboni didn't know what to do for her husband, Mike's big 30th. His birthday was coming up soon, and Mike worked hard for St. Paul's largest tax law firm. Tracy wanted to do something special for him. She hoped that he'd treasure her gift to him for his entire life.

Being brought up in the Bronx section of New York, she loved the area of the twin cities. It was very different from where Mike and she had come from. Her New York accent was detected whenever she spoke, but she didn't give a damn. One thing was certain, being brought up the way she was made her a tough girl

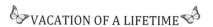

who wouldn't take shit from anyone, including her husband. Although he still had his accent, he tried acting polished in the field he was in, but she knew that one could never take New York away from a New Yorker.

She felt sorry for the many hours he devoted to the law firm, knowing that all his hard work would pay off someday. They both hoped that the practice would ask him to become a partner, and she knew that that day would come. She made it her business to be up whatever hour he came home. The dinner she prepared would be waiting for him at the dining room table. Tracy didn't want their honeymoon to go away. That was one way of showing her affection and love for him. She was Dr. Steven's physician assistant, and worked long hours. Even though she was happy and was a great physician's assistant, her first priority was her marriage. Like her husband, she was a giver. Tracy enjoyed their intimacy and hoped that this part of the marriage would always be great, especially the time spent in the bedroom.

One morning she was at work and overheard an assistant telling her patient about the trip her friend had been on. The way the girl described the vacation sounded wonderful. During lunch hour, she went to her friend and asked about her discussion with Mr. White. "You know Diane, Mike's 30th is coming up shortly and I want to do something special for him. What you told him sounds just the type of thing that I'd love to do for Mike. Not that I was eavesdropping, but would you mind telling me more about this vacation? I think it sounds like the solution to my predicament."

"Sure Tracy, let's go to Au Bon Pan, and while we're having lunch I'll tell you what Mr. White described."

While eating their Oriental, apple, walnut, chicken salad, Diane explained what her patient told her. "He portrayed the great adventure and weather he experienced on the sailboat. They visited different islands, having the sunshine on him all the time; they even had a gourmet cook making their meals. I'm telling you Tracy, this will be the perfect present for Mike," Diane explained. As soon as she got home from work, she explored the internet to find the various sailboats that she would consider going on. She made a list of five and then would narrow them down to the one that she thought would suit them best.

NEWTON, MASSACHUSETTS

"Surprise!" everyone yelled as Paul walked into the large suite that he and his wife Renée had gone to at the Marriot Hotel in Newton, MA. "I don't believe it," he exclaimed. "I came here thinking I was going to celebrate my nurse, Rose's 40th Birthday party." Shaking his head in bewilderment, his smile lit up his already happy face. "You sure fooled me," he told his fellow physicians and nurses as they congratulated him on his retirement. "We'll all miss you, Paul, especially your patients." "Personally," laughing at his next statement, Chester, another physician said, "it will mean more money for us. If you think we'll replace you, think again buddy." Rubbing his hands greedily in front of him, Chester continued; "I can see my new vacation home in Vermont now." Everyone at Paul's retirement party laughed as their drinks were replaced with full glasses of whatever beverage they had. "We were going to have some of us tell us what experiences they had working with you and how we'll all miss you, but nobody had anything nice to say," another doctor chortled.

"Speech, speech," all the guests requested. Clearing his throat Paul was obviously embarrassed. "I'm speechless, and as you all know, that's a first for me. I want to know if I can still give the present I bought for Rose to her or, in back of my mind I'm thinking, I'll return the present and get my money that I spent on it." He was joking as he handed Rose her gift. "Seriously, I've worked in this medical association for many years. I won't know what to do in my spare time. It's been a wonderful 25 years and I can't believe that I'll be having my 62nd Birthday next month. I don't feel a day over 45." Someone yelled, "You look well over 70. Who are you trying to fool?" As the jubilant crowd gathered around him, Chester came forward with an envelope in hand. "We didn't know what to get for a person who has everything, so we all pitched in and decided to give you something that you and Renée would never think of doing for yourselves. To say it kindly, you're such a cheap bastard that we know this would be too frivolous for you to do for yourself and your beautiful wife. By the way, we'll miss her more than you. When she visits us and brings in her homemade brownies, the entire office scoffs them down in no time."

"Don't worry gang, I'll still visit and promise to bring the brownies with me," declared Renée, as she took Paul by his hand and led him onto the dance floor. "Hey, wait a second aren't you going to open our present?" One of the nurses asked.

"I almost forgot. I'm so happy that you all pitched in and emptied your bank accounts for me." Everyone laughed as he unsealed the envelope in his hand. Paul's expression was one of surprise as he stood there with his mouth wide open. "Look Honey, I can't believe what I'm seeing. This is a vacation of a lifetime. Literally, it's a sailing cruise to the South China Seas," beamed Paul. "I don't know what to say, except thank you. We'll take lots of pictures and videos and have all of you to our house and show them to you when we return. How does that sound?" Applause was resplendent as various co-workers congratulated him throughout the evening, while he and his beautiful wife ate their dinner and danced the night away.

NEWBURYPORT, RHODE ISLAND

Joe and Sam were sitting on the couch, holding hands, watching America's Got Talent on the television. They decided to change stations and watch the Travel Channel. They weren't paying much attention to the show, but suddenly a vacation that was on the show appealed to them. They raised the volume without saying a word to each other; listening intently while the host described the adventure.

"Sam, when is your vacation time? I have two weeks coming to me this year and this looks like the perfect getaway. Look at these Islands and the sailboat! It's incredible! The food looks yummy! There's even a gourmet chef on board! Look at the scuba diving in the beautiful turquoise water. The unique fish look incredible! What do you think?"

"Gee, I haven't given a thought about my vacation yet. I do get four weeks' vacation that I can split up any way that I want to," Sam answered. "I see what you mean by this unusual trip. Wouldn't it be fun? Let me look it up on the internet or YouTube and see what I come up with. I bet we can afford something different like this."

The next evening Joe asked Sam if he had a chance to surf the web. Sam put the steak dinner in front of his partner of seven years, and sat down across the table from Joe. They were enjoying their food when Sam asked Joe, "How well do you know me? Don't answer, just listen to what I found out about our vacation," a proud Sam exclaimed. He went into detail about the sailing yacht that traveled throughout the China Sea. "I'm telling you Joe, you came up with a winner this time. I can't wait until I put in for the weeks I want to get away. We've been away but this is something different and exciting. When is your vacation time and how far in advance does your company need you to tell them when you want it?" asked a concerned Joe. "They're pretty flexible." Sam answered. "Luckily, I have a managerial position, so I'm really the boss of my department. You find out when the best time to go on this excursion is and I'll tell them when I'm taking my vacation."

After dinner they cleaned the kitchen, washing and putting away all the pots, pans and dishes. Once the area was cleared, they sat around the table and looked at the brochures Sam took from one of the travel stores near his office. "These are just some of the pamphlets on sailing cruisers. I think the next thing to do is go to the web sites of these companies and find answers to the questions we

have." Joe high-fived Sam and they retreated to the second bedroom where their office was located and scrolled down to sailboat vacations. "Do you want us to be the only people on board or do you want a few people with us. Not our friends, we see them all the time," stated Sam. "I agree with you whole heartedly. It wouldn't hurt us if we mingled with some other couples. I don't mind having some straight couples on board. We can be the token gays," Joe laughed as he got up from the chair and kissed his best friend and lover.

CHELMSFORD, ENGLAND, UK

Cole and Isabelle Towers' business was as busy as ever. When they opened their fastener company eight years ago they didn't think it would be the money-maker it turned out to be. Sitting in their shared office, the bright sunshine coming through the massive windows of the mill building they occupied, Cole turned to Isabelle and asked her if she'd thought of their holiday for this year.

"You know," stated Isabelle, "I've been in a slump for some time and I think a holiday is just what we need. While I'm out posting a letter to my friend in Alabama I'll think about a place where we could go."

"Who are you posting to?" asked Cole. "You remember the woman we met on our last holiday? Her name was Anne Marie, you know, the lady who was rabbiting all the time. She always ordered soda because she didn't want to get pissed. A fag was always hanging from her mouth."

"Oh yes, I remember her, always going to the lavatory, that one, I think it was from all the soda she consumed." Cole laughed, slapping his wife on her rump as she headed out the door. "I'm leaving my mackintosh here; it's stopped raining." Isabelle informed Cole waving to him, "Cheerio!"

Isabelle returned from her outing and sat down at her davenport. Addressing her husband, she brought up the idea for their holiday. "I've been thinking, I fancy a jolly time. I think I'll ring our holiday agent and see what he might butcher; something balmy for a change." Cole nodded his head in agreement. "Go for it governor!!" Isabelle smiled as she picked up the receiver while putting the diary in front of her. That evening, while in bed beside each other, Isabelle mentioned what the holiday agent suggested. "He knew that we are keen to find a scheme. He'll ring us later; the proctor will take charge of everything."

"That's jolly good," Cole told Isabelle. "Before we get too tired I'm gagging. I promise you won't be gutted!!" Cole teased Isabelle as he kissed her tenderly. The next day sitting at their davenports, Isabelle mentioned that the holiday agent called, "He talked my lungs off," she declared. "He didn't miss a thing. He came up with something that he knew would give us a jolly good time. We're going on a large rig for at least four glorious weeks. What do you think of that idea?"

"Whatever you say governor, just pack my valise and I know you'll want to find some good precincts that you enjoy going to." With a smile she returned to her work.

CHAPTER TWO

BROOKLINE, MASSACHUSETTS

Hope's sisters met two weeks later at Spencer's and Hope's beautiful, large, colonial home. After drinking their cocktails, they sat by the roaring fire that was burning in the stone fireplace in the family room. "Okay Taylor, what did you come up with?" Melanie asked. "Before I got any correspondence, I wanted to call Rich and ask him if he and Nancy had a definite date planned for a wedding. He started laughing and told me to go ahead with whatever we decided because they wouldn't be getting married for at least another year or so. I then went on the internet and also went to the travel agent to get some information. I sorted different vessels or sailing ships and then came up with the idea of a sailing yacht that is at least 108 ft. I didn't want them to feel claustrophobic. Then I called a few captains and after speaking to them, I picked three people who I wanted to discuss with you. Of course, they have to go someplace that has warm, sunny weather with lots of shopping. We'll also supply them with large hats, (to keep their faces out of the sun) and maybe baseball caps when they're sailing the seas to their next destination. "That sounds great, Mel, let's take a look at the brochures you brought," Hope said. Melanie passed the same literature to each participant.

Everyone had a different brochure that they liked. After much deliberation, they came up with the same conclusion. Putting their favorite brochure on top they asked Mel to call this "Vacation of a Lifetime," Captain, Bob Winters, and get details. Spencer piped in, "We need to know everything before making a commitment."

"We'll make this happen," pronounced Spencer. Two of the girls looked at each other, rolling their eyes after Spencer spoke.

Taylor said, "Before we call this Captain Winters do you think that they'll really like this trip? It's very different than most vacations. Personally, I haven't seen the entire Caribbean yet, and that's what I'd prefer. But both Nancy and Mom have been to many places throughout their lives that I think they'd be surprised and happy with this unusual experience. Sorry kids, I just had to get what I was thinking off my chest. Okay, who's going to call for the details?"

Addressing everyone, Hope announced, "Let's hope that we can reach this Captain tonight. I'm terrible at differentiating the diverse times in the world." Spencer started laughing at his wife, whom he adored. "Honey, I married you because you have other qualities that are more important to me than geography." The other sisters started snickering when they saw Hope go over to Spenser and hug him. Simultaneously, they all groaned.

"I'll put the phone on speaker so we can all hear what this Captain has to say. He might have an office with someone answering." Hope let the phone ring six times when she heard the telephone being answered. "Hi, I hope this is the correct number for "Vacation of a Lifetime?"

"Yes it is, this is Bob Winters and who might you be?"

"I'm Hope Johnson and I'm calling for information about a trip we saw in a brochure at a travel agency. Can you answer a few questions for me?"

"Of course, that's my job."

"From what we read, you're a licensed Captain. Do you have other ships or sail boats in your fleet? I saw that you have various sized vessels. On the trip we're thinking of giving to our mother, we want to know if you would be manning the sail boat yourself?"

"First of all let me ask you a few questions before I can answer correctly, all right? It depends which trip you're thinking of having her go on. I need to know how long you intend to have her on this vacation and the destination that you picked out."

"The holiday would be for my mother and her business partner and best friend. Just so that you know, they've had a lot of medical problems and I think that a long vacation will do them good. Let me assure you that these medical issues won't conflict with anything that they'd probably encounter on your sailboat. They've been to many places in their lifetime, and my sisters and I thought that a trip to the Far East that goes to Singapore, Vietnam, Hong Kong, Philippines, Borneo, and Saigon." Taking a breath Hope continued, "Then they would go onto Hong Kong, China, Manila, Philippines, Kota Kinabalu (that I never heard of) and Malaysia. I then read of some other places that I don't have the slightest notion about. I have heard of Singapore, Malaysia, Hong Kong, China, Borneo and, of course, the Philippines."

Captain Winters was laughing to himself. "That sounds like quite an excursion doesn't it? Let me assure you that I've personally been on that route so many times that I could navigate it blindfolded. Of course, I wouldn't do that. Yes, young lady, I would be the captain of the vessel. Besides myself, I'll be having a first mate, a gourmet chef, and at least four other crew members. They would consist of a Chief Engineer, a backup and two general deckhands. My

sailboat is 108ft. long, plus a motor, just in case we need it if we should get into any trouble. I haven't had to use it yet. The ship will take approximately 12 vacationers plus the crew that mans the ship. The reason I'll be on the ship is, truthfully, that's my favorite itinerary of all my excursions. I should tell you that this is a four, at least, week cruise. I'm flexible, and if the guests should want a little more vacation time, it being my ship, I can accommodate them. The reason is, with all the ports we go to in order for the vacationers to see the various places and get a feel for the islands, a month will be just perfect. For instance, traveling from Borneo to Singapore is 700 miles. Without getting too technical, it would take about 24 hours of constant travel and speed. Since winds are never constant it would turn into about 35 to 40 hours just to travel from port to port. So a four-week vacation allows for just that little bit of extra time a person needs to enjoy the ports and sights. I hope I've made myself clear. Please, ask me any questions you have and I'll try to answer them to the best of my ability," Captain Bob Winters spoke to Hope candidly. "There will be more questions, but for now I'll talk this over with my sisters and husband, and I'll get back to you," said Hope. "That'll be fine, Mrs. Johnson. I'll try to be as helpful as possible. Feel free to call me and I'll be there for you. Thanks for considering my sailing agenda and hope to hear from you soon."

Hope put the receiver down and looked at everyone in the family room. "Well, you heard the entire conversation. What do you think?" The girls were quiet and contemplative for a while and then, one by one, they said that it sounded like the vacation that their mother and Nancy needed and would enjoy. They all gathered in a circle and all high fived. "The next subject we have to consider is whether or not this should this be a one month vacation. Do you think that they'll balk at the idea of being away from the business for such a long time? Since they've been out of work for over three months, do you think we'll have a problem with them agreeing to take this holiday?"

"For me," Taylor gave her opinion, "I'd be thrilled to go on this incredible vacation. I hear Viet Nam is exquisite and I used to love watching China Beach on television." Melanie piped in, "I feel the same as you, Taylor, and I hope that they get as excited about it as we are. They haven't even gone yet, and I can't wait to see the many pictures that they take so we can drool."

CHICAGO, ILLINOIS

Sandy and Arthur were invited to their only son's house one week before their forty-fifth Wedding anniversary. Dressing in their bedroom, Sandy was spraying Eternity behind her ears and on her wrists. Looking behind her she saw her husband. "Arthur, I think that the kids are having a surprise party for us. What do you think, Honey?"

"Usually children make a big to do about the fiftieth. I think they're going to have a nice dinner for us with a cake. I'd be surprised if anything else occurs," Arthur answered.

Sitting on the living room sofa, she waited for Arthur to get himself together. She closed her eyes, thinking: *'at least I made it for our forty-fifth.'* Every time she thought of these last two years, a shiver went through her body. It was like living in a nightmare, when she heard Dr. Waters tell her that the results of her third mammogram and biopsy came back positive. The only word she kept hearing over and over again was "CANCER." All the way home, she wanted to talk the matter over with Arthur, who was not only her husband but best friend. She couldn't help feel the dread and heartache they both would go through. Dr. Waters had given her a choice of the few options she had and gave his opinion on what she should do if she were his wife. Sandy opted to have a lumpectomy and go through the series of chemotherapy and radiation treatments the Oncology Department prescribed for her. She always liked her doctor, whom, she had gone to since she was pregnant with her first child. Sandy had confidence in the entire team of doctors and nurses that had made her feel whole and better again, but, in the recesses of her mind, she couldn't help but worry that she was living with a time bomb that could explode her and Arthur's entire world.

All their children were at her son's and his wife's house when they arrived for their dinner party. When they finished the dinner, Violet and Gloria came out with a beautiful cake for the dessert that was going to be served. "Oh my," exclaimed Violet, "what's on top of the cake? I don't know how that envelope got on top of the frosting. Mom, would you please remove it and hand it to Dad?" Sandy looked quizzically at Arthur. Her brows knitted together, waiting for him to open the packet. The paper was inside. When Arthur opened the literature, his mouth flew open, but no words came out. Sandy looked at Arthur and gave him her opinion on what the letter must say. "Arthur, what is it? No, don't tell me, it's a sonogram of the baby that Violet's going to have. I could sense that something was going on whenever I spoke to you," she addressed her daughter. Everyone at the table laughed. "Sh!" Violet whispered, "Cut down the noise, I don't want Vincent's and Gloria's young daughter, Ellen, to get up and disturb this special event." Sandy took the letter from her husband and read it. Shaking her head she looked at the people sitting around, the family that was her entire life's reward. "I don't believe what I'm seeing." She started to cry. "Now, now dear," Arthur turned and hugged his wife. "This is a joyous occasion. Don't cry, be happy and say thank you. Then we'll ask all the questions and the kids, hopefully, will tell us what this is all about."

"We know that you, Mom, and all of us, went through Hell these last few years. It was a scare that we don't want to experience again. All of us got together and decided that we weren't going to wait until your fiftieth anniversary to do something special for you. We want you to enjoy this trip for your forty fifth instead." Sandy sat glued to her seat, in shock. Shaking her head, she said to herself, as well as the others around the dining room table, "Yes it's true that not only I, but all of you were involved with what I had to go through. I'm not denying that life has taken on a different perspective regarding the way I see the world. I'm not going to be maudlin and say anything else that has the letter 'c' involved. All I can say is (standing up, putting her hands in the air) she shouted, YES, YES, what a wonderful present and surprise! I'm not going to be practical and admonish you for spending this amount of money. I know it must have cost you a fortune. You are all young with families of your own that, thank God, are growing. But for once, your father and I will enjoy this trip more than anything else we've ever done. Well, besides having our wonderful family healthy and happy." Walking around the table she hugged her family and once again sat down beside Arthur.

"You all know that Mom is the vocal person. I have, and always will, go along with whatever she wants. But for myself, I can't thank you kids enough." Instead of going around the table, he stood up and blew kisses to them all. With their wide smiles illuminating the children's faces, Vivian stood. "Dad, please have a seat. I want to say that we love you so much and have been blessed with what we think are the two greatest people we were lucky enough to call our parents. We know that you and Mom never had a real honeymoon. So this is our way of saying, have a happy anniversary and honeymoon all at one time." The rest of the evening went by quickly, and Sandy and Arthur were the first to leave.

"I don't know about the rest of you, but Honey," Violet said to Glen, "I need a stiff drink."

"Yes," shouted the others as the drinks were handed out. As everyone sat leisurely in the family room, the dirty dishes still in the kitchen sink, everyone was discussing the gift that they gave their parents. "I couldn't have thought of this type of present by myself," Vincent announced to his siblings and their mates. "I feel that all of us made this dream of a vacation and honeymoon come true for them. Yes, Mom was right. We've all been through Hell and back these past few years with Mom's cancer. Let's think on the positive side and hope that we never have to go through this again."

"Vicky, where did you get this idea, and how did you get all the research that went into this wonderful plan?" Veronica asked her third sister. "It wasn't easy," answered Vicky. "I heard one of the women in the office describe the once-in-a-lifetime vacation her Aunt and Uncle went on when she came back from visiting during the Easter Holiday. I was curious to find out more about the trip she was describing. Now, let's not kid ourselves, we're all optimistic that Mom will be healthy and never have to go through cancer again, but I and you all know that the disease could very well return. I thought, why the Hell should we wait till their fiftieth, when we don't know how many good years they might have together. It was as easy as that."

Vincent interrupted, "I don't know about you guys, but when they come back, I want them to tell us every detail and show us so many pictures that our eyes will come out of everyone's sockets. I'm not going to wait till my twenty-fifth anniversary with Glory, but if, God willing, we can afford it, I'll take Glory on a vacation like the one we're giving Mom and Dad." After the chatter that went with a party, they left at different intervals, each thanking Vincent and Gloria for their hospitality.

When Arthur and Sandy were in the king-sized bed that they shared throughout their married life, they both looked over the itinerary for their upcoming trip. "It's funny, we couldn't afford anything when we first got married," Sandy declared. "If it weren't for my parents' generous gift of this bedroom set, we would have had to sleep on the living room chair."

"Isn't that the truth? As a matter of fact, we didn't have any other furniture in our first apartment except for the second-hand table and chairs that we used for the kitchen table." They both laughed at Arthur's last statement and went to sleep, their arms and legs entwining.

ST. PAUL, MINNESOTA

Tracy made reservations at Monticello's, a very fancy Italian restaurant, fifteen minutes from their house. "I'm glad that you didn't have to stay at the office late tonight. I'm looking forward to a good Italian meal. How about you?" Tracy asked Mike as he put on a different shirt from the one he wore to the office. "Yeah, you know that I could have Italian food every night of the week, especially when it's my thirtieth birthday and I'm spending it with my girlfriend." Tracy smiled and asked, "Mike, what excuse did you make to your wife this evening?" As he helped her on with the light-weight jacket he explained, "I told her that I had to work late." He opened their front door and as they walked onto the stone steps leading to the garage, he put his arm around his adorable wife, and they both giggled as he pushed in the numbers for the electric door to open.

Tracy put her hand on Mike's knee as they were driving to the restaurant. They let the valet service take Mike's new Lexus and went into the eatery. After being seated, they ordered the wine that they preferred and toasted each other. "Mike," Tracy asked, "Do you feel any older now that you're turning thirty?"

"Are you kidding? I feel I have the world in my hands and nothing but happiness will be ours. I'm not getting older, more mature maybe, but no, not older." Tracy pulled out a thick envelope with a card inside and told him to open it. She looked at her husband, who she still loved with all her heart and beamed at him when he saw what was inside the packet. "Happy Birthday, Honey. May you have many more happy and healthy ones," declared Tracy as she saw a smile appear on her husband's face. "The card is beautiful but I can't believe what I'm seeing. Do you know what this means? We would both have to take four weeks off from work? We both have responsible jobs, and I don't know if I can get a complete four weeks off."

Tracy had a smug look on her face. "Well smarty pants, I called up the president of your firm and explained to him what I was planning to do. He was as excited as I was! He then told me not to worry, that he'd call up your clients and re-arrange your schedule. As for myself, I begged my boss and, after considering my request, he said, okay, but make sure you don't have many sick days off during the rest of the year." Mike shook his head. "That sounds like something the doctor would say."

"I didn't care what I had to answer, just as long as he let me take the four weeks off," Tracy admitted. "I'll drink to that," Mike said. Their wine glasses touched and their meal arrived.

Mike moved his chair closer to his wife and, as they ate their dinner, they talked all about their impending trip. "What a great thirtieth birthday present! Only you could have thought of something this unusual. Have I told you lately how much I adore and cherish you?" Mike asked as he bent over and kissed her on the lips. As they were leaving the establishment, Mike turned around and whispered in his wife's ear, "I can't wait till we leave on our trip and especially until I can thank you properly tonight when we're in bed." Tracy squeezed Mike's hand as he held the door open for her to get into the car.

NEWTON, MASSACHUSETTS

Renée and Paul danced the entire evening. They went around to the various tables and thanked them for the gift. Paul joked with his co-workers about the

different situations that occurred at the office throughout the years. On the way to their stately home, they continued to talk about the party and how excited they were with the upcoming trip. When they were in their night clothes, they sat up in their bed and with diligence, wrote down the questions that they wanted answered when they called "Vacation of a Lifetime."

"I have to admit this was a very generous gift that your office gave you."

"Hell," Paul answered, "I literally gave all my life to that practice; this is the least that they could have gotten me."

"Honey, I'm surprised at you," Renée said. "I thought you loved what you did for a living and enjoyed everyone that you worked with."

"I do, I mean I did, but let's not forget the fact that I spent many hours at the office and the hospital. You don't find doctors with as much dedication as I gave to my co-workers and my patients anymore. That's all I'm saying. I can't wait till we go away for an entire four weeks and relax and enjoy ourselves. Throughout our married life, we've gone away every year. Our two week vacations were spent with either our parents, until they passed on, or to the Islands were we'd go for our regular two weeks of sun and excitement."

"I guess you're right, Paul. I'm glad that you retired at sixty two rather than wait until you are sixty-five. Think of all the fun we'll have during your retirement! It's sad that we didn't have children during our young lives, but on the other hand now we can go anyplace we want to and don't have to worry about children or animals. Yes, everything turned out for the best. I've also enjoyed my volunteer work at the hospitals and my oil painting has become rather successful from what once was a hobby. I'm glad that I took Art Appreciation throughout my college years. If I didn't, we would never have met." Feeling his wife's breasts, he bent down and kissed each one, sucking the nipples until they hardened. "Let's put these papers away and start doing what people do that have nothing else on their minds except having great sex with the person that they love," declared Paul.

NEWBURYPORT, RHODE ISLAND

Joe arrived home earlier from work then Sam and started dinner. When Sam got home, he was glad that he didn't have to do the cooking for this evening's meal. While they were eating, Joe informed Sam that he asked his supervisor at Verizon if he could take an extra 4 weeks for vacation time. "I had to practically beg; I felt like Fido begging for a dog biscuit. After practically promising him a blow job, (only kidding), he told me that it would be okay, since I didn't take any sick time for the last 2 years and have accumulated the required time.

Luckily, the company holds over the sick days and they don't eliminate them each year."

"I'm lucky you don't get sick. Although we work hard and see many people, it's surprising we're healthy and don't get many colds in the winter. I bet it's all the antioxidants that we take every day and we keep in shape by routinely keeping up our exercise program. I like Tai Chi Chuan best of all! With all the gay bashing (thankfully not as bad as it was a few years ago) I'm glad that we can defend ourselves. If people only knew that two guys that have an alternative life style isn't going to take shit from others!" Sam proclaimed. They both laughed. Joe (who didn't make as much money as Sam) didn't know how to ask the big question. Inhaling he blurted out; "Now the hard part; how much is this going to cost?"

"Joe, what the Hell are you worrying about? I saw your bank book and it's nothing to sneeze at. Christ, you've been saving money since you were a little kid. Your parents paid for your education and what does it cost you each month? Hardly anything! We share the living expenses and we don't have any kids to worry about. Relax, we only live once. Personally, I want to enjoy every day and not live for tomorrow because who knows when there will be no more tomorrows," Joe remarked. "That's awful and depressing Sam. I plan on living for many years and I want to have enough money to insure I'm able to live well in my old age."

"That's good for you. Honey, life is short; let's try to take a day at a time, that's all I'm asking."

"I guess I'm a worrywart, that's all. Don't mind me. Just let me know how much I have to take out of my account and I'll plan on having a great time. You know that as long as I'm with you, I'll always be happy," exclaimed Joe. "I'll call up the company and find out the details that we need. I'll also have to find out the time of year that they recommend. Damn, I don't want to hit any monsoon season."

CHELMSFORD, ENGLAND, UK

While Cole was grafting, confirming orders from the many customers that their business relied on for orders, Isabelle was keen on ringing the travel agent to see if he found a scheme for their holiday.

Isabelle was intently listening to every word the travel agent told her. "Let me discuss it with my husband and, if he agrees, I'll ring you in a few."

"Cole," Isabelle called him to gain his attention. She waved her hands indicating for him to get off the telephone. "I've spoken to Edward and he found all the information we'd need for our holiday."

"Who in bloody Hell is Edward?" grumbled Cole. "Don't be a twat, he's the holiday agent."

"Oh yes, now I remember. Tell me, beside him being a rabbit, what did he tell you?"

"He wants us to have all the information that we need to make a decision. There's one problem, the holiday that I was thinking about will take approximately four weeks' time. Do you think we can take an entire four weeks off or should I stash the idea entirely?"

"I've been thinking, since you mentioned the idea of a holiday I've been fancy on the idea. You and I, we've been deadbeats. All we do is graft. I think we'd both be gutted if we don't take time off. So what if it's four weeks? We deserve it! Give this Edward a ring back and find out all the details. We have to make room on our diary for this jolly idea you came up with." Cole got up from his chair and hugged his wife. "Get with it girl, I don't want either of us to be gutted." They both smiled as she lifted the receiver.

STONEY BROOK, MASSACHUSETTS

Suzanne was letting herself into the house after a full day's work. She plopped down on the soft sofa and closed her eyes. The first thing she noticed was the wonderful aroma coming from the kitchen. She wasn't hungry. All she wanted to do was go to bed for the evening. On the other hand, Mrs. Walsh would be disappointed if she didn't eat the meal she'd prepared for her. She wearily got up off the sofa and put a smile on her face as she approached the kitchen. "Well, well, I smell something awfully good. What might that tempting aroma be?" Mrs. Walsh looked satisfied with herself as she sat down with Suzanne to eat the late dinner. "Why did you wait for me? You shouldn't have."

"To be honest with you Suzanne, after I made the dinner, I took a little nap and got up just a while ago. Anyway, I enjoy hearing about your events of the day." Suzanne took a deep sigh and told her the mundane, routine happenings that took place at Metamorphosis Salon. "I have to admit that I wasn't hungry when I got home, but you outdid yourself with the pot roast."

"I cooked so much that we'll be able to have it for tomorrow night also. I'll freeze the rest because we'll both be sick of pot roast after a few days," said Mrs. Walsh.

"Come on, Mrs. Walsh, I'll help you clean the dishes and the kitchen. I think we'll both retire early tonight," said Suzanne.

Nancy got home and was happily anticipating the nightly phone call from Rich. She enjoyed being at the spa, helping with the bookkeeping and being the front person, greeting all the clients. She still got exhausted but didn't like to complain. *'At least I'm exercising on a regular schedule. I can imagine how tired I'd be if I wasn't keeping in shape'* Nancy told herself as she hurried to the telephone to hear Rich's voice. She deftly held her cell between her shoulder and ear and walked up to her bedroom, took off her working clothes, and put on her night shirt. She wiggled under the covers and spoke to Rich for over an hour before he realized that she was dead tired. "I'll call you tomorrow and I'll tell you more about what's happening out here. Till then, sleep tight my darling. I'll be dreaming of holding you in my arms. Until then I'll have to be satisfied with hearing your voice."

"That won't be for long," assured Nancy. "By the way, I spoke to the attorney that was in charge of Mr. Makino's estate. He left Mr. Yasuhito his place in San Diego. When Mr. Yasuhito heard about the tragic death of Mr. Makino, he couldn't help but cry." Nancy said out loud, "I wonder if he cried for Mr. Makino or all the money he'll be inheriting once he sells that large house?"

"Oh well," continued Nancy, "Did you ask him if he would like the idea of coming to Massachusetts and living with us?"

"He told me that anytime I want to relocate, I have a devoted servant and friend with me always."

Once more Suzanne's daughters gathered at Hope and Spencer's house in Brookline. Melanie told her sisters all about the phone conversation she had with the agent who would do the planning of the trip. "So far we've narrowed it down to the orient, to be exact, the South China Seas. We know that they go to Japan quite a bit, but it's not the same type of trip. They'll be going somewhere that they'd never thought of going. It'll be a complete vacation for them. For as long as I can remember, whenever they've been away, they would tell us it's a vacation or on business, but it was monkey business. This time they won't get themselves into trouble; only peace, sun, and complete relaxation." Taylor piped in, "I can't imagine Mom and Nancy being able to relax for four weeks. They'll go crazy."

"I bet there'll be many shopping areas on their excursions. They'll each have to take an empty suitcase to bring all the gifts and personal items that they'll buy," Hope told her sisters as they settled in the family room with large bowls of their favorite flavors of ice cream. "Now the next question that has to be answered is how this present is going to be given?" Taylor thought for a while and came up with a great solution. "Let's invite Mom and Nancy out to dinner. We'll make it a special 'getting better outing' at one of the fancy restaurants that they enjoy. Of course, we'll have to have the complete itinerary settled so we can hand it to them. We'll have to have a list of everything they'll need to bring and I'll bring a camera to capture the look on their faces when we hand them this gift." They all cheered as they brought the empty bowls to the kitchen sink.

In Hope's spacious kitchen, the girls thought of how to present the gift to their mother and 'Aunt Nancy.' They had doubts about taking them out to eat at their favorite restaurant. "I'll think of something better than going out to eat. I mean they're always going to a fancy restaurant. I'll think of something different and then I'll call you," Melissa said as they were gathered around the sink, rinsing the empty bowls of ice cream.

Suzanne was busy the entire day. She made sure to give her clients the treatments that they deserved, needed and wanted. They didn't want to hear about her and Nancy's confinement or what they went through in the past several months. It was best to let their 'other life' be known only to themselves and not let their family and best friends know what they really did to help the world be a better place. At least that was Suzanne's and Nancy's feelings about their life beyond their families. Helping people who didn't realize that a crime was occurring around them was something that Suzanne and Nancy felt they wanted to do. It had been a while since their first encounter with crime and working with the FBI in Boston, but now it seemed second nature. The new friends that these two best friends made were unique and now that a new aspect of their life had opened up to them, Suzanne doubted that either one of them could go back to being 'ordinary people.'

Nancy and Suzanne constantly talked between themselves about what they did. When they were confined in the hospital in Japan and then sent home to the States to recover from the many injuries they sustained in helping the team who worked diligently in the international art crime theft area, their conversations would last until the medicines they were given started taking affect. Suzanne knew that these new friends would always be there in case Suzanne and Nancy needed help in other crime-related issues that came up. Suzanne often thought of Madaline and her son Kyle and how happy he was since he let the world know that he was involved in and living in the gay world, which he wanted desperately to be in. Madaline often called Suzanne and kept her informed of Betty, her adopted daughter, who felt comfortable knowing who her birth mother was, being a part of her new family. Suzanne often felt sorry for Kyle's ex-wife, but heard from the magazines that she was happy in her world of modeling and now had a wonderful love life. She was living with some Prince in a far-off land, God knows where. Nancy often laughed when Suzanne told of the many exploits of their friends and what was happening in their lives.

Nancy often called Suzanne late in the evenings to find out if she heard from their friends. Nancy, when not working helping Suzanne at the spa, was often away visiting Rich in San Diego. Nancy still pinched herself to make sure that she wasn't dreaming when she thought of how she met and fell in love with Rich Colangelo, the spirited homicide detective that they met while in San Diego on their last caper. Their friends would call Suzanne, knowing that Nancy wasn't home to talk to them.

Now that Madaline Mason, her famous friend and actress, was performing her play, *Beyond Murder*, in the various cities in the United States, she was sure that Madaline and the troop would be visiting Europe as well. Suzanne would make it a point to go to some of the famous European countries to see Madaline and always continue to keep up their friendship.

Thinking back to that time in her life when she didn't know if she would be alive to appreciate everything in the world, she was happy with the way that her life turned out. She knew and appreciated that health was more important than being rich. Sure, being wealthy helped, it was nice, but in the grand scheme of things, Suzanne would rather have her health and make people happy than have all the money in the world. She looked back at when Nancy was rich but unhappy in many ways that money couldn't buy. Now that she had been fullfilled emotionally by being in love, she could take on anything that came her way. A smile came to Suzanne's face as she thought of Nancy, and she was thrilled that her best friend was now a happy person in all ways.

CHICAGO, ILLINOIS

Sandy and Arthur were beside themselves with excitement. Sandy called her close relatives and girlfriends and told them about the impending trip. "Can you imagine? An entire four weeks of rest and relaxation? I don't remember the last time Arthur and I have been able to relax. I forget when we took our last vacation, it seems ages ago." She told everyone the itinerary for the luxurious trip. All the friends and relatives wanted to know was how much money it cost the kids to give them a lavish vacation. "You know what?" Sandy answered, "I didn't ask them and frankly I don't care. We've gone through so much crap these last few years that I know Arthur and I need this getaway more than anyone can imagine. I think that the kids knew exactly what we've gone through as they were right beside us throughout it all. Anyway, if they couldn't afford this luxurious gift, I don't think that they would have been able to give it to us. We have to get

inoculations and I have to get new clothes for the trip. I've lost so much weight since my illness that nothing fits me. Thank God that my hair grew back. And guess what? It came back curly. I never had natural curly hair in my life; except, of course, when my mother gave me a home permanent. I used to be so embarrassed. I looked like a French poodle." The person on the phone and Sandy couldn't stop laughing as they reminisced about their younger years.

Arthur sat at his office desk, daydreaming of his vacation. It seemed ages ago that he and Sandy had been able to relax. He couldn't remember himself without having little ones following him and going to practices and games with his children. He was grateful that they're now grown up. He was proud that their lives seemed happy. Of course, Veronica and Tim had their own problems, but he knew that they were strong and able to handle troubles that came their way. *'I know people think it's our turn to live. Since Sandy's Breast Cancer, we've not been able to confront our issues straight on. We, especially me, kept our thoughts to ourselves. Sandy didn't want me to worry about her; she didn't realize that even if we didn't talk about her illness, I was always upset and concerned. She didn't realize why I was so upset. She thought it was the cancer, but now wouldn't be a good time to tell her what's really on my mind. Oh God, she doesn't even know how I really feel. Well, I guess I have to keep my thoughts to myself. Besides telling her my feelings would only make matter's worse. This isn't the time for me to unburden myself. Yes, this is going to be our vacation of a lifetime and let's see what will be, will be.'*

CHAPTER THREE

STONEY BROOK, MASSACHUSETTS

Suzanne was enjoying her hectic day at work. Between patients she went back into her office and brewed her tea. *'I'm finally on the mend,'* she thought as she looked over the rest of the client cards she had for the appointments scheduled for the day.

She was thankful that she had her regular clients for the entire day and it was going to be pleasant seeing the women since she came back from her vacation. *'Yeah, some vacation,'* she thought to herself. *'I'll never tell any of my clientele what really happened. That's all they'd need to hear. They have enough tsuris (troubles) going on in their personal lives; they don't have to hear about what happened to Nancy and me. I'll listen to what's been going on in their lives and make them relax and enjoy their facials.'* While Suzanne was looking through her appointment book she realized that she'd be giving a body facial to one of her standard customers and was happy that she'd be able to vary her schedule a bit. *'I really think that exercising has helped me get my stamina back to normal. I was getting sick and tired of always being exhausted after doing routine day-to-day chores. What a pleasure it is not to be worn out at the end of a day. I'd better not stop working out and I'll try to keep up with my new routine for as long as I can.'* The intercom buzzed and her next client was in the waiting area.

When Suzanne was ready to leave for the evening, Justin called. "Why don't you come over to my house and sit around and talk for a while. It's been too long since we have seen each other. I'll make a simple meal and we'll enjoy each other's company."

"What a great idea. I'll call Mrs. Walsh and tell her not to expect me home for dinner. I'll leave now. But Justin, how come you're home at 8:30 from the gallery?" Suzanne questioned her dear friend. "Even though Alan's worked for me for a longtime, it's different now that he's a full-fledged partner. Not that I'm getting older, but it's nice to have a younger person around to take care of the mundane responsibilities. I can leave the gallery and not worry about anything pertaining to the store. He closes up and I have the evening to myself. You'll understand what I'm talking about once your daughters take over the entire operation of the spas."

"I know just what you mean, Justin. I'll be over in less than twenty minutes. See you then." Suzanne walked to Justin's spacious condominium on Commonwealth Ave., leaving her automobile in the parking garage. She was pleased that Justin called her. It was nice that she didn't have to worry about vagrants anytime, day or night, because of the nice neighborhood and the various college students roaming about. "Justin, I thought that this was supposed to be a little pick me up. I don't think that I can budge. I hate you for putting out that scrumptious dessert. Everything was perfect. Let me help you clean up and then we'll talk more in the library."

"First of all, I won't tell a soul that you ate my special beehive dessert, which by the way was your recipe if I remember correctly." Suzanne laughed at that comment. "You're right, Justin, I did give you that recipe that was handed down to me by one of my aunts."

"Secondly, don't even think of helping me put away anything. It's my pleasure and what will I do after you're gone, play solitaire?"

"I can't stay much longer but it's nice to spend some leisurely time with you; it seems like the old days. Show me what new books you've acquired."

It was an easy ride back home to Stoney Brook, with practically no traffic hindering her arrival going to Route 3 and then navigating to her street. Suzanne opened her front door and was greeted by Boston and Simka. She called for Mrs. Walsh and realized that her surrogate mother was probably in bed, fast asleep. Quietly going into the kitchen, she plopped down on the kitchen chair and opened her mail. Tossing away the advertisements, she realized that she spent such a long time with Justin that it was very late. Following the two felines up the stairs, she didn't bother taking her nightly shower and fell into bed. *I guess I can't burn the candles at both ends,'* she thought to herself and was asleep within five minutes.

The following morning, bright and eager to leave for work, while eating her fast breakfast, she enlightened Mrs. Walsh about the previous evening with Justin, leaving out the delicious dessert presented to her. "What are your plans for today?" Suzanne casually asked her dear housekeeper. "To be honest with you, I haven't thought about what I'm doing today. I might call your mother up. She'll pick me up and we'll go to the mall and look around a bit. That's if Morris doesn't mind Dorothy leaving for a while."

"Are you kidding? He'll be delighted to have the apartment to himself. He can watch his cowboys without her nagging him to shut the television off and get out of the house and get some fresh air." They both smiled; knowing all too well that Suzanne was telling it like it was. "Anyway, that's my plan for the day," stated Mrs. Walsh, "I know that you're going to work and loving every minute of it."

"Catherine, you know me too well." She hugged the old woman, whom she loved with all of her heart and bent down and patted the two cats that were waiting for their treats. As Suzanne hurried to the door, Mrs. Walsh went to the kitchen phone and called Dorothy and told her when she would be ready.

Suzanne was already late for work and found herself in the midst of Route 3 traffic. She knew she wouldn't have the time for her morning tea before her first client arrived. She hoped that she would make it on time for her first appointment. She called her office to tell them of her dilemma. She received her schedule and made a mental note to make sure that she made time for lunch so she could enjoy the cup of tea that she wouldn't be able to have before her hectic day started.

Suzanne hurried down Newbury Street on the way to the spa, hardly noticing the early morning rush of people walking briskly to either their jobs or on Holiday enjoying the many shops along this famous street. While she was walking, she inadvertently bumped into a gentleman who was also hurrying to his job. She laughed to herself thinking: *'We're all in such a hurry, and so what if we're a few minutes late? Big deal, we'll still get everything done that we want to.'*

Suzanne put her bag into the office and looked over her schedule for the day. Before entering her domain, she went to the front desk and told them to block her off for an hour. *'If I don't make the time to eat lunch, I'll get busy with something else and then I'll be starving when I get through for the day.'*

Suzanne was ready to head into the treatment room when her receptionist told her that an important phone call was waiting for her response. She hurriedly grabbed the phone and realized that Larry was on the phone calling from England. "Hi, I know that you are probably busy, but I want you to know that I'll be coming to the States in a few days and want to invite you to lunch on Friday. Do you think that we can make it a date?"

"Let me look at my schedule. I'll rearrange my plans to make sure that we can see each other at that time. Let's make it for about one o'clock on Friday." With that said she nodded to her girl behind the counter and headed for her client who was waiting for a treatment that Suzanne would give her.

Suzanne was reading the new client's information and deciding on what therapy would be best for her. She decided to give her client a regular facial, analyze her skin and book her for a collagen treatment on her next appointment. While she was giving her client a great massage, thoughts she wanted to keep out of her mind kept reappearing. She didn't want Stephen's image or thoughts of

him to interrupt her serenity. She loved giving the massage and didn't want to have any negativity ruining her treatment. As much as she tried getting Stephen off her mind, she couldn't do it.

Yes, she realized that she and Stephen had made a beautiful couple and the way that they made love and the way he made her feel was too good to be true. Just the thought of their last physical encounter put goose bumps all over her skin. She chastised herself for allowing thoughts of him to disrupt her train of thought. When she shook her head to get these notions out of her mind, she then realized that making the date with Larry triggered these emotions.

'Yes,' she thought, 'I have every right in the world to see whomever I please, at any time I want. Stephen isn't my boss and who does he think he is, anyway? He's the one who didn't come back to Hope's reception. I'll never forgive him for what he did to me that day. Even if he comes crawling back on bended knees, I'll never forget how selfish he was. No, even though no one will ever take his place in the way I feel physically about him, his situation is too emotionally fucked up. It's not normal for a man who is not in love with his wife to stay with her because of his guilt feelings. No, unless he's willing to divorce her, there is no way in Hell that I can stay with him.'

Trying to suppress her inner thoughts, she concentrated on giving her client the best massage that she could give. Suzanne stayed with her client, even when the steam was opening her client's pores. She habitually would stay with her clients throughout the treatment.

After the facial was complete she walked Mrs. Jones to the front desk to set up her next appointment. She went into her office after Mrs. Jones left and felt overwhelmed. She realized that she and Nancy had gone through a terrible time and it took time to rehabilitate. She was glad that she and Nancy's experiences with the Yakuza were over. Time would heal everything, even her feelings for Stephen, she hoped!!!!

BROOKLINE, MASSACHUSETTS

Hope closed her cell phone. Finding Spencer in his home office, she seated herself on the brown, leather sofa, waiting for his conference call to end. When he looked as though he was through with the work, she told him to sit back and listen to what she accomplished after eating their breakfast. "I was finally able to reach Captain Winters, and I think most of the arrangements are finalized. The only thing that's still up in the air is to see if I can reach their pilots and find out if they'll take Mummy and Nancy to Taipei."

"Sweetie pie, they work for your Mom. I don't think you'll have any problem in telling them what you and your sisters are doing for their bosses, and they'll be

glad to oblige. Of course, after your Mom and Nancy find out, I'm sure they'll tell them where they'll be going. Now that that's out of the way, what do we have to do next?" Spencer asked, waiting for Hope to continue. "I found out the entire itinerary, and you'll love it." Spencer jokingly told his wife, "You don't care if I love it, the point is that Suzanne and Nancy will love it."

"Of course they will, silly. I'll arrange another meeting with Mel and Taylor and figure out how we'll give our present to them."

CHICAGO, ILLINOIS

Sandy informed Arthur that she'd be going to the mall after lunch to browse and most likely start buying clothes for their impending cruise. "You have a good time. I'll look over my wardrobe; I really don't think I have to buy anything new. Maybe if you see a bathing suit and two pair of shorts, I wouldn't be upset if you'd surprise me." He waved to his wife as she drove down the driveway and went back into the house. He was calling Sandy's doctor to find out for himself if, in the doctor's opinion, the sailing cruise vacation would be okay for her to do. Arthur didn't want Sandy to know what he was doing. Now that Sandy was out of the house he hoped the good doctor would call back and get on the phone with him before Sandy returned from her shopping spree.

He waited with bated breath until the doctor's office returned his phone call. Arthur finally got the physician on the phone and, after explaining their upcoming vacation, was pleased that he got the reassurance that Sandy would be fine. He was told to relax, get as much sun as possible, using at least 50% sun block, and have a ball. "If you have a chance to go snorkeling, take a few pictures and let me see them when you return," said the fine oncologist. With a deep sigh of satisfaction and a clear mind, Arthur was now able to relax and get ready for this much needed rest.

Sandy returned home and excitedly showed Arthur all her new purchases. "I'm surprised you could carry all these bundles with you through the mall," exclaimed Arthur. "Well, I did have to go back to the car a few times to put a few bags into the trunk, so I could shop for more items."

"Did you remember to pick up the clothes that I asked for?" Arthur was sure she did but wanted to tease her. "Now Honey, would I forget anything that you asked me to do for you? Come on, you know me better than to even ask such a question. Now what were those items you asked for? I thought for sure I looked for them, but come to think of it, I might have forgotten. Oh well, I'll go back tomorrow and get them for you." Getting up off his comfortable chair, he towered over his small, petite wife and messed up her now, short, curly hair.

Sandy pulled out a new shopping bag and displayed the new clothes he asked her to buy for him.

Lying in bed that evening, Sandy enthusiastically went over the itinerary they received in the mail. With a voice both apprehensive yet full of excitement, she went through the details of their impending vacation. "I'm telling you Arthur, the days can't come fast enough until we can board the plane to Taipei and know that we'll be having so much fun for an entire four weeks! Can you believe it, four weeks with no worries, bills to think of, children to worry about, and to just sun, swim, snorkel and have the times of our lives! What a honeymoon. Although it did take quite a few years to have one, this makes it all worth the wait." Arthur was happy as a pig in shit listening to his wife talk about their up-coming vacation with such enthusiasm. "Don't forget, there'll be a lot of sightseeing at the many places we'll be visiting. I'll make sure to have the camera all prepared for all the pictures we'll be taking. I'll also bring a journal along to write the entire trip, day to day."

"Oh Arthur, you're so methodical, that's one of the traits that I love. You keep me grounded with your practicality," Sandy softly spoke as she adoringly felt the soft hair on his expansive chest.

ST. PAUL, MINNESOTA

Tracy was glad that the work day was over. As much as she enjoyed her work, it had been a hectic one with not a minute's reprieve. It was so busy that she had to gulp her lunch down in less than fifteen minutes. While waiting in traffic to get home and make dinner for her and Mike, she mentally made notes for all she had to do for their vacation. They received the itinerary for the sailing and now had to make arrangements for the flight to Taipei. Tracy had to listen to all the ludicrous comments made to her by fellow workers about her and Mike's upcoming adventure. *'That's okay,'* Tracy thought, *'they're saying all these ridiculous remarks because they're envious and would want to be going on this vacation. Instead, I'll be having the time of my life while they're at the office doing their routine, everyday assignments. Oh well, such is life, then you die.'* Tracy made it home through, what seemed to be, the never ending traffic. She picked up the mail at the box in front of the driveway and opened the door to what she knew would be a quiet house. Mike was working late again. She realized it would be that way for a long time, until he was made a partner. Even then, she knew and recognized the fact that once he achieved his goal of becoming a partner, he'd still have to keep long hours. It was one of the facts of life of which she was aware.

At first it bothered her that he kept the hours he did, then she understood his wants and desires and put them into perspective. She would never squelch his dreams of wanting to become wealthy. He needed that assurance more than anything. *'I gave this gift to him because of who he is. Mike had been brought up in the projects in New York and saw how hard his family worked and how little they received for all the labor they put into their lives. He vowed and promised Tracy that he'd make it good in life so that they'd never have to worry about money as his parents did. He respected them for all that they tried to do for their large brood of children, but realized that they would always be struggling or wanting things that they knew they couldn't own. When he started college, he promised himself that when and if he made something of himself, he would pay his parents back for all the love and inspiration they gave him. Although they couldn't give him monetary items, the love they gave him was just as fulfilling.'*

Tracy understood Mike's inner thoughts and dreams and never gave him a hard time about his working the late hours he did. She also loved Mike's parents and siblings and hoped that one day his wishes and dreams would come true. *'I understand Mike like no other person. He came from the projects growing up in New York and made it through college all by himself. He received scholarships for law school and was third in his class. He wanted to repay his parents for all the encouragement and love they bestowed upon him and his siblings. There were times when his parents, who were hard working, but very poor, couldn't afford to get a birthday cake for his or his siblings' birthdays. That's why I wanted to do what I did for his special day. Yes, he works many hours in the hope that one day he'll be made a partner at the law firm. Sure, even when he does make partner, he'll still have to work hard, but at least he'll have fulfilled his goals, hopes and dreams. He wants to give his parents money so that they won't have to struggle anymore and work the hard manual labor until they get too old and crippled to be able to settle down and enjoy life. I know why Mike is working so very hard. The respect, admiration and love that I have for him can never be vocalized. I only want him to be happy and attain the goals he set for himself, his family and me. That's why I put every spare penny away to save and to show Mike how much I love him. I know this was a great surprise and birthday present. We'll have a vacation of a lifetime.'*

After eating a small dinner and everything was put away, she sat down on the comfortable, beige, suede, lounge sofa in their family room and removed the cell phone from her pocketbook. She called the various airlines finally finding an airline and flights that would get them to Singapore to begin their vacation. After the hectic day she had, she laid down on the large sofa and fell asleep, waiting for Mike to return home. When Mike finally opened the door, he immediately went into the family room, knowing that was where Tracy would be. He stopped in

his tracks, looking adoringly at his wife, who he thought was the most beautiful girl/woman he'd ever laid eyes on. Mike noticed that she was sleeping soundly, a big smile on her face. He thought to himself that she was probably dreaming of the upcoming vacation. He quietly walked over to her, gently shaking her to wake up so that they could both go to their bedroom and sleep together.

NEWTON, MASSACHUSETTS

Renée came home from the hospital where she volunteered after six long hours. Her feet were tired as she remembered wheeling the cart with the many books, through the corridors where the patients were. She quickly went to the sofa in the living room and put her feet up on the ottoman in front of the couch. She closed her eyes and didn't want to think of a thing until she rested for a half an hour. After resting, she found herself feeling refreshed. She knew that Paul was, most likely, down in the basement finishing one of the many projects he did to keep himself busy. She wondered if she should yell down the stairs that she was home or start making dinner and he'd smell the aroma of the food cooking for their evening meal. She decided on the later as she gathered the vegetables to cut up. Sure enough, Paul had finished using the lathe and sweeping the sawdust off the floor when he smelled the wonderful aromas drifting down the stairs from the kitchen above.

Paul walked up the basement stairs after closing the door to his workshop and put his arms around his wife's still-small waist. "Now you stop that; we'll have plenty of time for 'you know what' when we're on vacation. I don't want to get distracted and burn our meal." Slapping his hand, she turned down the burner on the stove and swirled around, putting her arms around his neck. She gave him a big kiss and told him to sit down while she finished preparing the food. "That's what I love about you," he announced. "You're never too tired to say 'No.' Maybe that's why we've stayed married for as long as we have. I love you, Renée, and if I haven't told you enough times, I'll tell you again how much you mean to me."

"Paul, you are a sentimental old fool, but I love it. What new project are you working on?"

"Corey, the young boy next door, is entering a mini scooter race, and along with his Dad's help, we're making a go cart for him. Won't he be surprised when we present him with this new scooter, all painted and polished, of course."

"When did you decide to make this speed wagon?" Renée asked. "Sam saw me in the yard last week and told me all about the race. Corey's birthday is coming up within the week, and we thought we'd surprise him. Sam will do the

painting and polishing of the go cart and then we'll be taking him down to the track at the high school and start training him," a proud Paul announced. "Aren't you the one who doesn't believe in racing?" his wife teased. "Yeah, but that was before Sam came up with this great idea." They both smiled as they sat down for dinner.

"It's not going to be long before our vacation, have you decided what you're going to pack? Remember, the airlines make you pay for any excess baggage. I hear that some airlines make you pay for any bag that a person brings on or have them put into the cargo section of the airplane." Paul remarked, "Hey, I don't give a damn what it costs, as long as we're going away someplace warm. All we have to do is relax, enjoy the sunshine, and buy you all the souvenirs you want. Oh yes, make sure you bring comfortable walking shoes because I bet we'll do a lot of walking to see all the sights in the various places we go."

"You're right Paul; make sure you do the same. I saw the list of the articles that we must bring for sailing and, luckily, we have everything we need. Anyway, we have shoes that have rubber soles; that's all we must have, except each other."

NEWBURYPORT, RHODE ISLAND

Sam came into the house waving the envelope that arrived. "I figured you didn't pick up today's mail and the itinerary is here. I'm so excited!"

"I thought you'd pick the mail up, and I didn't want to see any bills. So bring the packet over and let's see what we've gotten ourselves into." Waving his hand he said: "Just put the bills and junk mail on top of the entry table and come over, patting the couch and put that beautiful tush beside me so we can go through everything together," advised Joe.

Looking through the itinerary, they jotted down everything that was suggested and made notes on what they had to do to get ready for their big trip. "Whatever we do, we can't forget to bring the suntan lotion and some aloe just in case we get a little sunburn," suggested Sam. "Let's go shopping this coming Saturday and purchase the items that we know we don't have. After all, four weeks is a long time to be away. We're lucky that our work agreed it was okay to take such a long vacation." With a smile on his handsome face he mentioned, "Also, I'll make appointments with the doctors for any inoculations we might have to get to go on this God forsaken get-away," Joe told Sam.

That Saturday they went downtown to the center of Newburyport and shopped along the streets, finally stopping at their favorite restaurant for dinner. "I can't believe we shopped so much that we missed lunch," Joe remarked. "It was worth the wait." Sam ordered two Budweiser Lite's for them and looked over the diverse menu. "Before it's too late in the season, let's order lobster and to Hell with the budget. I've taken so much money out of my savings account that at this point what's $65 more," Sam admitted.

Both men enjoyed their meal and, taking out the list, went over the entire inventory until they were satisfied with what they purchased for the day. "Oh by the way, I made an appointment with Dr. Toomey for next Friday, after work, for the inoculations we need," Sam told Joe. "Now that's one of the requirements that I'm not looking forward to," admitted Joe. "You get so squeamish. I can't believe you faint at the sight of blood," Sam admonished. "Well, I do, and as long as you're there to pick me up who gives a damn," Joe laughed as he lightly tapped Sam's hand that was on top of the table.

CHELMSFORD, ENGLAND

Locking the office door, Cole and Isabelle went to the local pub for their customary fish and chips. They greeted their friends and neighbors at the general meeting place and after exchanging greeting with their mates, they sat down at the table that they always had reserved for them and started their regular waffling with their mates. "I hear you're going on holiday," a person yelled from across the room. "What's it to you, you tosser!" Cole jokingly called out. After much banter their meals were placed in front of them. As usual their beers were brought to them as soon as the barmaid saw that they had finished the other bottle.

"These chips are delicious, how about ordering a pudding before calling it a night," suggested Cole. "Let me go to the lavatory and order me another Bud, my beaker is empty," Isabelle expounded. After their usual game of darts with their queues and then singing karaoke, they decided they were a bit shattered and pissed. "Let's call it a night," suggested Isabelle as they said "cheerio" to all their mates.

They didn't remember going into their apartment, but when they awoke the next morning their heads felt heavy as a large weight. "Wow, that was some night, wasn't it?" asked Isabelle. "I don't remember coming home. I think when this holiday comes, we'll be ready for it," admitted Cole. "By the way the postman delivered the itinerary for the holiday. Why don't we take a look see at it and then make arrangements."

"That's sounds bloody good to me," admitted Isabelle.

They couldn't have breakfast the way both of them felt, but instead, sat side-by-side reading the various items suggested to them by the holiday company. By

the time dinner was to be served, they decided to wait a bit longer and put together a scheme to go by. "We can't be scrappy or be a rabbit, we'll never ace everything we have to do," suggested Isabelle. "Of course you're bloody right; let's get cracking," Cole admitted.

When Monday morning came both Isabelle and Cole couldn't wait until they got to work. They realized that the faster they finished processing the orders that had come in, the sooner they could start packing and be ready for their holiday. They made arrangements for their dogs to be kenneled and rang up their employees with orders for all to carry out. They didn't get a chance to go on holiday often and wanted everything to be in ship shape by the time they were to leave. Isabelle was beside herself with anticipation and Cole had all he could do to hold her down. The holiday couldn't come fast enough for either of them.

STONEY BROOK, MASSACHUSETTS

Suzanne got home after working another long day. She opened the mail box and realized that Mrs. Walsh had probably picked up the correspondence. Opening the door, she went into the kitchen. The odors were permeating the house. She couldn't understand how delightful Mrs. Walsh could make a delicious meal after shopping the entire day with her Mom, Dorothy. She called out, informing Mrs. Walsh that she was home. She saw the mail on the kitchen table and started opening the monthly bills. '*I'd better pay them now before our vacation and have Mrs. Walsh get the following months' bills in order, just in case they come in and I'm not home to send them out in time,*' she thought to herself as she sat at the table and sorted out the mail. She made notes for Mrs. Walsh to follow for next month's bills.

When Mrs. Walsh came walking into the kitchen, she spotted Suzanne and, with a large smile, told her what she and Dorothy had bought at the mall. Suzanne was half listening and felt badly about not paying attention. Didn't Mrs. Walsh see that she was paying the bills? Because she had A.D.D., she couldn't pay attention to what her housekeeper was saying when she was doing the monthly bills.

When she finished with the monthly charges, she then put her full concentration on Mrs. Walsh's articulations. She then asked to see what her housekeeper, (more like a friend), had bought and raved about her purchases. While she waited for the dinner to finish cooking, she called her parents' house to make sure that Dorothy had a nice day and to find out how her Dad was doing. She was worried about him, but hadn't said a word to her daughters about what her mother had confided to her. Of course, she was worried about

Morris, but didn't want her fears to be realized. If she did, then she'd have to own up to the real world and confront the issues that were plaguing Morris. She didn't know if she were ready for such a happening to manifest into reality.

After consuming the delicious meal that Catherine had prepared, she told her to watch T.V. and she would clean up the dishes and kitchen. "You outdid yourself on this meal, and now it's time for you to rest. Go, go, into the family room and I'll join you shortly," Suzanne gently pushed Mrs. Walsh out of the kitchen and into the family room where the television was waiting to be turned on. She heard Mrs. Walsh clucking, like her Papa's chickens about the bad events that she was watching during the evening news.

Suzanne finished cleaning up in the kitchen and joined Catherine in the family room, in time to hear the weather forecast for the next day. Suzanne didn't like the heavy rains that were predicted for the morning's commute, but there was nothing she could do but grin and bear it. She only hoped that all the rain wouldn't make the drive into Boston hazardous for all the drivers who had no alternative way to get into town.

Simka and Boston jumped onto Suzanne's lap, one cat on each side. She gently petted them and it mesmerized her. Before she realized what was happening, she felt herself dozing. When Mrs. Walsh shut off the television, she gently shook Suzanne and they laughed while walking up the stairs to their respective bedrooms.

After a hot shower, Suzanne was wide-awake and was mad at her-self for falling asleep downstairs. She tossed and turned, and before she realized what was happening, thoughts of Stephen and Lawrence were before her. She closed her eyes tightly, wanting both of their faces to disappear. Unfortunately, she couldn't will them to go away. The memories of her first encounter with Stephen mocked her as she tried to pull the covers up over her lightly-clad body. She could feel herself getting wet in between her legs as she remembered the sensations that he brought her. *'This has to stop, or I'll never get over him,'* she thought, as Simka walked over her chest and onto the soft, down, pillow she rested her head on.

Then she remembered the date that she made for Friday with Larry and a smile appeared on her face. The two men were so different in many ways. She hadn't allowed herself to be free with Larry, as much as she knew that he wanted her. She wondered how long she could hold him off or was it inevitable that they would become romantically involved. These thoughts kept plaguing her and she couldn't toss and turn because she didn't want to disturb Boston who was sleeping on her leg, without a care in the world. Suzanne shook her head trying to get the images out of her head, but to no avail. She finally reached over, disturbing Boston and took two Advil P.M.'s to assure her of sleeping through

the night. She found that since her accident and episodes in Beppo, Japan, that without her anti-anxiety pill, she couldn't fall asleep. She was frightened that she was becoming dependent on them and realized that this type of behavior was unacceptable. Boston waited for her to take a sip of water to make sure that the pills went down smoothly and then walked again onto her leg. He settled in and again was out like a light. She hoped that she would soon be able to follow him in his good night's sleep.

CHAPTER FOUR

BROOKLINE, MASSACHUSETTS

Hope shut off her cell phone and, with a look of smug satisfaction, went into Spencer's office to tell him the good news. "I just spoke to the pilots and gave them the heads up. Anytime we tell them we need them, they'll be ready."

"That's great," replied Spencer. "When are all of us going to give your Mom and Nancy the surprise?"

"I need your help with suggestions in order for this surprise vacation to go over perfectly. Of course, I'll call my sisters and, between all of us, we'll come up with something."

"Well you better make it fast if you want them to savor the idea and get ready for this get away. Personally, I suggest that you get going because before you know it, they'll be leaving to destinations unknown."

"Oh Spencer, you make everything seem urgent. I'll call the girls tonight and we'll think of something."

"Before you go, come over here." He pushed his chair back and with his pointed finger beckoned her. She went over to where he was sitting and with a look of bewilderment didn't know what he wanted. He got her to stand in front of him and slowly undid the button to her pants, pushing them down so she had no other recourse but to step out of them. He then stood up and one by one, undid the buttons on her shirt. She didn't disappoint him and, when she realized what he wanted, she obliged him by slowly taking his clothes off. When she stood before him, he kissed her slowly and softly and then put his arms around her and with his nimble fingers undid her bra. He then pulled on her string bikini panties and gently pulled them off. Spencer admired his wife as she stood naked in front of him.

As their kisses got more urgent, she fully undressed him. They caressed each other's bodies, and his erection stood at attention. She kneeled down in front of him and licked his entire body. When her mouth was in front of his manhood she stopped and took him fully into her warm, moist mouth. She could hear his enjoyment as she aroused him so that his wet liquid spilled into her mouth.

He took her hand and guided her to the soft, leather sofa and put down an afghan that was lying on the arm of the couch. She lay beneath him and he sought her large breasts and slowly took each breast. With his mouth, he suckled her nipples until they were large and stood erect. He slowly moved his hands until he found her wet spot and sought out her clitoris until he heard her moan with satisfaction and delight. He then entered her slowly and methodically let his fingers roam her body. He deftly felt her soft body, enjoying her curves and lingering at sensual spots that he knew she enjoyed. Before he realized what happened, he lost control as his body moved faster and faster. Hope kept up with his movements, and his semen shot out into the folds of her womanhood. She heard his groan of satisfaction and he lay on top of her, both of them satisfied and enjoying the delights of this unexpected sexual delight.

"This is one way to enjoy a morning of leisure," Spencer spoke softly as he lovingly kissed his sexy wife. All Hope could do was nod her head in agreement as she found herself kissing him back with earnest happiness. "What a nice surprise!" She lay in his arms, content and happy. After a while, with no phone interrupting their unexpected pleasure, they got up from the sofa and put their clothes back on. "I guess I have to go back to reality and let you finish your report," Hope commented as she looked back at her husband when he seated himself back into his comfortable leather chair.

Hope called Melanie and Taylor and between the three of them, they decided to send their Mom and Nancy flowers. Hope gave Melanie her charge card to give to the florist. "In the middle of the bouquet, there'll be the card with the itinerary packed inside." Hope expounded as Spencer, who was now finished with his report, sat down to watch the football game. During a break in the game, a commercial came on and he yelled: "Whatever you decide will be fine with me, honey. Just don't wait too long. They have to make arrangements for replacements at work, at least your Mom does. Be prepared for some hassle with her telling you, and your sisters, that the trip is preposterous."

"You know my mother all too well," Hope said.

"I can't wait till the flowers arrive at their houses. They won't know who sent them, each of them thinking that they're from someone other than us." Hope started laughing and put her arms around Spencer. "Hey, hey, watch out, you're interfering with my Patriots."

"You and your sports," Hope stated as she went into the kitchen to put away the dishes that she was taking out of the dishwasher. Turning back abruptly, she yelled over the television set, "Melanie will take care of sending the flowers. She said something about including a special note inside but I didn't ask her what. We'll find out soon enough."

Melanie got Hope's credit card and decided to make a quick run to the flower shop and enclose a personal note and put in a separate envelope some pictures that she printed off of the web of some places that were located on the itinerary.

STONEY BROOK, MASSACHUSETTS

The weekend was finally here! Suzanne loved not having to get up early and get ready for another day of work. She was looking forward to a leisurely Sunday and to do nothing but lay around in her pajamas. She realized that the spring flowers had to be taken away from the garden. *'I probably have to change my plans for today and get going. What a waste of a good, casual Sunday,'* Suzanne thought as she mentally made notes for arranging her day's schedule. "I'm so mad," she told Mrs. Walsh as Catherine walked down from the second floor stairs. "What's wrong Suzanne, you look perturbed."

"I thought I'd do nothing today; have a leisurely day and then I remembered I have to get the flowers taken away from the front walkway in order to put in the various colored mums."

"Suzanne, what on earth are you pushing yourself so hard for? You can always get it done next weekend," scolded Mrs. Walsh. "Yes, but what if it rains? It's a beautiful day and who knows when we'll have another nice weekend," rebutted Suzanne. "Just take it a day at a time. From all you've been through, I'd have thought you'd have learned a lesson. Think positive, and next weekend will be as nice as this one." Suzanne didn't need a lot of persuasion to change her plans back to what she originally wanted to do. "You talked me into it. I'm not going to get dressed for the entire day. No one's going to see me, and I really don't care. You're right Catherine; I'm positive I'm going to be lazy and not do a thing unless I feel like it."

Suzanne was leisurely reading the day's paper, taking her time and reading practically every article when the doorbell chimed. "I'll get it Mrs. Walsh, just sit tight. I'm closer to the door than you are." She got up off the sofa, put the paper down and went to the front door. Usually she asked who was there, but for some reason she just opened the door, not thinking of any consequence if someone were to rob the house or attack her. *'Don't be ridiculous,'* Suzanne scolded herself. *'What criminal in their right mind would ring the doorbell and announce: "I'm here to rob you."'* Suzanne laughed, as she saw the delivery man with a large, beautiful bouquet of flowers in his hand. "It's Sunday afternoon, what the heck is a florist doing open on Sunday?" asked Suzanne as she accepted the arrangement of flowers. "Well, Ms. Morse, there are always funerals and weddings that are on Sunday. My boss figures we might as well deliver the regular flowers as well."

"You have a nice day, and be careful driving," Suzanne told the gentleman as she closed the door with her foot.

Mrs. Walsh came into the living room and remarked, "What a beautiful vase of flowers. I wonder who sent them to you?"

"I agree; they are gorgeous and full. I love the various colors of the flowers. I'll put them on the coffee table so we both can admire and enjoy them for as long as they last."

"Well, what are you waiting for?" scolded Mrs. Walsh. Find out who sent them."

"They're probably from Larry, or on the other hand, Stephen might have sent them apologizing about his behavior. Although, come to think of it, Larry is always trying to surprise me with unusual presents!"

"Don't forget, and I know that you can't, that the cats love to eat flowers. We'll leave them for a while here but move them to someplace safe, once the cats discover them."

"Yes, I know Catherine, I get nervous whenever I have flowers, knowing that I can't display them as I'd love to because of these darn cats. Oh well, it's the price one has to pay for loving Simka and Boston."

Suzanne saw the envelope in the middle of the arrangement and casually opened the packet. Suzanne sat down, not believing what she was seeing. There were pictures of countries and she didn't know why they were sent to her. She opened the enclosed letter and started crying. Mrs. Walsh came running in, as fast as she could, that is. "What are those tears for? Did Stephen send you a Dear Suzanne letter?"

"No Mrs. Walsh, they're not from Stephen. The girls sent them." Handing the enclosed letter to Catherine she waited for a response. "I don't believe what I'm reading. This can't be possible. This is the most thoughtful present! Just when you think that everyone thinks only about themselves, your daughters surprise you with this vacation." Mrs. Walsh sat down beside Suzanne, tears dropping from her sparkling blue eyes. "Now who's the sentimental one?" Suzanne spoke as they both hugged each other.

As the two women were looking over the pictures, Suzanne's cell phone rang. "Nancy, what are you telling me? They sent you a bouquet as well. We're both going on this fabulous vacation. I can't believe it. The girls went beyond the pale. They're so thoughtful! I'll get off the phone. They're probably expecting us to call them. Nancy, you call Taylor, I'll call Mel. Wait a second, I think instead we'll do three way calling then we'll both be able to hear the girls at the same time," suggested Suzanne.

"Before we make the phone calls," blurted Nancy. "Did you receive the lyrics to the song by Christopher Cross' 'Sailing?' 'I think they're so appropriate! I couldn't stop crying!"

"I did get them, and when I read the words, I handed the paper to Catherine, with the words written out, we both sat like two babies and cried our eyes out," Suzanne replied back to her dear friend.

At the same time both women spoke the lyric to each other. "To where I've always heard it could be, just a dream and the wind to carry me and soon I will be free.

Fantasy: It gets the best of me when I'm sailing. All caught up in reverie; every word is a symphony. Won't you believe me? It's not far back to sanity; at least it's not for me. And when the wind is right, you can sail away and find serenity. The canvas can do miracles; just you wait and see, believe me!!!!!!!!!!"

"Isn't that one of the most beautiful songs you've heard?" Suzanne asked Nancy. "It was hand written and I know it was Melanie's handwriting. I know how she writes," Nancy explained. "Being her mother, or should I say, mother to all of them, Melanie is the most sentimental and that would be just like her to include that song. Did you get the instructions on which packet to open first?"

"Yes, I did," Nancy answered. "Well, the way she did it was very clever. When I first read the lyrics to the song, I didn't know what to make of it. Then in the second packet I read the girls meaningful words and how each of them felt about me being their mother and you being their dearest aunt. Then the third packet showed the itinerary and the various cities and ports that we'll be going to," a proud Suzanne expounded. "It all means so much to me, but to be called their favorite 'aunt' just blew me away," declared Nancy. "By the way, those pictures are beautiful; I wonder how they got them," asked Suzanne. "Oh well, that doesn't matter, we'll take our own pictures and we'll have a great party when we return and show off gifts and pictures."

"Come on, let's start making those phone calls," Suzanne suggested. The girl's phones started ringing their individual tones. When Suzanne got through talking to everyone she sat down. She took hold of Mrs. Walsh's hand and the two of them, without saying a word, keeping their individual thoughts to themselves, looked at the beautiful bouquet. Again tears of gladness, appreciation and joy ran down their cheeks.

Suzanne forgot about her plans for relaxing on Sunday and immediately got pen and paper in hand to write down items that she'd have to include in her suitcases. "I have to remember that this is a sailing vacation so that means I don't have to pack as if I'm going to be going on a regular vacation, (taking lots of luggage). I presume this will be a very relaxing and laid back time. I won't have

to pack nice evening clothes as I usually do. I'm sure that Nancy knows that as well," Suzanne announced to Mrs. Walsh. "I'll take care of the outside flowers next week and, with a little help, I'll be able to plant the mums in place of the ones that are out there now."

Suzanne finished the list of items and then proceeded to write down the essential items that she needed to take. She couldn't wait to get to work the next day to make arrangements for people who would replace her. *'I can't believe I'll be away from the spas for an entire four weeks! It's wonderful that it's not a mission that Nancy and I are going on (sleuths and all that garbage with murder and mayhem). It will be nice to be away and just be able to relax. That's if I remember how.'*

The next morning Suzanne didn't mind driving through the traffic in order to arrive at work on time. The operators at the Salon noticed how jovial their boss was and wondered why she was more joyous than usual. At lunchtime, Suzanne set up a meeting and had a catered lunch brought in for all to enjoy and eat. "Okay, I want everyone's attention, listen up." Suzanne remarked as she moved to the center of their lunch area. "I have some good news and maybe, for some of you, not so good. Nancy and I've been given a surprise vacation from my daughters. We were shocked when we saw what the vacation entails. While we're away, I want all of you girls to get in touch with the estheticians from the other areas, and make out schedules that will cover my time away. I realize it seems that I just got back, but all I can say is that these things happen. I guess we're all lucky, with the economy the way it is, that we've still kept busy and have jobs." All the girls at the Newbury St. Spa clapped with enthusiasm; gathered around their boss and couldn't find out fast enough about Suzanne's up-coming trip.

SAN DIEGO, CALIFORNIA

Rich was sitting at his desk at central when Nancy called. "Hey, I know I usually don't call you during work hours, but I have to tell you some good news." Nancy went on to explain what Suzanne's daughters did for her and Suzanne. "I'm telling you, with all the places that I've been to, it seems as if this will be the most exciting trip of any other. You and I know that, when we go on our honeymoon, that will be an entirely different type of vacation." Rich smiled with delight as Nancy read him the beautiful lyrics to the song 'Sailing' and listened intently while she went over the entire itinerary where the two friends would be sailing. "Honey, I'm at a loss for words. I'm really happy for you and Suzanne. You deserve a vacation after all the two of you have gone through. I

won't rag on you about this is the best vacation. We both know that when we go on our honeymoon, we'll be staying in the hotel room most of the time."

"Oh Rich, you're so funny."

"I'm serious." Rich exclaimed. "Okay, whatever you say. I know you're busy and I'll talk to you this evening. I just had to tell you the news. Till we talk tonight, I love you, be careful and stay alert."

"I love you too honey and yes, I'll be careful and not let those bad guys get me. Remember the goodies always win," with that comment Rich hung up the phone.

This evening, Rich would tell Nancy, when they spoke on the phone, that he made arrangements for Mr. Yashuhito to move into his apartment while recuperating. The two men had gotten close to each other, especially after Mr. Yashuhito saw how devoted Rich was to him while he was recuperating from his near-fatal beating. Rich enjoyed the older gentleman and appreciated the devotion and loyalty that Mr. Yashuhito had for his former employer. *'It's a shame,'* Rich thought, *'Mr. Makino was such an asshole. Someday I'll have to tell this wonderful man how things really were and how bad his boss, Mr. Makino, was.'* For now he was happy to see his friend start to get better and even see a smile on his serious face.

The weeks couldn't go by fast enough for all the couples waiting to go on their vacations. They made their reservations at the individual air terminals that China Airlines or Trans World would get them, eventually to Taipei and, after a layover, fly again to Singapore where their vacation would begin.

CHICAGO, ILLINOIS

Sandy and Arthur had a restless night before taking off in the morning to start their adventure. Veronica and Tim were driving them to O'Hare Airport and were as excited as a 'Honey moon' couple. When they picked them up at Sandy and Arthur's house, Veronica couldn't help but question them about the items they packed. "What, do you think we're idiots?" Sandy, trying not to sound belligerent, told her daughter. "I brought five children up and I think I did a good job. I don't have Alzheimer's' disease or dementia yet; don't be a wise guy!" She scolded her oldest daughter. "Now, now dear, Veronica is trying to be helpful, she didn't mean to question your ability to pack," Arthur spoke, acting as the mediator. Tim lifted the suitcase into the back of the Ford Wagon. They stayed outside for a while, waiting for the appropriate time to leave.

"So tell me Veronica, how's Jason doing? I don't want to get you nervous Dear, but you haven't said a word about Jason since he's been at the facility," a

curious and loving grandmother asked about her oldest grandson. "To be honest with you, Mom, he's very quiet when we are allowed to visit him. He goes to a lot of sessions, sometimes in group therapy and sometimes with individual councilors. I really think he'll be fine when he comes out. The staff is very nice and the man in charge of the place assured us that he's doing well. That's all we can ask for. Just hope and pray that he'll stay off the drugs and booze when he comes home," a loving mother told her Mom. "With that said, I think it's time for us to leave. We'll get you to the right terminal when we arrive at the airport," Tim announced. With the parents sitting in the back seat, they were off to go on the vacation of a lifetime.

ST. PAUL, MINNESOTA

Tracy and Mike had to race back from their respective offices to get back home to drive to the airport. Tracy had made all the arrangements and packed the suitcases ahead of time. She knew that Mike had to finish work for his clients before leaving and wanted to make it as easy as possible for him to enjoy his vacation. From beginning to end, she wanted him to relax and, knew that it wouldn't hurt her either, to just lay back and enjoy this sailing adventure. She had to take care of a few patients and made their appointments early in order to get home in time to take care of any last minute details. Tracy arrived fifteen minutes before Mike, just in time to have the luggage downstairs in the hallway, ready to be taken outside to their automobile. Finally they were on the highway going to the St. Paul International airport. They felt as if their vacation was now really beginning. They held hands as he drove, Mike knowing not to drive too fast and yet not so slow that they'd miss the two hour deadline to check in. They left the bags with the porter and then parked their car in the lot. "You know, we should have had one of our friends drive us, it's going to cost a fortune when we pick up the car," Mike reported. "Don't worry silly, I allocated the money for the parking when I planned your present. Relax and enjoy, this will be our vacation of a lifetime."

NEWTON, MASSACHUSETTS

Renée took time off from volunteering at the Newton Wellesley Hospital in order to make sure that she packed just the right clothes for Paul and herself. She was excited for two reasons. First, for the vacation that they were going on and secondly, to see the exotic places she never dreamed of seeing. She was happy that Paul finished the go cart in time for Sam to do the painting and finishing work he needed to do to get the cart presentable for Corey's birthday. Paul entered the front door, a wide smile on his already handsome, but lined face. "Corey loved the go cart that Sam presented him for his birthday present. It was quite a hit. Sam's going to go around the track with him a few times and I have a sneaky feeling he has a chance to win," Paul beamed. "I'm not wishing our vacation away, don't get me wrong," Paul announced. "We'll be away to some far off land and I won't know how Corey did in his race."

"Isn't there some way that Sam can get in contact with you? Maybe the sailboat will have a ship to shore radio or something that Sam can call you."

"You know, that's a great idea. I'll call up the company that we're sailing with and find out the information. If they have something like that aboard the sailing vessel, I will tell Sam how to contact me."

"Thanks for thinking of it," a delighted Paul said as he went over to his wife and gave her a big hug.

"Tomorrow's the big day, are you getting excited about it?" asked Renée. "I didn't want to get too wound up; but yes, I can't wait until we leave for Logan and are finally in the air. When this vacation of a lifetime is over, I'll have to go to the office and personally bring all the pictures and send some sort of arrangement of flowers for the doctors and nurses. That's the least we can do for sending us off for my retirement present," Paul verbalized.

"Now sit down at the table because this is going to be the last meal I'm going to cook until we get home. There might be a gourmet chef that's on board, but I made something special for our last night before our adventure."

NEWBURYPORT, RHODE ISLAND

Joe and Sam were both on pins and needles getting their luggage packed for their big day. "I'm glad that we're staying over at the Holiday Inn at the airport the night before so we don't have to rush getting to Logan from here. You were smart thinking of it," an admiring Joe blurted. "Oh, I'm so smart and thoughtful," Sam teased as he finished getting their dinner ready. "The bags are at the door and, by tomorrow afternoon, we'll be on our way to the hotel. While we're in Boston, I think we should go to one of the restaurants that we enjoy. What do you think about McCormick and Schmitt for a nice fish dinner?" Joe asked. "Great idea, amigo," Sam admitted as he went over to Joe and hugged him.

As predicted, the traffic was horrendous and it took over two hours to get to the hotel at Logan airport. "I'm not even unpacking, just wearing what I am to go out tonight, if it's all right with you."

"Sure, I think that's smart," Sam admitted. "Lucky we look presentable for a night on the town."

"Now remember, we have an early flight to catch, so we can't stay out as late as we'd like to," Joe advised. When they arrived at the restaurant, they ordered a glass of Merlot and toasted each other on their trip and to have a vacation of a lifetime. When they returned back at the hotel, they went to sleep in each other's arms and both had pleasant dreams of their trip that was ahead for them.

CHELMSFORD, ENGLAND, UK

Cole and Isabelle closed the door to their office and with a big sigh realized that they didn't have to go back to the hectic schedule for another month. "Did you remember to put a sign on the door informing anyone who wanted to swing by that we're on holiday for a month?" Isabelle asked her husband. "I have one right here and I also rang up the answering service advising them of our time away from the office," a proud Cole announced. "I bet you'll forget to put the timer on for the lights in the house if I don't remind you before we leave," a smug Isabelle declared. "For your information, no bloody skive or nick will try to get into the apartment. I have the timer ready to go and I informed the Bobbie's to keep an eye out and come about and run the street and apartment while we're gone. I even had Leon take out the trash on trash day bring in the empty trash bin. The postman will keep the post and bills at the post office until we get back," a smug Cole announced.

"Well aren't you the proctor. I can't pick a Hoo Ha with you now can I," Isabelle admitted as she put her arm around her well-rounded husband and they pressed the lift button to get them out of the building. That evening they got the paper out with all the scheme's written down. "I'm getting nervous, a bit," admitted Isabelle. "Oh, by the way, I have Leon driving us to Heathrow in the morning. I didn't want to spend the extra money for keeping our car in the lot. I'm not a twat you know," pronounced Cole.

"I wouldn't have married you if I thought you were. I want you to butcher the satchels before we take off. You have a good eye for seeing if I missed anything of importance that we may need. After all, I'm not much of a boob either," Isabelle laughed as they headed home.

Leon came by early in the morning to collect his charges before they headed out for Heathrow. "Now are you sure that we have enough appropriated for us to go shopping and get anything unusual we might like. I know we can't bring a lot home because of the restrictions limiting our purchases, but I'll feel like a tosser if we can't purchase something that we really want," Isabelle reminded her husband before they got into their car and put their satchels into the boot. "Do you think I'd ever gut you? I don't look like a tosser to you, do I? I wouldn't want you to cuff my lugs now would I," Cole said as they both opened their individual books to read on the plane and pass the time away until they boarded.

"Leon, I can't thank you enough for all you're doing for us," a grateful Isabelle told their neighbor. As they pulled off to start the journey, Isabelle said out loud: "I hope we don't hit any tailback when we get on the highway."

"The way I figure it, Governor, I'm the proctor and we'll take highway A 12. It might take a few minutes longer, but it has less tailbacks. It'll take approximately one hour and nineteen minutes if I figured right."

"Leon, you're the best next-door neighbor and proctor we could have ever asked for. We'll make sure to send post from everywhere we go," a jubilant Isabelle exclaimed.

"Bye Mate," they both said as they saw Leon pull off from their terminal. They waved excitedly as they brought their satchels to the porter and then went through the line of waiting flyers, ready to take off to destinations unknown, to have a vacation of a lifetime.

BOSTON, MASSACHUSETTS

Nancy arrived at Suzanne's house as scheduled. "I'm glad you're leaving the car at my house. Even though you live in a great neighborhood, you never know what might happen. I'll have one of the girls bring your car to Logan while we're away. I know you'll be anxious to get home," remarked Suzanne

"Suzanne, I could care less about my car, I called the police to alert them I'll be away for a while, like I did when we went to California.

"They'll keep an eye out, they're good like that," Nancy told Suzanne.

"I understand and I think you did the right thing. Even though Mrs. Walsh is getting on in years, with her temper, she'd probably deter any would be burglar. And she's around to feed Simka and Boston. I think I'll have peace of mind for an entire month. I still can't believe this is happening to us. Of course, in the back of my mind the Spas will always be lurking. I'll be wondering what's happening. I have a feeling that if this vacation is as good as I'm expecting it to be; I don't think that the spas will come to mind that often." They put the luggage into the trunk and back seat and drove off to destinations unknown.

Suzanne headed the car down Route 3 to Route 128 north and then they'd pick up Route 93 to Boston. As usual, the traffic was heavy. "I'm glad that we left early. People say that when a person is taking an airplane, you should allow a minimum two hours to get there," Suzanne told Nancy.

Nancy didn't want to burst Suzanne's bubble, but told her friend that they weren't going on any commercial airline. "Did you forget that we have our own plane and go to a different part of the airport than the regular passengers?"

"Oh my God, I did forget! How could I have been such a nut? Yes, I keep forgetting about your generous gift to the spas! We don't have to worry about those silly regulations. I do forget that we have our own airplane and we don't have to adhere to any regulations that other people must. Oh well, it still doesn't make the traffic that we encounter any less. It means that I won't have to be in worry-mode about all the cars. We can take our time and not care about the two-hour time frame. I don't want to keep thanking you for your gift but I still can't get over your generosity."

"Hey, it's the least I could do," Nancy proclaimed. "Most companies have their own planes for transportation and this makes life a lot easier with all the trouble that we seem to get into."

Suzanne looked over at her friend and just shook her head… "It's not that we ask to get into trouble. It just sort of finds us, don't you think?" asked Suzanne. "Yes, I guess so, if you say it enough times, maybe I'll believe it." With that comment, both women laughed as Suzanne maneuvered her car and put her directional on to move into the commuter lane.

CHAPTER FIVE

Sandy and Arthur were trying to kill time sitting in the plastic and chrome, uncomfortable seats waiting for their Trans World airplane to depart from O'Hare Airport to Boston's Logan airport. Sandy and Arthur were holding hands, glancing and wondering about their fellow passengers. They were waiting for about an hour before they could enter the plane that would be filled to capacity. After settling down, they took out novels and various brochures of Boston, hoping that the reading would distract them from their nervous reactions that flying usually brought on. It had been years since they had to fly and it showed in their anxious behavior. They decided that since they haven't been able to see much of the States and travel to places that would be interesting, they chose to sightsee in the Boston area. They made arrangements to stay in Massachusetts for an extra three days before starting their real vacation. They would stay at the Marriot on Long Wharf and walk around Boston to enjoy the sights about which they heard wonderful things. When offered a beverage, they elected to wait until their two next really long flights to indulge in something stronger than the customary tea, water or coffee and hope that the alcohol would relax them and put them to sleep, at least part of the way, for their extensive, lengthy journey.

It seemed as if the hours literally flew by when they arrived at Logan airport in Boston. The taxis were lined up waiting for people to tell the drivers where to take them. After finding out that their cab driver originally came from Pakistan, they talked about his homeland and what he likes best about the Boston area. It was interesting for them to hear from an immigrant the various reasons why he decided to move his family to the Brighton area. They had friends, who had relocated and lived in Pepperell, MA, who they hadn't heard from in years. When speaking to them over two years ago, they realized that Pepperell was a quant New England town; not the inner city that Brighton was. After what seemed like no time they were brought to the front door of the elegant hotel. They were impressed when they arrived and finally settled into their spacious room. Sandy took the initiative and wanted to rest awhile before doing any sightseeing. Arthur realized that resting was the sensible thing to do. They slept for a few hours and then went across the street to Boston's Quincy Market to walk around and see the different sights. They bought food from one of the many diverse eating booths from various countries and the meals that went with that particular country. Sandy found two seats and they put the food on the wooden table that they shared with other people. Sandy, being talkative, found out that many people came from Massachusetts while others were from foreign lands and were visiting this famous area for the first time, like them. Arthur went back to the Monkey Bar and bought the different fruit drinks to enjoy with their food. After more walking, they went to the Gelato stand and bought the Italian ice cream that they heard many good things about.

After walking for what seemed hours, they went back to the hotel and fell into a sound sleep. They slept in late and then made arrangements to walk the Freedom Trail in the North End. An Italian Restaurant was a must! Before the day was to begin, Sandy made sure that she called her friends and told them that they were in town. The two couples talked endlessly and made plans to get together on their return home from their vacation. When Sandy put the phone down, she felt good that they made contact with their friends that, at one time, they were very close to. "Time seems to fly by, and I'm glad that we've made plans to get together with the Millers. Just exchanging Christmas cards is nice, but to actually see them will be great," Sandy expounded as she closed the cell phone. The next day they toured China Town and dined on Chinese Duck and different dishes that they never heard of. "Before you know, this will get us used to the unusual meals that we'll be having at the various ports on our vacation," Arthur remarked. "You're right, Honey, I'm getting excited just thinking about the strange delicacies that we'll be trying for the first time," Sandy commented as she put an unusual dumpling in her mouth.

They hated to leave the Boston area and promised they'd come back to see more sights within the next few years. "I promise, now that the children are grown and we have our own lives to think about. Life goes by too quickly and we have to make the most of the time we have left." Sandy heard Arthur and wondered if he had spoken to her cancer doctor, but put that thought aside. She knew her husband well enough that if he knew that she was remiss in her dealing with this new situation, she would have heard about it immediately. "Arthur, you sound as if you'll be dead in a few years. My God, we're still young and have many more years ahead of us. Think positive and, yes, I agree with you, this is our time in life to enjoy each other's company and see and do things that we never dreamed of doing." Taking his arm, she walked beside him as the taxi headed for the terminal.

They asked the attendants where they were to go to get to China Airlines. It seemed like hours, but in reality not that long, to walk to the waiting area. They realized that they would be crossing the International Date Line and lose one day en route to Taipei where they would stay at a hotel until the next morning's flight to Singapore.

While en route to China airlines, they noticed a couple who seemed unlikely candidates, waiting to board the same airplane. Talking amongst themselves, they tried guessing the reasons why the various passengers were flying to Taipei. "I know we're not world travelers, but isn't it fun guessing why the different people would want to go to this unusual destination," Sandy spoke quietly to Arthur. "Well Honey, we're not part of the jet set, so I imagine most of the people are on the way to see family, while others are going there for business."

"Arthur, look at the couple that just came into the terminal. They don't look like either type. They're dressed casually, like we are, and if I wanted to, I'd say they're going on the same vacation that we are."

"Sandy, I have a great idea, why don't you go over to them and ask where they're going and why."

With that comment, Sandy punched him gently on the arm and smiled wickedly at her husband. "You are a wise guy and I'll ignore that I heard what you said. We'll see if they come to the same hotel that we go to and then I'll definitely start a conversation with them," Sandy assured her husband.

"Well," Arthur remarked to his wife, "Look at the Fruit of the Looms that just walked into the waiting terminal. "Either they're here to adopt a baby, or are going on a business venture."

"They don't seem the type that would go on a vacation, like we're about to embark on, do you think so, honey?"

"Now Arthur, let's not make quick decisions about anyone. You never know why someone would visit this area of the world. Let's see if they also go into the same hotel as us and then I'll have to go over to both couples. I'll ask them if they're on their way to Singapore to go on the sailing vessel, 'Vacation of a Lifetime,'" Sandy remarked.

"That's why I love you, honey, you make everything an adventure. Don't worry that pretty head of yours until we get to Taipei. Then you'll have something to look forward to," Arthur laughed as he tussled his wife's short, curly, dark hair.

Tracy and Mike decided to begin their journey by visiting Mike's relatives in the Bronx. From their local airport, they determined that if they left a few days earlier, they could see his folks and siblings in New York. Most of his family stayed within the vicinity of the city so it made it easier for them to stay with his brother Joey and his wife while doing the 'kin thing.' "I can't believe you were so thoughtful to book us on the flight to La Guardia. Even though I speak to everyone at least once a week, what a surprise for them that they'll be seeing us in person. Lucky that Joey has a large enough house that has an extra bedroom."

"Honey, it's not that he has a guest room. Remember Lisa got married six months ago and she and her husband now live in Manhattan." Oh yeah, I almost forgot. I remember that we couldn't make the wedding because of some stupid audit that had to be in the hands of the firm's bookkeeper by a certain date and time, which didn't leave us any time to go the wedding."

"But, if you remember, Mike, we sent a more generous wedding gift than anyone expected."

"Yes, I remember in the thank you note that Lisa wrote saying that because of our big hearted and kind wedding present, they were able to purchase the bedroom set that they had dreamed of but thought that they'd never be able to afford," reminded Tracy.

"I forgot all about the gift."

"Honey, I think you have more on your mind lately than to remember all the small details that I take care of," Tracy told Mike to jog his memory. "You know Honey; thankfully, I let you handle all the details necessary to keep our marriage and house intact."

"Thanks, I'll get you back one day and when I do, be careful mister, I'll have you wishing I was still doing all the mundane details that you thought were nothing to handle." They both laughed as they departed the terminal and, with their luggage in hand, got into a taxi which was waiting to whisk them off to the Bronx.

Joey, Mike's brother, picked them up and couldn't wait to bring them to his house. He had made plans for the entire family to bring pot luck dishes and they would have an old-fashioned get together. When everyone left for the evening, Joey and Mike talked for hours. Finally Mike and Tracy got into bed and were all revved up, not able to quite go to sleep. They both looked at each other and before you could say Jack Rabbit, they were hugging and touching each other. One thing led to another and as in the past, they couldn't keep their hands off each other. Mike, not so gently, took off Tracy's night gown and admired her curvaceous body as his fingers touched each part of her womanhood. Tracy was moaning with delight as she enjoyed being stroked by her handsome and adoring husband. Before he realized what was happening, he felt Tracy taking his briefs off. Their kisses lingered and without another word, Mike was on top of Tracy, his knees spreading her legs apart and entered her swiftly. Their movements were slow and steady and suddenly, Mike was beside himself with hunger. His hips were acting as if on their own, he couldn't control his desire much longer. Tracy

kept up with him and, before they realized what was happening, they both climaxed together. Before they fell asleep, Mike rolled off of his affectionate wife and with a smile on his face, held her closely, not wanting to ever let her go.

After three great days of visiting family and friends, Mike's brother, Joey and his wife Maria drove them once again to the airport terminal for China Airlines. Looking into his wife's beautiful large brown eyes, he hugged her tightly. "Tracy, if I haven't told you enough times, I'll tell you again, I love you. You are so thoughtful and caring. My family loved seeing us and I can't tell you what it means for all of us to be together again, not just for funerals or weddings. Thanks again." Tracy turned bright red and shrugging her shoulders, "Now don't push things too far, or you'll expect me to do everything for you and I'm not going to wipe your ass, don't even think about it," Tracy laughed as they finally sat down waiting for boarding to be called.

Renée and Paul locked the door of their large home in the suburbs of Newton and backed out of the driveway heading for Logan Airport. Before pulling out and making sure a car wasn't coming down the street, Renée again reassured Paul that the postman would leave the mail at the post office and their next-door neighbor had a key to their house, and would check inside periodically and that she set the automatic timer for the various lights to go on at certain times in the different rooms of the house. "Okay, now I can go in peace," Paul remarked as he angled out of the steep incline on which their house and driveway was located. They were both glad that they were leaving the car in the parking lot at the airport, not wanting to be beholden to anyone for the favor of driving them. "It was nice of Sam to offer, but I'm glad that you refused," Renée told Paul as he tried maneuvering amongst the heavy traffic along Route 9. "I'm not sure this is the easiest way to Logan, but with all the new construction from the Big Dig, it's the way I know how to go and we're leaving enough time to make sure everything will be fine," Paul reassured Renée as he passed the various malls on either side of the street. Turning to look at her husband Renée tried squelching her enthusiasm; acting as nonchalant as possible. She made small talk trying to curb her zeal for this coming vacation. They have been and seen many places throughout their married life, but this trip truly would be above and beyond anything or anyplace they've been before. Renée squeezed her husband's hand as he drove cautiously, concentrating on the road.

Paul was jubilant and couldn't contain his happiness any longer. Out of nowhere he screamed 'YES' and Renée almost had a heart attack. "What the Hell was that all about?" She asked Paul. All Paul could do was laugh and shouted, "We're actually going, I can't believe that we're going out of the box and going

to destinations unknown. I'm sorry that I scared you, but Honey, I'm so happy I just had to yell. I want to laugh and cry at once. I know that sounds preposterous, but I can't help it." Renée smiled at her husband and was happy that he could finally relax and start his retirement in such a wonderful way. She happened to be thrilled for him, knowing how hard he worked to gain the wonderful reputation he had among his peers and patients. She was proud and thrilled at the same time. All she could do was squeeze his hand and smile throughout the entire car ride.

Paul left his wife at the curb waiting with the luggage while he parked the car in the lot. He loved to walk and knew that this was the beginning of the many miles that he and Renée would stroll through the various cities, villages, and remote areas they've never been to before. They left their luggage with the porter and took their time waiting to go through security. "I don't know what all the fuss is about. In reality, we're hurrying to wait and wait for what?"

"Now Paul, since 9-11 the airports have to be more cautious. Hopefully, they know what they're doing," Renée spoke as she took off her shoes and put everything she could into the plastic bin she would pick up at the end of the conveyor belt. When they gathered all their belongings, they went to the gate where they sat in the vinyl and chrome seats that were commonly scattered among the various airport waiting areas.

They looked about and saw the various couples and individuals who would be among them on the airplane on the journey to Taipei. They noticed the definite effeminate couple opposite them and smiled. They got back a return smile and, out of the blue, Renée started talking to them. She told them about Paul's retirement party and their surprise sailing venture. Paul didn't know if it was because of her nervous energy or insecurity but he couldn't get her to stop talking. Joe and Sam were listening intently and when they could get a word in edgewise, advised this lovely, friendly, anxious woman they would probably be going on the same trip. She thought, the two men, a handsome couple, seemed as if they were delighted that they were able to acquaint themselves with someone who would be going on this unusual adventure. The attendant finally called all the passengers to board.

When it came time to board the plane, Joe was delighted that the lovely, but talkative lady was seated at the other end of the plane. Joe realized that they would be crossing the International Date Line and lose one day en route to Taipei. He was glad that he and Sam could experience this long flight without hearing the constant chatter of this lovely lady. Joe realized that over the four week long sailing voyage, her voice would become familiar to their ears. Laughing he thought, *God love her, she is delightful and very jubilant. It will be*

pleasant seeing her experience all the wonders that she, probably, hasn't experienced before. He had to laugh because he knew that he and Sam were also seeing and doing something out of the ordinary as well.

HEATHROW AIRPORT

Cole and Isabelle passed customs and Isabelle wouldn't let go of her carry-on bag. "Why did you have to bring that satchel with you, luv?"

"Now Cole, God forbid something should happen to our luggage. I had to make sure we had a fresh pair of knickers, your pants and all of our travel documents. I've heard many people tell horror stories of their luggage being lost for days at a time. I'll make sure I'll put the case in the bin up above, and I'll feel better. Let me go to the lavatory and then I'll be good for a few hours. It's going to be a long flight, so we have to make sure and guff about, so we don't get leg cramps. I hope they give us a rug and pillow to get comfortable during this long flight," Isabelle informed her husband.

Cole removed himself from the row of seats letting Isabelle take the window seat she asked for. They realized that they'd be crossing the International Date Line and lose one day en route while in Taipei. Cole couldn't wait till the lift off and then the unfasten seat belt sign was on. He was looking forward to the pretty flight attendant coming down the aisle with alcohol drinks. He didn't want to natter to anyone, other than his wife. As far as he was concerned, he couldn't wait to have a couple of brews, (not any squash for him), get good and tired and sleep for most of this long trip. Of course, he'd have to get up and walk a bit going to the lavatory and slash after consuming all the beverages he intended to imbibe. He hoped that he'd be able to get some bloody rest. Neither he nor Isabelle had been on an airplane for this extended amount of time.

When the flight attendant came by with the drinks, Cole wasn't shy when asking for his brews. After polishing off three of them in a row, he felt tired. Before he knew it, he was fast asleep, snoring loudly enough to cause some of the passengers to get a bit angry. He was depriving them of the precious sleep they also needed. Isabelle was used to her husband's noises. Nothing would wake her when she finally shut her light after reading her novel and got the much needed rest that the other passengers were trying to get when all the lights went out except for the few emergency lights throughout the massive jet.

BOSTON'S LOGAN AIRPORT

Nancy arrived at Suzanne's house before 5 a.m. She was glad that she left Ipswich early, avoiding the morning commute which was unbearable between 7:00 to 9:30 in the morning. She realized it would have been easier for her to go directly to the airport using route 93 toward Boston, but knew that Suzanne wanted company on the ride into Boston.

It seemed forever since they received the packet from Suzanne's daughters informing them of their upcoming vacation. Nancy shivered in anticipation knowing that they were on the way to a different kind of adventure than either of them had ever had.

They were lucky to be able to avoid the crowded terminal. Their attendants parked Suzanne's vehicle in a separate area. Suzanne didn't have to worry about theft with the guards looking out for the special patrons. Of course, a nice tip was always appreciated. People who traveled on their own planes or jets were seated in a separate room and given anything they desired. Nancy and Suzanne ordered juice, knowing that a magnificent meal would be awaiting them once they were seated in the luxurious eating area of their own transportation.

Once inside the plane, the pilots waited for the go ahead from the air traffic controllers. The private jet pilots were grateful that Nancy and Suzanne were exceptionally cautious when it came to maintaining their plane and equipment. They insisted on the latest radio, radar and other signaling devices to use to their advantage. They had the latest equipment and felt confident when traveling short or long distances. Ray, the senior pilot, had logged many hours, as he was a pilot for the air force for many years and his co-pilot, Dave, had almost the same amount of experience. When having the airplane specifically built for those two dynamic women, they decided to have an extra-large fuselage installed to enable them to go nonstop to most international countries. Nancy didn't let cost be a factor in any of her decisions when it came to this mode of transportation. Ray and Dave felt good about their boss and had no qualms when asked to go anywhere. They knew that they had one of the best private jets in the world. They often asked themselves who would have thought that a young lady, who wasn't even forty yet, could afford such a luxurious, extravagant airplane.

The plane was on auto pilot and flying at a high altitude. Suzanne and Nancy had finished their breakfast and were now completing their gourmet lunch when they decided to play some gin rummy. "I bet I beat you this time," Suzanne chided Nancy. "We'll see, I've been practicing and I have a feeling I'll beat the pants off you." After playing six games the score was even. "Okay, we'll continue this game at another time, if it's okay with you Miss Nancy. Now I feel I'll retire to my suite and doze for a while. We did get up early and you got up earlier than I did. Of course you're younger, but I won't take that into account."

"You know, Suzanne you're a wise ass; a nice one; but nonetheless a wise ass."

"You can say anything you want, I'm not listening to a young kid like you and I'm taking my novel, getting under the warm comforter and sleeping in La, La land shortly. Even though it's a long flight, I don't want to think about the trip or this plane. I do appreciate all the money that you spent on this mode of transportation," her hands flying out by her sides, showing the proportion of the jet; "but nonetheless, I still hate flying. Let me get into my own zone and veg. out. Good night, Nancy. Don't forget, I really love you, maybe not in the same way as I would a guy, but love can be determined in different ways about all sorts of people and friends."

"Are you through or do I need to hear more of your prattle?" teased Nancy. Nancy realized that no matter what she did or how much money she spent on any airplane, Suzanne would still hate to fly. She heard Suzanne talk a storm about if God wanted humans to fly in the air, he would have put wings on them like he did on birds. Nancy would shake her head and laugh to herself. She'd never want to hurt Suzanne's feelings.

While Nancy was in her bed waiting for Morpheus to take over, she thought of Suzanne and felt sorry for her friend's circumstance. It didn't seem fair that she was in love with a man who couldn't or wouldn't change his life to become the couple that Suzanne wanted to be. No one realized how much hurt Suzanne had gone through when Stephen didn't show up for the reception party at Hope's and Spencer's wedding. All Nancy could think about was how grateful she was that Lawrence was there to help Suzanne in her time of need.

Lawrence has been in love with Suzanne for years it seemed. Nancy couldn't understand why Suzanne couldn't feel the same way about Lawrence as he did about her. Nancy recognized that she couldn't experience the thought of being in love with your high school sweet heart, a sense that Nancy couldn't understand. It seemed that Lawrence had been in love with Suzanne since he first saw her on Louis and Beverly's boat, years ago. *'If I were in Suzanne's shoes, I'd say to Hell with you Stephen and fly into Lawrence's waiting arms.'* With that thought, Nancy slept like a log, adrift on smooth water.

Both women awoke and were famished. Nancy placed the linen napkin on her lap and waited for the stewardess to give them their delicious meal. Suzanne, knowing that all the food that she consumed looked good on her, enjoyed the taste of whatever she put into her mouth. She put her napkin like a bib under her collar. She laughed to herself thinking of Morris and how her mother, Dorothy, would also place his napkin on top of his clothes, not wanting to have to send whatever he was wearing to the cleaners again...

Before they realized what time it was, the airplane was descending to Singapore. They couldn't believe that all the hours in the air had gone as fast as they did. The women had just enough time to quickly brush their teeth and get ready to disembark. Suzanne had butterflies in her stomach as she thought of this wonderful and unusual vacation. She couldn't believe that her daughters had been so thoughtful. '*Yes, I guess that I did something right when bringing them up.*'

CHAPTER SIX

Sandy and Arthur settled in the plane and, with a huge sigh, Sandy was finally able to relax. Arthur smiled to himself as he watched his wife (who was constantly on the go) seated, with a book in hand, waiting for the lift off to begin. The rest of the passengers were seated in their assigned seats and were adhering to the lighted sign telling them to buckle up. Arthur and Sandy hated the lift off. From all they read, the most dangerous time for airplanes was when the plane took off and when it landed.

Sandy laughed to herself as she put her book down. She shut her eyes tightly when she heard the engines whirling, ready for takeoff. She heard a few people talking to themselves and took notice of the Serenity Prayer being spoken softly by people around her immediate vicinity. With a sigh, they both were thankful that the plane was finally airborne and they could take their seat belts off.

Arthur whispered to his wife that she shouldn't forget to walk around the plane to get the circulation going in her legs because of the many hours she'd be seated in the jet. "Don't worry about me, honey, I know I have to do that because the children already told me, but don't you forget to listen to your own advice." Arthur patted Sandy's hand as they both opened their books, trying to pass the time away. When the attendants came around with the offered drinks, they gladly accepted the liquid refreshments. They knew that they'd be in the air for quite some time and tried not to think of the next descent to be made for refueling so they could continue on their journey.

Arthur took his journal out from the storage bin and, putting his novel down, began writing the different sights that they saw in the Boston area. "I'm glad that I brought three journals with me," Arthur remarked to Sandy. "With this long, trip we'll be seeing some unusual sights that we may forget once we get home and try to relate everything we saw to our neighbors and family."

"Arthur, you think of everything. I hope that you brought along that beautiful new digital camera. I hear that there's a vast jungle in the Viet Nam area. I don't know what part of Viet Nam it's in, but I'd love to find out if we can go there and see for ourselves the many species of animals and get pictures of them in their natural habitat."

"That's a great idea! When we're settled on the sailboat, we'll have to ask the Captain all about this particular jungle that you're talking about. Since he's been there many times, I'm sure he'll know what you're talking about."

"I didn't want to say anything to you, but, now that we're seated, I have a confession to make. I had hoped that we'd be seated in the middle of the plane and sure enough, we're right by the exit sign. I know it's a crazy notion, but it's one that was bothering me." All Arthur could do was smile and pat his wife's hand. After a few hours passed, the stewardess came around once more and handed out the meals, (if you'd call it that), and again offered drinks to go along with the meal.

Sandy was pretending to sleep next to her husband. She loved the idea of the gift that the children gave them. '*It couldn't come fast enough,*' Sandy thought as she remembered the last appointment with the oncologist. She had gone alone to this visit because Arthur thought that she'd be fine with all the good reports that they'd been receiving. Little did either of them realize what a shock she would get when she went into Dr. Tower's office! Sandy was happy to have the doctor take care of her in her time of need. When Dr. Tower asked Sandy to sit down, she had no idea that this was anything other than a routine visit.

The news that Dr. Tower gave her took Sandy by surprise. "When you had your last CAT scan, we made sure that the other organs looked good. Unfortunately, we found two separate masses, one on each lung." Sandy felt faint. Words couldn't describe the sick, nauseous feeling that overtook her. The bile came up and into her throat. She was glad that Arthur wasn't here to hear the words that the oncologist told her. The grim projection was devastating. She didn't want to burden Arthur or her family and friends with this terrible news. Dr. Tower took Sandy's hand and held her tightly. The doctor had a great bed-side manner; that was one of the reasons why Sandy and Arthur chose Dr. Tower as her oncologist.

When Sandy left Dr. Tower's office she vowed that she wouldn't tell anyone about the grim news until there wasn't time for her to undergo any chemotherapy treatments again. She couldn't put herself or her loved ones through the torment of knowing that there wasn't any hope. She made friends with many patients and, unfortunately, the outcome was always bad when it came to Lung Cancer. No, she was determined that she would live life to its fullest. She vowed to herself that she would be upbeat and not tell Arthur or the children until it was the very end. She feigned sleep, knowing that Arthur was in the arms of Morpheus. Sandy was determined that she wouldn't spoil this wonderful and thoughtful trip that her children gave to them. '*At least,*' she thought, '*Arthur will always have good memories of this trip and will remember the*

great time and new places that we saw together.' With those thoughts she willed herself to sleep.

Paul and Renée felt comfortable seated in the back section of the airplane. Renée requested seats in the last few rows of the plane because she felt that if the plane went down, the nose of the plane would land on the ground first and thought that they'd have a fighting chance at surviving a crash. Paul thought his wife's idea was crazy, but didn't want to upset her or her way of thinking. *'Everyone had little quirks,'* he realized and let her believe what she wanted. He again opened his latest novel and tried to get absorbed in the plot. Paul found it impossible to do and automatically took out the latest medical journal that he brought with him. *'Now this is crazy, here I am retired and I'm reading a journal that has new medical techniques and information that I probably won't need. I mean, really, I'm older and won't need this new stuff. I don't know why I bothered to bring it. I know why, I'm such an old fool; it's a habit and one that's hard to break. Who knows, when I get back home, I might get a bit bored and want to work part time doing clinic work. Then I'll have to be informed of all the new medicines that the companies have come up with.'*

Renée looked to her right and saw Paul reading the medical journal. She saw him pack it into his duffle bag and didn't say a word. She knew that old habits were hard to break. Thinking to herself, she remembered the time when she was slightly bored with her husband when they had been married for eighteen years or so. Then she realized that the grass always looked greener on the other side, but everyone had habits and it's better to live with the ones you know then to test the waters and not know what's out there. She was glad that the wanderlust was past her and the more years she was married to Paul the more she appreciated what a kind, thoughtful, gentle man he was. *'And he's not bad in the bedroom as well.'* It was with these thoughts that she closed her eyes and tried to pass the time away waiting for the hours to, literally, fly by and then refuel and get back up in the air to finish their journey to Taipei.

Joe and Sam were comfortable in the seats that they picked. They enjoyed being in the front of an airplane thinking that the ride was smoother the closer to the cockpit one could get. Each brought various magazines and journals and tried passing the hours by not thinking of how long they would be in the air. Each man was lost in his own thoughts. Sam couldn't help think about his ex-wife and his children that he often got to see and play with on the weekends. They were his to take wherever they decided to go. His ex-wife, at first, was a real bitch, not understanding how he could give his marriage and children up for another man. It was not in her realm of thinking. When she got married, it was for keeps, till death do you part.

Sam also was brought up in a conventional household, being the middle child of three siblings. He was the only son, having two female offspring on either side of his birth. Sam played all the typical boys' sports and, even though (he had to admit to himself), he excelled in each activity he played, he was a good player and team inspiration. Thinking back to the way he thought then, he remembered his thoughts about other young men and suppressed the ideas that were hidden in the recess of his mind. He dared not tell a soul and kept his emotions to himself. He didn't tell his best buddies or his fellow teammates. As far as he could tell, they all enjoyed and talked about the conquests of the opposite sex. Sam felt he had to go along with the other boys or else they would make fun of him.

When he got older and found himself in college, he kept his thoughts, in what they now call, hidden in the closet. He wouldn't come out. When he started dating Lisa while she was a sophomore at Simmons and he was a junior at Bentley, it seemed the right thing to do. All his friends were serious with their girlfriends and started getting engaged and married. After much kidding from his roommates and fellow students, he decided to take the plunge and ask Lisa to marry him. He had his misgivings, but he did like her and it wasn't that he didn't like the intimacy they had. It was that, in the back of his mind, he knew that he would prefer to be making love to another male. He tried to keep his effeminate side of his personality at bay and let life slide by.

Before he knew what happened, he found himself having a family consisting of three young sons, a wife who, in his eyes, was still attractive and a wonderful person. She hadn't a clue to what his inner most thoughts were. He still participated in the older guys' hockey league and, whenever the guys played tag football, he was always there to be part of the team. Sam encouraged his young sons to play sports and Sam became a coach to the little league baseball teams. He let life fly by and, all the while, when Lisa wasn't looking, sized up the boys or men who walked by or business acquaintances or the men who were part of the couples they frequently found themselves out with.

On one of the fellows' nights out, having watched the Patriots on the Monday night sports channel, the guys decided they'd hit one more bar. Jokingly, one of the guys brought up the idea of going to a gay bar. After much drunken banter, the group entered the establishment. Sam knew that it wasn't a good idea for him to be going into a gay bar. Besides being smashed to the gills, he'd find himself looking at young boys in a way that most men would find inappropriate. After indulging in a couple more beers, Sam saw guys flirting and dancing with each other. Joking around, the guys in his group started dancing with each other and before they knew what was happening they were mingling with members of the gay community.

The other guys thought it was funny; but, to Sam, it wasn't a joking matter. He could feel his face get red and he was sweating profusely. He wanted out of there as fast as possible. Before he knew what happened, a young man came over to him and started a conversation. His name was Joe and he seemed like a nice, regular guy who, if one were to look at him, would never consider him gay. The other guys whom Sam was with were so smashed that they didn't know who Sam was talking to. Sitting at the end of the bar, the two men found that they had a lot in common. They both liked sports; although, Sam found it hard to believe that a "swishy" guy would like to participate and watch sporting events. They had the same political beliefs and were brought up with practically the same family values. Joe hadn't found it necessary to marry, but to most of his friends, he was odd but definitely not gay. Most of his friends considered him a man that was destined to be a bachelor and didn't want to be burdened with having a family of his own.

The only time that Joe allowed himself to go to the gay bars (and sometimes to the clubs that only men went to) was when he found himself not having anything else to do or wanted to enjoy his favorite past time being with other men. He had a few relationships with other men but as he told Sam, nothing serious. At the end of the evening the designated driver rounded up his pals and started driving them home. While in bed that evening and other nights to follow, he couldn't get Joe out of his mind. He made excuses to Lisa whenever she wanted to make love and found one reason or another to avoid having physical contact or activities with his wife. He didn't like the way he was behaving but found it difficult to accept that he enjoyed the one night that he had with Joe more than any night throughout his entire married life. '*That's sick,*' he thought to himself. In his mind, he made mental notes and lists of the advantages were of being married to Lisa or having to come out of the closet and finally be the person he really wanted to be.

He realized that Lisa would be crushed and his young son's confused and bitter at being involved with parents who were divorced. It was one thing to have parents divorced, but an entirely different matter when their playmates found out that their father was gay. He would lie in bed, his hands behind his head and feel ashamed of his thoughts. He didn't know what to do. Sam considered suicide but was too chicken to go through with it.

Walking home from work one evening, he had to stop at the supermarket to pick up some items that Lisa wanted. When he got to the store, Joe was walking into the supermarket at the same time. They shook hands and one thing led to another. Before Sam realized what was happening, he found himself going to a club with Joe that his new friend had suggested. Hours went by until Sam realized that Lisa must be going crazy. By now she was probably calling the police and the hospitals around the area. He made his excuses, but before going out the door, Joe wrote down his cell number and told him to call him at any time.

When he arrived home that evening, he found Lisa in a panic. She bombarded him with questions, all of which he couldn't answer. He saw that his sons had been crying seeing their mother upset and sat them down. He tried explaining that he met an old friend and time went flying by. He apologized to them and read them a story before tucking them into bed for the evening. Sam found himself sitting on the sofa when Lisa came over and sat beside him. "Okay, now let's have the truth, the real truth. I'm a big girl now and for a long time I have been thinking that something isn't right. We've been married too long to keep secrets from one another." Her voice went up an octave as she continued to talk to her husband. Finally she sat beside him, crossed her arms, waiting for an explanation.

Minutes went by, which to Sam, felt like hours. "I'm not getting off of this couch and neither are you until I hear an answer. I can tell when you're lying, so it better be the truth. No dilly dallying. We've been through a lot together, and I thought we could discuss anything with each other," said Lisa. Sam could see the tears brimming in Lisa's eyes. Taking a deep breath, Sam told Lisa everything from when he was a young boy to the present. A pin could be heard dropping. Lisa sat there, her face expressionless. Suddenly she turned and started hitting Sam with fists clenched. He tried defending himself, but realized that he deserved every punch given to him. When the barrage was over, Lisa slumped and started crying. At first a whimper and then sounds like Sam had never heard before, sounds that came from deep within Lisa's heart and soul.

After ten minutes of hysteria, all was still. He was afraid to look at his wife, not knowing what assault would come next. Taking a deep breath Lisa said, "I can't believe what I heard come out of your mouth. You certainly had me and everyone else who knows you fooled. I'm too embarrassed to see or talk to my family and friends. How are your parents and family going to take this admission? I thought I'd never say this to you, Sam, but I really, truly hate you. I despise you for all the lies, the pretenses, and most of all, I hate you for what you're doing to those children up in their beds, fast asleep, not knowing that their father is nothing more than a gay, fucking faggot. That's right, you never heard me swear before. But believe me, I know all the swear words. You're a gay, fucking faggot, and I hope that you rot in Hell. In a way it's better than having you leave me for some worthless whore with big tits. That would be humiliating enough, but giving up all you have for some guy?" She kept shaking her head. "You can sleep down here tonight and every night that you're still in the house. I'll be making an appointment with a lawyer in the morning. You can tell the boys anything you want. Eventually they'll have to know the truth, and I really feel sorry for you when that day comes. By the way, I really wish that you were dead. That way people would feel sorry for me, being a widow and all."

With that said Lisa went slowly up to the bedroom and quietly closed the door. Sam sat on the couch, elbows on his knees and his head between his hands. He didn't know where to turn. His mind was all fucked up. Sam didn't know if he should call Joe or wait until he got to work to tell him the details of what happened this evening. All he could think of was their parting kiss and the tingling feeling in his groin and crotch whenever he thought of Joe's tongue entering his mouth.

Lisa cried herself to sleep. When morning came and the children ran down the stairs ready to have their breakfast, they asked their mother where their Dad was. Lisa made an excuse telling them that he had to leave early for work. When she saw the boys enter the school bus, she sat down at the kitchen table and cried until there were no more tears to shed. The first person she called was her mother. Lisa made the barrage of telephone calls to the rest of her family and friends. The last person she wanted to speak to was her mother-in-law, but she realized she couldn't put this conversation by the wayside. She gathered her thoughts, and after agonizing over what to do, she called Sam's mother and told her to get coffee and tea ready; she had to discuss a very serious matter.

When Sam's mother shut down her cell she didn't know what to think. All sorts of terrible thoughts came to mind. She didn't know if Lisa, Sam or any of the boys had an illness or some other type of horrible disease. Lisa couldn't get to her mother-in-law fast enough, as far as her mother-in-law was concerned. Sitting at the kitchen table, their beverages in front of them, Lisa tried explaining the situation to Mrs. Robbins. Mrs. Robbins sat there, her mouth wide open, not believing what she was hearing from Lisa. She put her face into her hands and started crying hysterically. Lisa went over to her mother-in-law and hugged her tenderly. "I went through all the emotions that one can have last night. Whatever happens between Sam and me, I want you and dad to know that, as far as I'm concerned, you'll always be my in-laws. I've known you since I was a kid, and even though I think your son is an asshole, that doesn't take away the wonderful feelings of respect and love that I have for you and Dad." That speech made Mrs.

Robbins cry harder, and by the time Lisa settled the older woman down, they both sat there not knowing what else there was to say to one another.

Sam felt some turbulence and grabbed Joe's hand for reassurance. "You seem very nervous; it's only some air turbulence. We'll be out of this situation before you know it." Joe thought that Sam's somber expression was due to the airplane's reaction to the weather conditions outside. Sam let Joe think whatever he wanted, in his heart he knew the reason for his grim appearance came from remembering the heartache he caused his loved ones. If he had to do it all over again, he would have made the same decision. He loved Joe in an entirely different way than he loved Lisa. He'd always love his parents, siblings and especially his sons. He respected Lisa for the way she handled the situation with the boys, and thankfully, they maintained a somewhat co-existing relationship. He knew that she resented him but never showed it when the boys were around. When the two of them were together with no one around, she would always make snide remarks that Sam ignored. He understood her feelings.

Joe couldn't wait till they got off so that the airplane could refuel. He made many trips to the bathroom and was sure to walk around a bit so his legs didn't swell. He didn't need swollen legs during their vacation. Joe could tell that something other than the trip was on Sam's mind, but didn't want to probe. If Sam wanted him to know, then it was up to Sam to tell him. Otherwise he'd ignore his unusually quiet demeanor and let his loved one work out any problems in his own mind.

As far as Joe was concerned, he had never been happier in his entire life since Sam became part of his existence. It took a while for his parents to accept him coming out of the closet and especially his relationship with Sam, but after a year or so, they'd adjusted to the idea of Joe and Sam as partners. Whenever Sam brought his three sons to Joe's parents' house, they treated the boys as their own grandchildren. They felt sorry for the kids and realized it was hard for the boys to know that their father was living in a relationship that was not the usual situation. Mr. and Mrs. Lewis never asked the boys serious questions and kept their relationship on a fun and games level. The two older people knew that the boys liked Joe and felt as if Joe's parents were their own grandparents. Whenever Christmas or Easter came, the boys were included in all the families' activities. They finally made the adjustment that what was to be, would be and that was Joe's life. Either they accepted him as he was or they could disown him, which was out of the question.

Tracy and Mike were still on a high from visiting his relatives in New York. It didn't matter how long their flight to their destination was, as they were happy as pigs in shit. They played card games on the opened trays and put together puzzles that Mike's relatives gave them to take with them aboard the plane.

Tracy always liked Mike's family and felt as if they were her own. There was never any rivalry between sisters-in-law, and Mike's mother never made her feel as if she were an outsider. From Tracy's first meeting with her future mother-in-law, the older woman made Tracy feel comfortable and wanted. She made her part of her large family. She remembered the first time that Mrs. Razzaboni took Tracy by the hand and led her into the small but warm kitchen. There she spent hours teaching Tracy how to make Italian sauce and meals that Tracy had only heard of and ate in Italian restaurants. Tracy had to admit that when made from scratch, the meals couldn't compare to that of a restaurant's. Mrs. Razzaboni's special sauce and dishes could win contests, as far as Tracy was concerned.

Mike put all his work aside and concentrated on having the best time of his life with his wonderful and beautiful wife. Other woman couldn't compare to his wife in any possible way. He was expecting an unusual type of vacation and made sure that his new digital camera was always by his side. Mike couldn't wait (yes, he could) to bring the pictures to his office and let the other lawyers eat their hearts out. Sure, many of them went on different trips but he bet that the one that he and Tracy were going on would be the most exotic of them all.

Many evenings, while staying at the office till the wee hours of the morning, he often had conflicting thoughts regarding what he was doing for work. He questioned himself about working so hard and if it was worth the reward that would be at the end of the rainbow. With Tracy's enthusiasm and encouragement, the pressure he put himself under was dissipated. He'd keep grinding away, knowing that one day it would be worth it. Another thought crossed his mind. There would come a time when Tracy would want children. He also wanted to have a large family, like the one he came from. Mike often wondered how he could bring a baby into the picture when he wouldn't have the time to enjoy and play with it. His only hope was that before the time came for them to become parents, he would have fulfilled his goal and become a partner.

They reminded each other, after finishing either a card game or puzzle to take the walk, staying on their feet for at least a half an hour at a time. Neither of them wanted to spoil their vacation by getting phlebitis. As a physician's assistant, Tracy cared for many people who had ruined vacations from lack of circulation resulting in phlebitis. Suddenly, Tracy bent over the armrest and kissed her husband lovingly on his cheek. "What was that for? I should be the one kissing you and not only your cheek, but on other areas where you might have cheeks and also your feet. A husband could never ask for a better wife." When Mike said those words to Tracy, he truly meant them. Strangers would often remark, when seeing the couple walking down the street holding hands, that they made a picture-perfect couple. Once in a while when Tracy or Mike overheard the nice comments, a wide smile appeared on their faces.

As far as the couple was concerned, these air flights couldn't go fast enough so they could board The Vacation of a Lifetime sailboat and start their official vacation.

The Filipino fishermen gathered at Mario's bamboo house that was mounted on pillars above the sea. He told his wife of twenty-five years, to take their children to her mother's house for the night. He wanted the meeting with his cousin, Efren, and some other fishermen, who had seen their livelihood, diminish from making a good monthly income, to barely able to provide his growing family with enough rice to feed them.

When all five men gathered had settled down in hushed tones, they talked about their dilemma and what could be done to support their families that had, at one time, not a care in the world. Sunny Parades told his comrades of the experience he had just a week ago. "I'm telling you that I saw what I saw with my own eyes. These Filipino soldiers boarded this Chinese fishing vessel and shot those poor bastards without any warning. You know that I have no love for the Chinese fishermen, but this was awful."

The men were all ears as they listened intently at what Sunny was telling his friends. "These Filipino soldiers boarded the ship and told the Chinese that they were in Philippine waters. They then started firing, and I saw at least two men fall down, apparently killed. I heard later that the rest of the men dragged the dead bodies and put them into the refrigerator where they kept the fish."

"Come on Sunny, are you sure that this isn't one of your exaggerations?"

"I'm telling you, I saw the shots, shouting, and at least three to four fishermen dragging their fellow mates into the cold refrigeration in the boat." Ronnie asked, "Where was this supposed to have happened?"

"I was fishing in the Scarborough Shoal, you know it as West Luzon. These Chinese are really treading on disputed grounds. The Chinese are claiming that they have proof that a treaty signed years ago made them the official owners of this and other areas where we fish for a living."

They all sat in silence, all the while their minds were thinking of various ways to get around this insurmountable problem. Tolemeo, Ronnie's cousin, cleared his throat to gain the attention of his fellow fishermen. "Okay, listen up guys," Tolemeo said in all seriousness. "I hate to say it, but I don't see anything that we can do." He cleared his throat, looking at each man as he spoke. "You and I know that this way of living is driving us crazy. We're used to making money to feed our families and maybe save some money for the kids to attend college if they want. This living meagerly is not right. In my estimation we have to do something drastic." Trying to stop Tolemeo from saying anything more that would only bring trouble to the already angry men, Sunny started making excuses about the fishing industry in general.

Before he could finish his sentence, Mario, who was seated quietly in the rear, got up and moved to the center of his fellow seamen. "I have an idea of what Tolemeo is going to say, and if it's what I think, he's going to say, I have to admit that I've been thinking along the same lines. Looking at his friends, avoiding Sunny's eyes, he blurted out, "you're thinking of pirating, like we've been hearing and reading about in the papers, aren't you?"

Tolemeo, put his head down, ashamed of his thoughts but then straightened up and turning to each of his comrades shook his head and said "yes."

The murmuring went from a soft whisper to an outrageous sound of hearty approval. Efren stood up and, with his arms and hands clenched, told his friends, "Tolemeo is right, what other recourse do we have? I've been a quiet man all my life. I've lived and worked like a slave to enable my growing family to be proud of me. But instead of being the person that I used to be, I now go around the house humbled. I can no longer be the provider that I used to be and, to be truly honest with you; I'm ashamed of what I am now. I used to be full of pride, filling my wife's hands with coins that I gave her to go to the market. Now I walk around ashamed of what's become of me and my way of life. At this point, I'm not too proud to do anything that will give me the self-respect that I once had. I don't particularly like the idea of pirating, but if it gives us the money that we need to once again provide a living for our families, then I'm all for it."

Mario stood up. Looking at his fellow friends, he put his hands out, palms up and said, "If everyone promises not to tell anyone else about our plan, then I'm all for it." All the men murmured their agreement. Mario then assigned the men in the room things to do in order for their new adventure to begin. He designated his cousin, Efren, to get a boat that would enable them to maneuver their new vessel in and out of the waters without any recognition.

Ronnie stood up and told his fellow mates that he knew some people that were unscrupulous. "Let's say that they're "dishonest".… Everyone nodded in agreement. "They belong to some gangs and can get us the necessary weapons that we might need to prove our point. Not that I'm condoning any violence, I'm against that, but we have to put some fear in these people that we're robbing."

Before they left they made plans to get together at the same time and place in another week. With everyone given an assignment, they left the house without another word spoken.

CHAPTER SEVEN

Cole and Isabelle were ahead of schedule. They decided to have breakfast at one of the eating establishments at the Taiwan Taoyuaw International Airport that used to be called (and was sometimes, still called) the Chiang Kai Shek Airport. They enjoyed relaxing, people watching and guessing about the various characters that passed before them. Isabelle made sure that she checked her purse, gathering all the important papers and tickets they needed before checking in. They weren't in a hurry to go to the area where they were to board. They found it frustrating. The hands on the clock seemed to slow down, adding to their anticipation. She watched the bored and uncomfortable fellow travelers wandering about, eating for the sake of doing something and buying magazines to read other than the material they brought with them.

With no other option, they made their way down the aisle where their hand luggage would be checked for dangerous objects. Isabelle found herself grousing to Cole about the inconvenience of being treated like some criminal wanting to hijack the plane or kill someone on board the flight. "Don't talk loud. You don't want these proctors thinking you're some kind of weirdo."

All the way down to the waiting area, Cole heard Isabelle mumbling obscenities under her breath until her temper cooled down. After being married to Isabelle for over twenty years, he was well aware of her reactions and ignored them as much as possible. Cole was sure that he had many quirky habits that annoyed her as well. All he wanted was to get on the plane, no matter what discomforts he had to endure, to get to the final destination to start their Holiday. It seemed as if years had gone by since their last Holiday and he didn't want this to be the last one they'd be taking. When they returned to their flat, he'd make sure that every year they'd go on at least one vacation.

They sat in their assigned seats and waited for the plane to get the go ahead from the air controllers to start their ascent. Isabelle crossed herself and held onto the arm rests until her hands were white. Only after the buckle seat belt sign was off, could Isabelle take a deep breath and relax. She closed her eyes and thanked God that the plane made it up in the air without any trouble. Cole was calm as usual and laughed to himself when he saw his wife's actions.

Cole picked out a magazine from the webbed pocket in front of his seat. He didn't want to think how long the flight would be, but realized that it was the price that he had to pay for going on such an unusual excursion. Trying to kill time, he inadvertently heard people talk among themselves about various subjects. Not to be one to interfere with anyone's conversation, he listened attentively and thought to himself about the many people who waffled about nothing.

Isabelle made it a point to journey to the bog as many times as possible. It gave her an excuse to walk the aisles to make sure that her legs got as much circulation as possible without being too obvious to the other passengers. Cole followed her lead and walked up and down the aisles, making sure he didn't interfere with the attendants or other passengers. He finally sat down and put down the magazine he was reading. He closed his eyes and tried to get as much rest as possible until they landed for refueling. Not knowing how long they'd be delayed, he found out that they'd be staying on the same plane so their luggage needn't be transferred. He was happy about that because he didn't want to worry about not getting his bags when they finally departed for Taipei. In Taipei, they would have a hotel room during the layover between the flights.

Many of their friends had visited the Orient and found the visits fascinating. Now he could make his own assessment of the various places. Cole was looking forward to getting to the hotel in Singapore and getting a good night's sleep on a mattress. Isabelle once read an article about Singapore and she described this beautiful island that blended the eastern and western worlds to her husband who was trying to get some shut eye. Her babbling wouldn't let him accomplish his mission.

The couple decided that once they got their proper rest and had breakfast in Singapore, they'd have until early afternoon to walk around the island and see some of the attractions that their friends told them were a must see. Cole and Isabelle found it unbelievable that Disney and Universal Studios had attractions there. They hoped to avoid the ordinary sights and find unusual places that were unique to the Island.

SUZANNE AND NANCY ABOARD THEIR JET

After resting awhile in her own suite, Suzanne meandered into the cabin waiting for Nancy to finish her nap. She looked at her watch and realized that she had to adjust it because of the date and time difference. *'I really do hate this part of the trip,'* she thought to herself. *'Why do I feel inadequate in math when I excel in other subjects?'* she wondered as she found the attendant and asked her nicely to fix the Movado for her. Suzanne realized that the stewardess was used to doing this task for her and was waiting for Suzanne to ask her. After a while Suzanne realized that Mary Beth was aware of Suzanne's inability to figure out math equations and looked forward to helping one of her bosses. There were many times that Mary Beth asked Suzanne questions about skin care and advice on what to do. In her estimation, that made them able to help each other out without feeling foolish.

Before Nancy emerged from her cabin, Suzanne looked at her watch and a smile appeared. She remembered when Stephen presented the gift to her on one of their many trips overseas. It was one of the first times that Suzanne visited Italy and she made sure that it wasn't the last. She learned to enjoy and appreciate each area of this country that was shaped like a boot. She took pleasure in eating the food in both the southern and northern portions of Italy. She loved seeing the many Cathedrals of Rome and enjoyed being serenaded by the men who maneuvered the Gondolas in the narrow waterways in the old city of Venice. She shopped in Florence and brought many items back home to remember the wonderful trip that she and Stephen had shared.

Of course, she'd never forget the time she and Stephen visited Tuscany and the wine country. She had so many glasses of various wines that Stephen had to literally carry her back to their condo. One of her clients, who came from Tuscany and Milan, insisted on having Suzanne and Stephen stay at her beautiful condo located at the bottom of the mountain. Maria informed Suzanne that she only visited the condo a few times a year and most of the time it was empty. It would give Maria great pleasure to have her friend be her guest. The quaint village was perfect and many a morning the two lovebirds would wonder the small rural town and sit at one of the outside tables drinking their beverage of choice with the various assorted, freshly baked pastries or breads with homemade jams to spread across the delicious baked goods.

Nancy came out of her bedroom quarters and saw Suzanne sitting at the breakfast area of the plane and sat down across from her. "I don't have to give you a penny for your thoughts," a smug Nancy blurted out. "What are you thinking you little rascal?" "You think you know me so well, but I bet you don't know what I'm thinking about now," Suzanne confidently assured Nancy. "If you give me three chances I bet I'll guess your thoughts within two of them."

"You're on, wise guy," Suzanne challenged her friend. "Okay" putting up her index finger; "One, thinking about what we're going to see and do on our interesting trip. The children are on your mind and you are thankful and happy that they would think of something like this to give us. Two," adding her middle finger, "you're looking at your watch and thinking of Stephen when the two of you were on vacation and he presented you with the watch, which by the way, you always wear." Just as she was about to put up her ring finger Suzanne stopped her. "Okay wise guy, I bet you heard me talking to Mary Beth. You know that I ask her to change the time on it everywhere we go if the clock is different than it is in America. Whenever I look at my time piece, I can't help but think of Stephen, so kill me."

Nancy took a sip of coffee that miraculously appeared in front of her and put her two fingers up to Suzanne's face and chortled, ya, ya, ya, ya!!!!! "Get those fingers away from me you nut case. So you know me like a book, or so you think. I'll let you keep thinking that until one day you'll be very surprised. There'll be a time I'll make a monetary bet with you, beat you and take the money that I win from you, for sure, you can count on it."

After this funny episode, Suzanne got down to serious aspects that she smuggled on board the plane. She put the spreadsheet in front of her and started calculating the various monies that were derived from each salon. The expenses on one side of lined papers and then monies brought in and by whom. Suzanne thought to herself, *'how come I can't do math, but for some reason, I find this part of my mathematical skills are superb. Oh well, thank God I can do this part and I've always been on the money.'*

Nancy appeared in back of her and grabbed her by her shoulders. "I thought this wasn't going to be a working vacation. How did you get those papers on board?" Nancy asked. "You scared the living daylights out of me," Suzanne tried to put the blame back in Nancy's court. "Seriously, this is supposed to be a V A C A T I O N!!! Please do me a favor and put the papers away. You'll have plenty of time to do the calculations when we return."

"Okay, okay, you win. But, you can't stop me from thinking about the spas." With that said Suzanne picked up the spreadsheets and brought them back to her room and packed them away in the leather briefcase she smuggled on board. Nancy yelled from the main cabin, "Don't think of taking your case with those papers on the sail boat. If I catch you with them I promise I'll toss them overboard."

"You win, I promise," Suzanne came out of her cabin pouting.

"Now that that's settled, let's get down to the fun part of our trip and start planning the many things that we can see and do. There are different ports that we'll be visiting and I can't wait to see them all." Nancy miraculously brought out various maps and brochures from behind her back. "I sent away for these when I knew where the boat was going to be sailing. Come, let's catch a glimpse of what you think might be exciting and where you'd like to go." The two women were so absorbed in looking at the many brochures that, before they realized what time it was, the jet was declining, ready to land and refuel.

Suzanne exclaimed: "Before I put everything away, I want to show you these adorable pictures that I took with my phone before I left." She opened her cell phone and showed Nancy four pictures of Boston and Simka in her luggage. Then when the suitcase was full, she again caught a great picture of the two cats atop of her clothes. Then she partially shut the case and just their faces appeared underneath the suitcase cover. Then her last picture was one of the cats, their tails up and ignoring her as she headed out the door.

"You realize that I have more pictures of these cats than I do of my kids. I bet if I was to go to a psychiatrist and, he was to analyze these pictures and, the lack of my children's photos in my cell, they'd have something very interesting to say about me."

"We all love you," declared Nancy. "Yes, I have to admit that you are a bit of a fruit cake, but that's part of your great personality." Shaking her head she turned as she was walking away and told Suzanne that was part of her charm.

As Nancy was getting ready to relax, and the jet refueled, Rich's face appeared before her. She thought to herself that even though they would be apart while she was on vacation, she would be missing him but realized that they'd be together before she knew it. Her face turned beat red as she thought of the great time they had in bed the last time they were together. Not one to usually show her emotions, Nancy couldn't help but enjoy (and show how much she enjoyed) and loved making love to Rich. Thinking of him gave her goose bumps. She wondered how Rich was and if he had asked his new friend and father figure, Mr. Yasuhito, to join him when he came to live with her in Ipswich. These were thoughts that were going on in her mind when she realized that the jet was back in the air after being refueled. As she opened another book that she had brought with her to read, the last thought she had was of Rich and Mr. Yasuhito. She tried concentrating on the book and hoped that Rich would be able to talk Mr. Yasuhito into being a permanent member of their household. She shook her head hoping that no more thoughts would interrupt her concentration on the book in front of her. She loved reading a novel by Jonathan Kellerman and what adventure and mystery Alex Delaware would encounter.

Each of the couples was astonished at the sights when they entered the air terminal at Singapore's Changi International Airport. When they entered terminal one, there was no separation between arriving and departing passengers. They followed the signs to Immigration and the baggage claim, which was downstairs. After retrieving their luggage, they exited through customs into the arrival hall. There were reservations made at the same hotel for the five couples who traveled through different airlines. Three of the couples were coming from the Boston area, one couple from New York; the fifth was coming from Heathrow's London airport. The sixth couple was on their private jet. The last couple was staying at another hotel of their choice and would meet the other travelers when ready to board the Vacation of a Lifetime sailboat.

When three of the five couples got into the lobby and were registering at the front desk at the Oxford Hotel, they realized that they were on the same flights. Renée nodded to the two young gentlemen that she talked to at the terminal and then went over to Arthur and Sandy and introduced herself to them. Not one to be passive, she found it easy to ask the couple if they were going on the same trip as she and her husband. When they found out they were, the two couples then made their way to Joe and Sam to find out if they were also going on the same sail boat vacation. After leaving their luggage in their rooms, they made arrangements to meet at the Skylight Café in the hotel before retiring for the evening.

Over glasses of wine, the three couples talked about the various incidents that happened to them on their flight. They also discussed what they hoped to see and do on the Vacation of a Lifetime trip.

Mike and Tracy had the same thoughts and, after putting the luggage into their comfortable overnight space, decided to go to the Café and have a nightcap before retiring and see the sights in the morning. Mike, not one to eavesdrop, overheard the six people next to their table discussing their vacation plans and going on the Vacation of a Lifetime ship. He spoke softly to his wife and told her that they should go over to the table and introduce themselves to their comrades who, most likely, would be on the same vacation as they were about to go on.

Tracy and Mike left their table and introduced themselves to the other couples. Sandy invited them to join them. They all were enthusiastic about their upcoming adventure and nervous at the same time. The couples left at the same time, knowing that they'd be on their own for the day until they would meet again at the dock.

Going up the elevator to their respective rooms, Sam almost bumped into a woman who was entering the lobby on her way to the front desk. After apologizing for his clumsiness, Sam got into the elevator that Joe held open for his partner to enter.

Once registered, Cole and Isabelle were dead tired and decided to go directly upstairs, waiting until morning to make a day of shopping and sightseeing. While lying next to each other in bed, Isabelle had a hard time going to sleep. She kept tossing and turning, not able to find a comfortable spot. "Isabelle, what the bloody Hell is going on? We've had a horrendous couple of days, constantly on the go and by now all I want is to get some rest and be able to get up in the morning relaxed and feeling invigorated."

"I don't know what my problem is. I thought as soon as my head hit the pillow I'd be out like a light, but I can't seem to get comfortable. I'd read a book, but I finished them all on all the flights while in transit. Remind me tomorrow to pick up a few novels so I can read them while we're on the sailboat. I hope that the novels are in English, otherwise I'll have a Hell of a time trying to read the story in a foreign language." They both started laughing. "Let's not waste the night tossing and turning, I can't go to sleep with you the way you're acting." With that said, Cole moved closer to his wife, put his arm around her neck and started nuzzling, biting and kissing her neck, ear and then unbuttoned her nightdress and started kissing her chest and putting his mouth and suckling her beautiful erect nipple. "Cole, you're getting me randy, and if you're going to start something you'd better finish or I'll have to bonker off and I really don't want to do that."

"Would I ever do that to you? When I start making love to you, I never finish until we're both satisfied. Now take off your nightdress." Before she knew what was happening, his pants were off on the floor and his penis was standing up strait, and pulsating. Cole's hands softly caressed her smooth skin, kissing her all over, his fingers pinching her nipples softly, and moving to his side, Isabelle could feel his enlarged penis, pulsating against her upper thigh. He could feel the heat going through her body and she moaned with delight. At the same time, she kissed him, holding his hands down and with her tongue began at his mouth, then his neck, chest, and squeezed his hard nipples as she moved down holding his manhood with one hand while licking his testicles and shaft with her wet tongue, moving rapidly along his shaft and the head with pre-come emerging from the hole at the top of his penis. She took his wetness, licking it and rubbing it down his manhood, enabling her hand to slide up and down with a firm grip as he moaned with delight. Suddenly, he removed her hand and pinned her down onto the mattress. With expert hands he caressed her body, which was writhing with hot passion knowing that his mouth and tongue would soon be going down to the very core of her womanhood.

Through the years of their married life, Isabelle could never complain about their lovemaking. Cole always knew what to do to bring his wife to a dramatic climax and he loved tasting her juices that got him even hornier than he was at that moment. The lower portion of her body moved up and down, her hand holding his head to continue the pleasure she was deriving from his tongue and lips. While he was kissing the core of her existence, his hands went to her large, firm breasts and massaged them until her heard her moan with satisfaction. She wanted more. She turned herself around and put her mouth onto his pulsating enlarged penis and again while giving him a hand job put her tongue and mouth expertly onto his throbbing extremity. His eyes were closed and he expertly spread her legs, again putting his mouth and tongue nuzzling her soft pubic hair, spreading her lips that were swollen from delight and upon seeing her come once again, his sperm erupted and he rubbed his warm liquid between her large breasts.

They lay in each other's arms, not an inch between them. Cole could feel Isabelle's head slumping and hear her breathing at a constant soft mesmerizing tone that indicated that their activity made her satisfied and sleep well until they would wake in the morning, ready for a fun-filled interesting day.

Isabelle woke up well rested and smiled at her husband as she entered the shower ready for a busy day. She anticipated seeing many different and unusual sights she never thought she'd see in her lifetime.

Sandy and Arthur took individual showers and were getting ready to call it a night. They were wearied travelers who hadn't experienced the joys of mundane traveling as many people who constantly fly for business.

Cleaned and feeling refreshed, the couple were laying side-by-side, each engrossed in their own thoughts. Sandy was virtually exhausted, but her mind constantly thinking of all the various places they'd be seeing and things that they'd be doing. Finally, after playing out the different scenarios in her mind, she felt herself getting tired. She turned onto her side and within minutes was in dreamland.

Arthur watched his wife, who he still loved in many ways. Even after all these years of marriage, enduring ups and downs one goes through in life, he probably would have chosen her for his wife. The children who were good kids, (sure they got into trouble, but they would have survived), wouldn't have taken up extra time that he would have spent with his wife. It wasn't Sandy's fault that she felt that the children needed her and would go out of her way to please and help them. *'I wish that Sandy would have given me more attention than the kids. Of course, I realize she felt obligated since I was working most of the time. If only things had turned out differently, maybe I wouldn't have been unhappy and God forbid, anyone should know how I really feel. They would have grown up the same, only Sandy would have been able to devote her attention to me instead of worrying about the problems each child had.'* He'd have changed a few things, maybe making more money to be able to afford the luxuries that one can have if wealth were no object. He was happy to see her sleep so soundly and was thankful that God had given her a second chance, She was now healthy and not in pain as she was only a year ago. It was then that he realized how much he depended on this strong woman who was the other half of his life. *'She would die, feeling betrayed and, have nothing to live for, if she realized how I really felt. He didn't think that he could exist without her by his side but, on the other hand, who knows what would have happened if she didn't get better.'* With those thoughts, he went on his side, their behinds touching each other's, and fell into slumber.

Renée and Paul sat on the edge of their bed completely drained. Although they had gone to many different places on vacations, they didn't remember being as tired as they were at that moment. All they wanted to do was to undress and get a good night's sleep. After doing her regular bed time routine of washing the makeup off of her face, brushing her teeth and putting her hair into a pony tail, she was ready to finally call it a day. Paul thought the same, although all he had to do was brush his teeth. He looked forward to sleeping undisturbed and to take a hot, long, shower in the morning.

With those thoughts, they retired for the evening, with not a care in the world, anticipating a new and exciting adventure like nothing they ever experienced before. They were looking forward to meeting the other couples that would be joining them and fell into deep slumber.

Tracy and Mike were all revved up from the different stimuli, which was an unusual experience for them. They were happy that they met some of the other couples that they'd be traveling with on the sailboat. "I can't get to sleep, Mike. I have so many thoughts going through my mind," Tracy informed her husband. "I think I'll take a shower and maybe that will get me relaxed enough to get a good night's sleep." "Good idea, Honey. Do you think you'd like some company in the shower?" a rascally Mike asked. After pretending to have to think about it, her hand on her chin, tilting her head, she laughed and pulled him towards her. With that done, she started at his t-shirt and pulled it over his head. She then undid his belt buckle and unhooked his pants, pulling them down his muscular legs and leaving them on the floor. The underpants came next. Mike couldn't be the only one undressed. He pulled her shirt, leaving the buttons closed, and as he lifted the pink shirt over her head, some buttons popped because of Tracy's large bust. He then pulled her shorts off and turned her around unfastening her bra, exposing her beautiful, smooth, white breasts. He slowly pulled down her matching briefs and, taking her hand, led her to the bathroom.

The pulsating hot water felt good on their bodies and Tracy put delicious smelling soap onto her hands and, with expert hands, started lathering his back, bending her knees to put the suds onto his legs and thighs. Keeping her hands, for a long time, just beneath his scrotum, she then moved to his testicles and ended with enveloping his thick prick onto her sudsy hands. She then turned him around, and with round motions, cleansed his chest and with her other hand, again held his manhood deftly stroking him till she heard him moan with desire. "Let me take care of you, Honey," Mike huskily said as she gave him the soap to lather his hands as she had. He imitated her actions and parted her lips as he felt her clitoris and softly rubbed it and moved his right hand to her breasts, putting the soapy water under her tits and then massaging her heavy breasts while squeezing the nipples until they looked like eyes looking out at him. He could hear her delight as he continued caressing her womanhood. Without saying a word, he shut off the water and with a large dry towel dried her completely and she returned the service. He carried her to the turned-down bed and they continued their love making until they both were anxious to fulfill their needs. He expertly got on top of her and plunged his swollen penis into her wet and waiting to be filled wet crevice and pumped her till they both exploded at the same time. Although he was muscular and heavy, Tracy pulled him down onto her and massaged his back. After a few minutes, he rolled off of his wife and they kissed each other tenderly. "Wow," he said aloud, "if this is an indication of what our vacation is going to be like, we have to go on more of them." Tracy hit him lightly on his upper arm and smiled wickedly. They lay naked on the crisp, white sheet and found themselves spooning and falling into Morpheus.

The week couldn't have gone by fast enough for Mario. His kids and wife groused a bit after Mario asked them to leave for the night again. Maria, his wife, made sure that she hurried their children out of the house before Mario and his friends were meeting again. She realized that something different in their lives was coming, but she dared not ask her husband. As much as she loved him, she knew that he didn't want to discuss any of his business with her. She would look at him across the table when they had their meals and could see the unhappiness that his eyes reflected. She had discussed her fear with her mother, but Anna didn't know what she could tell her daughter. She only knew that Maria was unhappy with the way that her husband was acting, but she didn't have any answers to relieve her daughter's family situation.

As soon as the family left, Mario put the straight-backed chairs in a circle around the coffee table in the living room. That was the room of the house around which all of the families' activities were centered. The other men soon arrived and they carried sacks of unidentified objects with them that would be soon uncovered.

Efren, Mario's cousin, was the first to arrive. He put his sack cloth on the coffee table and nodded his head to his favorite cousin. Clearing his throat, Mario asked Efren what he brought. "You'll see soon enough, but if you are really interested, I'll show you." With that he emptied the sackcloth to reveal a shiny compass and some elaborate knives that he displayed with pride. The knives were surrounded by leather sheaths, and he proudly showed the various sizes of his weapons. "These are sharp and can split a person's head in two. These were handed down to me by my father and his father before him. He was very proud of these instruments. Of course, he used them for gutting the fish that he was catching on his big fishing boat." A look of reflection passed quickly, and he puffed out his chest as if this were a common occurrence. He realized that he was a fisherman by trade and what this group of men were about to do would normally be against his grain. But these were different times and in reality he had to face facts.

Efran was a proud man and he couldn't stand the way that his life's work was going to Hell. He, like his cousin, would come home and, instead of handing his wife a good day's pay, would avoid her eyes and drop what little money he received for his day's pay onto the table instead of directly handing his little compensation to her. So instead of playing joyously with his children at the end of the day or helping them with their homework, he would clean the knives that he didn't have use for anymore.

Ronnie and Tolemeo arrived together and, with pride, dropped their sacks onto the middle of the table. They greeted the other men with silence. They took the glasses of port that were offered to them. As soon as they were seated, Sunny arrived and greeted his friends with enthusiasm. He pompously dropped his prize in the middle of the other bundles and took the port offered to him with gusto. With a twinkle in his eyes, he clapped his hands and gained the attention of his fellow friends.

The glass of wine looked lonely on the table amongst the treasures that were hidden in the various sacks. He couldn't wait to start drinking, but knew that he had to gain the attention of his fellow mates. Clearing his throat, he announced: "My fellow comrades, I realize that we are about to undertake an assignment that we never wanted. But, in all honesty, I don't see another way out of our situation." He heard murmurs of endorsement from everyone seated around him.

With that said, he lifted his glass, and put it above the catches that were secretly hidden in the various clothes in the center of the scratched, wooden coffee table. He saw the men clinking their glasses. The men took a huge swallow of the wine. With that done, they sat down and let Mario start the meeting. Standing up he puffed out his chest and began. "I guess I am automatically the leader of this gang of guys because it's my house." The other men laughed with resignation.

CHAPTER EIGHT

Joe and Sam were tired. Although they sometimes had to be away for business, they remembered never having to be in the air for as long a time as this journey was. Joe remembers when the longest flight he had was going from Boston to California. In his mind, that was a piece of cake compared to these grueling flights. *'I hope this vacation is worth all the long and tedious air travel'* he thought as he crashed on the bed, not bothering to get undressed. Sam was also weary, but seemed to have more resistance than his partner. Before he let himself go to sleep he wanted to make sure that he talked to his sons. He was pretty sure that it would be either dinner time or just before they went to bed for the evening.

He was glad that the hotel had wireless internet access. He e-mailed his three sons. Sam was the oldest, Sean was the typical middle child and Matthew was the youngest, who seemed to take advantage of being the baby of the family. Although Sam and Lisa were divorced, it didn't take away his role of being a father and a good one at that, he thought, as his fingers quickly moved over the keyboard. He wrote to each of his children and asked them about school and how they were doing with their respective teams at their hockey games. Sam made sure that, when the boys started walking, he had them on the ice, pushing the plastic crate from one end of the rink to the other. He laughed to himself when he thought of the videos he and Lisa took of them as little ones during their first time on the ice. Lucky they had a lot of padding because otherwise their little asses would still be red and sore.

Sam tried not to miss any of their games; however, they were upset at this four weeks leave of absence from their game schedule. He promised to make it up to them. As of now, he didn't know how he would, but he was sure to find a way. He was almost certain that the sailboat wouldn't provide him access to the net, but hoped that by chance they might have it available. If not, he was sure that on a few of their excursions he'd find some store that had this service available to him. *'It isn't as if I'm going to places that are so remote that the internet is unheard of. If there's a will, there's a way,'* he thought as he fell into bed beside Joe. Within minutes he was sound asleep.

Suzanne still felt better when the plane landed at the separate Jet Aviation aircraft terminal. They were greeted and brought to the private lounge that had accommodations and catering ready for them when they arrived. Nancy called ahead of time for reservations at the Holiday Inn Atrium before they left for the trip. She also made arrangements for the plane's pilots and staff to stay in Singapore for the four weeks till they returned from their vacation. "In a way, it's like they'll have a vacation as well. We're lucky that everyone who works for us isn't married with family obligations," Nancy told Suzanne. "Duh, I remember discussing that with you. That was the reason we picked the people we did." Pointing a finger at Suzanne Nancy said: "yes, that was the reason that we picked them as our crew." With a smile Nancy started walking, Suzanne was running to catch up to her.

"We'll have the plane maintenance crew go through the airplane from top to bottom so it'll be ready for departure when we have to fly home. Now don't you feel better knowing that we're in control of the servicing?"

"That's why I made sure I have a great partner, a maven that has plenty of gelt to hook up with. I'm not some nebbish that doesn't know what she's doing," boasted Suzanne as she sat down on the comfortable sofa waiting for Nancy to finish her meal and get in touch with the car service that would bring them to their hotel.

When Suzanne and Nancy arrived, they went right upstairs to their suite and, after taking long hot showers, settled on their separate queen size beds and automatically put on the television. "I don't know why we put this foolish thing on. This is supposed to be the start of our vacation and that means no conveniences that we have at home. Yes, we can make one phone call or e-mail at each port, if so desired, but I'd love not to be bogged down with mundane details like we always are."

"I know that you're right, Nancy. Give me that remote. If this is to be a vacation like none other, than we have to make sure we adhere to our own rules. Okay, this is a sailing expedition and we'll get down and dirty if we have to. We'll do whatever the Captain tells us to do and enjoy the fresh air and the smell of the ocean," Suzanne agreed with Nancy.

"You're so full of shit that your blonde hair is going to turn brown if you don't stop lying. I know you really don't feel that way, but I'm glad you're being a good sport about this entire vacation. You know I'm supposedly the privileged young maiden who never had to lift her hands, get dirty or do anything she didn't want to do. Yes, a brat. But do you hear me balking about what I'm going to do? I'm sort of proud of myself, if you want to hear the truth. Yes, I've become a mensch, and I even do my own housecleaning. No sir, no maids or

cleaning services for me. So madam, this vacation is right down my alley," Nancy had a smug look on her face as she rubbed her hands together, covered herself with the light blanket and closed her eyes.

Suzanne had no rebuttal and like Nancy, closed her eyes waiting for Morpheus to take over.

Each of the couples went their separate ways after greeting each other and having a hearty breakfast in the Skylight Café. When Isabelle heard the three couples laughing and talking about their four-week sailing cruise, she poked Cole and told him that the couples were probably their mates that they'd be on Holiday with. "Let's go over and introduce ourselves and then we can be on our way for the day until we have to be at the pier," Cole suggested. "Good morning, mates," Cole cheerfully greeted the exuberant crowd eating their breakfast. After introducing themselves to the people, they sat down and joined the group for a light continental breakfast. When everyone was finished, they took off, going their separate ways and visiting the sights of their choices.

"Cheerio," both Isabelle and Cole said as they waved to their fellow sail mates and went to see a couple of the sights that their friends recommended to them. They had to be cognizant of the time restraint given to them by the travel company. There was no way they were going to miss going on the Vacation of a Lifetime sail expedition.

They both looked over the various sites and decided that Isabelle loved going to the various precincts and, while there, they'd take in the Fountain of Wealth. "It's supposed to be the largest fountain in the world, luv. The best thing about it is that it's in one of Singapore's largest shopping malls. Let's get us a taxi and have them run us to this fountain and the precinct. I'm warning you now, Isabelle, don't spend all your money here. We have four weeks of ports and places to go and it'd be a shame if you appropriate all your spending cash at this one place. Don't be balmy and a boob," warned Cole. Isabelle just looked at him as they were climbing into the taxi. "Who in the Hell do you think you're talking to? First of all I work hard for my money, just as hard as you do and if I want to spend money as I want to, I will. On the other hand, I wouldn't be a tosser and not have anything left for the rest of the trip." Isabelle gave Cole a good whack on his shoulder and ignored him until they were at Suntec City.

Once in the center of the precinct, they wandered around the different shops and finally came across the fountain. They couldn't get over the enormity of it and the fact that it's the tallest man-made fountain. After a few hours, both were tired and decided to go back to the hotel, pack up their belongings and head for the port. Their excitement wouldn't allow them to be late.

Sandy and Arthur left the hotel and wanted to go over the brochures before choosing one or two places that sounded interesting. After much debate, Sandy decided she would love to see the Esplanade. "I'd love to see the spiky roof and, besides, it's right near the Raffles Hotel."

"What the Hell is the Raffles Hotel?" Arthur asked. Sandy picked out the brochure and showed it to him. "Look, it's one of Singapore's most important landmarks. I mean it must cost a fortune to stay there for even a night. Can you imagine, people like Elizabeth Taylor, Queen Elizabeth II and even Michael Jackson have stayed here?"

"Do you know which husband Elizabeth Taylor brought here?"

"No honey, which one?" asked a curious Sandy. Arthur laughed and told her he didn't know, he was just joking. With that Sandy hit his arm lightly then kissed it. "You're such a kidder; I don't know when to believe you or if you're joking," Sandy exclaimed as she took his hand and watched the traffic as she crossed the street to see the legendary Raffles Hotel.

Tracy and Mike decided to go to Merlion Park. After much debate, they decided to see the symbol of Singapore. They were in awe as they viewed the statue that is a creature between a fish and a lion. They saw the imaginary beast spouting water out through the fountains mouth. They walked through the shops and decided to purchase a statue of Merlion which would grace their refrigerator as a magnet. After staying there for a while, they looked at each other and ran, trying to beat the other, to sit at one of the terraced areas to see the beautiful views of Singapore's city skyline and the scenic waterfront. "Isn't this romantic?" Mike agreed and held Tracy's hand.

Paul and Renée took a cab to the Old Parliament House, which housed many art exhibits. Both Paul and his wife were members of Boston's Museum of Art and could walk for hours admiring the different pieces of art. They went outside after seeing the many paintings and viewed the large bronze elephant, which was located at the front of the building. "Paul, it was a gift from King Rama V of Siam. or as we know it now, Thailand. It was to show his appreciation after a visit to Singapore in 1871. All I can think of is 'The King and I' with Yule Brenner." Paul laughed at his wife's remark and hailed a taxi to take them back to the hotel. "By the way," Renée remarked, "my Mom told me about the movie and play when I was a little girl. I'm not that old!" Paul only laughed at his adorable wife and tussled the hair on top of her head.

Sam and Joe decided to go to Chijmes, which was located on the grounds of a former convent school. After years of restoration, it re-opened in 1997 "Let's come back here when we return to Singapore," Joe told Sam as they walked through the rest of the area.

Suzanne and Nancy slept in late and decided instead of running around like chickens without a head, they'd stay near the hotel until it was time to leave for the dock. "I bet there're plenty of sites and shops to browse in around here," announced Suzanne.

While walking through the streets of Saigon, they realized that the architecture of this large city was mostly built by modern standards, like the United States. For the most part, it was Americanized with the regular Oriental flavor strewn about. "Suzanne, have you noticed that Taipei and Saigon are very similar? There was more of an Oriental feeling when we arrived in Taipei. The center reminds me of Times Square, only it reflects the Asian culture and I feel I'm in the heart of Taiwan. Although both places have high rises like many of our major cities in the States, I can't tell which location I like best," Nancy stated as she walked into one of the boutiques along the main street in Saigon.

"To be honest with you Nancy, I'm in such a state of shock by the cultural differences, that I can't determine which I like better. I wish we had extra time in each country to see more. I'd love to go to the various religious Temples and then go to the suburbs and see how the residents live. It's such a different way of working and living. I guess it's like our own society. On one hand, the people who work in the city don't reflect their true selves until they're back in their own homes and live a simpler lifestyle."

"Well then" Nancy announced, "why don't we make it our decision when we come off the ship. If we want to stay a little longer in each area we'll make our own conclusion."

"That's a great idea," agreed Suzanne. "Let's see how tired we are and if we're up to the extra days. You are just a bit younger than I am and I might feel more tired than you do after our long vacation."

"I don't believe what I'm hearing. You know as well as I do that you can run circles around me. I only hope that I'm in as good a shape as you are when I get a few years older."

"Nancy," Suzanne laughed, "the truth of the matter is we are only a few years apart in age. Even though we've both been through a lot of tough times in our short lives, I think you faired a little better than I did."

Putting her hands up so as not to hear a rebuttal, Suzanne changed the subject and walked into another beautiful boutique, Nancy ran to catch up. After examining a few pieces of clothing, Suzanne looked at her watch and told Nancy they'd better leave or they'd be late getting to the pier. With anticipation, the women left the store and walked briskly back to the hotel. Nancy informed the concierge of their impending departure and asked for a taxi to come for them within twenty minutes.

Both women packed what little clothes they had taken out of their luggage and got into more comfortable mode, checked their makeup and were downstairs waiting for the transportation to arrive.

The five couples made arrangements to meet outside the hotel and take two or three taxis, depending how many people could fit into the small vehicles. The excitement was sparking through the air as each person had visions, in their own minds, of what to expect once they arrived at the pier and saw the boat with the Captain on hand to welcome them aboard.

With mouths agape, the couples were looking at all the magnificent yachts and sailboats when they finally spotted the 'Vacation of a Lifetime' sail vessel. When they were sent the brochures, they saw various boats displayed. They had to admit that the 'Vacation of a Lifetime' sailing vessel was more impressive than they could imagine. The Captain didn't come up from the second level deck and they stood in front of the ship not knowing what to do. Behind them, they heard people coming their way and turned to see who was there. Running down the wooden walkway, they finally stopped when they came to the group. "I hope that you weren't waiting a long time for us to come," Suzanne spoke to all of them at once. "No, no, we just arrived ourselves. We're waiting for our Captain to make his appearance."

Extending her hand, Suzanne introduced herself and Nancy to the rest of the vacationers. After five minutes of looking around they heard footsteps coming to the top deck. A man, who they assumed was the Captain, climbed over the hull. Taking the cap off of his slightly bald head, he tipped it and bowed to the people who were going to be with him for this four-week vacation. "Ahoy Mates! I'm Captain, Bob Winters. You can call me Bob when you get to know me better. My crew will be coming up momentarily and I'll introduce you to them. Before I do, it will be awhile before you get to know them by name. Don't worry. It's the same for them. The crew will be very important to you. They handle the ship and sails. They've been with me for many years and know this boat like they know the back of their hands. Now some of them have had one of their hands cut off by a sword, but that doesn't matter, they remember what it looked like." With a smile, the crowd didn't know whether to laugh or take him seriously. He let them have their own thoughts until they saw for themselves that the crew was intact. "Have confidence that they know what they're doing. Within a few days my men will acquaint you with the ship and all the articles and nautical terms that will be necessary or fun for you to learn. As he was speaking, all was quiet. Each person was listening attentively while he spoke. I'd prefer it if you learn to climb the ropes, and learn how to handle the sails, which you've by now noticed are square."

"I'll explain to you what the difference is between a square sail and a triangular fore and aft rigs. But, for now, don't worry yourselves about the technical names. I do have a list of nautical terms and a packet for each of you to study, in case we need you to help us handle the sails and various parts of the ship. Now don't get worried. In all my years of sailing, my passengers have had fun climbing the rope ladder to the top and standing in the crow's nest or masthead. You'll be viewing the sea and sometimes a few creatures like dolphins or whales will trail beside us or in front or in back of the boat. If you should be wondering, you'll be safe because there are steel rails around you with your feet secured on a platform. You'll sleep like babes when the salt water gets to you. Is there anyone who has any type of impediment that would prevent you from climbing or hinder you in any way to help with the rigging, masts, or climb to the backstays that support the topmast, for instance; This looks like a little, square, box. When, in the seafaring days, the sailors would take their long binoculars to see if other ships were near. If anyone feels that they can't do a job for any reason, please come to me and it will be kept confidential. Just look over the papers, I'll be giving tests in a few days. Only kidding guys!! But in all seriousness, you'll have a ball and enjoy this vacation. I'll have a list at the end of the trip for signups for next year. Again, only joking!!"

"Let me and my crew, who are coming up now, help you aboard and we'll bring you and your luggage to your cabins." When the men came up from the deck below Captain Bob introduced the men to the passengers. "This is my first mate, Sean Bogaard from Norway and our chef, André from Paris, France." The men tipped their hats as they bowed and came forward in greeting. "My chief engineer is Jim Brown from Sweden, his backup man, Steve Bowman, also from Sweden, and our two general deckhands, Dick and Harry Boggart, as you can tell, they are from none other than Detroit, Michigan. Don't worry about telling them apart, we usually can't either." Dick and Harry after bowing, walked back to the line trying to suppress their laughter. They all nodded their heads and with their hands extended, helped the women first and then the men onto the large vessel.

Each of the couples was seated on their beds and had nothing to say. The packet that Captain Bob told them about was lying on their double or twin beds, whichever the travelers had asked for. After a few minutes, Paul said to Renée, "I already like this ship and the Captain. I hope I can master the physical requirements, but with all my tennis, racquetball, golf, and walking I think I'll be able to handle it. What about you, Honey?"

"Don't worry about me, Darling. I also golf and play tennis. Although we don't play as vigorously as the men at the club do, the gals do pretty well for themselves. Besides, don't forget the many hours I push that cart around to the different floors with the heavy books and magazines for the patients to borrow, buy, or read. No, I think I'll be able to handle it. I realize that we're the oldest people on board. Won't the rest of the passengers be impressed with the way we are able to physically hold our own?" With that said, Paul squeezed his wife's shoulder and hugged her endearingly, bringing her closer to him. "Paul, do you think you should go to Captain Bob and tell him you're a physician? I don't know if they have a medic on board, but it would be good just in case an emergency comes up. You never know what can happen during such a long vacation."

"My God, always the worry wart! Okay, you're right. I'll tell him after we get our clothes put away and get back on deck. After all, we have to see the ship, with the sails heading out into the ocean. That's one of the most invigorating things I can think of."

"Oh, yeah" Renée poked her husband with her finger in the middle of his belly, with one of her eyebrows raised. "Of course, that's not even in the equation." Paul smiled as he led his wife out of the polished wooden door. Renée stopped suddenly and turned around while asking her husband if he remembered to take the camera. He patted the pocket of his shirt and smiled as he hit her on her bum. He walked behind her as she ascended the ladder to the sun deck (the deck which is open to the air and sea).

Tracy and Mike were thrilled when they opened their cabin door. Tracy was surprised when she saw the beautiful bouquet of flowers on the main table of the room. "I wonder if all the passengers received this as a welcome present." she asked Mike. "Why don't you open the card and see what it says," he advised his wife. Suddenly a wide smile crossed her face and she ran into her husband's open arms. "What does the card say, Honey?"

"You know what it says. I can't believe how thoughtful you are."

"It's my way of saying thank you for what I know will be the most memorable time in our lives, except, of course, when you deliver our baby." They kissed passionately and Mike slowly broke the connection. "If we continue this behavior, and I wish we would, we're going to miss the sail away and I think we should be upstairs to see us leave the dock. What do you say, Honey?"

"Okay, but when we come back, we'll resume where we left off," Tracy made it known as they left the cabin and went to the main deck in time to see the other passengers. One of the crewmen unhooked the large, heavy rope from the iron holder or hook, and shoved the boat away from the dock. A lump was forming in Tracy's throat from all the emotion she was feeling.

"Honey, but the trip hasn't started and I love it already," Sandy announced as she was practically jumping on the bed from joy. "That's one of the reasons I love you, Honey, it doesn't take much to make you happy. I've never seen anyone who enjoys life the way you do and anything I bring home for you, there's never a whine or, but, just a large smile and a thank you. Then, at night, you really show your appreciation, and it makes me want to always bring a present home to you."

"Well, thankfully, that part of our marriage hasn't gone away like a lot of our friends' have."

"Thanks, because you've always excited me and always will. Now let's head upstairs and see the ship head out to the open sea." *'If I could only tell her the truth,'* Arthur thought to himself.

Joe and Sam finished putting their clothes away in the small drawers in their room. "Thankfully, I brought as little as possible knowing it was a casual vacation," announced Joe. "Do you think they could have spared another piece of space to enlarge the closet," Sam related as they packed away their toiletries and made sure that their cameras were intact before heading up the stairway to see the ship leave the dock. When the land was barely a spec, Joe sat on the polished wooden deck and felt the sun's rays attack his pale skin. "You better watch out or you'll get sunburned, and you'll be one hurting pup," warned Sam. "Who do you think you are, my mother?" Joe asked Sam as he listened to his partner as he put his short sleeve pullover back onto his body. "I did bring some Aloe Vera in case we get too much sun, but you're right as usual; I hate it when you're always right," Joe admitted to Sam. "It comes naturally when I have the kids and take them to their games or to the beach. I'm like a mother hen, always checking and pecking at them," Sam admitted as he put his body next to Joe's and enjoyed the warmth of the day. "I don't know about you, but I'm famished," Joe admitted as he smelled food down below. The Captain left his seat at the wheel and announced to the guests that there was a buffet downstairs and to enjoy it before they had their main meal in a few more hours.

Nancy and Suzanne looked out of their small window and saw the waves crashing against the boat. "I'm glad that we got to see the sail away. It's not a usual occurrence to be on this type of ship and have the pleasure and excitement of knowing that we're going to places that I wouldn't have thought to ever see," announced Suzanne. "I'm glad that you're happy, and yes, I enjoyed seeing everyone joyful once we left the dock," admitted Nancy. "Do I smell something good or is it my imagination?" Nancy asked Suzanne. "I smell it too. Let's go and see what's going on." The two women left the cabin and followed the aroma to the third level where there was a great buffet spread with all sorts of drinks available for everyone to enjoy. "I'm not going to be shy" Nancy told Suzanne. She took a plate, utensils and napkins and was one of the first people to fill her plate. People started lining up and, the drinks were abundantly available. Everyone was talking as if they had been friends for years and years.

Suzanne felt the rays of the sun and, for the first time in years, didn't get upset at having her skin exposed to it…She sat down and jotted a few things that were on her mind on the notepaper that she had brought upstairs with her. In her writing, she jotted a note off to Mrs. Walsh. She penned, "I know that at this moment you're sitting at the kitchen table and wondering what I'm doing. Well, to be honest with you, for the first time in years, except when I couldn't do anything in the hospital except lay like a mummy, I'm enjoying doing nothing. I'm inhaling the salt water and the smell of the air. The rooms are rather cramped, but I can live with that. I have to admit that I do miss Simka and Boston. They have become so much a part of my life. I'll be sure to bring them home some toys. I know that they'll ignore me when I first arrive home, but I also know that they'll be happy to see me once again. I'll miss calling my Mom and Dad every day, but that I'll make up for it when I return. I have to admit that the chef on board is remarkable. What little I've seen, the food looks great. I have to admit that, with the girls living on their own, I miss talking to them, but not as much as I thought that I would. Okay, okay, I miss you the most. I knew you were waiting to read that… I miss our little chats in front of the fire in the wintertime and the times that we'd sit out on the patio and just talk about anything and everything.

I'm going to try not to think about Stephen and Larry while I'm on vacation. Sometimes I think of Stephen and I have many mixed emotions. I can't seem to say or think of anything negative about Larry. He's such a giver and a wonderful person. Maybe this time away from home will be good for me. I'll be able to sort out my feelings and when I return, I hope I'll have an answer to my prayers. God, it's about time that I make up my mind. Nancy is a great companion and I guess that's why she's like a sister to me. As much as I love to tease her, she's a great person and I'm happy that she finally found someone who appreciates her the way a person of the opposite sex should. Seriously, Rich seems like a perfect fit for our Nancy.

Well, I better stop writing or I'll never stop. Send my love to everyone, give an extra treat to my babies and tell them that Mama misses them. Oh, okay, you can tell my parents and the girls that I wrote to you, and I hope not to slight them. I'll write to them when I'm in the mood. For now, Adios Amigo, stay well, and pray that nothing bad happens to us. It seems that there is always something or another that happens, but this time I think we'll be safe as babies in their mother's arms. I love you and I'll be writing again….Suzanne!!!"

Captain Bob and his crew ate separately, and the crew looked at each other with merriment in their eyes. "Well boss, it looks like we have a good bunch of passengers with us," Harry expounded as he filled his plate for the second time. "Hey leave some for the rest of us," Dick joked as he also filled his plate and his glass with another drink.

Captain Bob just shook his head and wondered how their mother got by with those two in the family. He truly enjoyed having them as part of his crew. Someday he'd have to talk to their parents and find out how it was raising twins and all the other members of the family. It must have been a hoot!!! He never asked the boys if they had a brother by the name of Tom. That would have made it a complete madhouse he thought as he got up from the table, emptied his dishes and put them away in the dishwasher.

When all the talking had died down; Mario stood up, clearing his throat, and once again, he gained the attention of his friends. "Well, we know why we're here and it's about time that we get around to the business at hand. I already saw the beautiful knives that Efren brought, but I'd like each of you to examine them and appreciate the workmanship that is displayed in every one of them. It's taken Efren a long time to polish and sharpen these knives to the best of his ability." He enjoyed watching the men take a knife and examine the workmanship that was in each individual piece. They each held the knives deftly and let each one lay on the inside palm of their hand to feel the weight of the knife. Mario already picked out the one that he wanted for himself. He enjoyed the sharpness and the weight of his lethal weapon, and, as much as he never wanted to use it, he knew that if he didn't have any choice in the matter, he would strike with not a second thought.

The other men picked one out that they admired and held them deftly in the palm of their hands. They then turned each one around as if wielding the most precious possession they ever handled. The difference in the length of the weapons varied, as did the thickness of their sheath. They realized that Efren had taken great pains in selecting and sharpening each knife that they would be holding to carry out the mission ahead of them.

Tolemeo stood up, got his bundle and overturned it. Out came an assortment of rope, twine and tape. As proud as can be, he displayed his prized possessions. "I know that this is not the same weaponry as Efren gave to us, but I assure you that we will be using these tools as much as any dangerous weapon that we can be carrying. I can envision the people whose ships we'll be overtaking, and

believe me, they won't be giving up their possessions as easily as we hope they do. We'll be using these ropes to bind their hands and feet and the tape to go over their mouths to stifle the yelling that might attract other boating people in the vicinity." He displayed them proudly. He showed the other members of his group how he made sure that they were sturdy and couldn't be taken off easily by anyone who they bound. The men took the rope and admired the thickness of the cord and twine. Each man took many rolls of tape and ropes to be put in their belts that went around their waists. With pride, Tolemeo sat down and poured himself another glass of wine.

CHAPTER NINE

Once everyone was fed and had enough liquid refreshment to be happy, they all took their papers with them to the top deck to read. Each person enjoyed the breeze and sun, which soaked their bodies with warm rays. There was not a cloud in the sky to mar the beautiful, balmy, gentle wind on the first day out on the beautiful turquoise sea.

Renée and Paul were sitting up against the open bow, enjoying the warmth of the delightful day while reading the pamphlet Captain Bob had left on their bed. "Do you think we'll be able to remember all these nautical terms described on these pages?" asked Renée as Paul was looking over the same booklet.

"It's not as bad as it seems. If you don't understand what a term means, and most of them are simple, then ask me or go to one of the crew and have them explain what you don't understand. By the end of a few days, I'm sure we'll both be like pros that have been sailing for years."

"You're always so upbeat, and you can understand the most technical language. I, on the other hand, have to be shown and then after seeing how something is done or doing it myself a few times, can master the task at hand. I guess it takes all kinds. That's one of the reasons I married such a smart, industrious man. Besides, I didn't want to have to go to a medical office every time I didn't feel well. Now all I have to do is tell you how I feel, and you tell me what I have to take to make myself better. Now that's what I call smart."

Paul pushed his wife gently and told her to study the words because in another hour or so, he'd give her a test on what she learned. With that said, she got up and gave him a look, and if looks could kill, he'd be a dead man. Renée saw Sandy and Arthur talking quietly and enjoying the glorious weather and didn't want to disturb them. She then saw Suzanne and Nancy, and they seemed to be enjoying the weather as was everyone else. She didn't want to feel intrusive by going over to them and starting a conversation. On the other hand, what did she have to lose?

"Hi," she said with all the excitement she could gather. "I'm sure you don't remember all of our names." Extending her hand, she told them who she was and again asked them their first names. Suzanne and Nancy re-introduced themselves and told Renée to please join them. When Suzanne found out that

Renée and Paul came from Newton, Massachusetts, Suzanne felt as if she'd known her for years. Renée told Suzanne and Nancy that she heard of the Metamorphosis Spas and was privileged to be on board with the two owners of the prestigious salon. "I've always wanted to go to your salon but never went out of my way to have a facial or have my hair done there. Now that we'll be together for many weeks, I'll have to make it my business to start going to your exclusive establishment."

"Thanks, Renée, but don't feel you're obligated to become one of our clients because of this trip. Honestly, we'll still like you, even though you're a traitor," Suzanne laughed, and she hoped Renée realized that she was teasing her. "I'm serious. My hairdresser just retired, and I've been going to Allen for years. I'm sure you've heard of Alan Hersh of the DeLorean Hair Salons. As for facials, I'm ashamed to say that I've never had one in my life."

"That doesn't make you a bad person," Suzanne tried to explain. "Yes, I've met Alan, and as a matter of fact, he's a cousin of mine. It might take too long to explain, but he's a great hairdresser and I felt bad when I found out that he was retiring. Many times I asked him to join our staff, but he didn't want to travel into Boston. I can understand his reasoning."

"Renée, I have to tell you that your skin is beautiful. I don't mean for a woman of your age. You happen to have a natural glow and your pores are small, and your complexion is beautiful. I wish all women had skin like yours. It wouldn't hurt to have a facial once in a while or a massage for that matter. It's not that you need one, but to have the experience and enjoy the pleasure of receiving a facial or massage would be a wonderful event."

"Thanks for the compliment, and when we get back, I'll be sure to make an appointment at your salon. I hope I can get you as my esthetician. That's what you call yourself, right?"

"That's right. A lot of people don't know that's the name of a skin care specialist. Of course, most people think of Dermatologists. That's all right and good, but they're for a specific problem or disease. I can refer to them if I feel I can't take care of their problem. Now let's stop talking shop. I'd love to learn more about you and your husband." The three women talked incessantly until they realized that it was almost time for dinner. After departing to their suite, Suzanne and Nancy got changed out of their bathing suits and dressed casually for an anticipated delicious dining experience.

Paul was waiting back in their cabin and, as soon as he heard his wife coming in the door, he sat on the bed with a broad smile on his face. "Well, that's one way out of getting you to take your exam. Don't think I'm going to let you off so easily. After dinner and whatever entertainment we might have, you'll eventually have to come back to the cabin and I'll have questions for you to answer," Paul told his wife as he buttoned his shirt. "Well, that's a shame because I thought of other ways we can have some recreation. But, if that's how you want to spend our first evening aboard this wonderful yacht, then be my guest."

"Well, given the choice, you know me too well. Maybe we'll put off the exam until another time." With that said he took his wife's hand and led her upstairs to the main deck where the dining room was located. They noticed that the food was presented to all the guests by the two general deckhands. Dick and Harry explained what they were being served and explained that, at each port, the Captain and chef hand-picked the food for the guests to have while they were at sea sailing to the next port. "It's quite interesting to enjoy the local cuisine and get a flavor of what specialties the different islands can provide." With that said, they told the guests to feel free to call them at any time. They would be frequently coming up to present them with the next course. All of the guests had a beautiful hand cut crystal bell at the end of their table to ring for the servers. The lower deck was where the crews sleeping cabins were located along with their own kitchen and dining area.

The six couples sat at the table for what appeared to be hours, as they were not being rushed after each course. Talking across the table to the people seated across from them, Arthur stated that he couldn't wait till the next day when they'd start their education on the various terms to be used for the various items that were aboard the vessel. "I know it will be exciting, but to be honest with you, I'd rather sit back, enjoy the beautiful weather and let the crew handle everything" admitted Joe. Most of the guests agreed with Joe (with the exception of a few people who wanted to know what to do in case of an emergency). "I realize we shouldn't think about such a scenario, but I'd like to know the different parts and what the correct names are, just in case we have to help the crew out," Mike admitted. That's when Paul informed the rest of the guests that he was a physician, and he'd be glad to help anyone out who wasn't feeling well, or had an accident. "Pooh, pooh, stated Sandy, I'm sure we're all healthy individuals and, even though it's nice of you to offer your services, I'm sure we won't have to use them." The others all agreed and, with that said, they saw a splendid looking array of desserts being presented to them.

When Sandy and Arthur got back to their suite, they stayed next to each other, holding hands and not saying a word. Finally, after what seemed a good fifteen minutes, Arthur broached the subject. "It was nice of Paul to offer his services in time of need, and I know why you sounded so put off. It's natural for you to feel the way you do after what you've been through. Thankfully, we're both healthy and won't need to worry about his offerings." With that said, Sandy put her head on Arthur's shoulder and he heard her whimpering and felt the wet tears through his shirt. He let her get out all of her misgivings and when he felt she was through, kissed her gently on top of her head. She came even closer to him and passionately kissed him on his lips. With that said and done, they shut off the lights and started undressing each other. *I might as well take advantage of this, while I can,'* Arthur thought.

"What do you think that was all about?" Tracy asked Mike. "I don't know, and frankly, I don't want to know. Maybe Sandy has gone through something pretty awful and doesn't want to be reminded of it. Or possibly someone close to her, like a family member, might have died or something. I'm certainly not going to ask her." Mike volunteered his reasoning. "I, for one, feel the same way that you do. Sandy will have to come to grips with whatever she went through, and deep down she knew that Paul was speaking through the goodness of his heart."

"I agree with you, Tracy. We're here to have a great time and I know the others feel the same as we do. Let's forget that ever happened and now let's finish what we started before we went upstairs." With that said they too shut off their cabin light and felt around for the shower, which wasn't far from their bed. With only the low light from the ceiling of the shower, they gently cleansed each other and stopped at areas that aroused their sexual excitement. When they laughed and realized that the shower was too small for any actual action, they moved to the bed where they finished making passionate love.

"Paul, do you think Sandy was offended by your offering your services this evening to anyone who needed you?"

"I don't know, but if she was upset, I think she's the one that has to get over it. I just meant to inform the rest of the passengers what I did as a profession. As a matter of fact, I really didn't have to mention it at all. In a way I wish I hadn't. But if, God forbid, something should happen, and four weeks can be a long time, they should know that someone's there to attend to their needs."

"I think you were right, and I think once Sandy thinks over what's on her mind, she'll be fine with you being a doctor and all. I'm telling you now, no testing; I think there's other ways to test each other out. What do you think, Herr Doctor?"

Suzanne got under the covers of her twin bed as did Nancy. Suzanne was tossing and turning and found the motion unable to put her to sleep as she thought it would. "Suzanne, are you still up?"

"Yes, I thought you'd be sound asleep once your head hit the pillow."

"I can't help thinking about Sandy. What was it that Paul said that would make her as upset as she seemed to be?"

"I really don't know. That's one of the reasons I'm having a difficult time going to sleep. Whatever her problem is, I'm sure she'll overcome it and we'll all have a wonderful trip. Arthur looks like the type of husband who will calm her down, and she'll soon forget the incident all together." With that said, Suzanne turned toward the wall and, within minutes, the motion of the ship put her into the state of Morpheus. She felt as if she were in her mother's arms as an infant and the constant motion of her rocking back and forth led the baby into a peaceful sleep.

Joe and Sam were still talking about the delicious dinner they experienced. Sam wondered if tomorrow morning the Chief Engineer could tell him if they had equipment on board that could get them in touch with land or if he could use his laptop to convey any messages he wanted to send to his three young sons. As he was thinking of his sons, Joe mentioned the incident that happened at dinner and wondered what it was all about. "I really don't know," answered Sam. "I don't think it's our business. I think that Paul was being nice and whatever is in Sandy's head is for her to work out. I'm sure all of us will have a great time on this vacation."

"I hope you're right," Joe agreed and started to get undressed for the night.

Cole and Isabelle closed the door to their suite and, as soon as the door was closed, Cole hugged Isabelle as hard as he could. "Watch it. I don't want to be breaking my ribs. Did you have as good a time as I did today?" Isabelle asked Cole. "I bloody did. You couldn't have asked for a better day. The meal was something to die for. I don't know about you, but I have a feeling every night I'm going to look forward to eating the great dinners they serve."

"So far this vacation is a real bomb. Now I know you're looking for great food and having beautiful weather, but I'm looking for a good bonk, if you know what I mean," Isabelle unashamedly spoke to her husband. Cole moved his eyes from side to side; a sheepish look crossed his face. After you said that my knob is pulsating! I'm going to bonk my slag and that's just for starters." They both lay exhausted after making love like two horny teenagers. "Come here, woman, and let me unfasten your buttons and feel your heavy boobs."

"I can honestly say you're good," exclaimed Isabelle, as they spooned each other on the double sized bed. "What do you think of those two batty's? I bet they bugger all the time," Cole told Isabelle. "Whatever, I don't give a shit if they both bonker off at the same time. They seem like nice guys and I don't give a rat's arse if they're buggers or not. As long as they don't come on to you, I don't care. We're here to have a jolly good time and, by golly, we're going to." With that said the two cuddled closer and fell into a fast sleep being cradled by the waves.

The next day was beautiful as the daylight shone brightly. Not a cloud marred the sky and the waves were gently lifting the sailboat while the wind was a bit gustier than day one out in the ocean. They could see the sails swaying in the breeze. They all couldn't wait for afternoon tea and buffet and then listen to what the Captain was to tell them on his lecture to be given at 3:30 in the afternoon. The six couples gathered on the deck, and with his first mate and chief engineer beside him, he got down to business. "First of all I hope that you had a great first day, and we expect many more good days on our great sailing yacht. When you first came aboard, you found a packet on your beds, which I hope by now you looked over. We don't expect any problems, we have not yet had any, but we'd like you to know a few essential nautical terms and functions that will help you if you ever need to use the knowledge that you're about to receive. Before I begin, are there any questions? None of them will be foolish to us, so feel free to ask anything you want to, and we'll try to answer these queries to the best of our knowledge."

The couples looked at each other, and at first, no one wanted to be the primary person asking questions that were surely on the other tourist's minds. Art was the first person to raise his hand. He asked Captain Bob to explain the different areas of the ship and what they were called. "It gets confusing when you're not a sailing person. At least if we learn the proper names, it will be easier if you or one of your men tell us to go to the front or back of the ship."

"Good question, Art. First of all I'll give you a pencil and a pad of paper so you can write down what I'm about to tell you. You might have a question or two, and instead of interrupting the conversation, just jot it down and one of us will explain what you are wondering about." Everyone nodded their heads.

"I'll try to tell you the phrases in alphabetical order to make it easier for you. First: when I say ABOVE BOARD: It's what it means, above the deck in plain view. Second: ABANDON SHIP! This means an imperative order to leave the vessel immediately. It's usually because of some imminent danger. It's usually the last resort after all of the other actions have failed. By the way, the crew and I have never had to give that order.

Third: ACCOMMODATION LADDER: It's a portable flight of steps down a ship's side.

Fourth: ADRIFT: it means the vessel is afloat and unattached in any way to the shore or seabed, but not under way. It implies that the ship is not under control and therefore goes where the wind and current take her. It's loose from moorings or out of place. It also refers to any gear not fastened down or put away properly. That's why it's important to make sure everything is put away. When someone yells: BATTEN DOWN THE HATCHES: That means to prepare for inclement weather by securing the closed hatch covers with wooden battens so as to prevent water from entering from any angle.

Fifth: AFT: That means towards the back of the boat. Sixth: AGROUND: Resting or touching the ground or bottom and it's usually involuntary.

Sixth: AHOY: A cry to draw attention. Seven: AHULL: When a boat is lying broadside to the sea. That's usually when we ride out a storm with no sails.

Seven and a half:" Everyone laughed at his attempt at making a joke. "This is an important one. ATON Aid to Navigation: It's any device external to a vessel or aircraft specifically intended to assist navigators in determining their position or safe course. It also warns us of dangers or obstructions! Eight: When I yell ALL HANDS: It means the entire ship's company, officers and our personnel, are to report to me. Nine: ALOFT: In the rigging of a sailing ship. It's above the ship's uppermost solid structure; overhead or high above. Ten: AMIDSHIP: sometimes called the middle of the ship. It's along the line of the keel. I know this seems like a lot to you, but we'll do it a few days at a time so it's not overwhelming. There's a few more and then you can look the list over at your convenience." Everyone shook their head in agreement.

"Eleven: ANCHOR is an object designed to prevent or slow the drift of a ship. It's usually attached to the ship by a line or chain. Typically it's a metal hook-like object to grip the bottom under the body of water. Twelve: ARMANENT: You do realize that every ship is now required to carry arms. You never know when you might need them. I'm sure a lot of you have heard about modern day pirates. They're usually in the Indian Ocean, but sometimes in the China Seas where we're headed. Most of them are fishermen that have had their livelihoods taken away from them from countries that fish in their waters. Knock on wood, we've never seen a pirate ship near us, and hopefully we never will. To be on the safe side, it's important that each and every one of you learn how to fire a rifle and defend yourself in time of trouble. Don't get nervous because you'll most likely never have to fire a rifle or pistol but when home, you'll at least have the knowledge on how to protect yourself from any would be robbers." With that said everyone laughed. "Thirteen: ASHORE: It's when you leave the boat and, hopefully, have a great time learning about the various places you'll be seeing and spending lots of money on the beautiful goods that each place has that's unique to the area. Fourteen: ASTERN: Towards the rear of the boat, behind the vessel. Fifteen: AVAST: It means stop, cease or desist from whatever is being done. Sixteen: AWASH: The boat is so low that the water is constantly washing across the surface. Seventeen: BACKSTAYS are long lines or cables that reach from the stern of the vessel to the mastheads. These are used to support the mast. Eighteen: BAR PILOT: Usually me, guides the ship over dangerous sandbars at the mouth of rivers. We'll be going by some rivers and you'll see what I mean. Nineteen: BARREL MAN: That's a sailor, or one of our guests, who is stationed in the crow's nest to see if there's another vessel in sight or if we see land. You'll enjoy climbing the ropes and rigging to go aboard the crow's nest or Masthead as it's often called. Twenty: BEAT TO QUARTERS: Now this command, hopefully, you'll never hear. It's to tell you to be prepared for battle. As I told you before, you'll all learn how to protect yourselves, so this is only an old fashioned saying and will never have to be used, I hope." Everyone laughed at his quip. "Do you think that's enough for today or would you like to learn more?" he asked the passengers.

In unison they said and raised their hands and shouted, "ENOUGH." "Tonight we'll look all of the material over and tomorrow we'll read anything else you give us. Is that all right with you, Captain?" Suzanne shouted. Captain Bob laughed and told everybody to enjoy themselves and told them that they can dive off the side of the ship if they want to. "If any of you are registered scuba divers, you can see some of the colorful fish down below. Or, if any of you want to swim alongside the boat, be my guest. Of course, you can also mellow out, enjoy the sun and wind in your face and eat to your hearts content. I'm expecting you to study some of those words that I gave to you."

"Our next stop will be Ho Chi Minh City, which used to be called Saigon, Vietnam. We'll be stopping here for a few days, so take your time and enjoy all the sights that you'll like to visit. There certainly are plenty of them. It's a dynamic city and one that you'll love. Feel free to explore on your own or join a guided shore excursion. Either way, I know you'll have fun. Before we go, I'd like to show you how to tie the rope to secure the ship to the dock. It's not hard, and I'm sure that you'll all master it in no time. But I figured this is as good a time as any."

The six couples were on deck as The Vacation of a Lifetime sailing yacht pulled into the dock. "We're lucky that Captain Bob knows his way around." Mike told anyone who was listening. Mike was told by one of the team members that he had to call 24 hours before they arrived to be assigned a dock. I guess Mike told Sandy that Saigon Port consists of three different piers and they're all in the center of town," Nancy whispered in Suzanne's ear.

Nancy told Suzanne that she was glad that they were able to travel a little further up the Vuag Tao River. "It takes about four hours to get to the port and the center of the town, but I guess the crew told one of the guests that it's worth the extra time. Wasn't it wonderful to see all of us enjoying the sights and our journey into the center of the city?" Nancy asked Suzanne. "You know I truly have goose bumps on seeing the city that I can remember seeing on the news. It reminds me of how my ancestors felt when their homes and villages were bombed to rubble. Many of my relatives, like these citizens and natives, had loved ones killed unjustly. Just think of all the unnecessary deaths of innocent people who didn't ask for such a war. Anyway, I'm glad to see how the city and all of Viet Nam has rebuilt itself for people to enjoy and try to understand the inhabitants and their traditions. I'm really looking forward to visiting this interesting place," voiced Suzanne.

The other couples were putting on comfortable clothes and walking shoes not knowing what to expect. As they were about to leave the yacht, Captain Bob halted them. "I want you to have a wonderful experience and learn the culture of these great people. Unfortunately, like many of our modern cities, there are lots of petty crimes, so be careful. I wouldn't wear good jewelry and keep your valuables locked in the safes that are provided in your rooms. While we're at dock, I thought you'd like to taste some of the food at the various restaurants that are different from our usual fare. Of course, if you want to come back to the ship, you're more than welcome, but tell us now, so we can prepare a delicious meal for you." Everyone looked at each other and nodded. "Speaking for the group, thanks but no, we'll enjoy as much as we can and see all the wonders while we're in this city. I can't wait till I can go and take a three-wheeled bike and be driven around to see some of the sights," elaborated Joe. "Oh yes," Captain Bob cautioned the group, "please leave your watches with your good jewelry. Buy a $5.00 watch and then, if someone should take it, you'll only be out $5.00." It took about ten minutes for people to go back to their cabins and deposit their good jewelry. "I don't know why I bothered to take my good pieces," Sandy told Arthur. "You did know that this wasn't going to be a highly glamorous vacation, but since we haven't traveled much, I can understand why you brought your pieces of jewelry. Let's put everything away and get down to business," Arthur said as they hurried up the stairs to walk and wander and see the sights that interested them.

When everyone was through depositing their jewels, they couldn't wait to start their journey to a new land to learn about the various cultures and the community they knew so little about. A few couples decided to travel together, while others wanted to see for themselves the different places and restaurants that would be a new adventure for them.

Tracy, Mike, Renée and Paul decided to team up and enjoy the sights together. Suzanne and Nancy told the two couples that they'd probably see them about and join them later. Suzanne felt like a little schoolgirl going on a field trip, but this time without the teacher to guide and tell them what to do. Tracy and Renée looked at each other after seeing their husbands with cameras and camcorders in hand. They laughed as they joined their mates walking through the crowded streets.

There was so much to see and do that Nancy and Suzanne didn't know what they should first visit. "You know Suzanne, I heard about the Cu Chu Tunnels. It's going west near the Cambodian border and it takes about two and a half hours to get there. What do you think?"

"Let's get a cab or whatever and, while we're driving, we'll have the guide tell us a little about the various areas that we pass on the way."

They were lucky to find a man who seemed honest and told them to write down the money he quoted them for the ride and tour. Getting out of the city was horrific with all the traffic jams, but they finally were on their way. Sam, the cab driver, told them all about himself and his family and the atrocities that he and his fellow countrymen had to endure. "I don't want to bore you and make you feel bad, so let me tell you about the scenes we're about to see on our way to the tunnels. These tunnels are in the Cu Chi region and I'll introduce you to some of the local people. It'll take us about two and half hours, and I'm sure you'll enjoy the scenery and all that you're going to learn."

When the two women got to the tunnels, they learned from Sam that these tunnels were built by local fighters during the Indochina conflict and were used as a base from which the Viet Cong could operate close to the South Vietnamese capital. Sam said, "The construction started in 1948 when we had to find somewhere to hide from French air attacks. By 1965, it consisted of 200Km's of various tunnels. Included in these tunnels were hospitals, schools, meeting rooms, kitchens and sleeping quarters. It was a difficult life for the inhabitants to protect against outside intruders. We had to place booby traps throughout the complex. As a matter of fact, during our war with the United States, part of our tunnels, were actually under some of the U S military installations. They had no idea about these tunnels. The people who lived in these tunnels faced many hardships with amazing ingenuity employed to maintain life, as normally as could be expected in these tunnels." Suzanne and Nancy were speechless when they heard Sam narrate the hardships and lives of these courageous people. "Come, we're here. Let's set you up with a guide to show you some of the tunnels, and you'll see for yourselves what I was talking about. I'll wait out here. I've been through the tunnels and many of my relatives actually were pioneers who helped build some of them. Go, and see for yourselves." With that said Sam took out a package of cigarettes and pulled one from the pack. Suzanne and Nancy followed their tour guide both with apprehension and a curiosity that neither expected on their first day in Saigon. In the kitchen area, they were seated and given some refreshments of which they were in dire need.

On the way back to the city, Nancy and Suzanne didn't have much to say. They let Sam prattle on, but both women were heartsick after seeing what these brave people had to endure. The two women also thought of the courageous military men that gave their lives for a war that the American people belittled. They gave Sam his allotted money and a very nice tip for his descriptive narration of the countryside. "Do you realize we've been gone for over eight hours?" Suzanne told Nancy. "No wonder I'm so hungry, and I'm sure you are as well."

"You could say that I agree," Suzanne admitted as they walked the streets wondering where they should eat.

Nancy seemed quiet as she thought of her own gorgeous home overlooking the beautiful ocean. She seemed to be in a different world than the one that she was used to. She never took for granted the many amenities that she had, but when she had visited the tunnels and learned of the atrocities that these people had endured, she appreciated her pampered life even more. "You seem quiet; anything bothering you?" Suzanne asked her friend. "Yes, I guess I realized how spoiled everyone who I know really is. Compared to the way these people had to live, it really seems sort of selfish when I complain about the little things in life that I take for granted."

"I see what you mean." Suzanne went on to tell Nancy her thoughts about what they just saw. "I have to agree with you. When I was a youngster, my grandparents and their friends talked about the 'old country' and what it was like living there. Now I can understand what they missed and couldn't put into words. Like you, I now understand how people of different countries, especially those that have come from war torn areas, feel when they first arrived in America. They do feel that the pavement is made of gold. Compared to what they had to go through, coming to America is like nothing that they were used to. I remember hearing stories from some of my friends that came over here to fight during the Viet Nam War. The horrific tales that they related were awful. Many a man that I knew had bad nightmares that even their nearest and dearest couldn't understand. The VA Hospitals are filled with many soldiers that went through Hell and back. Personally, when I see a service man, I revere him and what he and the men of the military had to go through to protect our country."

"I guess I'm getting too serious in my dialogue," Suzanne said aloud. "No, I understand what you mean. I have a new appreciation for the Asian people and how they left their homes to start fresh lives in America. It's like the settlers in the early days of America and the immigrants from Europe who had nowhere else to turn," Nancy spoke as a tear fell onto her cheek. Suzanne hugged her dear friend and they walked the rest of the way in silence.

"One more thing", Nancy said. "When I saw the play, Miss Saigon, I loved it, but it didn't really register as much as being here and seeing for myself what this country was really like." The two walked hand in hand, not caring what others thought.

Ronnie stood up and wiped his face from some spillage of the wine. "Like I told you last week, I know some men that are sort of criminals. I've known these men since we all played together in the village and swam and fished together. They went their way and I was lucky that one of my uncles was in the military and another cousin was on the police force. I went in one direction and they went into another. They are still good men, but they value life differently."

Lifting his shoulders Ronnie continued, "What I'm about to show you are things that I never thought I'd be handling in my life. We've all heard and seen these items, but to say that they are ours is alien to the life that we chose to live." With that said he took his cloth and emptied it onto the middle of the coffee table. "I want you to know that Sunny and I took what little money that we had and went to my friends and told them of our plight. They all knew of our dilemma and, because they are my friends, did well by us. They didn't have to charge us what they did, but they gave us a deal on this ammunition and assortment of weapons, and I couldn't ask for any better agreement."

With that said, he proudly displayed the guns and all the ammunition needed. The rest of the team just stood with their mouths open. Slowly they took the rifles, guns and semi-automatics that they liked and, like proud parents, held, caressed and looked at them with glee in their eyes.

He lifted his hands and arms and stilled the men, who all at once started talking. "I told you I had friends who could deliver the goods," Ronnie proudly uttered. "Put the guns down and I'll show the different ones and the ones that I particularly like." He displayed the Glock, Uzi, Baretta ARX 160, and M16 and the Colt 45. Also among the stash were some AK47 assault rifles and a few RPG rocket propelled grenades. One of the men picked it up and said: "Wow, these guys aren't fooling around. This is enough power to blow a hole into the side of a huge ship. I don't think that we'll be looking to go after those kinds of ships, are we?" Laughing in unison, they all agreed that they would only stick with smaller ships. There were also Semi-Automatic Rifles and a few Automatic ones as well. All the straps and holders for them were displayed. Like any parent, he told his men the good and bad aspects of each gun and told them that they had to learn how to shoot the guns and be proficient in learning how to clean and take care of them. "It's like taking care of anything that you cherish. If it's not taken care of correctly, then it could come back and haunt you and, like any type

of weaponry, you have to respect it. Now I suggest that we learn all about these instruments of destruction, and before we do anything else, find a place where no one will see us practicing." They all nodded in agreement.

CHAPTER TEN

Tracy, Mike, Sandy and Arthur were captivated by all the activity in the city. "I thought that New York was busy, but this beats it by a mile," Mike stated. "There's a lot to see and do in Ho Chi Minh City (Saigon). I'll leave it up to you to make the decision on where we should go. I'm easy, and Arthur, don't say anything because I know you're a smart ass." Arthur laughed as he took Sandy's hand and walked behind Tracy and Mike. They waited for Mike to make the decision on where and what to see in this vast city of history.

Looking back to Sandy and Arthur, Mike announced that he and Tracy looked at all the brochures, and he thought that the two couples would enjoy seeing the Notre-Dame Cathedral Basilica and then go to the Mariamman Hindu Temple, which is located in Ho Chi Minh City, Vietnam. "If we have time, there are two other Temples that aren't very well known, but they're supposed to be different. So let's go to the Basilica and then the Mariamman Hindu Temple. We'll see what time it is and then we'll decide whether to eat or continue." Sandy and Arthur said it sounded great to them.

While heading to the Mariamman Hindu Temple, they enjoyed the sights of the Japanese rickshaws being pulled by their Japanese coolies. The tourists pointed to the different tourist attractions as they passed the elaborately decorated figures and various articles mentioned in the brochures that they had looked through. On the way to the well-known Temple, Mike told them of two other Temples that were not as well known, but if they wanted to see them, they would be worth it. "Let's see how my feet are holding up and then I'll have a better idea on if I want to continue or maybe we can take a taxi to them," Sandy admitted. "I'm with you, Sandy. Even with all my working out back home, I think all this walking will kill me. I'm enjoying it, but we'll have to give it some thought when we're through seeing this magnificent structure," agreed Tracy. The guys just laughed and thought to themselves, '*What Sissies!*' "You know what, instead of hearing about your feet, why don't we take a cab and then the cab can take us to the three Temples in one day? I heard that the other two temples are not well known and most people don't even know where they're located. As a matter of fact, I had to go to the National Archives of Malaysia to find out how to get there and their addresses."

"When did you get off the boat to do that?" a surprised Tracy asked Mike. "Just call me Harry Houdini! Seriously, when you were in our cabin for one of your rests, I asked the Captain how to find the other two Temples and he told me how to go about finding them."

The two couples were in awe as they approached the Mariamman Hindu Temple in Hochi Minh City. They were surprised to find out that the practices and rituals were only partially followed. At this Temple, the practice is more like the Buddhist manner of prayers where the devotees kneel before the deity and pray with the joysticks. They could wear their foot-ware, but when entering the main sanctum, they had to remove their shoes or sneakers. "There's so much to learn about the different cultures; I find it fascinating," exclaimed Sandy. They learned that all the Temples were run by Vietnamese Hindus. There were no Sanskrit mantras chanted; nothing was chanted- just devotion. All the Temples in Saigon were at least 100 to 300 years old. They stayed there for a few hours admiring all the figurines, and then they decided to visit the other Temples. "This Temple is the Subramiam Swamy and a moderate one. The keepers of the Temple live here as well." Though it's not as famous, they admired the cleanliness. The same methodology, rituals and practices were done here as well. The Deities were different they noted. "Now, I'm saving the best for last," proclaimed Mike. When they arrived at the large Temple, they were in awe of the cleanliness and how it was maintained. "A Vietnamese man and his family live and take care of this Thandayuthapani Temple. The various statues and deities are different and give us a better insight of the religious belief of the Vietnamese people," Arthur explained to all of his friends who would listen.

After their long journey, they had to decide what restaurant they wanted to eat at. "You know, Tracy and I picked out the sight for today, so how about you picking the restaurant?" Arthur acknowledged the challenge and, after much deliberation, decided on La Villa Restaurant. "I hear it's isolated from the noise, dust and hectic craziness of the city. I've heard you feel as if you're in a home of a rich relative. It's supposed to be warm and embracing, and you feel you're an honored guest of Monsieur Thierry, who also happens to be the owner and an experienced chef."

"That sounds fine to me, I'm sure we're all famished. Look at the variety of dishes they have to offer. It's going to be difficult to decide which meal we should have. I, for one, am going to take a little portion from all of your plates and I hope that it doesn't gross you out," declared Mike. They all were in a great mood as they were seated and ordered the first of many glasses of wine. Tracy, after her third glass of wine, waved her hand around the establishment and declared how beautiful the pool villa was. With a little slur in her voice, she declared, "My, it's a quiet neighborhood. You made a terrific choice, Arthur." Tracy lifted her glass and proclaimed: "To Arthur and Sandy!" Sandy lifted her wine glass to click with the other three people at the table, in acknowledgment of her husband's choice of fine cuisine. She tried getting the doctor's voice out of her mind. She didn't want to think of her last visit, without Arthur, and didn't want anyone to know the dire result of her last scan. Putting on a smile, she blended in with the other members of the party.

Paul and Renée hooked up with Isabelle and Cole and decided to go to the Fine Arts Museum and to the Ben Thanh market after, which interested both couples. "I graduated as an art historian and we go to the Boston Fine Arts Museum at least every 6 to 8 weeks. We truly appreciate the different types of mediums and artists and hope that you do as well," Renée said to Isabelle. "Hey, we're up for anything. I'll endure the Museum as long as I don't hear you cuffing about my meandering about. As Cole told you, I love to natter with the locals, and I love to barter. This is the type of precinct that fits my fancy. So sure I might learn a bit of culture, and you, on the other hand, will enjoy seeing all of the art work." As much as Cole and Isabelle didn't think that they'd enjoy seeing the Fine Arts Museum, they were greatly surprised to walk among the paintings and sculptures of the three-floor facility. Isabelle was impressed by the ancient Buddhist artwork. She whispered to Cole that the beautiful piece of lacquered artwork in front of them would look gorgeous in their entryway. "Maybe there's a gift shop, and if you like anything in particular, buy it. But don't forget, we're going to the Ben Thanh market and you might change your mind." With that spoken, Isabelle bashed Cole lightly on his shoulder and said, "When do I ever buy anything that I don't like. As long as I have you with me, you can hold some bags as well." They walked fast to keep up with the other couple. "All this culture might do us some good. Who knows when we might need to use it," Proclaimed Isabelle. "Yeah, like we'd use it when we go to the local pub and spend the night getting pissed and playing trivia or darts with the rest of the gang."

Cole felt it was hours that they were at the museum and was glad when Renée announced that it was now time for them to visit the market. "I hope that you enjoyed the Art Museum as much as Paul and I did," Renée declared. "Oh, sure we did, didn't we, luv?" Isabelle inconspicuously elbowed her husband.

Just before they entered the Market place, Cole poked Paul and whispered to him, "now you'll see what turns my wife on. She loves to shop and you know that expression, shop till you drop? I've never seen her drop yet." Isabelle turned around and told her friends to make sure that they didn't forget which door they came through. "There are many different entrances and, just in case we should split up, we should make a specific time and place to meet up. Let's say at this vegetable stand where we're standing now."

Paul laughed as he saw Isabelle take off like a flying bat. "I really do believe she enjoys shopping more than any other pastime," he remarked to his wife. "Well, let her have a great time. I'm thrilled that we got to see the art museum and we'll have fun seeing the different items, and who knows, we might enjoy the bartering."

Cole followed Isabelle around like a chick following a mother hen. They'd been married for many years, so he knew how she shopped. With all the ribbing he gave her about the many items she purchased through the years, he loved to tease her about all the guff she brought home but had to admit that, once in a while, he rather enjoyed a purchase or two that found its way into their apartment. He realized that she was a grafter, and because she kept right up with him at work, he couldn't or wouldn't deny her anything. Laughing to himself he thought that if he did put up a fuss, she'd mince no words telling him where to stuff it.

The aisles were narrow and filled with shoppers browsing about. The locals were buying their foods and the various tourists were trying to bargain with the merchants on items that they thought interesting.

Cole tried to keep up with his wife who was going from stall to stall. "I didn't think that anyone could run so fast through a market, but I honestly think Isabelle would win a contest for the fastest shopper I've ever seen," Paul remarked to Renée.

When it came time for the two couples to meet, Paul felt sorry when he saw Cole looking wiped out. Paul hardly recognized his friend with all the bundles he was carrying and some of them were actually hiding his face. "Come on," Paul said to Cole, "let me help you with some of those bags, and Renée will take a few items from Isabelle. I can't stand here and see you guys bundled down with packages."

"That's awfully jolly of you old chap, and I'll make it up to you in some way. How about my paying for the fare back to the dock while we unload these 'items' and then go to dinner."

"That's sounds like a great idea," piped in Renée as she tried to ignore the grumbling in her stomach. Paul and his wife decided to wash up and change before dinner and knew that Cole and Isabelle would also take time to do so. When they met back on deck, they felt like new and couldn't wait to have a great meal. Isabelle admitted she was ready for a jolly good restaurant. With that stated the two couples got into the cab and described to the cab driver what type of meal they felt like having. "You sit back while I take you to my favorite place to eat. Food good and you have a good time. Here's my card; call me when you finish, and I pick you up. Okay?"

"Sounds good to me chap. Hey Paul, I'm going to buy you any drink on the house, you and your misses, that is. You were jolly good companions to help us out with all the articles and bags we had. I don't want any hoo ha from either of you. Now let's hope the maître d' finds us a table rather quickly because I'm famished." No one could disagree.

Paul and Renée were not used to drinking to excess and both felt light-headed and giddy by the end of the meal. Cole and Isabelle were used to going out to their favorite pubs. At least once a week they went out. They were not alcoholics, but could hold their own when it came to consuming liquor. They both drank, mostly beer, but weren't opposed to downing a few different concoctions. As Tracy was leaving the great eatery, she spotted their other friends and said hello. "Come join us. I'm sure that the waiter can add four more chairs to the table," Paul amicably proclaimed. Not wanting to make a fuss, the two couples decided to join their mates. They ordered some after dinner drinks, and after downing more than they had originally thought they would, the four couples felt no pain.

When Tracy and Mike entered their suite, they fell onto their backs, heads splitting from laughing so hard. "You know, Honey, I don't remember the two of us getting this loaded at the same time before. Too bad I'm so wasted because would I like to fuck the Hell out of you. However, I don't think I could find him." All Tracy could do was laugh and within five minutes both were sound asleep. They didn't change into their nightclothes and were snoring so loudly that the Captain was worried that something might be wrong. Captain Bob put his ear to the door and listened intently. He realized that the couple was probably inebriated and walked away with a smirk. He thought to himself, *'yup, everyone seems to be having a great time.'*

Suzanne and Nancy saw the other couples departing. It seemed obvious to them that Joe and Sam were off in their own world. "Okay, what's on the itinerary for today?" Nancy asked Suzanne as they were dressing for their outing around the city "Well, to be honest with you, the Notre-Dame Cathedral Basilica looked interesting. Although I love architecture and enjoy seeing the beautiful stained glass windows and the intricate designs, I feel like doing something different. The Tunnels were interesting, but I thought it would be nice to tour the Mekong River. I've heard so much about Mekong Delta that I'd love to take the trip. Are you up for it?"

"Oh great, I can see the headlines now: "Two of the most prominent business women in the United States died accidently while on a river tour along the Mekong River."

"Nancy, you are truly a baby. You are always teasing me about my fear of flying and you know that I can't swim a lick or for that matter float, but this is something different. If it wasn't a safe journey, I'm sure they wouldn't offer it. Come on let's be adventurous."

"Okay, but if I die, I'll come back and haunt the Hell out of you." With that said Suzanne shoved Nancy out of their cabin door and found the way to get the tour.

They left early in the morning after finding out that the tour lasted 10 hours. The gentleman conducting the tour spoke English, so it was easy for them to understand what was being said. The tour was from Ho Chi Minh to the Mekong Delta. They traveled along the canals and visited floating markets, which was a memorable experience. They saw the various species of fish and learned that because of contamination and mercury, the fish were now causing problems with the people who were consuming them as a mainstay of their diet. They cruised through the lush green vegetation of the Mekong canals to an orchard, where they were treated to a delicious lunch complete with tropical fruit. They continued along to the town of Vinh Long and took many pictures. The route that they took is really called the "rice bowl of Vietnam." At first, Nancy was a nervous wreck as she saw how shallow the boat was and how close it was to the water. Susanne tried calming her friend's tension. They saw many tropical fruits and flowers and took pictures to show everyone back home. The lush green vegetation of the canals leading to an orchard was spectacular.

When the two women returned to Ho Chi Minh City, Nancy thanked Suzanne for coercing her to take the trip. "You know, Suzanne, I would never have gone on such an exotic trip if you didn't force me. I can't believe the various and unusual sights that we saw and I can't wait to show Rich and all the gang our pictures."

"This is just the beginning of our trip. I'm sure there'll be more exciting things happening, and I can't wait to be part of this adventure. Now let's decide where we shall have dinner. Back at the boat, I have an extensive list of eateries that we can choose from once we clean up and change."

"That sounds good to me, oh wise one." They both smiled as they went back to the pier.

Sam and Joe stayed in bed a little longer than usual while looking over the various brochures that were available to choose which place that they would visit. They knew that they'd be in the city for at least one more day, so they decided to tour the tunnels tomorrow, and today they would take it easy and visit the Notre-Dame Cathedral Basilica and enjoy the various architecture of the beautiful Basilica. They first entered and saw the floor, which was imported from

France (as all of the building materials were). The bricks were from Marseille, France, and the bright red color was as vibrant as it was when installed. The towers enthralled them, as the six bronze bells weighed 28.85 metric tons. The crosses were installed on top of each tower. The total height of the cathedral to the top of the Cross is 60.5 m. They loved the pipe organ, which was designed especially for this Church to have perfect acoustics. They learned that a new player was installed in 1967 and blessed in 2005. They walked around the entire Church and admired the design. They saw the original Vietnamese writing when the Cathedral was built. The entire inside of the church, including the ceiling, were incredible. They picked up all the literature that they could, and with anticipation, wanted to go back to their suite to read all about this Christian Church in a country that was unfamiliar with its customs.

"I don't know about you, but I'd love to go to dinner and look over some of the literature while we're eating."

"Joe, that's a great idea. I understand that there are many great restaurants to choose from, so why don't we look over some of the menus that the Captain gave us and we'll pick one that we'll both enjoy," said Sam. With that said they started walking.

They decided on The Deck Saigon Restaurant and were famished when they finally got to the Saigon River Bank in the quiet neighborhood of District 2. As they sat down, they could see and hear the lapping of the waves on the dock. Both being romantic men, they couldn't wait to see the sunset as they watched the traffic on the River. The river traffic provided a pleasant, soothing, relaxing atmosphere while they listened to the French down tempo music playing in the background.

As they waited, they spotted Suzanne and Nancy entering the establishment. The men called the women over and asked them if they'd like to join them for dinner. "What a great idea," Suzanne admitted as they sat down beside the gentlemen, each party holding brochures in hand. After a 45-minute wait, they were seated. At the table, both parties expounded on the various and delightful wonders of their day. They ordered wine and toasted to a great trip. The two couples stayed for hours, not being rushed, as many restaurants have a habit of doing. As they talked, they found out about each other and liked what they heard. Going back to the pier the friends realized that two more great acquaintances were made.

SAN DIEGO, CALIFORNIA

Rich was happy that Nancy and Suzanne were having, he hoped, a wonderful trip. He missed Nancy immensely and selfishly couldn't wait until her return. There was so much to say and tell her when he finally would see her; it would be difficult deciding where to begin. The longer he was with Yasuhito, the more he became aware that the older Japanese gentleman had no relatives. Rich enjoyed his company and learned many nice things, mostly Japanese culture, from the elder man. Yasuhito had become like a surrogate father, helping Rich with philosophy, teaching him Japanese cookery, as well as his inner thoughts and beliefs. Rich had a hard childhood, one that he wanted to forget. Talk about dysfunctional families, he was lucky that he turned out to be on the good side of the law. Many times he thanked God and whatever it was that changed his attitude to be one of helpfulness. Rich could have turned out to be on the wrong side of the law.

Now, with Mr. Yasuhito's influence and the love he and Nancy found with one another, he felt life was wonderful. He became an optimistic person and realized, for the first time in his life, that life is what you make it.

The more he thought of transferring to Boston PD the sadder he was that Mr. Yasuhito and he would not be there for one another. Many a night Rich would lay in bed, hands under his head, and think of a solution that could accommodate everyone involved. After many agonizing and sleepless nights, he realized that the only scenario that would satisfy him was to have Mr. Yasuhito move with him to Nancy's house. The house that she lived in would afford them the privacy that was essential to both of them yet allow Mr. Yasuhito to be an elder to both Rich and Nancy. Nancy had not been brought up with loving parents or family. The only family Nancy considered as her own was Suzanne's. He knew in his heart that his darling would understand his feelings, and even though she probably wouldn't admit it out loud, she'd appreciate Mr. Yasuhito's patience and guidance throughout their years together. The three of them would make a great team hopefully for many years to come. With that thought, he made up his mind that when Nancy returned from her trip, that would be one of the first items on the agenda for them to talk about. Mr. Yasuhito entered Rich's kitchen and in broken English explained that it was time for their lesson in Taekwondo (a Korean martial art). Mr. Yasuhito was a student of one of the best teachers in the art form. He'd been taught this martial art since it was established in the 1950's and 1960's in the South Korean military.

Although he realized that Rich had many wonderful skills, he wanted to add to his defense arsenal and felt it his duty to teach this wonderful, popular, martial art to his new friend, whom he considered to be a son. Rich was surprised at the agility that the older Japanese gentleman possessed, with a natural nimbleness

and dexterity that one doesn't usually find in a man of his age. Although Rich didn't come out and ask him his birth years, for his records were long ago lost, he couldn't bring himself to raise the question to him. Rich realized that sometimes one couldn't tell the age of a Japanese person for some reason or another. They either looked older than their years or looked like a young person. Whatever, he knew that Mr. Yasuhito was very versed in many subjects and, he benefitted greatly from Mr. Yasuhito's expertise. *'Yes,'* Rich thought to himself, *'both Nancy and I will enjoy him, and she'll learn to love this older gentleman as I have. Whatever time we have left on earth we'll make him feel wanted and needed and not be taken advantage of.'* With those thoughts, he got dressed to get ready for his early morning lesson, shower and go down to headquarters where he was sure he'd find plenty to keep himself busy.

BACK ON SHIP IN THE PORT OF VIETNAM

All the guests were too hyped to retire for the evening. They sat on the second deck (which was decorated like a living room) around the large, round, mahogany, center table. They all started talking at once and, finally, after a few minutes, Suzanne stood up, clapped her hands, and feeling like a school teacher she told everyone to be quiet. "I take it we've all had a wonderful first day in Ho Chi Minh City and all have wonderful stories and events that we want to share. I suggest that we start with the couples that went together and starting from my right, get up and start their epilogue, everything from where they went, what they learned and why they liked it. Then they can tell us where they ate and what unusual dishes they might have had and anything else they want to talk about. We don't have any limitations so let's get started." Suzanne sat down and waited for Renée and Paul and Tracy and Mike to start the narrative. The guests were all ears and enjoyed listening to the different adventures everyone had. It was late in the evening when all were finished with their stories. "I don't think we have an alarm clock to wake us up. Let's sleep late and see what today brings," Suggested Arthur.

When they got up, they were treated to a great buffet that had all the customary Vietnamese dishes with a few other Far East delicacies awaiting them. After filling themselves like stuffed pigs, they were in no mood to start exploring anything for at least a couple of hours.

"Well, now that I have you at my disposal, I think we should go over a few of the nautical terms that I think will be important for you to know, especially when we're at sea," suggested Captain Bob. He heard groans from everyone but ignored them. "I know a lot of you have never been on a sailboat or, if you have, not one as large as this one. As you realize, we are an 108 ft. yacht and, in order to fit 6 couples comfortably on board, things had to eliminated, to make the extra suite. There's one combo room of dining and living room with direct connection to the kitchen. From the kitchen, there's a direct connection to my quarters. So, to sum up, there would be one large area below deck that contains the master suite, my cabin, kitchen, dining/living room and all the needed electronics that we call the server room. Then there is one lower deck below that contains the five bedrooms and a separator for the crew's rooms, which connect to a small engine room. For a four-week trip, we allow 24 to 36 hours per port and possibly longer, if you so wish it. If the group wants to cut the trip short, we can also do that."

Everyone was quiet listening to every word Captain Bob was saying. "The front of the ship is called the BOW. The back part of the ship is called the STERN. And for gosh sakes, instead of calling the male bathroom the HEAD, we'll call it the BATHROOM. I'll try to make it easy for you and give you the nautical names that I think you'll need to know. As I told you, the Stern is the back of the boat and, further aft. The AFTERDECK is the deck behind a ship's bridge. The person who works the aft sails on the quarterdeck and poop deck is called Afterguard. AMIDSHIPS is midway between the BOW and the STERN of a ship. A BACKSTAY extends from the ship's mastheads to the side of the ship. A BINNACLE is the case in which a ship's compass is kept. A BOATSWAIN is the crewmember in charge of equipment and maintenance. The BOLLARD is a short post on a wharf or ship to which ropes are tied. I already told you what an ANCHOR is and, to repeat myself, it's an object designed to prevent or slow the drift of a ship. It's attached to the ship by a line or chain; typically a metal hook-like object designed to grip the bottom under the body of water. Some of you might want to help in the Anchor watch. It's the crewmen assigned to take care of the ship while anchored or moored. Some of your duties are making sure that the anchor is holding and the vessel is not drifting. Every large ship should have armament. These are the weapons on board in case of an emergency. I'll get into that later, as I told you before. Maybe while we're at sea tomorrow, we'll show you the rifles and guns and make sure you know how to fire them in case of an emergency. Now don't get all riled up, so far we've never had to use them.

Now, in case of inclement weather, you'll hear one of us yell, BATTEN DOWN THE HATCHES. That's to prepare for inclement weather by securing the closed hatch covers with wooden battens so as to prevent water from entering from any angle. BEACHING is deliberately running a vessel aground, to load and unload (as with the landing craft) to prevent a damaged vessel from sinking.

The BEACON is a lighted or unlighted fixed aid to navigation attached directly to the earth's surface. A BEAM is the width of a vessel at the widest point alongside the ship at the mid-point of its length. BEAM ENDS are the sides of a ship. It may mean the vessel is literally on her side and possibly about to capsize, more often, the phrase means the vessel is listing 45 degrees or more.

BEAR DOWN or BEAR AWAY is to turn away from the wind, often with reference to a transit. BEATING or also known as TACKING is sailing as close as possible towards the wind in a zig-zag course to get an upwind direction to which it's impossible to sail directly. I want you all to learn to tie a BIGHT. It's a loop in a rope or line, a hitch or knot tied on the bight is one tied in the middle of a rope, without access to the ends. The BILGE is the compartment at the bottom of the hull of a ship where water collects and must be pumped out of the vessel. A BOUY is a floating object to define shape and color, which is anchored at a given position and serves as an aid to navigation. BUNTLINE is one of the lines tied to the bottom of a square sail and used to haul it up to the yard when furling. Now I want all of you, either today or tomorrow to climb a rope and go onto the MASTHEAD or CROW'S NEST and look out at the ocean. It's really a beautiful sight. I'll be there with you or one of the crew will be there to help. If you want to wear a life preserver, please feel free to do so until you feel confident to climb up the masthead. I think that's enough for today's lesson. We still have a lot of days ahead of us so please don't take anything that you heard today as hogwash. Learn and remember all that I've said."

The group looked at each other and groaned. "I feel as if I'm back in school," Sam announced. "Well, it's important to know these terms in case an emergency does occur," warned Sandy. "I, for one, will study these terms with Arthur and even at my age," raising her hand and shutting her eyes, "don't even ask if you know what's good for you," she warned the group. "I'll have him test me and I, in turn, will test him. Don't take this lightly. Even though we're all having a great time, you never know what can happen."

"I'm going to my cabin and all I can think of is the poem by Samuel Taylor Coleridge - - The Ancient Mariner – The Albatross. Good night all and I hope I don't have any stupid nightmares about the albatross hanging onto my neck and someone shooting it dead," announced Suzanne as she walked to her quarters. The other people looked on in horror as they sat in silence. "Oh she's just kidding," Nancy tried to quell their fright. She once told me that she had to memorize the entire poem in order to pass English when she was in high school and she never forgot the poem. Whenever she gets a little upset she quotes: 'Water, water, everywhere, not a drop to drink, water, water, everywhere and all the boards did shrink.' Don't worry, she's a jokester, that's all," Nancy reaffirmed Suzanne's idea of a joke.

Nancy left to catch up with Suzanne and everyone looked at each other with fear in their eyes. "I think we'd better learn what Captain Bob is trying to teach us, especially not wanting the albatross to hang on our necks," Tracy remarked as she and Mike went to their cabin.

It was late morning and the fishermen (Pirates), decided to meet at the dockyards with all of the equipment that they had. Each individual brought his gear and made sure that the apparatus would not be seen by anyone else but the men involved in this operation. When all the men were together, they chose a gathering place that they could target practice without being seen by anyone. They decided on a place where Tolemeo used to bring his young son in the deep woods and camp for the night. "I bought some target practice posters at the local store and told the man in charge that I was taking my son for some practice. I thought that would satisfy his curiosity."

"Good idea," boasted Ronnie as he embraced his cousin. "We'll put the targets onto the trees and each of you will take the weapons of your choice."

"After we practice for a while" Ronnie told the men, "we'll take each gun and the ammunition home, and meet every day if necessary, to make sure that all will be good marksmen. It's not that we intend to harm anyone, but just in case some of the people on the boat have their own guns, we can't look like morons and not know what to do with the weapons that we are carrying."

They shook their heads in unison. Efren laughed out loud and proclaimed to his fellow buddies, "It's not like we're the typical pirates and are out for blood and jewels. All we know is fish" They all agreed. "Now we have to get serious and, with Tolemeo's and Ronnie's help, we'll at least know more about marksmanship and know what the Hell we're doing. Speaking for myself, I'm sick and tired of not having enough money to bring home to my family who depend on my income to live the good life, at least put food on the table and indulge in hoping that my kids will be able to attend college. I want to be proud of myself again and be able to look myself in the mirror and not be ashamed of who is looking back at me."

With shaking of fists, they all agreed. They headed out of the dockyards and made their way to the parcel of land that was wooded. They let Tolemeo lead the way and were determined to become the best that they could be.

Tolemeo put up the posters and each man drew a straw, in order of length, to make sure that they had a turn at the range. Each man took about half an hour at

the shooting range and although not as proficient as they wanted to be, knew that with practice and patience they would be the best shooter that they could.

When all of the men finished practicing, they agreed to meet tomorrow, same time and place. Mario stayed behind and put his arm around his friend, Sunny. "So, what do you think? Do you see yourself as a marksman and pirate like the others do?" Contemplating deeply, Sunny cleared his throat and optimistically proclaimed that he did. He asked his friend if he could think of a better plan. With a shrug of his shoulders they both knew the answer. It was the best answer to the problem at hand.

"Good, good, that makes me feel better. You've been quiet, and I was hoping that you weren't getting cold feet. I'm glad that you're with us, my friend, and when this ordeal is finished, we'll look back on this entire episode and laugh while we're at the local pub having a few beers."

With that said they both went out of the clearing and headed to their individual homes, making sure that their family and friends would not find the hidden stash. Only one person knew where to find it.

CHAPTER ELEVEN

Nancy closed the bedroom door and grabbed the first object she could find, which happened to be a light comb, and threw it at Suzanne who was in bed reading. "Hey, what's that for?"

"You know, for an extremely bright woman you're really dumb at times. Do you know that you have every one of our companions afraid of a disaster because of your stupid poem? I'm not joking, Suzanne. I hope that they'll soon forget your little quip and go about their vacation not remembering that stupid albatross remark." With that said, Nancy went into the bathroom to get ready for a sound night's sleep.

Suzanne lay in bed, thinking of what Nancy said. She had to admit that at times she blurted out what was on her mind without thinking. She was mad at herself, but at the same time a certain dread was weighing heavily on her mind. The imaginary thought was like a toothache that wouldn't go away. She tried not to think of these vivid horrors, but nothing she did would remove them from her subconscious. '*Oh well, I'll try to ignore my imagination and enjoy the places we go to and learn about the people of the area. The pictures will be proof enough of our great vacation,*' she thought as she tossed and turned until Morpheus took over.

The next morning, while everyone was having breakfast, Suzanne got up from the table and asked for everyone's attention. "I'm sorry for that stupid remark about the poem I quoted last evening. It was only a joke, a stupid one at that. I hope all is forgiven, and let's go and have a great time. Again, I apologize." Everyone clapped and thought to themselves that it was quite a woman who will admit when she makes a mistake. "Hey, we knew it was nothing and don't you worry, we're all adults and know when someone is joking," Joe assured Suzanne as he started to eat the breakfast that he was enjoying. Looking around to make sure no one could hear him, Sam whispered, out of the corner of his mouth; "What a crock of bullshit. I know you and I were scared as everyone else, but you did say the right thing. Thanks."

Captain Bob came up from his quarters and informed them of the weather predictions for the day. "As usual, we have another bright, sunny day and, if you want, we can explore more of this great city and then I thought, as a diversion when we're at sea tomorrow, we'd head for Ha Long Bay, which isn't on our itinerary. It's in the province of Quang Ninh, Vietnam. The bay features thousands of limestone karsts and isles in various sizes and shapes. Ha Long Bay is a center of a larger zone, which includes Bái Tử Long bay to the northeast and Cát Bà islands to the southwest. These larger zones share similar geological, geographical, geomorphological, climate, and cultural characters. It's around 1,553 km2, including 1,960 islets, most of which are limestone. The limestone has gone through 500 million years of formation in different conditions and environments. The evolution of the karst in this bay has taken 20 million years under the impact of the tropical wet climate, it includes a tropical evergreen bio-system, oceanic and sea shore bio-system. It is home to 14 endemic floral species and 60 faunal species. Historical research surveys have shown the presence of pre-historical human beings in this area tens of thousands years ago. It's truly a 'rock wonder in the sky.' By the way it's translated to mean 'descending dragon bay' and is a UNESCO World Heritage site. It's also one of the most popular travel destinations, to those who know of it."

Paul stood up and said, "I hope that I can be the spokesperson for the group and say we would love to go to this impromptu visit. I take it we can dive off the boat or snorkel and enjoy the various specimens in the bay." Everyone cheered and knew that after another great day of adventure, they'd be going on to this glorious Bay that was practically unheard of, at least to them, who were novices to this area of the world.

The travelers wanted to see the areas that they hadn't seen the day before. When leaving, they all decided to meet at the restaurant that Sandy and Arthur had gone to, but then decided to go to the spot where Joe and Sam had dined to see the scenes that they described. They made a time for the meeting and all went on their way to the various places that they hadn't seen the day before.

The next morning, everyone got up, and after breakfast took one last look at the famous city that they heard so much about years ago. They had no idea how it made a turnaround while recovering from a ghastly war and was now a glorious, cosmopolitan place where one could enjoy all of its natural wonders.

"Okay, now that we're off and Mike was a good sport and undid the knot that was tying the boat to the dock, I want all of you to get a large piece of thick rope and make the knot that Mike so graciously undid for us. When that's done, I want you, or whoever thinks they can climb their way to the top of the crow's nest or masthead, to get ready to do so. After I see that you made a great knot that you'd be proud of."

Everyone took a long, thick rope and began trying to tie the knot as instructed. Suzanne whispered to Nancy, "Do you think I can get out of climbing up that stupid rope to see the water or whatever might be out there?"

"To be honest with you, Honey, I don't want to do it either, but I think it will be fun. We've been doing a lot of exercising and I think we're in very good shape, for the shape we're in," Nancy laughed as she thought her quote was funny. "I remember what Captain Bob told us about the various whales, dolphins and who knows what else we'll see. I, for one, will be ready to climb to the masthead."

"Well, you're a bit younger than I am," a stubborn Suzanne announced. "I think that Sandy, Arthur, Renée and Paul, who by the way are older than you, will be climbing the ropes. I really think it's an essential part of sailing to be able to do this exercise and know that we're all in this together."

"Nancy, when you talk that way, you make me feel guilty. Okay, I'll feel my way up with my hands and have my eyes closed all the time when I'm climbing. Does that satisfy you?"

"You can be such a jerk at times. You and I know you won't do that, so just suck it up and enjoy the fun."

"Okay, okay, I'll do it, not willingly, but I'm up for the challenge. Who knows, we might see a big storm headed our way or some pirates that will try to attack us."

"Oh thanks for that bright, optimistic outlook. You're sure making the trip a lot of fun for me. I think I'll nickname you Doom and Gloom."

"Can't you take a joke, Miss Serious One? Remember what Captain Bob said, he's never had any confrontation or, for that matter, sailed in a storm while having passengers on his vessel while on vacation. I'm taking him at his word and just hope my dire premonition is just a stupid insecurity." Nancy told Suzanne that she'd take it as such and went along trying to tie the knot. "You realize that this sailing doesn't do a manicure justice. That's who we should have taken along with us. Mai, comes from Viet Nam, and while visiting her relatives and provinces' along the way, we could have her fix our nails at the same time."

"You know Nancy, even though you profess not to be spoiled, I've come to the conclusion that deep down you're a spoiled brat."

"Thanks Suzanne, I appreciate that remark," she said as she gently shoved her.

While the wind was slight, the square sails were billowing in the breeze. The calm water was a gorgeous turquoise color and the vacationers were taking advantage of the sun shining down on them. Getting up from her comfortable lounge, Sandy went to the Captain and asked him if she could be the first to try getting up to the masthead. Elbowing Suzanne, Nancy exclaimed; "What did I tell you. Sandy is going to try to climb the ropes to the crow's nest."

"I really think that's great for her and I wish her well. I'll certainly not be one of the first to make that exploration," Suzanne admitted. After a few tries and some scrapes on her legs, Sandy finally made it up the masthead. Steve Bowman, the backup, went up after she was secured on the wooden plank that was surrounded by metal on four sides and handed her a megaphone and a large, long, spyglass. Sandy was in awe as she enjoyed seeing the vastness of the ocean and actually thought that she spotted a few whales that were spraying and flipping for her enjoyment. She stayed up there for what seemed forever and had to be coaxed down by Steve. "You know, I thought it was hard getting up the rope but, to be honest with you, I think it's harder climbing down." Steve was underneath Sandy in case she got into trouble and coaxed her until her feet hit the wood of the deck. She wiped the sweat that accumulated on her forehead with the back of her hand and was handed a white cloth by Steve. She gave a deep sigh, then, suddenly, she started jumping up and down yelling: "I did it, I actually did it." She ran to Arthur, both hugging, as he told her that he captured her on film with the video climbing up and down the rope for all their kids and friends to see.

"It's still early and we'll be getting to Ha Long Bay in about 4 more hours, so if anyone else wants to be as brave as Sandy was, come forward and try your hand, or should I say hands and feet at the task." Everyone looked at each other and then Mike volunteered to be the next in line for the duty of seeing that the ship was not in any kind of trouble. The clapping was extensive as he started up the rope, and he was full of pride when his feet landed on the plank. He also gave a narrative of what he saw and enjoyed the solitude of being alone, or what seemed alone, without a care in the world.

After a while, Mike thought he spotted a speck in the horizon. As they continued he yelled down to Captain Bob that he thought he might be seeing the bay ahead. "Good eye, sailor," exclaimed the Captain. Mike practically ran down the ropes, proud as a peacock, knowing that he was the first person that spotted the incredible Bay. He couldn't wait to see the wonders of the limestone karsts and their various sizes and shapes. He definitely wanted to snorkel or scuba dive through the limestone isles and hoped he'd see some unusual fish while he was under the water. When the sailing yacht finally anchored, Mike and Tracy were the first to dive off the side of the ship with their scuba diving equipment in place. They were glad that they packed a camera that could shoot pictures while under water. Both were in the sea for what seemed hours, viewing and weaving in and out of the formations and capturing on film the wonders of Ha Long Bay.

The others joined them and Nancy and Suzanne felt awkward not being part of the group. They tried to explain that they didn't know how to swim to anyone questioning them. Finally one of the deck hands, one of the twins, cautiously walked over to the two women. "My brother and I know how it must feel not being able to enjoy the water like your fellow passengers. Not meaning any offense, but Dick and I could supply you with snorkel equipment and we'll hold you up just so you can say you swam in the same waters as these ancient limestone's that are not known to many people." At first Suzanne and Nancy were apprehensive, but the twins' assurance gave them the confidence they needed to try it. "We'll put the ladder in so you can climb down, and I'll climb down first. Then with your equipment on, you'll be able to breathe and see like all of us. I'll have my hand on your stomach at all times so don't be afraid. My brother will do the same with Nancy. What do you think ladies?" Nancy and Suzanne looked scared and apprehensive. They went to the other side of the ship to talk between themselves.

"You know Nancy, with all the crap that we've done and gone through, if we can let these nice young fellows try to help us, I think we should go for it. What do you think?" "I'm scared as all Hell. But if you're willing to try, then I'll be right beside you. After all, would Robin not follow Batman into any situation?" Walking over to the twins, a small smile on their faces, they relented and told the boys they were scared but had all the confidence in the world that they'd be safe in, literally, they're hands. Harry climbed down first with Suzanne following him into the tepid water. Being a bay, there were no waves and the water was as calm as could be. Dick went after Suzanne and Nancy followed. They were amazed at how the water felt on their entire body and loved the feeling. Suzanne didn't get panicky because she could breathe without feeling as if she would drown. Her eyes didn't sting and she was able to see the coral and all the rocks around her. Finally, after a few hours, they decided they had enough and climbed back on board the sailboat. Their feet finally settled on the mahogany wood, they high fived each other. They thought that they just conquered one of the wonders of the world. The women thanked the twins and went directly to their cabin to take a shower and get into comfortable clothes. "I know that we're not supposed to tip the staff, but I think that Dick and Harry went far beyond their duties. I'd like to give them something extra in an envelope, on the q.t. of course." Suzanne stated. Nancy affirmed her partner's decision. With that said, Nancy waited on her bed while Suzanne could be heard singing 'A Sailors Life Have We' as she took her much needed shower. While Nancy was on the bed, thoughts of Rich popped into her head. Although she was having the time of her life, she still missed him. She hopped that he missed her as much. A lot of their escapades came to mind and she knew that she was smiling at the thought of him holding her in his strong, secure arms and feeling safe for the first time in her life.

Suzanne told Nancy that she left the water running so she could jump into the shower now. "I've done enough jumping for one day, thank you," Nancy jokingly told Suzanne. Suzanne put on some cotton pants and decided that in the next town they went to, she'd try to get some paints and an easel and paint a beautiful water and nautical theme to present to Captain Bob as a "thank you" for the wonderful trip that she and Nancy experienced. With that thought, she started blow drying her hair and didn't put any make up on. It felt good to be herself, without a care in the world and not have to impress anyone. It had been years since she felt so alive and carefree. She could not thank her children enough for the special gift they gave to their mother and their special aunt.

After dinner, Captain Bob informed everyone that they'd be sailing out of the bay shortly and back out on the China Sea. "For those of you who haven't yet climbed up to the masthead, I would advise you to do so. Besides feeling that you accomplished a mission, you really are helping out your fellow mates. So tomorrow morning we'll be off to Da Nang, which served as one of Vietnam's most important ports. During the war, it was home to a huge U.S. Air Force base. It's best known for its impressive art and architecture from the Cham Dynasty, dating from the 4th to 14th centuries. I think you'll enjoy it when you venture south of Da Nang and see the Marble Mountains. There are five marble hills representing the elements of the universe: water, wood, fire, metal and earth. On one of the mountains, Thuy Son, is honey combed caves containing Cham, Buddhist, and Confucian relics, pagodas and temples. I suggest that you enjoy your stay and enjoy this coastal city." That was when Suzanne made up her mind that this was the city where she would purchase the supplies necessary to start her painting. She hoped that the guests didn't get sick from the odor of the different paints and materials, but if she had to, she'd go ashore and do her painting. Suzanne was determined to make this painting for both the ship and Captain Bob.

Suzanne decided that if she could remember the formation of the various limestone rocks and flora under the water, she'd try to duplicate them as well. Suzanne remembered that some of the fellow shipmates had underwater cameras and she'd ask them for prints so she'd be able to duplicate the formations from camera to palette.

At sea, lying on the deck with the sun shining down on the occupants of the sailing ship, Suzanne made sure that she lathered herself and Nancy with 50% sunscreen. She realized that there really wasn't anything that was completely sun proof, but thought that the harmful rays wouldn't be able to penetrate her

delicate skin. She was mentally making notes of all the supplies she'd need when suddenly Justin appeared in her thoughts. She envisioned his hearty laugh and realized how much he taught her through the years of his tutelage. She honestly felt that without Justin's immense support and help, Nancy and she would have had a hard time capturing, and ultimately, eliminating Yoshirhiro Makino, the mastermind who commissioned many thieves, especially Curtis Jones, to perform his insane idea to steal many paintings and artifacts from all parts of the world. Unfortunately, his greed in stealing these masterpieces and artifacts from different countries for his private collection was his Achilles' heel and eventually the demise of his vast empire.

After all the funeral arrangements were taken care of by Yoshy's wife and only son, Kazuhiko, the family went into hibernation. Kazuhiko let Sam, our ally; take over many of the dealings of this vast corporation. After some time, Kazuhiko came back emotionally. He remembered everything that happened and it hit home. He brought his beloved mother back to the States, and eventually took over the empire that his father built. Sam was to become his right hand man, and Kazuhiko never found out the involvement that Sam played in the downfall of Mr. Makino. Toshiko, who would follow her son to the ends of the earth, stayed with him. When Kazuhiko fell in love and eventually married a lovely Japanese American girl who worked for the company, his mother stayed and took care of his baby and ultimately the other children that they had. Thinking back to all that happened, Suzanne was glad of the outcome. Unfortunately, it took a lot out of Nancy and her, both emotionally and physically, to get to where they were at this time in their lives.

Suzanne heard the shower and continued thinking back to all the dear friends who entered her life and made her a better person. Although she loved this trip, it didn't feel comfortable for her unless she was in communication with many of these dear people. She worried about them and hoped that they were well. *'After all,'* she thought, *'in four to six weeks away from home, many things could happen.'* She forced herself to stop thinking like a morbid old lady and just enjoy life a day at a time. She heard the water shut off and once again came back to reality. She realized that throughout her vacation, many of these dear friends would enter her mind and she didn't want to put them away, as if in a locked box, waiting to be opened upon her return home.

SAN DIEGO, CALIFORNIA

When Madaline heard of Suzanne's and Nancy's vacation plans, she and Kyle were delighted for them. It seemed as if mother and son became even closer than

they were previously, which was hard to fathom. Suzanne was on Madaline's mind, not constantly, but at least once a day. She didn't know how to thank her, Nancy, Justin, and Rich, as they were instrumental in clearing her son's name from murder charges. Since Kyle came out of the closet, it was easier for him to be more open with her. They seemed to enjoy the companionship and talks that went on and found it easy to stay at home and not have to be on exhibition for all their fans. Life seemed better and Madaline, in her mind and heart, felt that Suzanne, as nutty as she was, was the catalyst that got everything going for Kyle's defense. She didn't know how she would ever be able to repay her; however, she would find some way or another. Little did she know that it would be sooner rather than later!!!! Madaline was happy that Kyle and Betty were as close as they could be under the circumstance. They communicated with each other and would always make sure that they stayed in touch. While Madaline was Betty's biological mother, she realized that Betty would always cherish the parents that brought her up, as she would have wanted Betty to think of them as her real parents. Madaline would be Betty's friend and help her in her career as an actress. She would always be instrumental in making it easier for her to get ahead in the industry, be it theatre or the movies. She would always be there for her daughter. Madaline felt secure in her relationship with Kyle and was happy that Betty and Kyle would be as close as two people could be as stepbrother and sister who weren't raised together, but realized that there was a connection that would be forever binding.

DA NANG, VIETNAM

Suzanne and Nancy realized that Da Nang was one of Vietnam's most important ports. Suzanne told Nancy of her idea about bestowing a gift to the ship and the Captain, and Nancy wanted to go shopping with her to pick out the materials Suzanne would need. While shopping, they were amazed at the beautiful architecture from the Cham Dynasty. After touring the city and bringing back all of Suzanne's supplies, they decided to visit the Marble Mountains. They were awe struck as they viewed the elements. They visited the caves containing the various relics, pagodas and temples. "This is one city I'll never forget in my entire life," exclaimed Nancy as she took pictures of everything she could.

Suzanne heard that China Beach, which was also a part of Da Nang, was located there and was one of the U.S. recreation bases. They wore their bathing suits and put their blankets on the sparkling white sand. Both women were hoping that one day they would come back, but the next time with their significant others. "Do you remember the television series, *China Beach*? Believe it or not, that name China Beach comes up often when I talk to my clients. Its theme song was and still is one of my favorites to listen to. I try to watch Dana Delany's new show about a forensic doctor and try to have one of the girls tape it for me if I know I won't be home to see it. It gives me pleasure that she finally made it big in the acting world. She deserves it," an enthusiastic Suzanne told Nancy. "It feels kind of funny to be on this beach and remember all the episodes that they filmed here, or at least I think that they did. For that matter, they might have filmed it back in Hollywood. But I appreciate all the men that served in the military and fought for our country, even though they didn't get the recognition that they should have. So yes, I'm moved that I'm lying on China Beach, which I enjoyed for many years and never knew that it existed in Da Nang, Vietnam," voiced an emotional Suzanne.

"You know, Suzanne, I realize how fortunate that I am part of your life. Seriously, you're a very deep person, and many people who aren't part of your intimate circle of friends don't realize what they're missing by not knowing the real Suzanne Morse." Suzanne was dumbfounded by Nancy's remark. "If you keep talking that way, my head will become too big for my body. But thanks, Nancy, it's nice to know that you know the real me, and that makes a difference in my life. Does that mean that I still have to be sort of crazy and take on assignments that I have no business dealing with?"

"I'm not saying a word. Where you Goethe, I follow. It's as easy as that." They hugged, looking around, making sure that whoever might be watching didn't get the wrong impression.

They ran into some of the couples who were on their sail boat and they asked them to join them. Suzanne couldn't help but relate what she told Nancy about the television program, the theme song and everything else she could think of pertaining to the show. Everyone enjoyed hearing her story. Each person had a different version of the sights they saw and what it meant to them. They related stories about people they knew who had served in the Viet Nam War. Most of the tales were sad, but some were heartwarming and made everyone feel good after hearing happy endings for those soldiers that had to endure much pressure and anger from the very people they were protecting, or thought that they were protecting. Suzanne then told the people that where she lived, there was a large population of Vietnamese and Cambodian People in the surrounding cities. "I never got to know any of them personally until I hired an aunt and her niece as a manicurist and pedicurist for our salon. I really enjoy them and the stories they tell us. They put up a satellite television in their private room and sometimes on my breaks, or if I'm there as a client, I watch their oriental soap operas with them. I don't know a word they're saying, but I get the gist of it by their actions. Then I try to teach the niece to pronounce some of the English words, and she just can't enunciate them. She couldn't say five flags if her life depended on it. I'm not laughing or making fun of her because, believe me, if I ever had to live in a foreign country with a completely different language, I'd have my thumb up my ass, no lie," Suzanne explained.

Mario and the men were quiet as they went to their meeting place. They knew that what they were to embark on was totally dishonest and not something that they would go around bragging about. They attended to their business, making sure that each shot that they took was as if it were their last round. They became more proficient each time it was their turn to hit the target. While one person was shooting at the range, the other men did exercises to make their bodies stronger and more muscular.

They took the knives that Efren brought and so proudly displayed and handled each one with pride. They learned to handle the weight, using them like a sword, wielding them like they were the master of such an instrument of death. They learned to use the knives with precision, and in a matter of days, they were experts in the usage of these deadly weapons.

When it was their turn to shoot the target on the tree trunk, it was becoming common to hit the target where they intended the bullet or bullets to hit. They were proud of their accomplishments and silently thanked their Gods for what they were about to undertake. They didn't like the idea of what they were going to be doing, but they were left with little other recourse.

With what spare time they had, they became more proficient in tying the rope than ever before. After a few weeks, they decided that it was now time for them to start implementing their knowledge.

They decided to meet at Efren's house to finalize their plan of action. Efren asked his wife and children to go to his in-law's house and stay there for a few hours. He would come and get them when his meeting was through. His wife knew from his actions that something was about to happen that would change her husband's life and, ultimately, her family's way of living.

She quickly obeyed him. As she was leaving, he hugged her as if they were young lovers, never to be severed from each other. She thought that was odd, but kept her feelings to herself. She hurried her children along and took one last, long look at her husband whom she loved with all of her heart.

They all were seated around the coffee table in the center of the living room. With drinks in hand, they boasted to each other how they were proud of their accomplishments. Mario told them of a fairly large vessel that was in good shape and was for sale. He knew the owner and would be able to purchase the craft at a bargain price and in installments, if they needed to acquire it that way. "Only because I know the man and his business has been next to nothing, can I buy it from him. He thinks that I'm crazy to pay for it, but I let him think that it's just for me. Laughing, Mario said, "Little does he know that we will paint it a different color and put our own sails on the vessel."

Putting his right leg over his left one, Sunny piped up. "The only thing that I'm going to ask is, if we are to be pirates, we get or make sails with the pirate logo on its sails. I think that people have to realize that when we come aboard their vessel, they know that we're not fooling around and we're in business to take their possessions, money and jewelry." The rest of the men in the group listened as Sunny spoke and then nodded their heads in agreement. They all started talking at once.

Plans were made to go to the dock, pay off the present owner and then start painting the boat and have sails made and then paint their own pirate logo on the sails. Tolemeo asked: "The only thing I'm going to request is, can we paint a fish above the cross and bones? That will be our trademark, if that's possible." The other men contemplated his solicitation and nodded their heads in assent. "Then it's a go. Tomorrow I buy the vessel and within a few days, we will be ready to embark on our new adventure," Mario boasted. They all raised their glasses with congratulatory bravado.

When the men left, Efren went to his in-law's house and acted as if nothing of importance had happened. His wife knew her husband and realized that the meeting at their house was a very important matter. Whatever her husband decided to do, she would go along with his plan and try to help him as much as humanly possible. She knew he would never want to involve her in anything illegal. She also knew that she would do anything she had to do to insure that he was happy and what made him happy was to make a decent living, for he lived to insure his family's happiness and future.

Suzanne and Nancy were back in their cabin after having another great day. Suzanne was extolling Nancy with her excitement of finally sunning herself on China Beach. She then told Nancy that she was excited and, when on land, would definitely make a few paintings: One for Captain Bob and some for their friends as well. "I can't tell you how proud I am that I can do this for the people that I love."

"I never told you of the people that I knew and friends that I lost in the war. I won't dwell on the negative. I know a lot of people who wouldn't step foot on the soil that our boys fought and died on. But I, for one, can see that we did win.

When I see all these people, most of them happy to be liberated, and know that some of them have moved to America, I'm happy that the results are now evident. They think like my ancestors thought, that America's streets were paved in gold. Of course, we know it's not true, but these people came over with hope and not despair. Most Americans took them in and embraced these people who came with only the shirts on their backs. Sure, some people looked down on them, but they proved to be hard workers and, like anyone else, there are good people and bad. I guess I'm lucky that I've met the good ones."

"That's one of the things that I love about you, Suzanne. You are always the optimist. Yes, I'm looking forward to seeing the paintings that you do, and, hopefully you'll make one for my home as well."

"If you put it that way, Nancy, do you think that I wouldn't make you a picture for you to look at and always remember this great trip?"

Nancy went over to Suzanne and hugged her affectionately. "When Rich moves into the house, I'm sure he will love looking at the picture as much as I do. I don't care what you decide to capture, whatever it will be, will be beautiful and made with love."

With that statement, both women tried to sleep. Each had thoughts that would keep them awake for a while, but then Morpheus took over and they slept the sleep of the good.

CHAPTER TWELVE

Suzanne and Nancy were excited that they could tell and show their friends and relatives that they actually snorkeled and got to see the wonders of the various limestone's at Ha Long Bay. They even had pictures to prove to everyone that they swam among the flora and various fish and were able to capture the sights on the special camera that they purchased in Saigon. The caves were magnificent. "I can't believe that we're actually seeing the eighth wonder of the world," exclaimed Nancy as they got back up on the boat and took off their gear. "At least we don't have to really swim in order to snorkel," said Suzanne.

Mike and Tracy were looking forward to snorkeling and were not opposed to doing some cave exploration. They later found out that there were floating villages in Ha Long bay with people on it who had never set foot on land. They were born and will die on these floating villages.

The next day they were going to be at sea and Suzanne and Nancy were positive that Captain Bob would have the passengers learn more nautical terms and also have each person climb the ropes to man the crow's nest and get the self-assurance that they could conquer their fear of heights. The two women were nervous as Hell thinking of the task at hand.

The other members of the group were very interested in seeing the Five Marble Mountains. They especially wanted to explore the honeycombed caves and were excited about seeing the various religious artifacts and the temples. They decided to stay two days in Da Nang to get a good feel for this strategic port and enjoy the coastal city.

On the second day, Suzanne gave into Nancy and agreed to visit the Five Marble Mountains. "Only after we go into the city and purchase the necessary equipment that I need to paint, I can capture them with my camera and then copy them onto canvas with the oil paints." Nancy went along with Suzanne and carried the products back to the ship before taking the excursion to the hills representing the elements of the universe. "I know that we'll be impressed and Nancy, please, bring your camera so we can seize the opportunity to capture the essence of this remarkable wonder of the world."

"I wouldn't think of going anyplace during this trip without my trusty camera," a determined Nancy spoke.

When the two women got to the Marble Mountains they found themselves speechless. They took their time exploring the mountain, which contained the honeycombed caves, and they stayed for hours enjoying the relics that they saw. "You know, Suzanne, I don't think I'll ever forget this trip and the different aspects of life that I'd never have known about had it not been for this vacation. I'm truly indebted to your children for including me as part of your family."

As they and the other passengers (who were now more like friends) were leaving the port, tears were flowing from the eyes of most of the people. Captain Bob and his crew were aware of the emotional attachment the guests had formed for this unusual city and port and knew that this type of reaction was a normal one.

The rest of the passengers learned more of the navigational phrases while they were at sea. "I feel as if I'm in a school room again," Sam chided the rest of the group as they all listened intently to Captain Bob's nautical terms making them as easy as he could to coincide with their everyday language. Cole and Isabelle piped up and mentioned that, although they also spoke the English language, some of the terms were different than the Americans, but they did admit that a lot of these words were slang. "Well, if you have any questions or are unable to understand my terminology, just ask me to explain it better to you so you'll be able to recognize the expressions." "That's fine with me governor;" Cole spoke out loud for both of them.

While at sea, the rest of the crowd eventually made their way to the crow's nest and were very proud of themselves when they climbed down the heavy, rough rope and landed firmly on the deck. Suzanne and Nancy looked at each other and didn't have to say a word. "Do you think if we don't say anything the Captain won't make us go up there?"

"Suzanne, as much as you'd like to make yourself invisible, I don't think we have a chance in Hell of getting away without climbing the rope and sitting on that crow's nest with the spyglass. I mean, yes, it's going to be nice to see what's out there, but I do know how you feel, Honey. Just suck it up. I'll go first and then, when you see me, it will give you the confidence to go up there by yourself."

"Nancy, will you promise me that you'll wear a life preserver and make me happy. Neither of us knows how to swim, and I'll feel better if I see you wearing one. I know that when I go up, my poor legs will be chaffed as Hell, and you can bet your booty that I'll be wearing a life preserver. The Captain will probably insist we put one on, and I also heard that you have to attach a harness to protect anyone from falling down onto the deck or into the water. We do have fear of the water, even though we're on this sail boat, like the crazies we are," Suzanne said.

Nancy and Suzanne were lying on deck when Dick Bogart came over to the two women and asked who wanted to go up to the masthead first. "You're the last two passengers who haven't been there, and unless you're really afraid to or have a disability, the Captain would like you to try. If you want, one of us can climb up the rope behind you to give you more confidence. I'll be glad to do that for you," insisted Dick. "Oh no, that's okay," Nancy bravely answered for the two of them. "I'll go first and stay up there for a few hours, and then Suzanne will be glad to do her share, won't you, Suzanne?" With a little hesitation, Suzanne submitted to her friend's urging and said she would go up after Nancy came safely down from the crow's nest.

Before Nancy was about to make her journey, the Captain gathered all the passengers together and told them the story about the Crow's Nest. "The crow was an essential part of the early sailors' navigation equipment. These land-loving fowl were carried on board to help the navigator determine where the closest land lay when the weather prevented sighting the shore visually. In case of poor visibility, a crow was released and the navigator plotted a course that corresponded with the birds because it invariably headed toward land. The crow's nest was situated high in the main mast where the look-out stood watch. Often he shared this lofty perch with a crow or two since the crow's cages were kept there; hence the crow's nest."

The Captain continued his story: "So, it is a lookout spot from back in the day, but no longer applied, since all modern sailing ships now have electrical equipment to guide them along their path. The rope that leads up the main mast is usually a climbing net style. On a modern sailing ship, as ours is, we use pulleys and ropes to get ourselves up rather than climb up using the rope netting as they used to do. With all the modernizing, the workings on board have drastically changed, and, therefore, unless you are on a restored old sailing ship, things do not work that way anymore. Sometimes I think it's unfortunate. The only reason we have you climb to the crow's nest is for you to see how the sailors used to have to work the older ships." Captain Bob laughed heartily. The rest of the guests enjoyed the story about the olden days and how the older ships worked.

Nancy took a deep breath and made sure she didn't look down. She kept her eyes either on the rope that her hand was wrapped around or looked up at the upper, square sails, swaying in the wind. She thought that they looked truly beautiful. Without thinking how much further she had to climb, she reached the platform without realizing it. She felt alive and loved the wind in her face. She could see the white caps of the waves as they broke and thought she saw a blue whale or two who were following the ship. At one time she thought she saw them jumping and spouting and was amazed at how playful they were. Before she knew what was happening, her three hours were up. Nancy didn't want to leave, but she realized that tea was being served with little sandwiches and pastries put out for all to enjoy.

While everyone was at the table, Suzanne jabbed Nancy in her rib and quietly asked how it was up there. "If you want to know the truth, I loved it. I never thought in a million years that it would be so beautiful but it was." She then told her about the whales and the sea and how peaceful she felt. "Well I guess if you can feel that way I shouldn't be such a coward and get it over with. First, I want to finish the snacks."

"Suzanne with all the crazy and wild things that we've been through, believe me this is nothing. If you trust me, you'll love it as much as I did. I know you like a book and you're putting off going up there because of fear. Honey, don't be afraid; nothing can happen, especially when Dick or Harry is behind you while you're climbing."

"Okay, give me a while and then I'll go over to Captain Bob and tell him that I'm ready. But I'm going to insist on wearing a life jacket."

"I'm sure he'd want you to like I did. I also think that they'll attach a harness to you, just in case you should fall in the water."

"Oh thanks," blurted Suzanne. "Nothing's going to happen to you, so just take a deep breath and get it over with," encouraged Nancy.

Suzanne sucked up all of her strength and, walked to the Captain and told him that she was ready for her shift. A huge smile appeared on his face. "I know that you're afraid, but believe me, Suzanne, there's nothing to be fearful of. We're all here and anytime that you want to come down, we'll cheer you on. Make sure you wear your life preserver and enjoy the scenery." All Suzanne did was shake her head up and down; words wouldn't come out of her mouth. "I promise you that this will be something that you'll remember for the rest of your life." Under her breath Suzanne muttered, 'I bet it will be.'

As promised, Harry was a few feet behind her as she climbed the frayed, heavy rope. Her heart was literally in her mouth as she inched her way slowly up to the platform. She thanked Harry and picked up the spyglass that Nancy had left for her in the holder. She settled in and although she was petrified, she understood Nancy's jubilant feeling when she looked out at the sea and saw the birds flying above. She wondered how they could fly all the distance from their land and admired their elegance as their wings fluttered to get them to their final destination. She looked through the spyglass and saw the same pair of whales that Nancy told her about. Maybe they're not the same pair, but whatever, they are magnificent creatures. Suzanne felt calm and at peace, something she hadn't felt in years. In a way she didn't want this exuberant feeling to ever go away.

Suzanne again took the spyglass and thought that she saw dark clouds coming their way. The entire trip had been full of sunshine and she was surprised to see the puffy clouds that looked like pieces of fluffy cotton rolling in. She tried thinking back to her school days and tried to remember the different types of clouds and their names. For the life of her, the only ones that she remembered was the cumulus. Well, what are a few clouds she thought to herself, as she felt the wind becoming more than the gentle wind that she felt before. She noticed that the swells and waves were getting a little larger and that the ship seemed to be rocking a bit more. Thinking to herself that it was her imagination, she disregarded her basic instinct to worry. Nervously, she shifted slightly and made sure that her life jacket was securely on her. She didn't want to appear fearful or a baby, so she watched the clouds come her way and the various forms that the clouds were making. She started laughing nervously when she saw that the tops of the soft white cotton balls begin to look like the heads of cauliflower, she thought, as she started getting fidgety.

Before she realized what was happening, she heard Captain Bob yelling to her to start climbing down the rope. Harry was climbing up to help her down. The nice white, fluffy, clouds that she admired were now turning dark and ominous. It seemed funny that the wind was picking up and everything happened quickly. The rope that she held like a lifeline was beginning to twist and turn as the sudden storm became more violent. The beautiful waves were definitely not the same calm sea that she remembered and now the squalls were becoming more aggressive and the air currents were now accompanied by rain that was pouring down on her, like needles pricking her exposed skin.

She felt her body go out of control. Not willing to let go, she clutched the rope but couldn't hold on. She felt for her life jacket. Suddenly she felt the clasp break or come loose from the harness that was connected to her jacket. She wasn't sure what was happening. Harry tried climbing faster, realizing that the harness must have had a faulty or weakened connection to the clasp. Her hands felt shaky and automatically released themselves from the twine that she felt was her lifeline. Suzanne was aware of her surroundings, yet she thought of herself as an angel, or a bird, flying on her own. Instead of going with the airflow, she was fighting the tough force that was increasing her motion, down, down, like a butterfly suddenly caught in a spider's web. All at once Suzanne saw her entire life pass before her, like a film with all the events ever encountered passing in fast motion. She couldn't breathe. The salt water hit her face. She could barely hear what was being said above her on the sailboat. She tried not to open her mouth, but she had to in order to breathe. She felt the high swells of the salt water automatically pushing her lips open. She couldn't close her jaws because she was now panicking and she had lost control of her entire body. She felt herself splashing and the large waves were trying to push her down into the darkness. Her hands were splashing and going all over the place. She tried not to go under and was pushing her palms against the water. It was in vain, but she didn't realize it. Because of the salt water gushing and entering her body she felt she was bloated and felt out of control. Her entire being was in spasms, she felt herself chocking, dread of death assaulting her. She swallowed salt water and experienced it flowing into her lungs. The rain was coming down like bullets entering her body. Her hair was plastered to her scalp and the rain felt like tiny pin pricks over her exposed body. As much as she tried keeping herself afloat, the sinking of her body was overcoming her instinct for survival. She felt as if she were one of the toys in the children's bathtub. Suzanne was bobbing up and down; she was losing her battle to survive the elements that were surrounding her. She tried not to lose consciousness, but was not winning. She felt nothing, her body slack and lifeless.

Captain Bob was aghast. "Man overboard, man overboard," he shouted as the crew got the rest of the passengers below and out of harm's way. Pelting and driving rain assaulted them to the core. The chief engineer got on the radio to try to S.O.S. for help. Jim Brown, the chief engineer, heard a crash and saw the wires of the electrical antennas break. Jim realized that their radio was dead because of the antenna's lack of existence. The dome that contained the radio antenna satellite dish for GPS tracking and the radar had washed off. Jim Brown ran to the Captain and informed him of their dilemma. "We've lost everything and we're become basically helpless. We'll have to rely on our primitive skills to get back to land. Luckily, we know the old school ways of sailing and we'll put them into effect immediately. Of course we'll need the crow's nest and a sextant to guide us back to land."

The crew could feel the boat becoming unmanageable as it tilted and pitched from one side to the other. The passengers were now crying and screaming, depending how scared and injured they were. The vessel was now tumbling and rolling from side to side. The crew could feel this reliable sailboat swaying in the storm. The crew could see the swells, no longer waves but the water chopping and coming over the top of the boat. The captain gave orders for the men to strike the sails, i.e., to shorten, drop or lower the sails. The motion was making the passengers sick to their stomachs, and they got paper bags to use if needed. Captain Bob yelled for Dick to get and make sure Suzanne was out of harm's way and back on board. Captain Bob was yelling to the passengers and all of the men on board to: "Batten down the hatches."

The boat was on its side, the water coming into the yacht as fast as the men were trying to bail the water out without any success. Suddenly, they heard some of the sails tear and rip in the violent winds and rain.

Nancy tried walking back and forth below, but couldn't keep herself up. She never felt so helpless. All thoughts were about her best friend and how she could help her, but saw she couldn't. Images came before her eyes and what they both had gone through in their young lives. She was crying hysterically at this point. Paul Murphy tried braving the erratic behavior of the boat, forcing himself to be by her side and give what little encouragement he could. Nancy remembered the ironic poem that Suzanne quoted and it seemed, at that instance, like her famed albatross poem. 'Water, water, everywhere and not a drop to drink' was becoming a reality.

Downstairs the people were being whipped around like they were dry rags. Renée was pushed forward and could feel her head hit a hard surface. Blood started pouring out of her forehead. Paul saw Renée and automatically ripped his shirt and tried compressing the blood flow that was pouring out of Renée's deep wound. He was also trying to leverage himself and stay on his feet but the violent currant and the ship's motion had him moving from one side to the other. It was if he had no control of his body.

Suzanne's hands and arms were automatically flailing, her body being dragged down under the violent sea. The life jacket didn't seem to be helping. All she saw was darkness, and she realized that she couldn't breathe. She felt as if death was upon her. She felt at peace and knew that she'd be at rest and back with her grandparents again. Without thinking, Dick dove into the violent sea, unaware of the swells slamming into his body. It was difficult to find Suzanne with the pelting rain attacking and stinging his head and eyes. Dick was a strong swimmer. He knew that if he could attach the safety line to her life preserver he could, somehow, lift her up onto the now slick deck. Even though the boat was keeled, he knew his vessel and had confidence that she and everyone else on board would weather the storm.

The sea was dark, and Dick couldn't see anything under the violent water. Suzanne was out of sight as much as he tried looking for her. The wild, high waves inhibited him from finding her body, which he hoped wasn't lifeless. The hard driving rain assaulted his entire upper body when he came up for fresh air after diving to find Suzanne. He kept going under the sea and wouldn't give up until he thought it was useless and no longer viable for him to maintain himself before he got tired and weak fighting the raging ocean.

Dick felt himself drained of all energy and tried one more time to find his passenger. He dove deeper and suddenly just as he was about to emerge he spotted Suzanne's form. Adrenaline gave him the speed he needed to reach her and he placed his arm under her chin, bringing her along with him. He found her life jacket, half off her now and attached it to his. He yanked as hard as he could, hoping that Captain Bob would feel it and assist him in bringing Suzanne's motionless form onto the crippled ship. Even though the ship was on its side and the driving rains prevented him from seeing less than a foot in front of him, the Captain felt Dick's tug. Captain Bob knew that the rest of the crew was attending to the vacationers, and it was his job and duty to try to save the life of this defenseless woman.

Captain Bob bent over the bobbing boat and with all his might pulled Dick and his unconscious guest over the rail. He helped Dick lay Suzanne carefully on the deck. Dick was glad that the Captain was there waiting to help him to perform CPR on her. He wasn't sure how long she was in the water, but he was confident that she was unconscious and probably had cardiac arrest. It was very important to know how long she was comatose, but he had no way of knowing. To him, it felt like hours, but reality beckoned and he realized that it could only have been minutes. Dick wasn't sure. His only thoughts were that everything happened so fast that he wasn't sure how long Suzanne had been in the tumultuous water. Now was not the time to ponder; action had to be taken immediately. He knew for a fact that she consumed enough water that she was a victim of drowning. The crew was agonizing and wanted to help their Captain and the pretty blonde woman, but they knew it was best to leave the Captain and Dick to do whatever was necessary to bring her to consciousness. He hoped that between the two men they could bring Suzanne out of her motionless state. The Captain ordered Dick to quickly lift the board and both of them dragged Suzanne off the main deck that was unsafe and drenched with pools of water; to the second deck. The two men spontaneously began to perform the straddle CPR. "We don't have much room and time. Okay, make sure that her legs are straight. Place the arm near you at a right angle while I do the one near me. Bend those elbows and palms up. I'll bring the far arm across her chest and hold the back of the hand against her cheek near me. I'll grasp the far leg above the knee and pull it up. Make sure you keep her foot on the ground," Dick ordered.

"Dick, press her hand against her cheek and pull the far leg," and then the Captain yelled, "Roll her towards you onto her side. Make sure her upper leg is so that both the hip and knee are bent at right angles. I'll tilt her head back to make sure that the airway stays open. Adjust your hand under her cheek to keep the head tilted and face downwards to allow the liquid to drain from her mouth." Both men were trained in CPR. Then the Captain told Dick, "It's going to be important, as you already know that we have continuous compressions while giving ventilation. Give five initial rescue breaths before we start chest compressions. You might have to use two hands to achieve an adequate depth of compression. Okay? Go, five initial breaths, and one minute of CPR." They kept up the CPR, and within minutes, Suzanne started sputtering and coughing while throwing up all the water that was preventing her from getting the much needed oxygen. Dick alternated putting her onto her other side to minimize damage to the arm and hand that was underneath her body. When Suzanne started breathing with more regularity and they felt that all the water that was in her body was thrown up, they gently put her onto her back and told her to rest. Dick, go tell the rest of the guests that Suzanne is okay and will need rest for a day or so."

"Aye, aye sir!!!"

They made sure that Suzanne didn't have hypothermia and were confident that was one issue they didn't have to worry about. As long as they kept her warm, they were convinced that she'd be back to herself shortly.

Suzanne was back in her suite with blankets that Nancy got for her neatly tucked around her. "I still don't know what happened. I remember looking out at the sea, enjoying the beautiful tranquility of it all and, the next thing I saw was a storm brewing and coming our way. What occurred? I feel like Hell; that's one thing I know. I saw and felt Dick and the Captain on me and my chest felt like an elephant was on me. I'm still quite dizzy and feel like crap. Nancy, tell me what I've been through. I need to know."

Nancy realized that Suzanne was still half out of it; reality hadn't settled in yet. She knew that Suzanne would need plenty of rest and warmth. When she woke from her much needed respite, she'd then tell her the entire ordeal. *The poor thing, the more rest she gets, the better she'll feel.'* With those thoughts, Nancy closed the door to their suite and left Suzanne alone to get the rest she needed.

Nancy found the others below deck huddled around the Captain and his crew. She heard him explain the damage that transpired and how they were going to take care of the situation. "As fast as the storm came is how fast it left." Captain Bob explained that it was unusual for something like that type of eruption to occur. "We're lucky that it passed by quickly, but I'm glad that it did. I would say we're very lucky that more damage didn't occur. From the looks of you, it seems you all did well; except for some bruises, scrapes and cuts everyone looks okay. Thanks to the doc, we got the necessary medical attention that we needed. Now all we have to do is try to get this vessel back to port to get the broken and cut sails seamed and mended, or we might have to order new ones, if they don't have what we need in Hong Kong. But I must say that I feel we'll find everything we need in this fine metropolis and we'll be fit to finish our excursion. I know a lot of you are shaken up, but I assure you, something like this doesn't usually happen. If you'll bear with me and the crew, we'll continue on our way and finish our vacation. It might take a little longer to get to Hong Kong because of the condition our sail boat is in, but with patience, we'll get there."

After hearing the inspiring speech, everyone felt better and gave a round of applause to the Captain and crewmembers. Suddenly, all the people were talking at once of their individual feelings. "I thought for sure that we were goners or fish food," admitted Tracy. Everyone laughed at her remark but then told the rest of the people their emotions and the mood of the ship returned to almost normal. "It's going to take a little longer to get to the port of Hong Kong where we're supposed to dock. As you know, our radar and radio equipment was severely damaged and a few sails aren't able to get our boat to the designated port in the normal amount of time. I ask you to have patience and I'll make it up to you somehow," Captain Bob explained their situation.

The passengers were thankful that the damages to their yacht, although bad, could have been much worse. They were determined to amuse themselves by helping the crew members as best that they could, and for recreation, they'd dive off the boat and swim along the ship, hoping not to spot any sharks along the way. It took them an extra few days as the crippled ship ambled to dockside. All the guests were relieved that they finally made it to the incredible city of Hong Kong. There were many stories about this famous metropolis. Each couple couldn't wait to get off the sailboat and see the sights of world famous Hong Kong.

They realized that the Captain and his crew had a lot of work ahead of them to bring The Vacation of a Lifetime yacht back to its full potential. The rest of the people on board felt selfish wanting to see everything they could. They would get to see the many colorful signs and buildings that were displayed in many magazines that they had read aboard the ship. They got over the feeling of guilt when they went as a group and realized how crowded this amazing city was. The population was astounding and it seemed to take forever to get from one block to the other. Each person pointed to the different sights that interested them with the rest of the group gawking at the beauty. They couldn't believe the heights and various colors of the businesses that were practically on top of one another. "The buildings look like a rainbow of paints, and the neon lights are beyond spectacular," said Joe.

Suzanne was surprised that she felt as good as she did. She thought that there would be after effects from her ordeal and was happy that she felt none. She enjoyed accompanying her now good friends on the experiences they were having. "We should make a plan on what sights would interest us the most and then find out what restaurants we will eat at to enjoy the different flavors and unusual dishes that we'll be experiencing. I hate to be a sore sport, but I'm telling you now that there is no way in Hell that I'm going to eat sushi. Don't try to persuade me, because it will be useless," exclaimed Suzanne. A few of the people sided with Suzanne's feelings, but most of the gang wanted to experience as much as they could in the allotted time schedule. "I have a feeling that we'll be staying here longer than the brochure stated. With all the repairs that have to be made on our sail boat, I think our excursion to Hong Kong will be extended, which, between us, is fine with me," expressed Sandy. "We're actually a very lucky group. We experienced relatively little damage. It could have been a lot worse," Arthur admitted.

Meanwhile, the group of fishermen, who now liked to call themselves the 'new age Pirates' were walking toward the woods, ready for another challenging day of practice with the weapons allotted to them.

Mario walked ahead of the group of men with Efren hurrying to catch up to his cousin. With a huge hand, Efren slapped his cousin gingerly on his back. "Hold up and wait a second," commanded Efren. "You're walking so fast that not one of us can catch up to you." Mario looked at Efren, now walking quickly beside him and boasted, "I want to get to our designated spot. The sooner we can get there, the faster we will be ready to start our real mission."

"I know what you mean," Efren agreed with Mario. "But we don't want to hasten our marksmanship until we are all proficient in shooting. Each of us should know how to use each weapon with precision, so when the actual time comes for us to perform our duty, every man will know his job well. We all have to be perfect, and by that I mean we have to know how to use each weapon the correct way. I may be good at marksmanship and firing a gun, but not so good when it comes to handling a knife or sword or know how to tie a person up so that ropes and tape can hold them tightly with no fear of them escaping. Let another ship find the poor bastards. What do we care as long as we get our loot?"

Mario nodded his head in agreement. "I know what you're saying is right, but I want to start our escapade as soon as possible. I know I have to have patience, and I'm fighting myself every day that we have to show control and not prove to everyone that we are amateurs. By the way, I think that the boat we bought is looking very sturdy and good. Now all we have to do is finish the painting and hoist up the sails and make sure that we have two sets. One when we leave the dock and one when we're at sea to change them to our own logo! There will be no look of wonder when we approach a boat that we want to seize."

Sunny heard Mario and nodded in agreement. "I too want to start our adventure as soon as possible. I see my family and how down-trodden they are, and I want to sit down and cry. I am mad at myself and the world. I just want to provide a decent wage and hand my earnings to my wife. I want to see the look of pride again on her face when she sees me. Of course, she won't know the nature of how I am able to suddenly be a good provider again, but that's just between us." All the men shook their heads in agreement.

"In a couple of days we'll take the ship out on a trial run and then we'll have a better idea of what boats are out there. I want to make sure that we wear cover so no one will recognize us. I don't want to get reported to the authorities about our actions." With that said, they started their daily routine of getting ready for the biggest workout that they ever had. "And we thought that hauling the fish and nets were hard. Well, my friends, this will be both difficult and teach us how to use restraints on our "guests," boasted an eager Ronnie.

CHAPTER THIRTEEN

Captain Bob took his backup, Steve Bowman, to the different docks and shipyards to see what could be done about the ripped sails. The rest of the crew were repairing the vessel, making sure that no structural damage was sustained and if so, fixed. After going many places, and listening to the advice of other professional boatmen, they finally found one that would help them. The only compromise that the Captain had to make was to either have the original sails repaired or buy new ones. After contemplating, he decided to keep the initial sails because he knew that the electrical equipment either repaired or if they were forced to buy new apparatus, would cost a fortune. The people of the shipyard assured him that it would probably take a good three days to fix the damaged heavy canvas. The Captain had no choice but agree to wait for the repairs to be done.

"You know, Steve, we'll have to tell the passengers about our dilemma and let them decide if they want to forgo one of the ports or take a bit longer to finish the vacation. It'll be up to them. Personally, I have nothing else on my agenda, so I don't care one way or the other. Do you have any feelings on the matter?" the Captain asked. "Speaking for myself, I'm single and free as a lark. I know that most of the guys are like me and wing it. So, as far as I'm concerned, whatever you and our passengers decide will be fine with me. We'll have to ask the other guys, but I have a feeling they'll go along with anything."

The rest of the crew was on their hands and knees, with hammers and other necessary tools before them, ready to use these implements when needed. The bright sun was beating on their bare skin, but they loved it. The sun felt better than the pelting rain they experienced that got them in the situation they now faced. "I hope the Captain can get those sails fixed. We're doing our job and this ship will soon be like brand-spanking new," declared the first-mate, Sean. Meanwhile, the chief engineer was going into the appropriate shops to replace the battered and unusable equipment that had to be put back onto the boat in order to navigate the sail vessel in the right direction and also make sure they had the necessary tools in case another emergency arose. The Captain, not a betting man, would have staked his vast millions, (ha, ha), that nothing dangerous would occur during this trip again.

After exploring the multi-colored buildings and complexes that were like nothing any of them had seen before, the passengers decided that they should go to a restaurant and tend to the hunger pains they were experiencing. Knowing that the crewmembers were busy fixing the ship, they didn't want to interrupt their efforts to restore the ship to the way it was. Suzanne and Nancy made a pact with the other guests not to mention the storm or any of the danger that they experienced. Mike told his fellow shipmates to "Let bygones be just that and not bring up this unpleasant experience. They're doing all that they can under the circumstances. Let them go on with the work at hand and we'll explore this great place on our own." They decided to try the Yan Toh Heen restaurant that was recommended by some of the merchants they asked. The facility overlooked the harbor and also showed them how crystal flour (used in the casing of dim sum dumplings) makes them translucent. Spinach and carrot juice provided the color. The shrimp and pork dumpling was beyond delicious. The group gorged on sweet barbecued pork buns, steamed rice-flour cannelloni and diced scallop and crabmeat. They didn't think there was any room left in their stomachs, but they all managed to eat the crispy spring rolls with shredded chicken and the glorious zing of pickles. "I don't know about you," Suzanne said, waving her hands to the rest of the group, "but, I don't think I can walk. I feel like a stuffed pig." She headed for the rest room with Nancy following. While on the way to the bathroom, Suzanne whispered to Nancy, "I'm glad that I'm not an Orthodox Jew and don't feel bad when I eat pork."

"Why is it a woman has to ask another woman to accompany them to the bathroom? I've never seen a woman go to the powder room alone," Paul razzed them as they walked away telling the rest of the vacationers to wait and they'd be right back. "Nancy, you know what I'm thinking? Since the vessel is in disarray, I'd love to foot the bill, and have all of us get rooms at the famous Landmark Mandarin Oriental in Hong Kong for a few days. I understand it's one of the finest hotels in the city. I'm sure that the guys on the boat and the Captain would appreciate us not being underfoot while the repairs are going on and, if we have to stay at the hotel for another day, we'll do so. I'm sure that the other people won't mind, especially when they find out that I'm footing the bill."

"I think that's a great idea but, Honey, that's going to cost you a fortune. You just had the wedding and since we're partners I'll split the bill with you. I know you'll probably try to dissuade me, but I'd love to help out. Please!!" Nancy waited with baited breath for Suzanne's answer. "Okay, only if you're not doing it because you feel you're obligated," Suzanne reiterated.

When the two women rejoined the group, they told them what they wanted to do. Everyone was astounded! Sandy and her husband, Arthur, didn't have money like the other guests and they felt embarrassed. After contemplating their decision, Arthur explained to his wife that with the kind of money that the two women obviously had, they most likely wouldn't feel a drain on their bank account. Sandy couldn't comprehend the kind of money that some people had, especially when she went food shopping and had to choose between buying the brand name or purchase the grocery store label. She shook her head in disbelief and went along with the crowd, feeling a bit overwhelmed by it all.

Suzanne had the Captain's cell phone number and called to tell him about the decision to stay at the hotel for one or two days. "I don't want you to feel upset. We understand the pressure you're all under to get the ship fixed. We realize that you feel obliged to make us feel welcome and indulge us in the warm manner that you do. You have all the repair work that has to be done. It's impractical for us to stay on board while you're working hard to put the boat back into working order. I don't want to hear any argument, and when I make up my mind, there's nothing you can do to dissuade me," Suzanne adamantly stated. Captain Bob was overwhelmed and grateful at the same time. Although he'd never admit it, their overture was a tremendous help and he thanked Suzanne profusely.

Talking to their friends outside the restaurant, Suzanne and Nancy told the people that they should pack a minimal amount of clothing and they'd find out from the concierge at the hotel what options they had while in the area.

It didn't take the vacationers long to pack small suitcases and meet Suzanne and Nancy outside on the dock. Nancy called the hotel and explained their dilemma and the entire gang was accommodated. They were told it was an unusual situation, but under the circumstance, the hotel would make provisions for the six couples.

When the two women walked into the lobby of this luxurious hotel, they whispered to each other about how lucky they were that they were able to get rooms. "I have to admit that this hotel is one of the prettiest I've seen in many years," confessed Nancy. "I don't think it's shabby at all," teased Suzanne as they walked to the front desk and got the room assignments for their party. The other couples were in awe as they looked around. They couldn't believe their luck! When they opened the door to their rooms, they were dumbfounded. They sank into their deluxe beds and within minutes were fast asleep. Suzanne and Nancy fought to keep awake while trying to figure out what could they do with the couples for a few days while the boat was being repaired.

While lying in bed, Sandy and Arthur lay in each other's arms. Arthur felt her wet tears on his ample, hairy chest. He lay still, not saying a word, hoping that Sandy would tell him why she was crying silently. Sandy couldn't tell him the reason she felt the way she did. Many emotions and thoughts ran through her mind. She was glad that no one in her family had gone to her last doctor's appointment with her. After all, it was the last visit for at least six months. When the doctor asked her to sit down in his private office after taking her last scan, she could tell that his words to her would not be what she anticipated.

He said that he was surprised that he found another growth, and it looked as if it were malignant. It was on the same breast where she had cancer before. He wanted to go in and take another biopsy to confirm his thoughts. Sandy, knowing that they were about to leave on this glorious trip, didn't want any bad news to get in the way of their children's anniversary gift to them. No, she decided, she couldn't put herself or her family through the difficult emotions that they all went through in the last two years. Anyway, she also didn't tell him that she was having difficulty breathing, and without the doctor telling her, she knew that the cancer had already spread to her lungs. Her oncologist confirmed her worst nightmare. '*Too many growths, and I won't worry at all. What will be, will be,*' she thought to herself.

She wanted this trip to be as perfect as it could be with no thoughts of illness bogging them down. She realized that God had given them this extra two years. She was grateful that she and Arthur would have this time together and didn't want any thoughts of the big C word to get in the way of their happy union. The only problem she now faced was making sure that Arthur didn't find out about the return of her malignancy.

She made light of the situation and told her husband that her tears were of joy. "I've never felt as free and calm as I do now. This is the best present that we could have asked for." She didn't know when, but she wanted to tell him the truth. Hoping that he would do anything for her, she prayed that she would find the strength to explain her feelings to him. Now was not the time, of that she was sure. She wanted to find the right time to tell him her feelings. Sandy held him tightly and kissed him lovingly. The kisses lingered and before they realized what was happening, Sandy found herself under her husband and lover's mature body. He slowly took off her nightgown and let his fingers explore every inch of her fine, still toned, womanly curves. He couldn't believe that after giving birth to five beautiful children, she still kept herself in good shape. He tried to keep his mind free from all other thoughts that he hoped wouldn't get in the way of his making love to his wife.

The lovemaking started out slow and sensual. Suddenly, the excitement eliminated their unhurried, deliberate lovemaking, and without another thought, Arthur's desire to consume was all he thought about. He took her long, lovely fingers and put them around his throbbing and pulsating penis. His wetness astounded them both as they moaned with excitement. He touched the core of her being with fervid passion and waited for her to climax. When she was in the middle of taking in a deep breath he entered her wetness and filled her with his thick liquid. They lay in each other's arms, their thoughts kept to themselves. Arthur had no idea of the turmoil that his wife was living.

The next morning everyone met at the MO BAR for breakfast. "I have to tell you, Suzanne and Nancy, words can't describe what a surprise treat you provided in addition to this vacation of ours," Paul Murphy exclaimed as the others chimed in. "I don't know about all of you, but I can tell you that when I get home I'll never be able to fit into my clothes. Luckily, I brought comfortable and larger clothes on the trip, otherwise I'd have to go out and purchase new outfits," admitted Tracy. All the women laughed and agreed with her. "I can tell you that you women aren't the only ones that will have to worry about their weight," admitted Sam. "Well, I hate to tell you, but you are in one of the world's finest countries for clothing. Either custom made or already made outfits, you're all set," Nancy assured them. "After breakfast, why don't you have another cup of coffee or tea and Suzanne and I will go to the concierge and find out what we can do for the next three days or so. I think we've seen most of Hong Kong, and it's about time we visited other cities and areas of interest to get a better insight on just what some of this continent is all about." "We'll be in contact with Captain Bob to find out how the ship is coming along and then we'll head back to the boat. How does that sound to you?" Suzanne asked.

The concierge recommended that they fly to Shanghai, and from there, they could visit some cities of interest that have a lot of beautiful canals that they'd appreciate. "Nancy, the reason we bought our own plane was that you promised me I wouldn't have to fly on a commercial air plane again. I'm already having heart palpitations."

"Suzanne, this is an unusual circumstance. Honey, first of all, our plane isn't registered and to get permission from the Chinese authorities will take days. We might as well stay in Hong Kong. I promise, you can squeeze my hand till it turns blue, but from what I heard from the nice gentleman, it will take less than two hours to fly to Shanghai from here. Then once were in Shanghai, we'll ask around for another means of transportation to some cities and areas near Shanghai. I assure you, you'll be fine."

"Thanks, I know I should be grateful, but I can't help not liking to fly. And I haven't made up my mind about Larry or Steven. What a dilemma I'm in. If we should croak during this vacation; I won't feel complete until I've made up my mind between the two."

"You know, Suzanne, most people would love to have that as their only problem in life. Get real and be thankful for what you have. Look around and see what poverty is really like and how lucky we are with what we have."

"I know Nancy, but I guess everyone, even a saint like me, has misgivings in life. I realize that we've helped many people without them realizing what we've done to make their lives better, but give me a break, I'm human and I'm telling you how I feel. Don't let me feel guilty about blurting my true confessions out loud." With that said, Nancy hugged her dear friend. "You'll see, everything will turn out fine and someday you'll laugh at your misgivings. Who knows, you might go back home and tell them both to go to Hell and you'll find someone else that you'll fall in love with." Suzanne pushed Nancy and then straightened up when the hotel clerk filled them in on the details.

Isabelle sidled close to Cole and whispered in his ear, "Suzanne and Nancy are certainly working graft. They're certainly not cheap and definitely act as proctors. I'm rather happy that they're taking charge. We're very lucky that they're holidaying with us. We'd be in a fine mess without the two of them. I have to admit that they have a scheme, and I feel it will be a jolly good one." With that said Cole hugged his wife and waited for the two women to return.

"Okay, we're going to take a flight; it's less than two hours to Shanghai, and from there, people told us to find out from a few townspeople where we might find a China Junk that can take us to a few places that we'll find interesting. What do you think?" Suzanne asked her friends.

While on the puddle jumper, Mike asked Nancy if what he read in one of the National Geographic magazines was true about the China Junks. "I remember reading that sometimes families live on these boats and that they are made of bamboo and are very sturdy. They sometimes have two to three masts and the reason bamboo is the main material used is that it is tough and durable. Do you think we'll be able to find a person who'll take us on?"

"Are you kidding?" Nancy asked Mike. "Money talks, Honey, and anyone in these villages will be glad to accommodate us. Wait and see how many people want to have our business." Nancy was sitting next to Suzanne who was quiet and had her eyes closed the entire trip. Nancy couldn't help laughing to herself but kept patting her dear friend's hand, and said, "We'll be landing soon and then you can take a deep breath."

SHANGHAI

When the plane emptied, the group, who were all carrying their small suitcases or gym bags, left the terminal. Suddenly, Suzanne found herself feeling

claustrophobic among the crowds of humanity. Most of the citizens didn't understand or speak the English Language and they didn't know that, in order to board a bus, taxi, mini bus, or other form of transportation, a certain card was necessary to pay for almost all kinds of vehicle transportation. "Okay, first we have to find a designated office for an application for the transportation card," Suzanne tried to pretend that she didn't understand what was being said. (she really didn't). Finally, a kindly gentleman stopped in his tracks waiting patiently for Nancy to verbalize that she and her friends needed a transportation card. Not only did he tell Nancy, but took her hand and physically pulled her along to the building where she could purchase the cards necessary for her and her friends to get around the largest city in China. Suzanne and Nancy later found out that Shanghai was larger than both Singapore and Hong Kong. It was the largest city and populated by vast numbers of citizens and was dominant in the Asian continent. Once they received their tickets, the group gathered together to formulate a plan on what they wanted to do. "I think we have to all stay together because if we get separated we'll have a hard time finding each other," declared Suzanne. They all agreed and as they walked down another commercialized street, they spotted a small restaurant and gathered there for lunch. While eating they found out that Shanghai was located in the Yangtze River Delta in eastern China. "I guess you can say it's a coastal city, and if we're going to stay here, we should find out if there are any other areas to see that will get us out of this vast metropolis and get some tranquility and see what the people of the smaller villages and towns are like," Suzanne suggested. Tracy, Mike, Joe and Sam were the first people to agree while the others chimed in.

Speaking to a few of the people, who actually stopped for the tourists, they got the answer needed to go ahead with their plan to see other parts of China. "I know that I was terrible in geography, but this is ridiculous," stated Suzanne. "Who knew that Shanghai and the smaller villages sit at the mouth of the Yangtze River?" Addressing the group, Suzanne pointed at them and half joking said, "I don't want any of you to tell me that you know this bit of information, it will only make me feel more inadequate. I was smart in school, but I have to admit that geography was not my strongest subject. Heck, when Big Brother Bob Emery used to pull out the map of the United States and these kids would come up and name them with that long stick, I wanted to throw up." Everyone started laughing and those who remembered the popular show laughed while the other people had no idea what Suzanne was talking about. They found that they could find people who would be willing, for a fee, to take them to other locations by means of a Chinese Junk, which can get to the smaller bodies of water and the various outskirts of the old Chinese culture as well as some of the Provinces that they felt would educate them on how these people live and think.

They managed to find some docks where the Junks where located. After going to three locations, on their fourth try they hit pay dirt. They found a couple who were delighted to show these Americans, including the English couple, who were part of the group, onto their Junk, which they soon learned was also their home.

Suzanne went over to the father and introduced herself. The father told her his name and the names of his wife and children. Suzanne made the introductions and instructed the Fangs on which islands they wanted to see.

It was obvious that the married couple and their children didn't speak English. It made it difficult to communicate with them because they thought that they didn't understand English. It was apparent that the father was the head of the household and his wife was subservient. They had two sons and one daughter. The children also deferred to their father. It was obvious to the people of the group that the father was revered and was the head of the clan. Suzanne hoped that the family knew the islands they wanted to see.

Suzanne and Nancy saw that the family was in a huddle. The father reminded Suzanne of Tom Brady, leading quarter back to the New England Patriots, explaining and telling the rest of the team what to do. The group dissipated and the father came over to their guests. When the father started speaking Suzanne was astonished that he could speak a little English. Speaking softly, he made it known that he and his family would gladly take the travelers anywhere they'd like to go via their Junk, but wanted to be paid in Yuan. Suzanne, who had exchanged her dollars into the Chinese currency, knew that the Chinese Yuan was worth less than the dollar.

She and Nancy told the group to be formal and show them respect. They should refer to them by their given names. An electric excitement went through the group as they headed out on their unexpected adventure.

Mr. Fang, who wanted to be called Sunglo, explained to his guests that the first water town around Shanghai was Luzhi. "It's an ancient town and around one square kilometers. You see the small water lanes we are on?" Not waiting, he continued, "It has a long history of more than 2,500 years. There are many stone bridges. About 41 of them are well preserved, many of different styles and sizes." Tracy and Mike were enthralled when they saw the multi-arched, large bridges and some that were solo, well ornamented and twin bridges that almost looked the same. Paul and Renée, and a few other married couples kissed as the junk went under the various stone catwalks. The Fangs stayed in Luzhi for many hours letting their passengers off to explore the town and walk on top of the stone structures while seeing the houses that looked like shanties.

It was a small island, so the group could go off to do their own thing. Suzanne took a large pad of art paper and with charcoal sat on a knoll and captured the quaint town with the Chinese people walking along the small, narrow streets. Nancy was happy to go along with Suzanne and admire the way she captured the unusual settings through an artist's eyes. "I've always loved to draw Oriental people, especially the older folks. They have many lines on their faces that can tell a story in itself," Suzanne remarked to Nancy as she filled in the shadows and stopped a small, older woman. With hand motions, Suzanne asked the woman if she would sit down while she drew her face.

Nancy was fascinated when Suzanne was finished and couldn't take her eyes off the artwork that her friend so effortlessly drew. Nancy saw the money, held securely in the old woman's fist. Suzanne got off of the grass and the two women slowly walked around the village admiring the quaint streets and old style dwellings. "It's so peaceful with tranquility all around us. I could stay here forever," Nancy told Suzanne. Turning to her friend she asked, "Would you mind sketching the bridge over there? From the map it looks like it's called the Zhengy and Bridge." They stood to the side and read that it's the biggest stone arch bridge in the town. It was built in the Wanli era of the Ming Dynasty. (1368-1644). Suzanne noticed that she could capture the entire landscape of the water town from the site where she started. Suzanne knew that Nancy would hang this handsome picture in her home with pride. With sadness, Suzanne realized that years before there were a lot of American soldiers fighting these people of peace and humbly wandered off with thoughts of these soldiers bringing warfare for God who knows what. She was glad that those awful times were now a sorrowful point in history.

Before Suzanne finished her drawing, she spotted a young woman wearing a distinctive traditional costume. She noticed that the clothes were pieced together using different cotton materials in a variety of designs. The kerchief worn around the girl's head was beautiful, as was the embroidered shoes she had on. Suzanne walked up to the youthful looking teenager and asked her, using sign language, if she could draw her sitting on or leaning against the bridge.

It seemed to take a while, and when Suzanne was finished, she thanked the girl and put money into the palm of her hand. Shui Iv, was her name. At first she was embarrassed and didn't want to take the money offered. After Suzanne's insistence, Shui Iv, bowed graciously and walked away with a large smile on her face. Suzanne turned to Nancy and handed her the colored drawing. "It's my gift to you, so you'll never forget this incredible town and the beautiful costumed young lady who sat in front of one of the oldest bridges in history." Nancy hugged her friend. "I know where I'm going to hang it on my living room wall when we get back home," exclaimed Nancy, as she walked leisurely around the rest of the town.

When the two women returned to the Junk, they realized that they were the last couple to return. When they were traveling through the waterways again, everyone seemed to be talking at once about their experiences. Suzanne looked around the group and realized what happiness was all about.

The elder father's name was Sunglo. He perfunctorily asked the people on board, if they enjoyed seeing the ancient town and told them where they would be going next on their journey. Mrs. Fang welcomed her guests and motioned them to their humble kitchen table. Suzanne noticed that the children erected another wooden plank on which the rest of the party could be seated. The wife and children brought rice, fish and food different than anything Suzanne had seen before. She didn't want to appear rude, so she ate what was served and without saying a word, took a small portion of the fish without asking anyone what kind of catch they were eating.

The vegetables appeared to have been stir-fried and Suzanne quickly devoured the rest of the meal, no questions asked. They had been so enthralled with the first town that they visited and Suzanne was busy drawing that she and Nancy forgot to eat. At this point, she didn't want to know what kind of food she was consuming. She just wanted to fill her stomach so the growling noises would cease. Sunglo informed the passengers that after they finished their meal, they should relax until they arrived at the next town on their journey.

When they arrived in Zhouzuang, they realized how ancient the town was. It was small but quaint. Again they saw many stone bridges and waterside lanes. When Suzanne and Nancy left the boat, they walked along the narrow streets and enjoyed seeing the houses with courtyards. Some of them had arch gateways made of carved bricks. "I don't know about you, but I'd like to go back to the Junk and relax after walking through a few of these ancient buildings. Does that sound good to you, Nancy?"

"I couldn't think of anything I'd like to do better." Before going back, they found a tea house, sat outside and enjoyed a little pastry and tea. "This seems to hit the spot." Nancy admitted. "Even though we had lunch, I didn't eat as much as I usually do and this treat fills the bill." Each gave a high five and walked slowly back to their temporary home.

When the rest of the gang came back, Sunglo told them that their next visit wouldn't take them long to get to and they would probably stay the night. When Suzanne found out that they were going to Suzhou, she became excited. She'd read about this ancient and moat city many years ago and always remembered it. She couldn't believe, after all these years, she was going to somewhere that she never dreamed of seeing. It seemed that the other passengers were excited as well.

When they docked at the town, they noticed that it was built on a network of interlocking canals where beautiful gardens could be seen. Everyone was anxious to walk through the grounds and find out where they could acquire some silk garments to take back home with them. Even though the people realized that they were going to go to many other well-known countries, there was something different about this special place.

Sandy hooked her arm around Arthur and found Cole and Isabelle. The two couples went off the junk and the two women could be seen talking a mile a minute. It seemed that Sandy wanted to bring back some unusual silk garments for her children as a thank you for their generous gift of the trip. Isabelle loved shopping as much as she enjoyed eating and going to the local pub. The two couples made a great match. Suzanne noticed Joe and Sam walking through the beautiful flowers and talking intimately. Tracy and Mike, along with the Murphy's, were enjoying the sites and decided to visit many of the various places they noted on the brochures that they had picked up. They enjoyed seeing the ancient temples and the waterways. Both couples decided to go onto a small boat and see the houses that were along the water's edge. They hadn't realized that Suzhou was called 'little Venice.' The various pagodas were breathtaking and they took many pictures of all the interesting sites. When they got to one of the more populated areas, the couples couldn't believe what was starring them in the face. "Am I going crazy, imagining or having delusions?" Tracy asked Mike. "No Honey, let's go in and have us some good American food!"

Renée and Paul ran close behind. They sat at a booth of the two-storied structure and laughed until tears were seen in the couples' eyes. "Can you believe a McDonald's is located here? I wouldn't have believed it unless I saw it for myself," Paul Murphy stated. He abruptly got up and took everyone's order. Mike went with him. The two women finally stopped laughing and before the food was brought back, they decided to go to the bathroom. "We'd better go now or else I don't know where or when we're going to find another facility," advised Renée. "Who am I to not take advice from an experienced woman," Tracy exclaimed, as they made their way to the rest rooms.

"I don't know about you, but these fries taste delicious. I'm glad we each ordered two large double Macs with fries. Who knows what they'll serve us when we get back. I'm not one to complain, but I like to know what I'm eating," Paul stated. Everyone agreed as they stuffed their mouths with fries, hamburgers and drank coke as if it were going out of style. Feeling very full, they left the establishment and were ready to take in more sites. As they were leaving, Mike spotted Joe and Sam and told them they had to go to the McDonald's down the street. Looking back over his shoulder, Mike was happy to see the two guys walking into the familiar archways.

Suzanne and Nancy found the town had many stores and had a ball looking at all the beautiful silk garments. Knowing how hard it was for Nancy to make up her mind on purchasing anything, Suzanne grabbed a silk scarf off of the table and put it into Nancy's hand. "I don't care what else you purchase, and you can hem and haw all you want, but at least I can make up my mind on what I want."

"Well if that's the case, my dear friend, how come you haven't made up your mind on which of the gentlemen friends you have a notion to wind up with?" Nancy teasingly asked Suzanne. "That's a low blow."

"I know, but who cares, no one knows who we are and as far as I'm concerned, anything goes, that means I can say anything I please and probably no one here can understand one word I'm saying." All Suzanne did was shake her head.

PHILIPPINE ISLAND

It was early morning, the dawn just breaking. It seemed as if people were still sleeping in this small town, and the people who were up were heading for work or preparing for a busy day.

The men decided to meet outside of the town, at the edge of the deep green forest. When Efren arrived all the men clapped. He was the last to appear. Mario, who seemed the leader of the group, greeted the men with a shrug of his head. "Well, it seems the last of the work that we had to do is finished, and now is the time that we've been waiting for."

"I don't know about you guys, but I'm not going to lie to you and say that I'm not scared. I'm scared shitless." The men laughed and nodded their heads in agreement. "I have a plan and want your input. I think that we should head out, and put the regular sails up as if we're out for a normal day of fishing. When we are at sea and no one is around, we take down the sails and put up the sails that we designed. Let the people who we surprise know that we are pirates and are nasty. We are pirates and will stand for no nonsense. I would like to start off small and get a smaller yacht with a few couples on board and take as much as we can."

Tolemeo interjected and said, "We all know our strengths and weaknesses, and as long as we do the job that we've been practicing for a while now, I don't see any problems." The men agreed. "So like Mario has told us a dozen times, let's keep our cool, and show that we're united and mean business. These people are out on vacation, and all they want is to have a good time. Let's get our gear together. We know that we have to start out slow. By that I mean we'll go and hi-jack smaller crafts and go from there. It's easier to commandeer smaller vessels and then get money for the electronics and gear from their vessels. Any money and jewelry that the passengers have will also be ours. We'll get working capital and split everything among us." They all agreed with what was said.

The day was beautiful; the storm that had ruined their plans a few days ago was long gone. The Millers and their friends the Stevens were out to forget about all the issues at home and enjoy this leisurely vacation. It wasn't often that they were able to coordinate the vacation time with their best friends and they were thrilled that this time the Stevens would be joining their old and dearest buddies for this thrilling two weeks of fun, sailing, scuba diving and enjoying the sun.

Sal Miller was coming up from viewing the unusual fish below the ocean's surface. His wife, Anne, was preparing a light meal after she and Linda spent the day sunning with not a cloud in the sky. Anne Miller was down below changing into clothes to go ashore after her husband surfaced. Wayne was waiting for Sal to ascend from their scuba diving session.

Sal and Wayne got out of their wet outfits and joined their wives down below for the lunch that Anne and Linda had made for their mates. After showering and eating their sandwiches, the men showed the women the beautiful fish that they captured on film and picked out the ones that they wanted to have blown up to showcase on their walls back home in Philadelphia. Sal and Anne Miller met Linda and Wayne when they moved into their elegant new home in Bella Vista, Pennsylvania. Anne had grown up in the city of Philadelphia and was lucky to have been accepted into MIT in Cambridge, MA. It was there that she met her future husband and best friends, Linda and Wayne. After graduating, they were lucky to have found prestigious jobs back home. The two couples rented small apartments while saving up their earnings to hopefully purchase beautiful homes in the suburbs.

Both couples put off having children until they could afford their future homes in order to bring their children up in an environment unlike the one that they knew. Often times Linda and Anne talked in their dorm room until the wee hours of the morning, planning and hoping for a brighter future than the one in which they had been brought up. They were both lucky that dysfunction wasn't part of the problem. It was that their parents were of lower, middle-class backgrounds. Neither parents had furthered their educations and were laborers and housewives. When the high school councilors had them apply to the prestigious schools in Massachusetts, they were both excited, as they had worked hard in school to be accepted to this wonderful university. Of course, getting great scores on their SAT's didn't hurt either of them. Now that their homes were purchased, the two best friends were planning on starting their families.

Linda and Anne were on deck sunning, after having cleared up the dishes from lunch, when they first spotted a large boat coming toward them. Jokingly Linda blurted out that if that boat didn't slow down and change their course, a collision was imminent. "Hey Anne, am I going blind, or is that a skull and bones on the sails of that ship?"

"Come on Linda, you've seen Captain Phillips in the movies too many times," Anne laughed nervously. Linda was amused, trying not to show concern, when the boat in question was upon them. They saw the men with swords, guns and other weapons of destruction and heard them yell while they deftly jumped onto their boat.

The men were definitely not the type to aggravate, as Anne had a habit of doing when she didn't like a situation that was about to happen. Instead of acting indignant, Linda smiled and tried to make light of the situation. Linda said a little loudly, "Hey fellows, what is going on here?"

Efran, wielding a long knife, put the blade to the neck of Linda's heavily tanned skin. "Don't you utter a sound or this knife will make sure to puncture this beautiful long neck of yours." Commanding his men, Mario told the others to gather the people down below and bring them up to the deck.

The two men were startled when they saw a bunch of guys coming downstairs where they were playing a game of cards. "Hey, what's going on?" A surprised Sal asked and was hit across the face by a fearless Ronnie. "Shut your mouth or I'll shut it for you; now sit down so this guy can tie you." Ronnie motioned with his head to Tolemeo, and his cousin went on with his business tying the two men.

Sal and Wayne were taken by surprise, and before they knew what they could do to alleviate the situation at hand, they found themselves tied to the posts and couldn't move. The men were proud that they had trained as hard as they did and went about the cabins collecting any money that they found in the wallets of the couples who couldn't conceive of being in the situation they were in.

Sunny got more rope and tape from Tolemeo and started tying the two women on the deck. Anne, who by now was frantic, didn't know what was happening to the men down below and started fighting like a wild cat trying to get away from these obvious pirates. Before Anne found herself hogtied, she raked her fingers across the face of Sunny and tried kicking, but to no avail.

Blood started dripping from Sunny but he ignored the obvious cuts and pushed Anne down. He thought to himself, '*What a bitch! If I had my druthers, I'd rape and then kill the bitch and see how brave she'd be then.*' He went about his business, not allowing the obvious blood to prevent the task at hand.

Mario, when he saw that the four people were bound, with hand motions, told who should take the electrical equipment and anything else that wasn't tied down. The radar would get them good money on the black market. Grabbing any jewelry and taking off the wedding rings or any trinkets that any of the captors were wearing or had in their rooms, Mario stuffed them in the canvas bag that he brought with him. The other equipment was put into a different container and was held by a few of the men who were thrilled with the objects that they had stolen.

When the men were satisfied with their loot, they made sure that their captives were secured and couldn't get away. The men jumped back into their boat and with booty in hand, started laughing amongst themselves, and opened the cooler and brought up cans of beer to their mouths. Toasting themselves, they sang and laughed as they made their way back home. They made sure that they undid the sails and put up their old reliable ones so no one in the village could be aware of their venture.

The two couples were separated and didn't know how badly injured or even dead their partners were. The women tried undoing their ties but to no avail. Finally, when all hope eluded them, they saw another sailboat in the horizon. Anne hoped that the sailing vessel would sail near them and help them out of their dilemma. Sure enough, about after an hour went by, the other sailboat came near the Miller's boat. "Hey, are you guys having a good day?" One of the men yelled.

When no one answered, the men got worried and put their boat beside the sailboat that they had come across. In the recesses of their mind, they hoped that they didn't find people either shot, dead or otherwise injured. They jumped onto the boat to discover the women, tears streaming down their tanned faces, tied and tape over their mouths. Jokingly, Chad, one of the men who climbed on board, told his friend, "now this is the way all women should be treated," as he deftly untied the two women and then went down below to find the men, also tied and taped.

When the two couples were untied and got the feeling back in their extremities, they told the members of the other boat about the incident that occurred. The men couldn't believe what they were hearing. "No shit!" When they saw the electrical equipment and the radar not on board, they called in a mayday and waited patiently for the police boats to appear.

Mario and the others were delighted with their first adventure. They kept the jewelry in the sack and gave the equipment to Ronnie and told him to get the best price he could from the underground gangsters. "We'll divvy up the money and be as surprised as anyone else in the village when word comes back about the new pirates that did the horrible job of stealing from tourists." Mario took the sack of jewels and told the men that he would find a good place to hide it until they had enough jewels to get a lot of money for them. He divvyed the money among the men and told them to lay low for a few days and then they'd meet on the weekend to plan their next adventure. Mario headed home to his wife and family, whistling all the way to his bamboo hut.

CHAPTER FOURTEEN

Suzanne was happy that she hadn't thought of her dilemma back home. Admittedly, she was angry that Nancy brought up the subject of her love life. *'I'm going to forget that she mentioned that subject and concentrate on having a good time. That's what we're here for and, by golly, that's what I'll do.'*

Suzanne had a hard time concentrating on the shopping and couldn't wait to return to the junk that Mr. Sunglo and his charming family shared with all the guests on board. Although Suzanne enjoyed seeing the many old styled bridges and the ancient houses, she was anxious to return with her new family and start organizing the various pictures and notes that she'd taken along the way. She couldn't help think of the dilemma of her love life. *'After all, I'm not a youngster, and the way that Stephen acted or by his lack of actions, it's obvious that Lawrence is the man of the hour.'* Suzanne laughed to herself as she waited patiently for Nancy to purchase her silk scarf.

Once back on Mr. Sunglos' junk, Suzanne craved privacy to think of all the various new places she and Nancy visited and to start writing in her journal. She found concentrating difficult, as everyone it seemed, was talking at once. Nancy gave Suzanne the eye, and even though a word wasn't spoken between the two best friends, Nancy realized privacy was what Suzanne needed.

Suzanne went downstairs to hide and have some alone time. She threw herself on the small twin-sized bed, and not even realizing it, the tears started flowing down her cheeks. She didn't know what made her feel this sentiment, but somehow she couldn't stop crying. *'Maybe it's that I'm finally by myself, I'm healed physically, and now I have to learn to relax and like being by myself. After all, I've really never been alone, except when recuperating in the hospital. I wouldn't consider that a great time in my life. In my heart, I keep asking myself why I put up with this nonsense of love and being on a roller coaster ride. Here I am in the prime of my life and instead of liking being by my lonesome, I don't know what to do with myself.'*

The journal Suzanne brought along, with places for pictures, sat untouched. She closed her eyes, and various thoughts and visions floated before her, as ancestors of the past and the loved ones, who were no longer alive to guide and help her, just smiled, as if encouraging her. She fought off the depression and realized that she was the only person who could help herself out of the various predicaments she found herself in, both personal and professional. She loved her profession but realized that she only had a few more years left in her career. Sure, she could teach other young estheticians their profession but really didn't get the same satisfaction she derived from solving crimes. *'Now that's sick, she thought to herself. What am I thinking about when I get fulfillment helping people out in certain situations. Yes, making people feel good about them-selves in my profession of esthetics is nice, but it's not the same feeling that I derive when I'm in the middle of a scary and hurtful crime. I don't think that's normal!'*

Nancy came and sat down on the small bed beside her. "Hey, do I see the remnants of tears?" She took Suzanne, and like an older sister, held her tightly; the two women didn't have to say another word. After a while, she let Suzanne down gently and told her that most of the people were coming back on board. "Mr. Sunglo told us that his wife prepared a delicious meal, and we should all come upstairs and enjoy her excellent cooking." Nancy prodded Suzanne to come upstairs with her and told her nicely to enjoy herself and life. *'Don't think of sadness, just enjoy the moment. Come on, there's a whole world out there to see and enjoy. I don't want to see any more tears throughout this entire trip. Now come on." Nancy took Suzanne's hands and pushed her upstairs to join the rest of the group.

Everyone told the collection of guests of their day's events and what they thought of their experiences so far. Suzanne couldn't help but feel enthusiasm when she heard what the others had to say about their journey through this vast and beautiful countryside and waterways.

The next morning, Mr. Sunglo told them that they would be journeying to Shaoxing and what sights that they would see there. On the waterway, Mr. Sunglo told the tourists about the unique landscapes belonging to the area in South Yangtze River. While they were traveling down the waterway, Nancy could feel the rain drops on her head. "I don't want to be a pessimist, but from what I remember reading, isn't this the famous rainstorm area during May thru October," Nancy whispered in Suzanne's ear. "Oh just suck it up. We're lucky that most of the flowers are still in bloom. I have to admit that this is a gorgeous area. Maybe that's why many of the famous politicians, authors and celebrities, such as China's first Premier, came from this very area. I have to admit that it's a classic old town with very narrow water ways," Suzanne spoke softly to Nancy. "Well, from what I read," interrupted Renée Murphy, when she heard Suzanne and Nancy talking, "the best meals are prepared at the stalls where many local dishes are served for a very cheap price."

When Isabelle Tower overheard Renée mention the fine meals, especially at the local shops (that were really stalls) her ears perked up and she was ready to have Mr. Sunglo leave them to tour the area for a while. Suzanne saw Isabelle go over to Mr. Sunglo and the next thing she realized, the junk was stopping and letting people off to tour the island for a few hours. He told his guests that they should take advantage of the wine called Shaoxing Yellow Rice Wine. "This wine is made from a certain type of rice, and the amounts of food cooked in this special wine, adds to the flavor. Very little cooking oil is used because of the unique flavor of this wine that is added to the dishes of prepared food."

Suzanne and Nancy took advantage of the rain's sudden pause and wandered through the various shops to take advantage of the many delicious scents emitting from the locals stalls to their hearts' delight.

Sandy and Arthur held hands as they wandered through the various narrow streets and stopped at the same stall when they saw Suzanne and Nancy. They were enjoying the various vegetables and chicken being served to them from the owners of this quaint establishment.

After they were all back on board, everyone couldn't help but talk over one another as they explained the magnificent wares and foods they saw and ate while wandering the narrow streets. It sounded to Suzanne like her relatives who seemed to yell at each other from the different sides of her grandmother's kitchen and living room, whenever members of her family gathered for a party or get together.

Meanwhile, Sandy was lying on her bed, hands under her head, and going over in her mind her last visit with her oncologist. She and Arthur decided since her last reports were good, he didn't have to go with her to this meeting. She thought to herself that she was glad that he hadn't accompanied her on this particular appointment.

When the nurse called her in Sandy was full of joy, knowing or thinking that all of her treatments were behind her. She entered the office and was surprised that Dr. Silk wasn't his usual cheerful self. The smile she expected to see was not visible. She then remembered her last scan and thought that something was amiss. "Have a seat," Dr. Silk motioned for Sandy to sit on the chair in front of his desk. There was a grim expression on his face. He was one of her oncologists and motioned her to sit down.

All thoughts went flying through her head as she waited for 'the grim reaper' to tell her what she didn't want to hear. He started the conversation with little quips, about his thoughts on life and where he and his wife went on their last vacation. Suddenly, he became serious. He put out his hand and expected her hand to automatically go into his. She had to admit that he did have a great bedside manner, a lot better than a lot of doctors that she had seen throughout her lifetime. She often wondered how some doctors chose their profession. She disliked some physicians that had no finesse or could not relate to their patients. She automatically put her hand into his, somehow transforming his optimism and sincerity into her body.

"Sandy, we have known each other for many years and I don't have to tell you how much you and your family mean to me. When we performed this last PET scan, I honestly didn't think that I'd be relating what I have to tell you on this visit. Unfortunately, something showed up that surprised me. When I looked at the x-ray to verify my findings and what I thought that it looked like, I had my associate also view the new scan." Shaking his head he then told Sandy that he wanted to perform a biopsy to confirm his suspicions. "I honestly hope that what I think it might be is wrong. But we have to prepare ourselves for the worst. I don't want to say it's nothing when I look at the history that you've had. Now it could honestly be nothing and we will laugh at all of this at another time. But for now, I want you to schedule a date and time, as soon as possible, to have that biopsy done."

Sandy was speechless. She and Arthur had, thanks to her children and their significant others, bought their trip that they were looking forward to going on. '*This has to be a bad dream,*' she thought to herself. When she walked out of the office, she deliberately didn't make an appointment for the date of a surgery. She knew in her heart that Dr. Silk was a great doctor and known throughout the world for his work as an oncologist. No, she decided, she wouldn't tell Arthur or for that matter, anyone about this latest crises. She didn't know what to do, but did know that something had to be done, and she didn't want to put herself or her family and loved ones through any more ordeals that she had been through. She was thankful that she had lived all these years on, what seemed like, borrowed time. She was able to see her children walk down the aisles with their betrothed, and so far, no divorces were imminent. She had wonderful grandchildren that she adored and was a firm believer in fate and God.

Sandy decided that she and Arthur would take this trip, and she would do nothing about the stupid whatever that appeared on the scan. She felt fine, or as fine as she thought she should feel. Sandy didn't want to burden her family with anymore heartaches about her health. She would put her faith in God and decided that what will be, will be. So far, she felt great and wouldn't mention her doctor's visit to anyone. If any of her children or Arthur asked, she would tell them that everything was fine and it was just a formality that she had to go for a checkup. Yes, that's what she would do. With her mind made up she entered her house, put her purse where she always left it and started preparing dinner for herself and Arthur. She was sure that he'd ask her about the doctor's appointment and was preparing herself to lie to him for the first time in their life as a couple. She always told her husband what was on her mind and what was happening, but this one secret would be forever in her heart and soul. She didn't want to have any pity from anyone, especially her family.

The cabin door opened and in walked Arthur. He had a great smile that was evident now. She patted the bed and instead of sitting next to her, put his body next to hers. They always had a great sex life and now it seemed that she would try to get all thoughts of ill health out of her mind and go with the flow. Arthur started snuggling and kissed her neck and his hands automatically undid her robe. She loved the way his lips felt all over her body. She let him make love to her and she responded as she always did. She could feel the tingling in her opening, and suddenly her fingers were caressing his body as well. She moaned with delight as his hands encompassed her large breasts. She felt his manhood and besides enlarging, his member contracted, waiting for it to be caressed by her slick hands and then she would encompass his erection with her warm, soft mouth. They lie in bed examining and fondling one another until she wanted his penis to enter her. He lifted her buttocks with his firm hands and gently filled her to capacity with his organ. At first his movements were slow and deliberate, but suddenly he couldn't control his emotions any longer. With a fastness she hadn't experienced in a while, they both climaxed together. They lie in each other's arms, something that hadn't happened in a while, Sandy thought. They woke when they heard movement and noise outside their cabin door.

"Well, sleepyhead, I think we should get up and join the others. They might get worried not knowing what is keeping us from joining them on deck," Sandy told Arthur. "To tell you the truth, I really don't care what the others might be thinking." With that said Arthur took a hold of Sandy's hand and let her feel his erection once again. "My, my, I wouldn't mind staying here for a little while longer. He took her nipples, one at a time and could feel the bud get hard. He left one and went after the other, hearing her groan with delight. He kept his hands roaming, meanwhile suckling on each nipple at a time. After another session of love making, the two spooned each other and slept for another few hours. Arthur wouldn't allow other thoughts to enter his mind, realizing that he was acting like two different personalities.

"This time we'd better get up and dressed," Sandy announced as she started putting on her clothes, not waiting for her husband's response. "Put that way, I guess I don't have much choice," laughed Arthur as he also grabbed for his clothes and started dressing for the evening that lay ahead.

Meanwhile, as Sandy and Arthur were in their cabin sleeping in a fog of sexual delight, Mike and Tracy were up to their own enjoyment. "So far, this vacation has been nothing but colossal. But I like it when we're alone and no one can disturb my wanton thoughts," Mike declared as he brought Tracy close to him and pushed her gently on their bed. "My, my, what, pray tell, are you thinking of doing?" asked Tracy, teasingly. "You'll see. Now off with your clothes you little vixen, and I'll show you my wares if you show me yours." With that said, it didn't take Tracy long to undress and wait for her husband to show her his aggressive side that she always desired. She didn't bother to bring her monthly supply of oral contraception, thinking that this was a perfect time for them to start the large family that they both wanted. Aggressively, Mike took hold of his wife's firm breasts and sucked one and then took her other breast into his warm, mouth. His hands caressed her smooth, long legs and lingered at the opening of her crevice, knowing that she would encourage him further in his exploration. After another fifteen minutes of lovemaking, Tracy begged him to enter her and with a rapid movement found that their needs were being fulfilled. Holding onto each other after their experience, she looked over to her husband who was sleeping the sleep of the dead. She thought to herself that she couldn't have asked for a better mate and hoped that during this vacation of a lifetime they would have a great significant reward that would be arriving in nine months. With that thought, she closed her eyes, took a deep breath and slept the sleep of the satisfied.

The sunrise was a splendid sight to behold. Suzanne held her breath as she saw the brilliant day beginning. There was something magical about the way the world looked when one was on the ocean and saw the sun's first ray of hope. She nudged Nancy, telling her to look at the sunrise. They both were speechless. Nancy, appreciated beauty, as did Suzanne, but never in her life had she experienced such a magnificent sight. It reminded Nancy of the many times she looked over and saw Rich sleeping soundly next to her. She heard the waves crashing when the windows were opened and between the lovely sounds and the heavenly sight of Rich, how could one ask for more. She loved the trip but was getting lonesome for Rich. She always enjoyed Suzanne's company, but she missed her lover each day a little more. She didn't want to spoil Suzanne's and the girls' gift by seeming ungrateful, but in reality she couldn't wait till Rich held her closely again.

The gang couldn't have asked for a more accommodating person than Mr. Sunglo and his beautiful family. But, the couples couldn't wait until they returned to their sailing vessel and were again on their way to see the sights and new wonders to enjoy. Renée was especially anxious to get back to their scheduled vacation. Paul was being a wonderful companion, but she thought of her neighbors and the little boy whose small mini car Paul and his dad were building for his first big race. She didn't want to seem ungrateful, but although she enjoyed seeing all the new sights, she was getting anxious to return to her home in Newton. Paul, although he didn't verbalize his restlessness, wasn't used to this long a vacation away from home. *'Yes,'* he thought, *'we will bring many beautiful pictures and treasures from far off lands home with us, but I can't wait to get back home.'*

All the other couples felt the same as Paul and Renée but kept their thoughts to themselves. Although the trip was something magnificent, they all had agendas that they wanted to fulfill.

Suzanne was lying out getting some sun, making sure that she had an eighty sun block on her exposed body. She thought of her situation at home and, although she enjoyed the company and all the attention that Larry was giving her, her mind kept thinking of Stephen and wondering what he was doing. She realized she had to keep thoughts of Stephen at bay and enjoy the times she had when Larry was dotting on her. *'Yes,'* she thought, *'get Stephen out of your mind and concentrate on how wonderful Larry has been. I couldn't ask for a better companion.'* She had not yet slept with him, as she was afraid in many ways that she would be betraying Stephen. Suzanne realized that it was a stupid reason and wanted to show how much Larry's affection meant to her. What better way of showing her delight than finally making love to a man she knew would do anything in the world for her, if asked. She closed her eyes and tried to put her mind at rest. For once she didn't want to think of anything but enjoy the moment. *'If you can't be with the one you love, love the one you're with.'*

Nancy was beside Suzanne on the blanket, soaking up the rays, aware that her light skin could take only so much of the sunshine. The diary she kept was up to date on their excursions and the people that they met. She was also getting anxious to get home and tell everyone about their latest adventure. With that thought, she could feel herself dozing off and thinking of Rich's arms holding her tightly.

Suzanne felt the vibration of her cell phone and picked it up. It was Captain Bob telling her that all the repairs were finished, and the crew was putting up the sails as they were speaking. "I guess we lucked out on the expense and how fast we were able to order and get all the necessary equipment that we needed."

Suzanne woke Nancy and told her the good news. "Now all we have to do is get a flight back to Singapore and then we'll be free to continue on our way," a jubilant Nancy reacted to the good news. "I really don't want to go onto another airplane, but under the circumstances, I know there's no other way. Let's tell the others and we'll make arrangements for the airplane to take us back to Singapore. From there, it won't take us a long time to be back in Hong Kong and see the captain and the crew again."

When they were about to depart from Mr. Sunglo's Chinese Junk, Suzanne had everyone on board posed so she could take their picture. She also had separate pictures of Mr. Sunglo and his lovely family pose and was lucky that they had just caught a large fish. With the fish still on its fishing pole, a boisterous Deling was proudly holding the fishing pole with the fish caught still hooked on the pole. This would be the family's dinner and everyone clapped at a proud Deling.

It was good being on the sailboat again thought Suzanne as she was writing in her journal. She wanted to call Larry up and tell him the good news about their wonderful, sudden adventure on the Junk, but decided to wait until they were in another port.

The other members of the group were also pleased with the smooth trip back and couldn't wait to begin their adventure again. Cole and Isabelle were restless back in the cabin and couldn't wait till they were under sail once more. Sam and Joe were excited to continue on the voyage and couldn't wait to take more pictures of other adventures that they would be having. Renée and Paul were standing by the railing of the vessel waiting for the anchor to be lifted. Tracy and Mike were in their cabin and were like two rabbits in heat. Every chance they could get, they were back in their room making love and hoping that the little sperm would find its way to the egg that lay in Tracy's womb. They found themselves laughing all the time and would never forget this wonderful vacation.

When they were on the seas, Sandy found herself back in the room, laying on the made bed and trying not to think of her predicament. Her mind kept going back to her problem and as much as she tried not thinking and let her mind be blank, nothing would stop her mind from terrible thoughts.

The last time she was at the oncologist she felt fine, but if she thought about it, she would have realized that she really wasn't feeling as well as she did about six months before her visit. She started coughing, and knew that she had been having a hard time catching her breath. It felt as though there was a large elephant on her chest. She ignored her inner thoughts and didn't want a doctor to confirm her worst fear. She was having such a wonderful time and was surprised that Arthur hadn't noticed her trying to catch her breath. He probably thought she was anxious at the thought of going to all the new places.

She didn't want to discuss her feelings with Arthur but knew that she couldn't keep him in the dark for much longer. She had to find the right time to tell him how she really felt and that she didn't want anything more done to her if she had a reoccurrence of the disease. Now she felt and had a sudden knowledge that, not only was the cancer back, but also the nasty cancer was probably in a new place, her lung. She knew many people who tried to fight the dreaded disease, all to no avail. She wanted to live her life to the fullest and not be bothered with all the treatments that in all likelihood would not work. She lived each day at a time all of her life and she would continue with that way of living. It was going to be hard telling Arthur, but she wanted to stay strong and she knew that he would do anything that she wanted. Sandy felt lucky that her husband was as wonderful as he was. Yes, finding the right time and place would be her next concern.

The group couldn't wait until they were finished with all the expeditions that lay ahead. It was great that they were able to take the junk and visit all the unusual places that they had, but all at once they realized that they were going to be in one of the most beautiful and exotic places in the world. Hong Kong had a plethora of sights that city lovers, worldwide, would enjoy seeing.

As they made their way to visit the fine eating establishments that were recommended to them by a few of the crew members, they took as many pictures as they could so they would never forget this wonderful experience.

After eating to their hearts content, Suzanne and Nancy, along with the rest of the group, couldn't wait to get back to the ship and fall fast asleep. They all knew that tomorrow would be an experience that they didn't want to miss.

Looking over the various brochures, Sandy decided that she wanted Arthur to take her to the Chi Lin Nunnery and the gardens that were adjacent to the Buddhist place of worship. It would give Sandy a chance for the peace and tranquility that she craved. Arthur would do anything she wanted and was always amenable to anything she desired, well, almost anything, with the exception of the Cadillac car that she wanted them to buy.

Cole and Isabelle wanted to meet them in a couple of hours after Sandy and Arthur visited the sanctuary and gardens. Sandy estimated that it would take them about one hour to go through. Isabelle wanted to go shopping at the Plaza Hollywood. She couldn't wait to go to the third floor and see for herself all the dining places she could choose from.

After all the excursions, the entire group decided to visit and take a ride through the entire district of Hong Kong using the efficient and economical public transportation called "ding-ding" by all the locals.

After agonizing decisions, all the rest of the gang decided to join Arthur and Sandy on their journey. In a way Sandy was disappointed that she couldn't go to the Temple by herself with her husband. She thought that this was going to be the time that she would be able to talk and explain her feelings to Arthur. She kept worrying when a good time would be to tell him about her ill health.

Sandy and Arthur and everyone that joined them held hands as they made their way through the magnificent Gardens that they were told would blow them away. They found out how to go on the Metro and, after they arrived at the Kwun Kwun Tong Line, they would find the entrance to the Gardens that were about 100 meters away from the MTR Station line.

Sandy wanted to get away from the crowds and took Arthur's hand as they silently walked to the Chi Lin Nunnery. She found out that it was a Buddhist place of worship. She craved the peace and tranquility and found that she was praying to a God she knew nothing about. All she knew was that the Buddhists were people of serenity and peace and that's all that she wanted at this time. Arthur saw his wife's mouth moving silently without words coming out. He knew her well enough that he surmised that something was bothering her. In time, she would confess to him her thoughts and prayers. Knowing her as well as he did, she would confide in him when she felt the time was right. He held his breath, leaving her to tell this God, who he knew nothing about, what she had on her mind. Until then he left her alone, in her own thoughts. He didn't want to think or feel at this particular moment. He saw the dark circles under her eyes and when she wasn't watching, he saw the hard time she had breathing and taking in the needed oxygen she so desperately wanted to inflate her lungs. '*No,*' he thought to himself, '*I'll wait until Sandy is good and ready and it's the right time to tell me what's on her mind.*'

Isabelle had a great time looking at all the stalls and beautiful items at the various stores. She couldn't make up her mind which of the items she wanted to take back home. Her friend's daughter had just given birth to a baby and she needed no excuse to indulge in buying a beautiful pram set for the summer outings. That's the only thing she regretted about her and Cole's marriage. When they wanted offspring, the doctors told them that after all the testing, there was nothing responsible for her not conceiving. Isabelle thought that it was God's way, and she took it in stride that they never had children. But, she didn't have many relatives to share the festivities with her and Cole. She knew that Cole loved her with all of his heart and soul, and she felt the same towards him. '*What will be, will be,*' she said aloud, not realizing that other people heard her words of lament. Isabelle always thought of herself getting married and raising a family. The thought of them living to a ripe old age without having children really bothered her. Especially around the Holidays when all of her friends spent their extra hours with family, they were invited as friends, not the family she envisioned herself and Cole having.

Joe and Sam ate at a vegetarian restaurant after visiting the Nunnery and Gardens. They admired the bridge, but after seeing all the beautiful bridges on their excursion on the Junk, they weren't that excited about seeing another one. They bided their time, walking around the mall and enjoying all the various stores that had magnificent goods for sale. Sam talked Joe into going into a tailor shop and watched as his best friend and lover got fitted for a custom made suit that in the States would have cost Joe a fortune. He also told Joe that he would pay for a shirt that would go on the tab. They talked the tailor into making this special outfit to be picked up at the end of the day. Sam understood the anxiety that this small, bent over Chinese man was going through, but told him that he would pay the extra money if this extra service could be accomplished faster than normal. They left the shop knowing that Joe got a deal of a lifetime. The two men couldn't wait to tell the others what they had accomplished.

When everyone was back on the sailing ship, they were exhausted and couldn't wait until they were fast asleep. The gang would have a full day at sea and then go on to Manila, Philippines. Suzanne was secretly excited to personally see all of the wonders of this great port. She remembered when she was a youngster and had heard and read all of the gossip about Imelda Marcos and her collection of shoes. Suzanne always wondered if the rumors about Imelda having an affair with JFK were real or if it was just more publicity. She knew that JFK was a lady's man and always felt sorry for Jackie. '*Oh well, water under the dam,*' she said to herself as she took off her swimsuit to take a shower and get ready for another great dinner served by the crew.

They landed at the port of Manila, and everyone was excited. Not being busy bodies, Suzanne and Nancy still couldn't help but hear the rumor from the crew that there was a ship that was robbed by modern day pirates. Suzanne and Nancy talked amongst themselves and hoped that what they overheard was only a rumor. "Let's not kid ourselves," Suzanne whispered to Nancy, "we came here to vacation and not get involved with any crime. That's all we need to have happen to us."

"Well I, for one, hope that it isn't true. What we've been through is enough excitement for a year at least," Nancy laughed and whispered in Suzanne's ear. "All I want is for a nice vacation and not to get involved in any high sea drama," exclaimed Suzanne. "Besides, neither of us can swim. How can we solve any crime when we're starting at a disadvantage?" asked Nancy.

The five men met just outside the woods of the town. They walked with a different strut than they did a week ago. They no longer felt that they were being taken advantage of and now had a purpose that they didn't have before their adventure began. Mario said, "I know we're really not pirates, but it did feel good to be able to hand Maria some good money for a change." The rest of the men nodded their heads in agreement. Efran asked, "Did Maria ask you where you got all the money?" Mario answered, "She looked at me a little strange, but didn't question how I got the money. I don't like to lie to Maria, but I would have if I felt it necessary."

All the other men in the group shook their heads simultaneously. "Personally, I like the fact that no one really got hurt. None of the passengers or us was injured. I wouldn't have liked to see any bloodshed," Sunny spoke out loud. Ronnie admitted to the group that he'd be feeling horrible if anybody was injured or for that matter killed. "I don't mind doing this and, as long as no one finds out that we are doing this sea-robbing, then I'll continue to go along with you guys. Let's hope nothing of bad consequence happens to anyone. I mean a little tying up and taping is fine, as long as we keep coming home with something to show for it. When do we go out again?"

They all concurred that they saw a boat with other vacationers and had fishing equipment on board. With bottles clinking together they made a pact to meet by the woods again tomorrow and would be acting like the new age pirates again. With that said, they all left vowing to meet at seven o'clock tomorrow morning.

Barry and his group of couples from New York just landed in Manila as part of a thank you retreat from their boss for having another good quarter and year in their new start-up company. Reading the letter of congratulations from Mr. Cohen, the six couples were happy and relaxed and enjoyed the exhilaration that they felt when Ben was reading the letter from the President of the Company, Mr. Cohen. "Let's make a toast to the best boss we could ever have asked for," Tony shouted over the tumultuous noise that all the couples were joyously touting. "I'll drink to that," Marianne shouted over the other people who were enjoying themselves on this first vacation as a collection of the higher management in the fairly new company.

They had been on the Island for about two days and decided, instead of shopping in town, that they would enjoy the beautiful weather and get some fishing in. Bennie told the others, "Hey, the locals will enjoy the fish that we catch, and we can dine at one of the nicer restaurants that I've heard great remarks about."

"Hear, hear," shouted the jubilant crowd as they were out on the open seas. They had passed some fishing trawlers but knew that they wouldn't be catching the huge amount of fish that the fishermen were vying for. All of the couples were happy and doing their own thing.

Mario and his gang of hardy men were leaving the edge of the woods and were in an excellent mood. They carried the concealed weapons in two large canvass bags. They were jubilant that another day would mean a good payday for them once again. They each knew their job and were sure that what they were doing was for a good cause. Once again on the open sea, they changed the sails and put on different clothes, more like what a pirate of today would wear.

They soon spotted the large sailboat and knew that these were the people that they had heard about in town. "I bet these people have a lot of spare money on them and won't miss a bit of it," laughed Sunny. "Yeah, they seemed like rich people who wouldn't mind giving to the needy," Telemeo boasted.

They were happy that the swells weren't high and the wind was moving their ship along at a good clip. Marge yelled to one of the women, "Hey look at that boat, it seems to be coming close to us. Maybe they'd want to party with us!" With their string bikinis soaking up the sun, the two women started waving to the other boat. "Now isn't that a nice welcome," hollered Efran. "They'll be singing a different tune when they realize that we're not here to party," Mario yelled to his men.

The boat was next to the large sailing ship, when all at once, the men jumped on board the other ship. Before the couples knew what was happening, they found themselves being beaten if they gave any resistance to the men who wielded the destructive instruments of doom. When all people were subdued and tied and taped, the men went about the business at hand. They found the money in wallets left haphazardly on the beds and bureaus in the individual rooms. They tore apart the electrical equipment that would get them good money on the black market and put everything in the right containers that they had brought with them.

They tore the necklaces from the women and men and made sure that all the rings that were worn were taken off the people's fingers. "Who would be stupid enough to bring this kind of jewelry on a trip like this?" Tolemeo asked his fellow conspirators. "People who think that they don't have a care in the world and would never think that anything like this would happen to them," Mario laughed as he jumped aboard his own fishing boat that didn't look like a fishing boat any longer.

"I don't know about you guys, but won't our wives be happy to see us bring them home all of this money again," Mario boisterously spoke as he picked up a beer and toasted his fellow conspirators. "At the end of a few weeks, we'll divvy up the jewelry and that will make friends who will pay good money for the equipment. When we have enough apparatus for our booty, then we'll get real hard cash to divvy up amongst us." They again pulled up to the dock, their canvas sails once again changed. When they were sure that the boat was tied correctly to the dock, they walked with their loot to the forest where only they knew of the hiding place.

Once again the police were called after another vessel came to the vacationers' rescue. This time the people were too drunk on board to give any meaningful descriptions of the men. All they told the police was that they looked like Pirates of the Caribbean. The Police couldn't get anything of significance from the couples.

"Now make sure that our wives, who tend to have big mouths, don't tell any of their friends or relatives about this extra money that we're giving them," warned Mario. "That's all we need to blow our cover," a serious Efran told his band of merry men.

CHAPTER FIFTEEN

Suzanne was thrilled to be back on the sailboat once again. They would be what seemed home to them, once again. Hong Kong was a wonderful experience, but now it was time to move on to the next leg of their journey. They were looking forward to being on the sea once again, and after all the controversial things that they heard about the Philippines, they couldn't wait to see for themselves if these rumors were true or not. Once again they would be on their journey in the South China Seas.

While on the sea, Nancy remembered when they were in Hong Kong and she took Suzanne's hand and brought her to the high skyscrapers and then they wandered to the stalls that were housed next to the shiny new architecture. These alleys were crammed with all of the traditional vendors' stalls, and Nancy couldn't wait to dicker with the people selling their wares. She made sure that she had bought an ornament from each place she visited. She was glad that she packed an extra suitcase with nothing in it, which she intended to fill with all of the new trinkets she wanted to bring back to her home with Rich.

Suzanne was putting lotion on her face and extremities and couldn't help remember how happy she was when they visited Hong Kong. She was happy with the new purchases she had bought and was glad that the producer would deliver and send home the new furniture that she purchased. She couldn't wait to see how it looked in her home! Of course, she also made sure that she was able to fill her empty suitcase with souvenirs for all of her loved ones. When they were in Hong Kong, she debated whether or not to buy Stephen anything and, because of her stubbornness, decided not to. '*The Hell with him,*' she thought as she picked up a pretty ornament for Larry and had it wrapped in beautiful Chinese paper that she knew he would keep as a reminder of her thoughtfulness. Suzanne tried to quell her giggles as she remembered all the things that she had done. She bought some outfits for her daughters and also knew that they'd appreciate her knowing their sizes. Mrs. Walsh and her parents would get something when she and the gang went to Malaysia and the Philippines. She was excited to return home and see the faces of her loved ones as they opened their presents!

Of course, she had to buy Justin something unusual for his dwelling. She wanted him to think of her each time he looked at the item. Suzanne couldn't wait to find just the right piece for her favorite art gallery owner.

She was excited about going to Manila. Suzanne had many friends of Philippine heritage and couldn't wait to visit this country that had such a diverse mixture of ethnic groups and foreign influences. She remembered how her girlfriend had married a Philippine dental surgeon while they were interning at Dental Nursing School. They had to go back to the Philippines for three years to take some courses that had to be made up.

The seas were calm, and it was if they were being rocked by a loved one as the darkness, with just the stars to illuminate the sky, put them into a well-deserved sleep. Before Suzanne fell asleep, her mind would not rest. She anticipated the rest of the vacation with awe thinking of all the places and unusual sights she would never had seen if it weren't for the thoughtful gift that the girls bestowed upon her and Nancy. Yes, she admitted, she had problems, but when she thought of all the people in the world with their troubles, hers were nothing in comparison. Yes, she had to come to a conclusion about her love life, but in the grand scheme of things, she knew in her heart what had to be done. She had to once and for all make up her mind and stick to her decision.

She looked over at Nancy, who was sleeping the sleep of the dead and laughed to herself. She was glad that Nancy had found happiness with Rich and that she had a bright future ahead of her. All the money in the world couldn't make up for love, devotion and peace that she has finally found.

A complex map of the Philippines was being examined and a lot of the guests on board the sailing vessel gathered around Suzanne. They couldn't get over how large the Philippine Islands were and how it had more islands than they ever imagined. Suzanne couldn't wait until they landed at the capital city of Manila. "I want to go to Old Manila," Renée told the crowd looking at the map. "I've heard wonderful stories from some of the Philippine men and women who worked at the hospital where I volunteered, and now I can come back and tell them my own stories." Paul was smiling ecstatically as Renée told her new friends about some of the things she couldn't wait to participate in when they reached the shore. It seemed like hours had passed until they moored their vessel to the docks.

Joe and Sam sat quietly waiting to disembark. The evening before, they read terrible stories about some of the independent ships and sometimes larger vessels being high-jacked by the new age pirates. They huddled together glancing at the news items that they found in some of the newspapers and tried translating the words from the many newspapers that they had taken aboard Vacation of a Lifetime.

"Do you think that most of these stories are just hyped up to discourage people from taking their private sailing boats into the area?" Joe asked Sam. "Half of me doesn't want to believe the stories we've just read, but the other half wants to dismiss this all as gibberish and tell myself that the articles are a scare tactic to make sure that people don't sail on their own in these seas," Sam remarked as he was getting dressed and ready to experience another adventure on their vacation.

"I don't know where I heard or read an article once that stated that the new age pirates are really fisherman. They're trying to control the people who are infringing on their rights. They find themselves catching less fish and thus making less money to take home to their families to provide a decent living for them in order to maintain their lifestyle," Joe told Sam. "Well, let's hope that we won't be bothered by anyone and that the remainder of the trip goes smoothly."

"I didn't want to frighten you, but I have heard awful stories about large vessels containing cargo that the pirates took. They overtook the ship and later found a way to fence the products. The crew had to get onto the dinghy and row themselves to the main island. Just thinking about all the various accounts of stealing, mayhem and all else that is attributed to these pirates makes me want to throw up. I hope that nothing like this will happen on our great vacation," a now anxious Sam blurted out.

Cole and Isabelle were anxious to explore this beautiful island and couldn't wait until they met up with Tracy and Mike to have as companions on this wonderful new expedition.

Sandy and Arthur lay in bed, still in the glow of experiencing a night of love making, the likes of which Arthur couldn't remember ever having with his wife. He wondered, although he enjoyed every moment of this session, what had brought about the change to his wife. She had always been a passionate woman, but this was going over and above anything he had experienced in their married life. '*Maybe it's mid-life crises and she doesn't want to admit that she's getting older and wants our loving to be like it was when we were kids,*' he laughed to himself. He looked at his sleeping wife and knew that he had to wake her in order for them to be on time as the ship pulled up to their docking spot.

Sandy was lazily washing herself in the small shower, trying not to think of where and when she should tell Arthur about her condition. She didn't want his pity, or for that matter, anyone feeling sorry for her. The less people who knew, the better she'd feel. Sure she had compassion for other people when she heard of their plights, but in her circumstance, she only wanted Arthur to know the truth.

"Hey, what's taking you so long?" Arthur asked. "We have to be ready to leave the boat as soon as we get docked."

"Okay, okay, I'm just about ready to get out of the shower. I'll be dried and ready to go before you are dressed," Sandy answered back.

Sandy tried to make it as fast as possible. When she looked into the mirror in their small room, she saw a beautiful woman who looked back. But she knew better. Inside of her body were cells that were being destroyed by the dreaded cancer. She knew all of the heartache and pain that she had put her family and friends through when she went through all of the chemo and radiation treatments. The infections were hard to fight off and her friend Margaret had set up a special e-mail posting asking for donations and food to be brought to the house. Margaret was a good friend. Sandy hated being a person who was down and out. She was and always had been a fighter. She received get-well cards and special letters from people who she had heard of but didn't consider them her true friends. There were Novena's being made by people of the church and special masses said for her good health to return. She hated all of this attention when she knew that there were people and situations that were worse than hers. But she appreciated all of the help, especially when she found herself so tired after her chemo sessions.

Sandy told Arthur that she would be a few minutes more and told him to go up on deck and wait for her. After he left, she sat on the edge of the bed, her hands on her face and couldn't stop crying. She was distraught and didn't know what she could do to mask the unhappiness that she was feeling.

When Vacation of a Lifetime was docked, all aboard couldn't wait to go to the places that they heard of for years. Their own dreams and aspirations would shortly be fulfilled. Suzanne was telling Nancy how thrilled she was that they'd be spending two to three nights at this exotic Island and couldn't wait to finally see the palace that she had wanted to see for years. "I heard that Rizal Park is magnificent," Nancy piped in, "and that is definitely on my want-to-see list."

"Okay, that's a deal," Suzanne answered back.

While walking to Rizal Park, Suzanne told Nancy about her desire to see former First Lady, Imelda Marcos' shoe collection. "I've heard that she has a collection of shoes that is over 300 pairs and they are at the Marikina Shoe Museum." "I read about Ms. Marcos in one of my classes and have been dying to see her fetish foot wear," declared Nancy. "On our way back from the park, we'll go to the Museum, is that a deal?" Nancy asked Suzanne. They shook hands as they walked to the largest urban park in Asia.

They saw the statue of the Philippine National Hero, Jose Rizal, and saw the scenic Chinese gardens. While they were walking, they both decided that there wasn't much more to see, so they went to find a place to eat lunch. While eating at the Café Juanita, they saw some of the other passengers who decided to walk the streets of Manila and see some of the sights of this great, yet multi-cultural city consisting of Malay, Spanish, American, Chinese and Arabic influences. They sat at adjoining tables to tell the other people about the various places they visited so far.

Joe and Sam told their friends about visiting the 64-hectare stone citadel, founded by the Spanish in 1571. They couldn't believe how this citadel had withstood wars, natural disasters and successive waves of colonial invaders, and as such, stands as a metaphor for Manila itself. "Then we walked to a villa for breakfast. It was delicious." "Talk about delicious," interrupted Nancy, "I've heard that we have to go to someplace that has Halo-halo. I guess it means jumble-jumble and is a great dessert. I think it's a concoction of shaved ice and evaporated milk, mixed up with any combination of sweetened beans, candied fruit, nata de coco, Filipino créme caramel, purple yam concentrate and jelly, among other ingredients. And we can't forget to top it off with a scoop of ube ice cream." Their mouths were watering. "Let's set a time to meet back here," suggested Tracy and Mike. "The food here is so good! I guess it's like having the best home cooking next to going into someone's house to eat," recommended Tracy as she patted her bulging tummy. "Well, even though I like Manila, there certainly is a gumbo of different nationalities, and personally, I really don't enjoy or maybe fully appreciate the busy traffic. It's stifling, and the poverty and the urban sprawl is daunting" cut in Sam.

Suzanne and Nancy said their good byes to their friends. They agreed to meet them in three more hours back at the Café for their Halo-halo. The two friends decided to visit Chino Roces Avenue. It consisted of world-class exhibitions from the Philippines and beyond. Suzanne loved to walk the various isles and enjoyed the various artists' impressions as she decided on what print she wanted to take back home and show off. Nancy got a big kick out of watching Suzanne enjoy the various art exhibits and the shops along the famous Avenue, which was noted for its contemporary art. She also enjoyed looking at the superb photography.

When the time was right, Suzanne and Nancy went and met the others at Café Juanita. Other people from the ship were also there. They all talked about their adventures, and with mouths watering, all ordered the sumptuous dessert. Arthur and Sandy told of the Greenbelt Chapel that they saw. Cole and Isabelle happened to meet Sandy and Arthur in the area. Isabelle and Cole enjoyed strolling through the luxurious shopping complex where commercialism and Christianity got together. Isabelle enjoyed the local design talent that was on the entire top floor wing and had to buy some of the country's homegrown brands.

Cole teased Isabelle endlessly until she elbowed him in his protruding bulge of a stomach.

Arthur watched Sandy make her way to the domed church, the Greenbelt Chapel, which sat like a jewel in the middle of the carefully manicured grounds. He thought to himself that it was if she were compelled to visit this Holy place. Sandy insisted on staying for a Mass. It was as if Sandy were by herself, the way she prayed silently, mumbling and getting into the service. Arthur was religious, but not as much as Sandy was. The Catholic upbringing that they had when growing up must have had a great impact on Sandy, more than himself, he thought, as he watched his wife's pious act of devotions.

He hadn't realized that his wife was so devoted to the Holy Spirit. Arthur subtlety looked out from the corner of his eyes as his wife genuflected, as if she were being compelled to talk to God and to him alone. He didn't understand her sudden devotion and was perplexed. He saw a lone tear fall onto her cheek. He didn't want to embarrass her, so he let her alone in her private thoughts. His own mind was bewildered, as he couldn't understand her sudden obsessive behavior with the church and God. He and the family were always religious, and even when the scandals of the priests came to the media's attention, their devotion couldn't be deterred. He only hoped that Sandy's fanatical behavior would soon be a thing of the past.

They all walked through the streets and stood still while watching the beautiful sunset which was supposed to be one of Manila's prime assets. Joe and Sam decided to visit the White Moon Bar at the Manila Ocean Park to listen to the soul music as they enjoyed their liquid refreshments. "I don't know how we can think of putting another thing in our mouths after that delicious dessert," exclaimed Sam. "Well, let's put it this way, we're not having anything else to eat until tomorrow, but a drink is different," Joe emphasized. Sam nudged his partner, and as they were enjoying the music, they also watched the sun setting as they walked along San Miguel by the Bay. "I bet Isabelle would have died if she knew that this Mall of Asia existed," chided Joe as he held onto Sam's hand as they walked back to the sailboat.

Lying in their small room, Suzanne couldn't stop talking. She was fascinated by the various stories about Imelda Marcos and her dictator husband, Ferdinand. Nancy thought that her friend was losing her mind as she was forced to listen about how the Marcos' were sent or fled to Hawaii when the revolt or uprising happened in 1986. "I mean, she was obsessed with shoes and other objects as well. So much so that she even had a telephone made up to look like a shoe! Now most of these items have been destroyed by termites, mold and floods. Can you imagine the money her people would have enjoyed having what was spent so frivolously on things that only she enjoyed?"

"Isn't that always what happens when a dictatorship is in government? Money that should have been spent on the people of the country instead went into their own pockets."

"I guess one would call it greed. Most dictators are like that," Nancy proclaimed.

"I understand that she is now a member of the House of Representatives and a lot of the clothes that she wore at major official events can't be on exhibit because of the destruction of them." Shaking her head, Nancy sadly agreed with Suzanne.

Sandy and Arthur were enjoying the down time and discussed the many wonderful things that they saw during the day. Arthur didn't want to discuss the change that he saw happening to his wife. He wanted to believe that she was the same Sandy who he met as a young man in college and their life, as they knew it, would not be a thing of the past. He loved the change that their lovemaking had taken and wanted them to continue in this new vein. He thought to himself, '*if only it were that simple.*'

Sandy lay in bed; her mind was a million miles away. She felt her soul was cleansed, and no matter what happened next, she thanked God for the life he had given her. She realized that Arthur was a wonderful husband and she could never have asked for a better companion, father or faithful husband. They had gone through a lot of happiness in their life together, but when sickness overcame her, she appreciated his help and couldn't help but be thankful for the wonderful family that gave their all in her time of need. She hadn't asked to be sick, but realized that these occurrences were all meant to happen in the grand scheme of things. She had taken a lot of comparative religion classes and realized that maybe the Jewish people had it down pat. When a person is born, it is written in the Book of Life when a person is to die and from what. That's why the Jewish Holidays of Rosh Hashanah and Yom Kippur are so very important in the Jewish faith. Sandy remembered when she read some of the Meditations from the Jewish, Gates of Repentance, that a friend of hers had given to her when she was going through her illness. She often said the Serenity Prayer but also remembered the reading from Chasidic, 18th. Century. It said: "Just as the hand, held before the eye, can hide the tallest mountain, so the routine of everyday life can keep us from seeing the vast radiance and the secret wonders that fill the world."

With tears now rapidly flowing from her eyes, she remembered reading what The Baal Shem Tov said: "The first time an event occurs in nature, it is called a miracle, later it comes to seem natural and is taken for granted. Let your worship and your service be your miracle each day. Only such worship, performed from the heart with the enthusiasm of fresh wonder, is acceptable." (Chasidic, 18th. Century.)

She asked herself how she should approach the subject of her knowledge that her cancer has returned to Arthur. There were many methods she could employ to start the subject, but she didn't want to ruin this wonderful trip that they were having. Yet, she realized that she had to tell him and the sooner the better. Pretty soon he could see for himself that she was getting sick again. She especially didn't want to put her family through the agony again of holding her hand, washing her after her many bouts of being sick to her stomach with her head in the toilet after another chemotherapy treatment. She didn't want to get another wig when her hair disappeared from the many treatments. The cough was just starting, and she could blame it on a cold that she might be getting, but sooner or later Arthur would realize that something was wrong with his wife.

Arthur didn't want to upset Sandy, but he realized that she was going through something that she didn't want to share with him. The only thing that he could think of was that her health problem had returned. This time he realized it probably has returned with a vengeance. How could he get her to tell him what was on her mind? He had to wait until she felt prepared and was ready to share her new grief with him. He hadn't a clue until he saw her at the Greenbelt Chapel and realized that something was amiss.

Sandy turned to face Arthur and looked him directly in the eyes. She didn't know where to begin. Taking a deep breath she started: "Do you remember when I had an appointment with the oncologist?"

"Of course I do. You didn't want me to go with you because you've been getting a clean bill of health and thought it would be a waste of my time to accompany you. After all, we are taking so much time off for this great trip." Sandy didn't know how to tell Arthur, but proceeded as if possessed by demon-like tendencies. "Well, I went to the doctor's and when he gave me my usual PET scan, he saw something that shouldn't have been there. He also wanted me to have a full body x-ray. He wanted me to come back and do a biopsy. I left his office as if I were in a trance. Arthur, you have to realize that I'm not going to go through with this cancer treatment any more. I don't care if you stand on your head and spit nickels. No, I'm determined that what will be, will be."

Sandy had been courageous up until now. The tears that were welling up in her eyes were starting to fall, as much as she tried to suppress them. She shook her head to clear her thoughts. She didn't want Arthur to caress or hold her. She wanted to say what was on her mind and did not want his sympathy or caring to interfere with what she wanted to say.

"I know that you love me more than life itself. I feel the same way about you. I'm proud of the way that we raised the children and now that they are grown, we should be proud of the way they turned out. Yes, there are times when I want to tell them what to do, but then I realize that they have to find out the hard way, and do things by doing it themselves and, if not right, then right the wrongs. Those things will always be there and there is nothing we do or say that can help them. But, now this is our turn in life. As much as I want to be with you forever, it's not meant to be."

Arthur started shaking his head and tried holding his wife, the woman who he once loved with all of his heart and soul. She bore him five wonderful children, and Sandy had a large part in bringing them up by herself. Sandy pushed him gently away. "No, I want to say what's on my mind, and I don't want anything to interfere with what I have to say."

"You are a wonderful person, Arthur, and I couldn't have asked for a better person to have for a husband, confidante and the father of my children. At times I could have been angry with your hours at work, but that was to be expected. But you know as well as I do that when the time comes for me to depart from this earth and go into God's arms, that you made me the happiest woman in the world.

I know what lies ahead of me and it isn't going to be pleasant. I don't even want to mention the word cancer, but we both have to face reality. I don't want to go through the Hell that we lived with while I was doing the necessary treatments to get rid of the cancer cells that were invading my body. I thought that we won, but it was only a reprieve. I'm not going to feel sorry for myself, although I do. Do you think I want to end my life while I think that this is the prime of our lives? No, but I have to face reality. I know that my lungs are harboring these unwanted cells as well as other organs. Yes, it started in my breasts, and we all thought that I fought the fight and we won. But Honey, its back and we have to face reality. I want to be brave but it's hard. I'm going to need your help while I still maintain the dignity that I have left. It's not going to be an easy road. That's why I was happy that the kids did what they did for us. We'd never have taken this kind of vacation, and we wouldn't give ourselves the opportunity to ever go to these places or see the things that we've been lucky to see. You and I will never forget this vacation ever.

I want you to remember this happy time in our life because, all too soon, the agony of defeat will be upon us. I don't know how much time I have left on this earth, but, by golly, I want us to enjoy each day. Christ, each hour of every day is precious. Sorry that I used the Lord's name in vain," expressed Sandy. They both laughed in unison amongst the tears that were now flowing openly between them. Arthur felt like such a hypocrite, and yet he did love his wife, after all, they did share all those years of marriage. Some good, some not so good, but he couldn't abandon her at this crucial time in her life. While she was talking, besides crying he kept shaking his head, not wanting to hear what she was saying.

"How can you be sure that you can't still fight the fight of the good and come out of this terrible tragedy intact?"

"You know, Honey, I've thought everything over, believe me. A person, at least I do, knows when I have to admit that I've lost. I don't want any sympathy, and I don't want the kids to learn about this until it's apparent that I don't have much time to live. I'm certainly not a courageous woman, but I do know when to stop fighting and start living for the moment. I want our last days to be happy, not mournful and with regrets." At that moment coughing started racking her body. "I thought you told me it was only a cold?" Arthur moaned. "Well, it's not," Sandy yelled. "It's this God forsaken cancer that is taking its toll on my body!!!"

Arthur didn't let Sandy push him away this time, and she wanted him to hold her. He wanted to stop the hurt, anger and Hell that they were both going to go through.

They lay spent. Not from lovemaking, but from all the bitterness and hurt that they realized would be ahead. In the middle of the night, Sandy took a hot shower and got control of her-self once again. The hot water felt good, and the pulsating water was burning her skin, but she didn't care. She liked the feeling of being able to hurt herself and having the ability to stop the pulsating hot water on her skin any time she wanted to. She didn't want to be a slobbering idiot and a person who felt sorry for herself. She wanted control, and at that moment, she didn't want anyone to feel sorry for her. She cried plenty when she was alone and didn't want the sympathy of those she loved. She wanted to die with dignity, and by golly, she was determined to try to have it that way. She realized that soon enough she'd be in hospice, and there would come a time when she would not be conscious of those around her. She wanted to tell Arthur that she didn't want a wake or funeral. She hated the thought that when she died, people would kneel by her side and tell other people that she looked good. She knew that wouldn't be the case. She was a small woman as it was, and she knew that she'd be losing weight the more the disease took control of her body. Now all she had to do was convince Arthur that she didn't want a wake, but instead a memorial where people would remember her as she was. She was a fun-loving person and one who didn't take pity easily. The only problem was her convincing Arthur to go along with her plans.

She wanted a real party, no crying from anyone, not Arthur, her children or grandkids, just a fun time. She wanted plenty of liquor and food to take away the real reason why people would be gathering at her memorial. Now the hard part, how could she play the part that she dreaded acting out? She only hoped that Arthur could keep himself contained and still have a great remainder of a vacation. She knew that it would be the last one that the two of them would be having and she wanted this to be one that Arthur would always remember.

The group was back on the boat and enjoying the many stories that they listened to as each couple told the others of their day's experience. Arthur and Sandy came from down below and the others wondered what had taken them so long. Most of the couples thought that they had been having a second honeymoon on this vacation and laughed to themselves as they watched the Swartz's come upstairs.

Suzanne was attuned to people's feelings and saw the red marks beneath Sandy and Arthur's eyes. She didn't say anything to Nancy or the others and decided maybe they had a disagreement, but doubted it. *'How could any couple have an argument on this great vacation,'* Suzanne thought to herself as she tried ignoring the obvious distraught feelings that the Swartz's displayed. Nancy nudged Suzanne when she saw the couple appear but ignored her friend. She'd talk to Nancy when they were in the privacy of their room.

While the others were talking, Suzanne tried remembering the different places that Sandy and Arthur visited on the different islands on the tour. Come to think of it, she thought of the different sights of interest that they visited, and besides the regular tourist attractions, Suzanne remembered how enthralled Sandy was as she told everyone about the cathedrals and houses of worship that she was determined to visit. At first Suzanne thought that it was unusual for a person to be that obsessed with visiting the different places of worship, but thought that it was their choice to do that. Who was she to dictate what a person or couple enjoyed visiting during their time to themselves?

Suzanne tried putting all negative thoughts out of her mind and enjoyed listening to the tales that the different couples were telling of their adventures.

When all were finished, Suzanne couldn't wait to get down below and tell Nancy of her observation. She realized she was being foolish and didn't want any more drama in her life. Nancy and she had gone through enough drama in their past experiences to last a lifetime. They finally made it back to their cabin and Suzanne told Nancy what she observed. "Oh Suzanne, I think you're making too much out of it. They might have had a disagreement, and you and I know that this can happen anywhere and anytime."

"Yes, Nancy, I guess you're right. I'll try to ignore the terrible feeling I have in my gut. But don't you think that since we've been on this trip, Sandy isn't looking as good as she did at the beginning of this vacation?"

"You know Suzanne, now that you mention it, Sandy does look a bit pale. It might be that she misses being home and it's too long of a voyage for her. Yes, that's probably all that's wrong."

With that said they both tucked themselves into their own beds and tried sleeping. Suzanne had a difficult time getting to sleep and kept having terrible thoughts of Sandy. The more she tried ignoring her feelings, the more awake she became. Finally she went to her suitcase and took out three Advil PM's and hoped that the magic blue pills would do their job. Before she realized it, she was sound asleep and her terrible thoughts and images had disappeared and she didn't remember anything when she awoke for another beautiful day on this magical Island.

Suzanne had received the addresses of her girlfriends' husbands' families and persuaded Nancy to go with her to say hello. They were very educated people, and Suzanne remembered that Mario's father was at one time the head of the Philippine University. His other brothers and sisters were lawyers, doctors and engineers. Yes, it meant getting a cab to take them to the suburbs, but she figured it was worth it. Nancy, at first, was skeptical, but Suzanne talked her into joining her on this adventure. "I know you really don't want to go, but think of it as a learning experience. This will show us how the wealthy Philippines live and it will be interesting. Besides, Ellen told them that we were going to make an effort to visit them, and I just happen to have a few telephone numbers that I took just in case we decide to go there."

Nancy could have killed Suzanne if she didn't love her so much. "Okay, but what a coincidence that you just happen to have their number with you. Sometimes you can really exasperate the shit out of me," she said to Suzanne as she gently punched her friend on the upper arm. "Good, I'm glad that you are coming with me. Now let's see if they're home or away on a Holiday as we are."

"Suzanne, you know as well as I do that they'll be home, so cut the shit and just make the phone call. I realize that we're going to be on this island for about three days, but I agree, in part, with what you're doing. How much shopping can one do? That is except for Isabelle!" They both laughed at Nancy's observation of one of the guests on board.

While Suzanne was making the phone call, Nancy happened to overhear one of the crewmembers relate an incident that happened on the South China Seas in and around the Philippines. She tried not to eavesdrop but couldn't help but listen to the two men talking. She didn't want to tell Suzanne of this but was debating whether or not something of this type of gossip was only gossip or if it really happened. Nancy hoped that it was only gossip, and she didn't want to have to go through another bad experience.

Suzanne was speaking to Alicia, one of Mario's sisters, who was a lawyer in Manila. She was thrilled that Alicia had made arrangements for her driver to pick the two women up at the dock when Suzanne called her. Suzanne was surprised but happy that everything was coming together. The two women were impressed by the large, beautiful house, which was located in one of the better suburbs. After eating a lovely breakfast prepared by Alicia's cook, they were mesmerized when Alicia took out some photo books from years ago and showed them what the old Manila looked like when she was a youngster. Alicia told them that she was a lawyer, which they already knew, but didn't know that she kept an apartment in the city and stayed there for the week and only came home on the weekends. Suzanne exclaimed, "Well, I can honestly say that I don't think I'll need any judicial representation while on vacation, but if we did, you would be the lawyer that we would call." Alicia was pleased with this pronouncement of their faith in her, although they didn't see her in work mode. After spending a good part of the day, the driver drove the two women back to the boat's dock and Nancy admitted to Suzanne that she had a wonderful time and thanked her profusely for including her.

The other couples were still out and about when the two women came back. They made their way to the cabin and on the way downstairs Suzanne overheard the hands gossiping about another ship that was hijacked and their goods stolen. She told Nancy of her inappropriate listening, but it still didn't discount her fear of what might happen if their sailboat was taken over and the pirates should take their new equipment and who knows what else from the ship.

Nancy advised Suzanne not to pay attention to idle gossip. For all they knew, that is all that is was. "Well, I hope that you're right Nancy. After all, I don't want to feel any negative energy and just want to think positively. It's when you think negatively, that energy will become a reality. Don't you dare tell the other people on board what you happened to hear;" Suzanne promised Nancy that she would keep that type of gossip to herself.

When the guests came back from the various places that they visited, they gathered around the living area of the ship and told every one of their experiences. Suzanne and Nancy were happy to hear that all had a great day. They also told the others what they did and the other guests were all ears listening to the women relate their experience of being with a resident of the Island.

Captain Bob informed his guests that they would go out fishing tomorrow and they'd leave early in the morning so they should be prepared to get up early. Chef André will make you a great breakfast to start your morning, although his breakfasts are usually great, this particular one will be extraordinary. As if she were asking permission, Renée raised her hand. Captain Bob acknowledged her. "I don't know how to bring this subject up, but I personally don't like to put those slimy worms or whatever you use on the end of the hook." Captain Bob laughed to himself and told Renée, or for that matter, anyone else who felt funny about handling the worms or dead fish bait that any of the crew members would be glad to assist them in doing that chore. "As a matter of fact, if anyone doesn't want to experience this fishing expedition, you can wear your bathing suits and lie on deck and soak up some nice rays of the sun. Would that please the people who aren't interested in fishing?"

The people on board were happy to hear of their options and not another word was spoken. As Sandy and Arthur were going down to their cabin, Sandy told Arthur about the gossip she had overheard while walking the streets of Manila. "I was with you all the time and I didn't hear that kind of news. Tell me more of what you heard when we're in the cabin because I don't want to frighten any of the other passengers with this idle gossip."

When they were alone, Arthur told Sandy, in no uncertain terms, that she wasn't to mention a thing that she overheard. Sandy promised her husband she would abide by his wishes. While in bed lying next to one another, Sandy brought up her wishes, if and when she became sick. She wanted no extraordinary life support measures taken because she felt that what will be, will be. "Like I promised you not to say anything about what I heard, I want you to promise me that you'll abide by my request." With a heavy heart Arthur shook his head and held Sandy tightly.

A few days went by and the Pirates met again at Mario's house. They couldn't stop talking and made sure that none of them had mentioned, even kiddingly, to any of their relatives or friends what they were doing. With affirmative nods, they made preparations for their next outing.

They would meet at six o'clock a.m. at the woods the following morning and then walk to the dock and have another fruitful day.

CHAPTER SIXTEEN

Tracy and Mike were full from all the food they ate and exhausted from walking from one end of Manilas' city to the other. The sunset that they observed was magnificent. Tracy wondered if it was the same sunset as she had always seen back in the States but never took the time to appreciate. After seeing the poverty and crowded conditions that people lived under, she was thankful that she was living where she did. She'd never take for granted how they lived and made a vow never to complain of mundane things that used to bother her. No, she would be grateful for everything.

While Mike was taking a well-deserved shower, she looked back at the wonderful vacation she had given Mike for his special birthday. It made her appreciate all the amenities that she took for granted. After seeing how most of the people lived here, she realized that she was spoiled and would never complain about the small things in life that used to haunt her. She made a vow never to be one of those princesses who always had to get everything her own way and didn't care who or what she hurt in order to get it. This vacation taught her that people are people all over the world and they each have their own problems.

When Mike came out with just a towel wrapped around his waist she knew that he wasn't thinking the same thoughts she was. He had something else on his mind, and she was just the person to make his wishes come true. He dropped his towel and she could tell that he was aroused when she was only in her underwear. "I'll be right back," she told her husband as she took a hot shower and was ready for him when she dried herself off.

He started kissing Tracy on the top of her head and gradually went lower and slowly kept going down. She was groaning with want. She could feel her inner being get wet with anticipation and stopped him when his head was between her legs. She took his hands and put them above his head. Tracy wouldn't listen to his protest as she nimbly kissed his nipples that were getting hard and erect. She went lower and started nibbling his abdomen and then his stomach. Then she went to the heart of his manhood and put his pulsating erection in her mouth. Mike was now emitting a noise that she had never heard before from deep within his body. Suddenly he pushed her aside and put her on her back. He mounted her and shoved his hard manhood into her wet, waiting, deep opening and together they moved in unison. Suddenly they both exploded at the same time. Later, she lay huddled in his strong arms; the feeling of protection was all around. She felt safe and knew that she had married the man of her dreams.

Renée and Paul were exhausted from all the places that they managed to visit this afternoon. She was glad that they met up with everyone and had that sumptuous dessert. Paul laughed at her when she got out her camera and took a picture when the desserts first arrived at the table and then managed to get a picture of everyone in their party, eating and enjoying the delicacy that was presented before them. She wished that they could have that type of concoction where they lived, but realized that it wouldn't be so intriguing if she could have it anytime she wanted. That was the beauty of this trip. She and Paul got to see how people from other countries lived and ate. She would never complain about little things again, she vowed. She appreciated that Newton wasn't as crowded as most of the places that they visited on this outstanding trip. She was excited about having many people at their house to show them all the pictures that they brought back. She was sure that people wouldn't have believed her if she didn't have this proof in hand.

Sam and Joe were lying in bed, relishing all the sights that were bestowed upon them. "You know we are two lucky people who have now been to places one only dreams of seeing," Joe spoke to Sam. "I've always loved where we lived. I mean Newport is surrounded by water. But some of the villages that we were lucky to see on the Junk and the various bridges that are thousands of years old are unimaginable."

"I agree with you one hundred percent. People at Verizon won't believe some of the pictures that we show them. Unless we had the proof, I'm sure that they would have thought that we're making this all up. In a way, I can't wait to get home and show off all of the things that we've seen."

"Well, I know how you feel, but for now we're here, and let's enjoy what time we have left." With that said Sam rolled over and started caressing his lover and the only person who could make him feel so loved and wanted. They fell asleep after making ferocious love in each other's arms.

Cole and Isabelle were deep in conversation and examining all the new items that Isabelle put carefully into the empty valise. "I can't wait to get back and show all of our mates these great items," Isabelle told Cole. "I'm sure that when we get back, that's the first thing that you'll do," chuckled Cole. When they lifted the valise off of the bed, they lay exhausted in each other's arms. "You know, luv, in a way I can't wait to get home. This Holiday has been wonderful, but after a while, how many river ways and crowded cities can one see?" Cole asked Isabelle as he slowly drifted off into oblivion.

Isabelle laughed to herself when she saw the deep sleep that Cole had gone into. She wanted to make love, but knew that he needed his sleep. Otherwise he'd be a bear in the morning and she didn't want any confrontation when they woke. She took a novel that she was reading and opened it up to the last page she had marked. When she started to yawn, she shut off the night light and dreamt wonderful dreams.

Nancy went off to sleep and she dreamed of Rich and the wonderful life that she anticipated having with him. She saw their future children and relished the idea of playing games and going clothes shopping with them. She knew that her time clock was ticking day-by-day. She also knew that in order to start a family with Rich they would have to start trying sooner rather than later. Then she thought of Mr. Yasuhito and the great time that the old Japanese gentleman would have living in their mansion. She was glad that he was recovering and was sure that when Rich asked him to come to Ipswich and live with him and Nancy, he would surely enjoy the challenge. She would not expect him to be at their beck and call like Mr. Makino often expected of his dutiful employee. She couldn't wait until he was living with them and could enjoy the peaceful walks along the hidden beach. He would be wonderful with their future children, she just knew it. He would probably teach them the art of self-defense and had visions of him teaching her how to cook the various dishes that she would relish learning. Little did she realize that Mr. Yasuhito cooked sparingly and enjoyed take out Chinese food like any other American.

Nancy was having a wonderful time dreaming while she slept and Suzanne felt awful when she had to wake her friend to tell her that it was time for another day of sightseeing. With a smile on her face, Suzanne gently nudged Nancy to wakefulness. Nancy was slow to rise. Suzanne could tell that her partner and younger best friend and sister dreamt about home and Rich. The smile that Nancy showed in her sleep confirmed what Suzanne was thinking. Suzanne was happy that Nancy finally found happiness. Now it was time for Suzanne to have the same. As much as Lawrence or Larry, as she liked to call him, had the patience of a saint, she realized that he couldn't wait for her to make up her mind forever. She was still angry with Stephen for his not getting in touch with her when she needed him. She realized that, although she would always love Stephen, they couldn't make their union last. She wanted a commitment that he couldn't give to her. No matter that he knew that commitment was the only thing that she asked for, he was either too selfish or didn't know why he couldn't fulfill her wishes. If he lived in the past, then let him. She had a future ahead of her and she was damned if she would live it alone. She wasn't getting any younger and when she got back home she would make up her mind, once and for all.

The group extended the day until it was getting dark. They realized that the end was nearing for this fabulous trip. They would be at sea and then would see Kota Kinabalu and Borneo, Malaysia. Suzanne was thinking that they were lucky that Bandar Seri Begawan, Brunel was very close to Malaysia. Then they would be heading back to where the trip started in Singapore. Suzanne and Nancy made sure that the pilots would be waiting for them on their return. As much as the two women enjoyed the vacation, they were anticipating going back home.

Using the highest sunscreen, Nancy made sure that she didn't get a sun-burn like a lot of the people of the group seemed to have. Suzanne laughed at Nancy as she saw her applying the heavy duty sun screen, but deep down, she also made sure that she protected herself as well. Too many times she saw the effects of what sun damage can do to one's skin. They lay on the deck, enjoying the rest and didn't want the pleasure of fishing. Yes, they would be two of the few people who'd rather be sunning than trying to catch a poor, unsuspecting fish from becoming the main course for a person's dinner.

Meanwhile, unbeknownst to everyone aboard the sailboat, six hungry fishermen were making their way back home to Manila where again they would split and divvy up the proceeds from their latest victims. That morning the Pirates had planned to take more money and equipment and then take a few weeks off. They didn't like it that the authorities were now warning most vacationers about the sordid actions of these criminals. "We're not criminals," shouted Sunny. "We are taking what we deserve, and rightly so," exclaimed Efran, as they got their weapons and walked quickly to their boat.

Mario explained to his friends, "You know that we've been lucky that none of the vacationers have put up a fight, but we have to be ready for that one day we'll encounter some passengers who won't be as easy to handle as the people who we've been taking from.

I've been hearing stories all over town about the 'New Age Pirates' who are making a bad reputation for turning what was once a vacationer's dream into a place to try to avoid."

"I don't like that type of talk. Let this be one of our last excursions and let a week or so go by and then we can start again," suggested Ronnie. They all shook their heads in agreement. Telemeo said; "We've been lucky that no one has been hurt so far, and let's try to keep it that way." All of the members of the group nodded their heads and made a pact to have this job be one of the last for a few weeks or so.

"Do you know that the police are getting involved and have issued warnings to other fishermen in the village to try to find out who these men are that are robbing these unsuspecting tourists," a serious Sunny said.

They walked quietly to the dock, keeping their inner thought to themselves, as they got ready for their last job for a few weeks.

Captain Bob and his crew got up early as usual and had a large, delicious breakfast waiting for the guests on his ship. Most of the people had signed up for the fishing expedition, and the few who didn't would enjoy the nice peaceful sunshine of the day. Chef André planned to make fish stew and serve the fish that people caught for their meal. He made sure that he had all the preparations waiting when they served their home-cooked meal. This was the meal that he most enjoyed because the people appreciated the fact that they caught the fish and would be proud that they were part of the planning of this fantastic dinner.

Mike helped Dick and Harry undo the knots and push the sailboat out from the dock. The anchor was pulled up, and Mike was excited about going fishing for the day. Tracy was beside him when he helped her hook the bait at the end of the line. He realized that she was a bit squeamish about the bait, but as long as she was a good sport about their expedition, that was all he could ask for.

The day was beautiful. It was bright and, sunny, with not a cloud in the sky. There was just enough wind to have the sailboat moving at a good clip. Captain Bob knew where there was a good spot to stop the boat and anchor it down for a while to see if the fish were biting. They were out about an hour when Captain Bob gave the order to anchor and see if any fish could be caught. The few people who decided to forgo this part of the trip were enjoying getting a great tan.

The pirates were heading out and made sure that they left the dock early, not to be seen by any of the local fishermen that knew of their hard times. They didn't want to have any attention drawn to them by others who they didn't trust. They made sure that they were the first ship to leave the pier. The men were used to getting up early, as when they were legitimate fishermen, they always left early to start their day. This was like an old habit.

When all the men were on board and the vessel was underway, they slowed down and changed the sails to show the hand-painted skull and cross bones that they cleverly made. They couldn't wait to change into the appropriate clothes and wondered whom they would encounter and surprise. The seas were calm, and the men leisurely got all of the necessary tools ready for them to make their surprise attack on an unsuspecting ship.

Sandy and Arthur were standing side by side with Cole and Isabelle next to them. On the other side of the ship, Joe, Sam, Mike and Tracy were all set and knew that patience in this particular sport was a virtue. Dr. and Mrs. Murphy were lying down beside Suzanne and Nancy exposing their skin to the sun's ever present illumination. Suzanne warned her fellow guests that they had to make sure that they had put on the proper strength of sunscreen lotion so not to get any needless exposure.

Dr. Paul Murphy assured the ladies that, being a doctor, he was well aware of the dangers of the sun. With that said they took out the books that the two couples were reading and relaxed for a pleasant day of doing nothing but enjoying the sun. The two couples were in their own worlds, reading the various books that they liked. Dr. Murphy enjoyed the Travel and Leisure magazines, while the women enjoyed the various authors and the characters that were created by famous authors that intrigued the seasoned readers. The rest of the guests on board were taking their time, waiting for the fish to take a bite of the various baits that were attached to the hooks at the end of the fishing poles. Sandy was getting aggravated and frustrated by just standing waiting for the fish to bite. "Hey, do you see that boat coming our way?" asked Tracy out loud. "We've been lucky so far that we've been the only boat in this area nearly all morning," Cole answered back.

Joe said: "Personally, I hope that they don't try fishing near us because I don't want any competition." With that said, they waited to see what the other boat would do. Sam exclaimed, "They seem as if they're coming our way. I wonder why they'd come so close to us?"

Mario was all pumped up with adrenalin going through his body. He hated doing what he knew had to be done, but still the thought of being a pirate was an unpleasant thought. He was waiting patiently for the ship to get by the sailboats side so they could board the ship. His mind suddenly went to his family, and just before he jumped onto the other vessel, he closed his eyes tightly, trying to rid his thoughts of his family waiting for him to come home.

Efran looked at his cousin Mario and was remembering all the fun times that they had as children in their village. He was lucky to have had close family living nearby. He too thought of his family that depended on him for their living and didn't like what he was about to do. There was no turning back. For that he was sure. Efran didn't want to harm anyone. He just wanted to do what he had to and get the Hell out of the financial hardship. He felt the adrenalin rush as he soared over the side of the fishing vessel onto the sailing ship. With deft hands he would do what he was trained to do and that was to fight with all of his might to keep the respect of his family and loved ones.

Sunny was pumped up with nervous energy as he thought of the job ahead of him. He didn't like this part of his life, but realized that he had to do what he had to do. His mind was full of all the good times that he shared with his family and friends, before his world came crashing down. His finances were a mess, and if this meant he had to become a pirate and steal, then so be it. He shook his head to remove any obstacles that were flooding his head with remorse. He leaped aboard the sailing vessel and knew what had to be done.

Tolemeo and Ronnie looked at each other with anticipation. There were all sorts of thoughts running through both men's minds. Tapping his pockets and holding onto the canvas bag that held the tape and rope that would tie their victims; he nodded to Ronnie as they vaulted over the side of the vessel, ready to do their job.

Before they realized what was happening, the Pirates from the other ship were coming closer than Joe wanted and before he realized what was happening, they jumped onto their vessel.

Cole yelled: "What the Hell is going on?" He got attacked by Sunny and was down on the floor before he knew it. The crew members of the expedition tried hurrying down the staircase, attempting to reach the rifles that were hidden in the storage compartments down below. Dick and Harry had seen the flag displayed on the other ship's mast and made a fast decision to reach the ammunition before the pirates climbed on board. As they were rushing down the staircase, Efran grabbed Dick by the back of his shirt and turned him around. With one mighty blow, he knocked Dick down and put the muzzle of the riffle to his throat. Harry turned around quickly when he saw that his twin was in trouble. Mario saw what Efran was doing and, while Harry grabbed hold of Efran's hair, to catch him off guard, Mario put the end of his rifle butt to the back of Harry's skull and knocked him out. Captain Bob, not as young as he was, was now bleeding profusely from the back of his head. There was a terrible scuffle. Suzanne and Nancy closed their eyes tightly, not wanting to see more bloodshed.

They opened their eyes, and Suzanne shook her head as to say "Don't say a word." Suzanne and Nancy looked at each other and without a word spoken, didn't make any movement to try and hide from these obvious intruders. Nancy whispered to Suzanne: "I don't think we're in a position to impose any of our learned techniques on these guys."

"Duh, you think so," Suzanne whispered back. "Let's see how this will play out." The two women watched as the pirates acted quickly tying up the people who were taken by surprise. Nancy saw some people running down below. It was if she was paralyzed and couldn't move. Everything was happening very quickly but as if Suzanne was seeing it in slow motion.

Paul and Renée had been the first to see the pirates, and before anyone could see them, they dropped their fishing rods and ran down the stairs to try to get the ammunition that they knew was kept there. Sandy and Arthur, who were beside the Murphy's, saw what was happening and were right behind them. Sandy was petrified, but at the same time, a feeling of calmness went through her body. She helped get the guns and whatever she could out of the closed cabinets that she was handed by an efficient Paul and Renée. She and Arthur took the weapons that were handed to them and saw that Tracy and Mike were behind them. Arthur diligently handed the ammunition to the others and found that in his haste, was dropping some of the weapons. He found that he was very nervous and had every right to be.

André, the cook, held his cleaver as a weapon of destruction when he came in contact with some of the thieves. He felt like one of the Three Musketeers. He wielded his cleaver as a bat, not really wanting to chop off one of the men's heads; he just wanted them to leave this vessel and be done with them. He found himself one person confronting two men. He kept swearing in French and with closed eyes, kept waving his cleaver as a sword. He was a bit out of shape and found it difficult to maneuver as well as he wanted to. These men were in good physical shape. He didn't know how long he could keep these thieves at bay. He hoped that someone would come to his rescue and relieve him.

André was still yielding his cleaver as a sword when one of the thieves dived to the floor and literally had the chef fall flat on his ass. On his way down to the floor he felt his cleaver hit one of the pirates' arms and heard the man yelp in pain. With that done, the pirates took the cleaver from the pudgy chef and hit him hard across his face with the wooden edge of the weapon. André could hear the crunch of his cheek. A good hard hit, connecting with his chin, knocked him out. He was down for the count. A man took his feet and dragged him up the stairs to join the others who were now subdued and hog tied to the bottom of the rails that were under the cushioned seats.

Meanwhile Sandy was holding the guns and loading the ammunition into the cartridges of the rifles and guns. Her fingers were trembling and she was seeing the ammunition fall to the ground faster than she was filling the cartridges. She was shaking like a leaf in a terrible wind. She doesn't know what happened next, but she suddenly got hold of Arthur and dragged him into their cabin and closed the door. "What the Hell are you doing?" asked a befuddled Arthur. She was talking quickly and it was hard for him to understand her. Her mind was going and thinking a million miles an hour.

"Arthur, I don't want any remarks or questions on what I'm telling you to do, but somehow I want you to shoot me. I'm not kidding." He looked at his wife as if she were crazy. "I know you think I've lost my mind, but I haven't. I know that my time is going by quickly and I won't be here in less than a year. I know you think I'm nuts, but I'm telling you I know my body and I know how I feel. We've worked too hard for what we have and I want you to kill me so you'll have all of the insurance money that we've put aside. I know, in the grand scheme of things, that you are the person, the man, who is supposed to die before his wife, but God didn't see it this way." With tears now streaming down her face she continued. All the while Arthur was shaking his head no and didn't want to face the facts that his wife was crazed. "I'm telling you, this makes sense. I will go quickly. I will be happy and know that you are well taken care of. We have to make it look like one of the pirates shot me in a scuffle. Don't argue with me, Arthur. Take me into the hallway and I want you to shoot me. You never were a good aim, except when your sperm would travel to my egg, so you better make this shot count. I'm hearing all sorts of yelling up stairs and, in a few seconds, we'll be confronted by these hooligans who will do all sorts of things to us."

Arthur was now shaking his head, denying what he was hearing come out of the mouth of Sandy. "I want you to shoot me and wipe your fingerprints off of the trigger and the gun." Being in control, she adamantly kept repeating instructions on what she wanted him to do. "You don't want me to suffer in agony from the cancer, do you???" He kept shaking his head no. "This is the only way that I know to go quickly and I won't have to suffer. Just make sure that you hit an organ. You know that I love you and I'm thinking of your future. You better not have any misgivings because this is the only way I know that will make me happy. Yes, it was something that I didn't think of, but when the opportunity arose, I want to make it happen. Can you understand my point of view, Arthur?" Tears were now running down both of their faces. "I hear the men coming, and I don't want any worries that I'll have to live in a vegetative state. I don't want the kids and our friends that I love looking at me with pity and saying, 'She was such a nice person and so young.' I don't want that kind of sympathy. Can you understand it?" He nodded his head in submission. "Quickly, I want us to leave this room and outside of our cabin, you shoot me in the back. Then confront the pirates and even if you get beat up, it will be your word against theirs that they killed me. So far they haven't been caught, and maybe they won't this time either. Now let's go." Before she opened the door she embraced Arthur with all of her might and kissed him as if this was the last kiss of her life. Tears were now on their faces but it didn't matter. Arthur knew that his wife was still sane, and he knew that she wanted to go out of this life in a way that was courageous and not having people fawning over her. She asked God to forgive her for what she asked her husband to do. She realized that she was being a coward to go out this way but she could see no other recourse. With a deep sigh, she helped Arthur open the door, and for a second had remorse over how she wanted to die. Maybe she was wrong in asking Arthur to kill her. Her head was spinning and she didn't know what she wanted. Was it crazy for her to act on impulse and to take advantage of the moment? Her head was spinning and before she could take back her desire, she turned to close the door and she knew that Arthur was going to shoot the rifle. *'Oh God,'* she thought to herself, *'Please forgive me!!!!!'*

After their embrace, Arthur opened the door and saw the pirates coming toward them. Before they could confront the couple, Arthur fired his rifle into his wife's back and neck. She fell instantly. He turned around and faced his adversaries. The men were shocked at what they saw. He quickly wiped his prints off of his weapon and started battling the men who were quickly upon him. He heard yelling, and then he was whirled around and hit on his body and face. Arthur put up a good battle but soon he found himself being dragged up the stairs. His eye was already closed and puffed out. His nose was bleeding profusely and it hurt him to move. He was sure that a rib or two was broken. He heard the men yelling at each other in a foreign language but didn't want to know what they were saying to each other. Tracy and Mike, Joe and Sam were captured, but not before the men gave the pirates a good fight. Tracy used her nails and clawed the faces of the men who tried to tie her down.

Suzanne and Nancy, ran from their cabin after not being seen sunning themselves by the pirates. They wanted to get their computers hidden so they wouldn't be confiscated by these evil and nasty men. But before they ran, Suzanne thought that she saw Sandy and Arthur closing the door to their quarters. Was she seeing things as she saw the pirates run down the stairs, and suddenly she thought she saw Arthur shoot his wife in the back! Sandy fell instantly, blood already pooling around her. They tried running upstairs but were being shoved by some of the pirates. They saw their fellow guests tied like hogs with tape across their mouths. The Captain and crew looked like they had looked when Rich and the rest of the detectives and police found them in the home of Mr. Yoshy at the beautiful cabin in Beppu, which was in Kyushu, Japan. Suzanne was glad that the awful brutal beatings that she and Nancy endured were part of the past and she didn't want any more occurrences like that happening to them again. Memorizing the pirates' faces, being an artist at heart,

Suzanne looked for any distinguishing marks on which she could focus. She was looking at the other members of the party and didn't see Sandy among them. She tried elbowing Nancy but found that Nancy was trying to stay calm and not let the gruesome peoples' faces get in way of her meditation. Anything that helped her not face reality was okay with Suzanne, as she didn't want to see Nancy get in another tailspin of utter dismay and humiliation.

She saw that Arthur was coming to, and he kept saying Sandy's name. As awful as the other guests and crew looked, Arthur looked devastated. She saw the pirates hauling electrical equipment into their boxes and realized that they probably found the money that was stashed in each person's cabin. The pirates then came back upstairs and literally ripped off any jewelry that anyone had on them and put the items into a canvas bag. Suzanne could only assume that the rest of their money was taken from her and Nancy's wallets. Most of the people had exchanged their currency to Travelers checks so they could get their monies reimbursed. She saw that the weapons that were on board the ship were now in the hands of the pirates and were being taken off the boat.

Suzanne noticed that one or two of the pirates had large gashes on their arm. She also noticed that some of the intruders had been injured during the mélée, they certainly didn't leave in the same shape as when they jumped aboard. For that, Suzanne was happy. She couldn't wait to be rescued; by whom she didn't know, but that couldn't come fast enough.

Suzanne realized that Harry and Captain Bob were badly injured. The rest of the men didn't look so good either. But the blood that was dripping profusely from Harry's skull was starting to slow down. Maybe his body's clotting power was starting to work? She didn't want to see any of her friends, who had already been man-handled, injured to the extent that they would be injured for life. Dr. Murphy, when he was released would help the injured, she was sure of it. She would do her part in helping people who were in worse shape than she and Nancy were. Suzanne was grateful that they knew better than to get into a fighting contest with these barbarians, knowing that the outcome wouldn't be a good one. She saw Chef André coming to and noticed that he was groaning from the injuries he sustained. His chef's outfit was a bloody mess. She then noticed that Isabelle and Cole were still groggy from all of their fighting with the pirates and then noticed that Cole had a deep gash across his cheek. The blood had poured onto his chest and was now not dripping as intensely as it was when she first saw him. Isabelle was crying and the more that she looked at her husband the more she cried.

The people were coming around, trying with all of their might to untie the ropes that were holding them in place. The more that they struggled, the tighter the bindings were becoming. They couldn't talk to each other for the tape was held across their mouths. Suzanne could feel the adhesive on her skin. She suddenly went slack, realizing that the more she fought to free herself from the bindings, the tighter they were becoming. She prayed that they would be found shortly, before the flies that were now gathered around the dying fish on board, could start crawling on her own unprotected skin. She saw the flies swarming on her friends' bodies and wanted to throw up. She realized that her vomit had to be contained due to the tape holding her mouth closed. She saw the other people closing their eyes at the gross pillage and decided to do the same. She looked at Nancy, their eyes communicating concern, but she realized that they had no control over the situation that they found themselves in.

Nancy felt as if she were having an out-of-body experience. She looked around her and saw destruction and bleeding people everywhere. Tears were now flowing down the face of Renée as she saw Paul for the first time, not able to do anything to help people who were injured and hurt. She knew that Paul was incapable of helping those people, who had become like family, and felt the helplessness that he was experiencing.

Renée wanted to swat the flies that were crawling on her face, hair and exposed body parts but was incapable of lifting a finger. Cries were emitting from her tired and hurting body. She closed her eyes, trying to ignore the helplessness that she was feeling. She saw Isabelle crying and her body heaving up and down. She wanted to hug those people that she had grown to love and felt vulnerable and weak.

It was at that point that Tracy opened her eyes and noticed that Sandy was not among the people who were on deck. She looked all around but couldn't imagine what or where Sandy was. She saw Arthur, who was white as a ghost, his entire body shaking uncontrollably. Because of the gauze, she couldn't ask Arthur where his wife was, and she was afraid of the answer she'd hear. She did remember hearing the sound of gunfire from down below but thought that it was a figment of her imagination. Now she wasn't sure if it were real or imagined. She kept praying that someone or some boat would come to their rescue before any more damage occurred.

About three hours had gone by and then another fishing boat spotted the lone sailing ship drifting with what seemed like no one on board. The vessel got closer and then realized that the people were on the deck and tied and couldn't utter a sound. With swift movements the men climbed aboard and started untying the shipmates and people who were injured. Everyone started shaking their hands and feet to get the circulation back. The good doctor, who was injured himself, went to the first-aid kit and started swabbing the injured and then ran downstairs to get his medium-sized black bag. "You know that Renée yelled at me for taking this on board, but God knew that I'd need it one way or the other. I'm glad that I didn't listen to her," Paul said aloud to anyone who was listening.

When they were being pulled back to the dock by the other ship, Suzanne ran downstairs and stopped abruptly. She pulled Nancy close to her chest so Nancy couldn't see the body of Sandy, lying in the middle of the aisle, in front of her cabin door. Suzanne yelled for Arthur, who was halfway down the stairs, when he spotted his wife. "She died instantly and didn't suffer," was all that Suzanne could say to Arthur who cradled his wife's now cold body into his warm one. He hadn't wanted to do what she wanted him to do, but now that reality set in, he wanted his body heat to give her life. Suzanne tried to console him, but realized that nothing she said would have any effect on Arthur. At that moment, Suzanne hated the pirates and wanted retribution for their acts of inhumanity. *'How could they have shot her like a piece of meat, an innocent bystander'* she thought to herself. *'She was one of us. Sandy was enjoying this cruise and she was an innocent victim of violence.'* Suzanne kept shaking her head, not wanting to believe what she saw before her. Then a minute or two elapsed and something she didn't want to remember suddenly appeared before her. Was it a fantasy that she was thinking of? She thought that she saw Arthur shoot his wife in the back? That couldn't have been what she really saw, she thought to herself. *'No it was just a figment of my imagination.'* It was then that she smelled the iron that was blood pooled around poor Sandy.

The people were escorted to the local police station. The people on board were lucky that Dr. Murphy was one of the passengers and had helped with the stitches and cleaning of the wounds sustained in the mêlée. They were then taken to the hospital where the doctors and nurses would perform a more thorough evaluation of the sailors and the guests aboard 'Vacation of a Lifetime.' Nancy overheard Captain Bob exclaim that in his career he never experienced such a cruise.

'This is supposed to be fun for all. With the sudden storm, Suzanne going overboard and now this, I'm thinking of retiring. This is ridiculous!!!' Captain Bob was talking to the authorities and couldn't believe that Sandy had been shot. In all of his life, nothing like this had happened. He heard stories, but never thought that his life would be impacted in such a way as this. When he heard about Sandy, he literally threw up. He remembered the happy couple and how their children had called and made the reservations for their parents' fortieth or forty-fifth wedding anniversary (his mind was in shambles). He felt sorry for Arthur, who had to be the one to go home and tell his children about the tragedy

that happened. '*They won't be able to forgive themselves. They'll think it was their fault that she was killed. She wouldn't have taken this sailing vacation if her children didn't give them this trip as an anniversary gift.*'

Suzanne and Nancy called the pilots and crewmembers of their plane and made arrangements for them to meet them at the airport in Singapore. They realized that this trip was now officially over. Suzanne still was beside herself with grief and wondered how Arthur was holding up. Nancy went over to Suzanne and held her like a mother consoling a child. Suzanne went back into the cabin when they finished up at the hospital and police station. She imagined that she was still in shock but wanted to go to the others, and especially Arthur, and tell him how sorry she was. Of all the people on board, it was Arthur who needed all the support that was now necessary for them to give him. Suzanne fell onto her bed and cried like a baby. She didn't know why she was taking this incident so badly, but really didn't care. This was how she felt and if she wanted to cry, then by God, she would cry until there were no more tears left in her body.

All the guests and people who were civilians and lived in the village came on board to say their farewells. The mates and the people, who were vacationing on board Vacation of a Lifetime, thanked the people of the village for all of their generosity and condolences. Everyone on board thanked the people who had helped them in their time of need. Suzanne and Nancy knocked on Arthur's cabin door and realized that it would take a few moments for him to gain his composure and greet them. When he opened the door, the two women could see that he was crying. His eyes were still swollen with red blotches all over his face and especially around his eyes. The women didn't know what to say to this grief stricken man.

"Come in, come in. I think everyone is avoiding me because of what happened to Sandy. I couldn't do a thing. She wanted to go that way." He kept repeating and repeating the same words. Suzanne and Nancy looked at each other with questions that they knew shouldn't be asked. After trying to console him, Suzanne and Nancy went upstairs to where the other people were gathered. They didn't tell the others that they had visited Arthur in his cabin. The rest of the party thought that the two women were in their own cabins resting. Once the police questions were answered, it would take a few days to travel back to Singapore but the festive mood was no longer an option.

Captain Bob and his crew, as soon as they left the hospital, went to the various equipment places and replaced the parts that were necessary to guide the ship back to its port in Singapore. Chef André was very quiet when he was preparing the meals for the people on board. He wasn't his jolly self and the more he thought of his confrontation with those awful men, the angrier he became.

Suzanne and Nancy were lying in their cabin, their minds thinking of all the happy times that they and everyone had experienced. Suzanne had to tell Nancy of Arthur's strange behavior and the words she kept hearing him utter when he didn't think anyone was listening. She didn't know when a good time would be for her to tell Nancy of Arthur's strange behavior. Suzanne knew that Nancy would make excuses for his actions but there was something that didn't make any sense.

Suzanne had asked different people who lived in the village about these New Age Pirates and the various boats that they had attacked. In listening to their reactions, not any of the victims had been attacked as viciously as the way that Vacation of a Lifetime was. It didn't make sense to Suzanne why the response was so very different in this circumstance. She didn't want to bring up the subject of her questions to Nancy but knew that the subject had to be mentioned.

The police appreciated the help that Suzanne offered to the police artists when asked if she could help them with the drawing of the pirates. They had heard of Suzanne and her artistic talent and thought that she would be able to assist them. Suzanne was more than happy to oblige. Suzanne closed her eyes and, after a while, she was able to come up with the various shaped faces, their features and in some cases little variations that distinguished them from other people. She remembered that one man had a large brown birthmark on his left arm. Another pirate had a slight variation on his eyebrow, which was different than the other side of his face. On another man, she remembered a definite broken nose and how it was distorted. It left an impression of the way it took away from the beautiful eyes that were above this hideous punched, mangled and flattened nose. On another pirate, she remembered the definite cleft in his chin that enhanced his good looks.

With most of the pictures finished, Suzanne took a look at what the artist was able to accomplish and appreciated the work. She went back to the ship and was proud that she was able to do her part in helping the police apprehend the New Age Pirates.

CHAPTER SEVENTEEN

Mario and his gang of pirates hadn't wanted to cause the destruction that occurred, as it would ultimately bring mayhem and unwarranted notoriety. They walked glumly back to the forest where they put down their loot and made a fire. It was getting cooler and it seemed right for the men to talk around the hot, yellow and blue, flames that were spewing over the dead branches and logs.

Mario started off by clearing his throat and, with his face downcast, broke the silence. "I don't know what to say. I'm as dumbfounded as I'm sure all of you are. We all had our designated jobs, and I really believe we've been efficient in doing them. Who the Hell would have thought that such a fight would ensue?" He looked up and told the men that he saw were visibly wounded and that they should go to a local doctor they could trust. "We have to find a doctor who won't tell a soul that he fixed our wounds. We know all the locals, and as long as we say that we got into a fight with each other and got carried away, (he showed the men the deep gash in his arm, thanks to chef André) we might be able to let this incident go by."

Sunny shook his head vehemently, "I don't think it's going to be as easy as we think it is. We are now wanted men. These bozos will think that we killed that poor woman, who we don't know from a hole in the wall. I don't know what to do and I'm honest enough to admit it. I have a friend who went to medical school and for some reason, didn't finish. We'll all go to him and he'll patch us up."

The others nodded their heads in agreement. It was apparent that they weren't the happy, enthusiastic men that came back from their other ventures slapping each other's hands and anxiously waiting to divvy up the loot and money. Efran, was listening intently to the conversation, but in his mind all sorts of wild thoughts were filling his brain with confusion. Efran spoke softly, until the others asked him to speak louder so he could be heard.

"I really am not ashamed to admit that I'm scared shitless. I almost crapped in my pants when I saw what was happening with these people, who we all thought, would be as complacent as the other people we robbed. But no, they acted like the devil himself, fighting back with all the muster and gusto within them. Yes, thankfully, we won, but at what price? Now we have the police looking for us with as much zeal that is possible. It would give the department nothing but pleasure to see all of us apprehended and see our asses hauled off to jail."

The rest of the group nodded in agreement. Tolemeo spoke his piece: "Not only are they looking for pirates who are ruining their tourist season, but now we're considered murderers. I didn't kill anybody, and I don't care what those people say they saw, they didn't witness what I saw before my very eyes. Will they believe us when we tell them that we didn't shoot that woman?"

"Of course not!!" screamed the rest of the men. The others nodded their heads in agreement as they tore their shirts to make tourniquets for their body parts that were visibly sore with blood coming out of their wounds.

Tolemeo continued, "Those people acted as though they were possessed. What the Hell caused that man to shoot that woman in the back like he did??? I didn't see that coming," announced Tolemeo, with tears in his eyes.

Ronnie put his arm around Telemeo's shoulders and didn't mind the others seeing his affection for his cousin. "We'll hide out for a while, after the doc fixes us up. Then, when we return to our homes, not a word of any of this will be discussed. I don't care if you think that what you tell your spouse will stay in confidence. All women have big mouths and don't know when to shut them. As for the rest of you guys, I don't care if we go to the bar and get loaded as shit. We're not to glorify what we've done or let anyone know that we are the pirates or that you are one of them. Do I make myself clear?" Each man nodded and when Ronnie put his hand out the other fishermen grabbed their friend's hands and made the pact of a life span.

Ronnie continued; "In another six weeks, after this incident subsides, we can continue our quest to get enough money. No old contract by the Chinese government or whoever is going to take away my right to make a living! Would I like to go back to fishing and having it easy? Sure, I'm like all of you; we've been hit between our eyes and feel terrible that we can't do what we really want to do."

Mario got up and, with diligence, started putting out the roaring fire. He felt the chill in his bones when they were trudging out of the woods and was no longer comforted by the flames of the roaring blaze. They followed Sunny to his friend's house, hoping that he was home. With individual thoughts running through their heads, they silently walked the walk of the defeated.

When Sunny got to the neat little cottage on the outskirts of town he knocked demurely. His friend's mother answered the door and Sunny asked if Phillipe was home. She ushered the men into the house as if she had blinders on. "I guess she's used to people knocking on her door," Mario whispered to Efran.

The men smiled when their wounds were fixed to the best of Phillips ability and given antibiotics that he dispensed. They patted Sunny with affection when they left the house. "Now be sure, we go home and give our wives the money and don't say a word to anyone about this incident. If we see each other in the local tavern, only our eyes and hearts will know what we know. I think that the coast will be clear enough for us to resume work. But the next time we go out, we'll make sure that the people that we want to rob will be only a few in their party. I never want to get myself involved in mayhem like we've experienced. Is that clear to everyone? We'll be seeing each other at the tavern and we'll know when the time is right for us to head out to the open seas once again," declared Mario as he turned off the main road, headed for his small but clean home and refuge.

Efran spoke loudly so that Mario and his friends could hear, "If any of our families should ask how we got our wounds we should all have the same story. I think we should tell them that we were jostling." With that said they all shook their heads in agreement, and Mario shook his head also as he walked wearily to his cottage on stilts.

The police were baffled after they interrogated the crew members and the guests of the 'Vacation of a Lifetime.' This wasn't the first time that the new age pirates had violated the waters of the South China Seas. They still didn't have a clue about these new hoodlums. Usually word gets out on the streets about the banditos that someone knew or had an idea of the people that were causing the mayhem on this lazy and perfect island that many sail people used as a stopping ground for supplies on their trips.

There were many branches of police departments that had been established in 1991 in the Philippines. Officially it is now called the Philippine National Police (PNP). The PNP was formed when the Philippine Constabulary and the Integrated National Police were merged. It is part of the Department of the Interior and Local Government. The national headquarters is at Camp Crame in Quezon City, Metro Manila. It has 140,000 personnel. Part of the branches included the PNP Maritime Group.

Chief Raul Luna was sitting at his desk, reading the latest report given to him by one of the police captains and kept putting it down, picking it up, and reading it again. He was furious. With his network of informants on the streets, not one had come forth with names of people who could be the latest thieves who were acting like the pirates of years ago. He pressed the intercom and told his secretary that he didn't want to be disturbed. He shook his head and pressed the intercom for his secretary to get the Police Brigadier General Antonio Bautista on the line and into his office immediately.

It took about fifteen minutes for Brigadier General Bautista to knock on Chief Luna's door. "Come in, come in, Antonio." Raul motioned for the General to take a seat in front of his desk. "As you know, we have had terrible press about these robberies, beatings and now the ultimate disgrace, a passenger on one of the sailboats has been killed. We cannot afford such publicity. It was bad enough when the departments had scandals, shootouts, blackmail incidents, torture, massacre, failed hostage rescue operations, and worst of all, our secret detention facility, 'Wheel of Torture,' was discovered. Now another embarrassment plagues the department! We can't afford such bad talk and gradual resentment towards the PNP. Before you know it, we'll be having Interpol and a lot of outsiders in our midst and sticking their noses into our business." Brigadier General, Antonio Bautista, could see the redness creeping up from Chief Raul Luna's neck onto his entire face. "Do you have any suggestions or are we going to sit back, make a half-assed effort to find these banditos or wait for Interpol to come and take over the department and find the people who are responsible for these incidents?" Antonio Bautista could tell that with each accusation and assessment of the case involved, Chief Raul Luna was getting more agitated and angrier with each passing minute.

Clearing his throat, hoping that he didn't notice the heat coming from the top of his Chief's head, he gave his opinion on what he would do. "If you don't mind me saying, sir, I agree with you that we have to capture these banditos as soon as possible. I've been having my officers get in touch with their informants, and so far, nothing is happening. I understand your frustration. We've heard about the new age pirates who have been attacking the boats outside of Somalia. Everyone knows about the Philippines attacking the Chinese fishermen. But this is altogether different. These pirates are most likely Philippine fishermen who need the money. Our Naval officers will be on the lookout, I assure you. I realize that the antipiracy efforts are also greatly hindered by the system of ship registration. I truly believe that the ship these pirates are using has falsified documents. They probably change flags when they are out to sea. What I need to do is use more men and ships to scour the area for any vessels that are not up to par. Years ago there was an IMO survey that found over thirteen thousand cases of falsified documents of sea-farers; most of them were from Indonesia and the Philippines. They are probably using false identities. I really don't believe that these men are from organized crime. If they were, then they'd be hijacking larger vessels and cargo ships. That's my take on it."

Chief Luna listened intently to what General Antonio Bautista was saying and nodded his head with agreement. "Okay, we have to bring the sailing ship into port and not let it go anywhere until I question all of the passengers on board. That will include the ship's crew as well. I want all the registration numbers of their equipment, if they have it, and I think that the captain will have that information written down somewhere. We'll have our police check all the shops and fences that we know of and really come down hard on them. They'll have no other choice but to tell us or inform us if they hear anything from their friends. Something is bound to show up. We'll find out what jewelry was taken and go to all the pawn shops and other places where they can get money for these pieces. I'll want a memo circulated to all of the department heads, and they'll give the list to all of their men. First, let's get the crew and the party on board that vessel in for interrogation. I'll personally conduct the questioning and find out all that I can about what happened. It certainly didn't go as those pirates thought it would." With a shake of his head he dismissed General Bautista and waited for the arrival of all the people involved in the crime.

Suzanne and Nancy were lying down on their bunks when they heard a knock on the door. Nancy got up to open the door and found Dick Bogart, one of the twins, with hat in hand, moving from one foot to the other. He was obviously nervous when Nancy invited him into their small quarters. "Oh that won't be necessary, Ms. Tremblay, I just wanted to inform you that Chief Luna from the PNP wants everyone that was onboard ship to go down to their headquarters and tell them, in your own words, what you saw and what happened. All of the crew is also going so you won't be alone. Let's say we'll all meet on the top deck in about fifteen minutes. Is that okay with you ladies?" Suzanne spoke for both of them, "Of course it is. We'll meet you up on the deck." When the door was closed, Suzanne and Nancy looked at each other and didn't know what to say. "We have to get our stories straight you know. We can't go in there and not tell them what we saw. Before we go, I think it best if we go to Arthur's room and try to talk to him. I wasn't hallucinating when I saw Arthur shoot Sandy in the back. I wasn't hallucinating was I?" Suzanne asked Nancy as much as telling herself that she wasn't being delusional. Nancy put her head between her hands and spoke. "You and I know what we saw, but they seemed like such a wonderful couple. What would make Arthur do such a thing to his wife? Kill her in cold blood! It doesn't make sense." Suzanne then said, "Well, everyone always says you never know what happens behind closed doors. Maybe what we saw of them when they were in mixed company wasn't what their life was all about. I don't know. If I had certain powers, like being psychic, we wouldn't be facing this challenge." (little did Suzanne realize that as she matured her psychic powers were increasing!) Come on let's go to Arthur before he goes up to the deck." With that said both women got off the beds and closed the door behind them. Looking both ways, they made their way to Arthur and Sandy's room, hoping that Arthur was still there.

Suzanne knocked on the cabin door and Arthur hesitantly opened the door. Suzanne cleared her throat and asked Arthur if she and Nancy could come in before they went up on deck and go to the police headquarters with the rest of the people on board the ship. "Of course, how rude of me, come in, come in, gestured Arthur. Pardon the appearance of the room, but Sandy usually straightened out the cabin so it was habitable."

"We won't take a lot of time," Nancy assured Arthur. Nancy didn't know how to approach the subject and looked at Suzanne for assistance. Suzanne inched forward a bit and spoke. "Arthur, Nancy and I were running out of our cabin when the pirates were running and a lot of yelling, screaming and chaos happened. But I must admit that when we were running out of our room, we saw you and Sandy coming out of your cabin. We saw that you had a riffle in your hand, and you shot your wife in the back. Now we consider you more than acquaintances and almost like part of a family that we've grown to love. Please, we implore you to tell us what the Hell happened."

Arthur was dumbstruck that someone had seen the actual shooting. He was at a loss for words. He realized that it would be his word against theirs. "I don't know what you're talking about," Arthur stated. "Sandy was shot by those awful pirates that came aboard the vessel, and besides killing my innocent wife, they looted all that they could and ran away. You must have been imagining what you saw because we were in the same situation that you were in." Suddenly, Arthur started crying and trying to hold back the tears that were falling from his eyes. The two women could see his fragile state and realized that it would be their word against his. Suzanne and Nancy looked at one another; not trying to argue with this man who they could tell was distraught. "Okay then, let's all go upstairs and go to the police station and give our statements," Suzanne said, as she opened the cabin door for all of them to make their way to the top deck.

Suzanne and Nancy let Arthur go ahead of them and Nancy shook her head and looked at Suzanne as if to say, *'what the heck was that all about?'* The two women let Arthur go upstairs and they stayed down in the aisle for a while. Nancy asked Suzanne what she thought was going on. "I really don't know, but I do know that we are not crazy and we saw what happened. At this point I don't think we should go to the authorities. But I, for one, am going to find out more about Sandy and Arthur and get to the bottom of this. What happens if the police do find the pirates and then bring them to trial for murder? We know that pirating is awful, but, on the other hand, I don't want to see a person being convicted for something that they didn't do."

"I'm with you on that," Nancy affirmed. "Let's see what happens when we go to the police station and then we can talk more about this state of affairs when we're alone and no one can hear us," Suzanne stated.

It was a glum group that traipsed into the police headquarters led by Captain Winters with everyone else following behind him. He was greeted by a policeman at the front desk and told where to go. They saw the man in charge of homicide and then the group of policemen that were searching for the pirates came over to the sorry-looking group. The introductions were made and then they were led into a conference room. It contained a long table with chairs around it and no other accessories, except a large mirror, which Suzanne and Nancy thought would be a two-way mirror with others able to look into the room and hear what was said.

Introductions were made and the people all took their seats. Captain Winters took the lead and told the policemen what had happened. From there, the men of authority took over and asked the group to make out individual lists that consisted of their jewelry and money that was stolen and asked the Captain to make out a list of his equipment with their serial numbers on it. They asked the people who had jewelry stolen to give, as best that they could, a precise description of the pieces stolen and about how much each piece was worth. Suzanne and Nancy were glad that they hadn't brought very much jewelry with them and certainly not any that was worth that much in monetary value. They didn't suspect that the others had, but couldn't be sure. When they were packing for the trip, Suzanne had told Nancy what kind of vacation it was going to be and cautioned her about not taking anything significant in the way of jewelry. She was glad that Nancy had listened to her.

Suzanne's head was spinning, as if everything was on a recording device and going out of control. Everyone's voice was in high pitch and she couldn't stop the voices that were giving her a headache. She heard Arthur telling the police his version of the shooting and Suzanne was sickened when listening to his story. She knew that he was lying, and also realized that it would be her and Nancy's word against Arthur's. When the detective came over to write down her account of what she remembered happening when the pirates took over the ship, she of all people, was suddenly at a loss for words. Suzanne shook her head and closed her eyes. She didn't want to divulge the horrendous act that she saw happening before her eyes. She realized that before she uttered another word, except for the money and jewelry that she had lost to those awful men and the small trinkets that she had brought on board, she and Nancy would have to discuss what to do about the deceitful act that happened before their eyes. The police kept the crew and all the members of the party about two hours before they let them go back to the ship. They reminded the people on board that they were to stay in port until the complete investigation was finished and they would have a chance to apprehend the pirates.

Going back to the ship, Nancy and Suzanne were quiet. They both knew what they saw, but wanted to discuss what they would say and do when they were in their cabin, behind closed doors. Everyone was talking at once. Arthur was walking with Cole and Isabelle and listened to their pity and condolences for this man, whose wife was shot in the back running back into the cabin. It sickened the women as they heard Arthur's response when they knew what really happened. Suzanne didn't care if the other members of the group didn't understand how the two women could be so cold and uncaring during Arthur's time of need and grief. *'If only they had been there and seen for themselves what really took place, maybe then they could understand our situation'* Suzanne thought to herself.

Suzanne and Nancy excused themselves after everyone else climbed aboard The Vacation of a Lifetime sailing vessel. Everyone else was at the tables waiting for a nice meal and wondered why Suzanne and Nancy were back in their cabin. Arthur realized that they were having a hard time with what they saw, but he promised Sandy he wouldn't tell anyone why he did what he did and he was a man of his word. He kept hearing what the people around him were saying, but was in a world of his own. He realized that Suzanne and Nancy had seen him put the fatal bullet into Sandy's back but he promised his wife that he wouldn't tell anyone what happened and, by golly, a pledge was a pledge. It was their secret forever!!!

Suzanne and Nancy sat on their respective beds and looked at each other. Not a word was spoken. A lone tear dropped from Nancy's eye and suddenly she couldn't stop the agony and heartfelt feelings that were raging through her mind and body. She started sobbing bitterly and Suzanne went over, put her arms around her friend and hugged her tightly. Patting Nancy's back, Suzanne kept saying over and over again that she understood. Suzanne calmed Nancy down and told her that, when they returned home, they would get to the bottom of this tragedy. Nancy didn't want to wait until they returned home and wanted to get everything attended to while they were still on the Island of the Philippines. "I have a feeling that Arthur won't say anything to us about what really happened unless he's forced to," Suzanne said aloud. "I think you're right about that, but we have to find some way to get him to tell us why he did what he did. Do you think we'll be able to get him to confess to us?" Nancy asked Suzanne.

"I think tomorrow morning I'll give our friends in the FBI a call and see what they have to say about what we saw. If they have to have us go to Interpol and get their help in the matter, we'll do it. We can't sit around and do nothing."

"I agree with you, Suzanne, but I want to find out a few things from Arthur before we involve Interpol. It's going to take a few days for all of the information that everyone gave to the police to get absorbed and then to try to get the pirates is another project. We'll be lucky if we get through with this terrible scenario within two to three weeks."

"I'm afraid that I agree with you," Suzanne said as she sat glumly on the bed.

"Let's go upstairs, and if anyone should ask why we went to our cabins, which I doubt, we'll tell them that we wanted to straighten out a few matters at the shop. People will understand," a determined Nancy replied.

"Lucky that we can use the computers and that will explain how we're keeping abreast of our salons' operations from day to day," Suzanne spoke as she re-applied her make-up and motioned for Nancy to come with her.

When the two women were seated around the table, Arthur refused to look their way. Suzanne didn't make much of this and realized what he must be going through but still knew that she had to get hard facts. Like Joe Friday from Dragnet used to say, just the facts!!! Well, she understood those words and, by hook or by crook, she'd get to the bottom of what happened and why. She knew that it was going to be a tough assignment, but heck, she and Nancy had more than their share of rough missions that they had to get through. This was going to be a hard one, but she knew that they could get it done. It was a matter of time, and then she wondered if they had enough time to obtain all the information that they needed before they left the port.

While Suzanne was in bed, hands behind her head, she tried thinking of Alan, and how wonderful a friend he was. She'd be forever grateful for his introducing Suzanne to Nancy. Instead thoughts of Stephen and Larry entered her mind. She realized that Stephen was as stubborn as she was and wouldn't contact her until she made the first move. Then she became agitated because he wanted her to call first and she was damned if she would let herself be the first one to make contact. Larry's face came before her and a smile became visible. He was such a wonderful person and, as hard as she tried not to have a physical relationship with him, the more she realized that it was getting more difficult each time she saw him. If he had his way they would be seeing each other on a regular basis and by now an intimate relationship would be happening. She was getting to the point where every time she thought of Stephen, feelings of disappointment, frustration and finally anger would take over her thoughts. She didn't want to think of her own life at this point when she knew that she should be thinking of the present situation and knew that Sandy's unexpected death (or murder as she saw it) should be paramount on her mind.

Nancy was on the next bed and thoughts of Rich couldn't be reined in. She saw his face in front of her and suddenly her womanly assets were tingling and she would give anything to be in his arms. She wondered how much longer they would be detained at port, and by now, she couldn't wait to get home and be in his embrace, loving him and knowing what they had with each other. Nancy looked at Suzanne and realized that her friend was having conflicting feelings herself. By the look on Suzanne's face, Nancy could tell that all sorts of tensions were whirling within her. She wished that she could take all her confusion away, but realized that only Suzanne could do that. She was her best friend, but Suzanne had to separate her feelings and emotions and differentiate between the two. She hoped that her friend could do that without killing all the passion within herself. Nancy willed herself to start thinking about the present situation at hand and tried sorting out what would make Arthur kill his wonderful wife. Nancy saw the way he had looked at her throughout the trip. He couldn't have been that good of an actor to be able to put those expressions of love, gratitude and devotion on without someone realizing that they were not his true feelings.

Nancy wondered if she could use her phone, and with Suzanne's help, asked herself if she should try to call any of Sandy's family members and get some details that might have been overlooked. When she looked across the aisle, she saw that Suzanne was sound asleep and didn't want to wake her. She'd ask Suzanne about her thoughts in the morning.

The next morning, the sky was bright and clear. The sun was shining with not a cloud in sight. They all had a great breakfast prepared by the wonderful chef. After they ate, Nancy and Suzanne got off the boat and that's when Nancy mentioned her idea to Suzanne. "I think that her immediate family knows of Sandy's demise, and it's been a while since they found out. I don't think it would be a bad idea if we get some of the questions that are on our minds answered. I don't think that we are the ones that should make the call. Let me call our friends up at the FBI. Maybe they have contacts in Chicago, Illinois at the FBI headquarters that can help get information for us?" "What are you waiting for, dial," commanded Nancy.

When they finished their phone call, Suzanne told Nancy that Tim would call them back as soon as they made contact with the FBI in Chicago. "I hope that Interpol doesn't have to get involved. We can do all the messaging through the computer."

"It's lucky that we put the computers away under the mattresses in the beds. I for one am glad that the pirates didn't confiscate them and didn't know that they

were on board when they took all of our money and jewelry," Suzanne spoke with a smugness she usually didn't have. "I don't know what made us keep the computers hidden, but I'm now glad that we did." Nancy agreed.

They waited for hours until they heard from their friends. When all of the information was given to them, Suzanne decided to call one of Sandy's children, Veronica Owens, and express her sympathy on the loss of her mother. "I won't get into what we suspect, but I will, underhandedly, try to pry information out of her. Like where and who Sandy's doctor was and what arrangements the family will be making once the body comes back home."

Suzanne called the Owens' household but no one answered at first. After many tries Veronica finally answered the phone. Suzanne told her who she was and sent her condolences to her and her family. She also told them that Arthur was being cared for and not to worry about him. "We are making sure that he is well and everyone on board is trying to keep his mind on other things. While we're in port, we go to other various places that we wouldn't have been able to see if the group had gone on to another port." Suzanne tried making small talk but then when she felt she had all the information that she needed, she gave Veronica her personal cell phone number and told her to feel free to call her at any time.

"Whew, I hate to be dishonest, and in a way, I wasn't. But I think I got more information out of her than she realized she was giving me. Like the insurance company's name that they had and I now have the doctor's name that Sandy was seeing."

Nancy was glad that Suzanne made the call, but still felt awful about the underhandedness they were using in order to get information that might be useful in determining what made Arthur shoot his wife in the back.

CHAPTER EIGHTEEN

Suzanne and Nancy went back on deck and decided that, as long as they were in Manila, they'd make the most of it. "You know Nancy while we have to stay in the Philippines we might as well take advantage of the other sites that we haven't seen. If you want to mention it to the other people on board, that will be fine with me."

"You know, I think it would be fun to visit some other places that we thought we would never see once we left the Island. If you want to invite the others, that's fine with me, but I wouldn't ask anyone else. How often do we have a chance to just be with each other? It's not that I'm antisocial, but with your busy lifestyle and me being with Rich, when we finally make it home, I think it would be fun for the two of us to make these trips. If the other people want to take advantage of these extra days, then they will," Nancy gave her honest opinion.

Suzanne declared, "That's fine with me. Let's see the tourist attractions and pick out a few that will be of interest to us." After looking the guide over, they decided to take the tour from Manila to the WWII Corregidor Island. Nancy suggested: "Let's get a separate cab and get our own tour guide. I really don't want to go with a bunch of people. It's not that I'm a snob or anything, but I don't have to go to lunch with more people than I have to."

"That's fine with me. I'll go down below to our cabin and change into walking shoes and something comfortable."

"Sounds good," declared Nancy as the two women walked briskly to their cabin. While they were getting dressed, Nancy said aloud: "I wonder how the police are coming with getting an idea of who those pirates are."

"Well, tomorrow we'll call the police station and get some input on what's happening. For now, let's get a cab and see the Corregidor Island."

Their driver took them to the ferry dock where they boarded the one-hour ferry to Corregidor Island. They found out that this Island guards the entrance to Manila Bay. Its nickname was 'The Rock' and provided the first line of defense for the Filipino and American soldiers from the invasion of the Japanese soldiers during WWII.

Nancy looked at Suzanne as they got off of the ferry and headed to the Malinta Tunnel, which they found out was built by US engineers as a bomb-proof storage and hideout bunker and then was later converted to a hospital. Both women found it interesting when they explored the tunnel's ruins and relived history. They saw the Malinta Tunnel light and sound show. It was as it was described, an Experience, and they learned of the events that shaped American operations during the war.

The two friends were walking to the life-sized dioramas with complete voice-overs, lights and sound effects. It showed people what it was like living in the tunnel during the war. Suzanne was in awe at the footage of important events that led to two epic battles involving the invasion and retaking of Corregidor by the Filipino and American forces from the Japanese.

On the way to the Mile-Long Barracks, a now roofless, skeletal three-story concrete building that served as the quarters of around 2,000 American troops, including General Douglas MacArthur, Suzanne cleared her throat and asked Nancy if she wanted to hear a very interesting story.

"Sure, we can hold back awhile and our guide will tell us all about the barracks once your story is finished." Suzanne then told Nancy the story that she grew up hearing about her uncle. "Years ago there was a lot of prejudice against my nationality. Being of Jewish heritage I was well aware of the unfairness. After all, being brought up in Dorchester, I was well aware of the discrimination and bigotry that I lived with day in and day out, but getting back to this interesting story:

My uncle was in the first graduating class from Bridgewater State College. He was very smart. As a matter of fact, all of my uncles, including my Dad, Morris, were always on the honor roll in high school. Not to get off the subject, but if my Dad didn't meet my mother, he was accepted to Northeastern University and would have gone on to pharmaceutical college. Instead, the war was going on and he went to the Fore River Ship Yard to help build ships during the war.

Anyway, all of my uncles joined the army and my Uncle Arnold made first lieutenant during WWII. My other uncles were also there, and one of my uncles never wanted to travel again, once he got home from the service. My other uncle was a cook and fed all the troops. When my Mom asked him how he makes a cake, he started out by giving her the recipe using so many dozen eggs and bags of flour that she laughed and realized that he only knew how to make cakes for the entire troop. That is a funny story. But before I go on, I always cry when I relate the story of my Uncle Arnold. He graduated from Bridgewater State. I remember telling you that he was in the first graduating class. Anyway, instead of looking for a job, he enlisted in the service.

He was a First Lieutenant and was in charge of getting the food to the men who were enlisted. One day he met a very nice nun who happened to be in charge of the Leper Colony in New Calidonia, which I think is in the South Pacific, but I'm not sure. Anyway, this nun was telling my uncle about the lack of food she had for her patients and that no one wanted anything to do with her or the colony. My uncle understood. When I watch the Ten Commandments, Moses' mother contracted the disease and she had to live in a Leper Colony."

"Come on Suzanne, get on with the story, I know that you can't help saying what's on your mind because of your A.D.D. but finish the story about your uncle," reprimanded Nancy.

"Okay, okay. Well, my uncle went to his men and made sure that for the entire duration of his stay (which I believe was five years) the nun got plenty of food to feed the entire colony. She was very grateful for his help. Anyway, when he was about to ship out, she asked him for his entire name and his address and told him that when she got back to the States, she would look him up. He didn't think anything of it. He thought to himself that she was being kind and generous, and he probably wouldn't see her ever again. Well he went back home and my grandparents, God bless their souls, didn't have any money, but managed to get him a suit for interviews for schools in the area. He wanted to be a teacher. In those days, it wasn't spoken, but there was a lot of prejudice among people. Everyone stayed in their neighborhoods and really didn't have friends outside of their religious circles. Anyway, my uncle went from interview to interview and was told nicely that they would consider him. He knew, from the way the interviews were going, people saw what his last name was and automatically rejected his application.

One day my grandmother received a telephone call from Cardinal Cushing's office that was located in Jamaica Plain, near Dorchester, MA. They asked to speak to her eldest son. She was so proud of him being the first person to graduate from college. Anyway, he got on the phone and was asked if he was the Lieutenant who was stationed in New Calidonia? He answered yes and he was given a date and appointment to see the Cardinal. He was stymied and couldn't understand why Cardinal Cushing, would want to see him. He went there, all dressed up in his suit, and the Cardinal's secretary asked him to go with her. He went into the study and sat down. The Cardinal came in and started talking to him...After about 10 minutes, Cardinal Cushing said to him: "Wait a second, I think someone you know would like to thank you." You've guessed it!! Out comes the nun who he befriended and she gave him the biggest hug. She told the Cardinal how my uncle helped her and her people out when no one would look at them. Cardinal Cushing was a wonderful man. Within a week my uncle received a call from a school in his town, Quincy, and was offered a position as a teacher. He stayed his entire life teaching in Quincy and even made Assistant

Principle years later. I had one of his friends as my Biology teacher and I got straight A's in her class. It didn't hurt that I happened to love biology and understood everything she taught. I already graduated high school when I found out that Mrs. Monohearn was ill. I loved her very much, and I visited her in the hospital. I later found out that she didn't survive her bout with cancer."

"You never told me that story before! It's beautiful." "Yeah, sometimes I tell my clients, and when I do, I cry. I'm surprised that I didn't this time when I told you the episode," Suzanne responded to her friend.

They walked behind their guide and finally got to the barracks. It felt eerie to sit among the deserted, skeletal building that now only rats and critters scurried about. They then went into the Spanish Lighthouse, which was located at the highest point of the island. They walked up the steps, which was still hard for the two women to do, even after all their months of physical therapy. They viewed the spectacular view of Corregidor, Manila Bay and the South China Sea and all of the neighboring provinces of Bataan and Cavite.

They then visited Battery Way and Battery Hearn, where they saw the display of the various guns from the war. Suzanne's thoughts were of her uncles and the years of hardship the country endured during this difficult time in history. They walked back to the cab and were quiet for some time… "Hey, I don't know about you but I'm famished," declared Nancy. "Okay, let's get a bite to eat at one of the local restaurants before we head back to the ship."

"Sounds good to me," declared Suzanne as they got back to the city and made plans with their cab driver to pick them up tomorrow at the same time and go on another sightseeing tour of Old Manila and New. The cab driver told them that he would include the Intramuros and Fort Santiago. The two women waved goodbye and then took the short walk back to the sailboat and their new friends.

Suzanne was exhausted when they got back from their tour and opted to sleep for a while after they had a great dinner at a local restaurant in town. While Suzanne was on the bed, various thoughts kept going through her head. She couldn't get the romantic moments that she and Stephen shared, especially when they first began seeing each other. As hard as she tried, those romantic interludes kept reoccurring in her mind. She put her mind on other things, but nothing helped. With her body responding to her thoughts, the tingling sensations she felt down in her crotch wouldn't go away. She tossed and turned and then said to herself, 'the Hell with it,' and got up. She had to get Stephen off of her mind. She realized that there was no future for them unless he left his wife and they could start anew.

She found Nancy upstairs on deck, and while Nancy was admiring the beautiful clear sky and stars that were shining up above, Suzanne stood next to her. While Suzanne also watched the beautiful stars, she said a silent prayer to God that he would know what the best thing for her would be. She put her faith in His hands. Not knowing that Suzanne was in her own world and was silently meditating, Nancy told Suzanne of her hopes, dreams and all good things to come when she got back, and she and Rich would make their dreams come true.

After Suzanne came out of her trance, she apologized for not listening to Nancy and asked her to repeat what she had said. "I thought you looked like you were in your own world," an aggravated Nancy responded. "Okay, I'll only say this one more time and you'd better get what I'm saying." She then started to repeat her prediction and after she did, Isabelle came over to the two women and stood beside them. "Sorry, luvs, but I have to tell you what Cole and I did today." She then proceeded in her diatribe and both women looked at each other and couldn't seem to stop Isabelle from babbling on. Nancy said, "That's wonderful. I'm glad that you had such a lovely day." She then started to tell Isabelle what they did.

Nancy asked, "If you and Cole would like, we'd be glad to have the two of you join us tomorrow when we go on our own sightseeing tour of old and new Manila. Then we'll go on to Fort Santiago." Isabelle thought for a moment and then begged off, describing how she just heard from Tracy about a new market that she should see. At that moment, Cole came up beside her and listened to his wife's ramblings. All he did was laugh, as he knew that his wife couldn't pass up another shopping spree.

When Cole and Isabelle left, Nancy wiped her brow in an exaggerated way and said, "Phew, I thought that I'd be stuck listening to Isabelle the entire afternoon. Thankfully Tracy told her about the new shopping area, and I hope that she has fun. But while we're out and about, I think we should go to police headquarters and try to find out how they're coming along with their investigation."

"That's a great idea, and I was going to suggest it as well, so I guess we're on the same wave length," Suzanne spoke as she headed downstairs to go to her cabin.

While the women were in their respective beds, Nancy told Suzanne that they should call the eldest of Sandy and Arthur's children and find out about some things that shouldn't have to wait until they got home. With that stated, both women got ready for a peaceful night's sleep. They knew that tomorrow wasn't going to be an easy day after they went on their tour, but realized that they had to try to find out what really was the cause of Arthur killing his wife. With that stated, the two friends slept the sleep of the good. No bad dream interrupted their night's sleep.

Before going to sleep, Suzanne suggested that they ask their friends, Kevin and Tim from the Boston branch of the FBI, to find out how to get the number of some of the other children and also to find out, without giving anything away, the name of the doctor who Sandy was seeing and go from there. "That's a great idea. I only hope that what we want to find out won't be hard for the guys." Within a moment of her statement, Nancy was dozing, visions of Rich appeared before her eyes and then she was sound asleep.

The women grabbed a quick breakfast and headed out to meet their cab driver who would take them through the city of Makati and then visit Old Manila. Even though the women had been to the financial district of Manila, they found a new perspective from their driver. They received a guided tour of the financial center and drove past Forbes Park and the American Cemetery and War Memorial. They found out about the Spanish colonial period and walked through the ancient fortified area of Intramuros to see Fort Santiago. They marveled at the intricate Baroque architectural designs of UNESCO, (which is better known as the World Heritage) that was listed at San Agustin Church. He even took Suzanne and Nancy, unexpectedly, to an exclusive residential enclave dubbed 'Millionaire's Row.' It was on the way to visit the American Cemetery and Memorial that paid tribute to the fallen soldiers of World War II.

The women were awestruck when they went into Old Manila and passed through the Roxas Boulevard. They remembered passing through this when they saw Rizal Park. They loved the cobblestone paths. It reminded them of some of the streets that various parts of Boston had, especially near the State House and on the way to the North End. They found out that Dr. Jose Rizal, who the park is named after, wrote his famous poem, "My Last Farewell" when he spent his last days in incarceration. He was the Country's national hero.

The women told their driver, Mario, to let them off at police headquarters when they were finished with the tour. They enjoyed the tours and made sure that they were extra generous with the tip that they gave him.

While they waited patiently for Chief Inspector Hector Gomez to receive them, they reviewed the questions that they were going to ask him. "Now don't forget that we have to tell them that, besides being tourists, we also work with the FBI and Interpol. Tell them how we were involved with the capture of the criminals, (or some of them at least) of the International Art Crime Thefts and how we were able to stop a gang of the Yakuza." "That should impress him," stated Suzanne.

"I agree with you," Nancy answered whole heartedly. "After all, he would think us ordinary women or sailors on a vacation and I want him to realize that we are very interested in the involvement of the 'New Age Pirates.' I see the way that these Philippine men treat the women. It's not as bad in this country as some of the countries that we've been to, but still, women are second-class citizens." Suzanne shook her head in agreement and Chief Inspector Gomez's secretary informed them that he was free to see them.

Nancy and Suzanne walked into his office with all the determination that they could muster. They saw Chief Inspector Hector Gomez sitting solemnly at his desk, writing some reports when they entered. They waited a good minute for him to acknowledge them. He finally put his pen down and, while looking into their eyes, asked: "How can I be of service to you ladies?"

Suzanne asked if she and Nancy could sit down. "How rude of me, of course, have a seat ladies." He waited, then cleared his throat, and indicated with his hands to continue. Suzanne was the spokesperson for the two women. "I don't know if you realize that we were aboard the Vacation of a Lifetime sailboat that was taken over by the pirates, for a short time. But in that time, there were a lot of personal items, money and valuable electronics stolen. I also believe that there was an incident where a woman was shot in the back. I don't know who killed Mrs. Sandy Swartz, but this is a disturbing issue that has to be addressed. Can you tell us if you've found out who these pirates are and tell us if you've come anywhere close to getting to the bottom of this horrific situation?"

Suzanne cleared her throat and told him about dealing with the FBI and Interpol in other situations, indicating that they were not novices in the field of crime or criminal investigation. After she told him their story, they waited for his reply. He listened intently and nodded his head in agreement, the women not knowing if he was really understanding their involvement or just being courteous.

Chief Inspector Gomez spoke to both women, trying to be as diplomatic as possible. "You have to understand that being located in the Philippines is a bit different than dealing with the United States or other countries. We have our own way of dealing with these types of investigations. As you told me that you were involved with the Japanese Police and Interpol as well as the FBI. I don't want to be rude or tell you not to help us, but we are searching and using our sources for information. I will call up your friends, not that I doubt your involvement, but I have to confirm that what you have told me is accurate."

He then told them that they were doing all that is possible to solve this horrific crime and would keep everyone involved abreast of the situation at hand. "My secretary will call the numbers that you gave me and I will find out if what you have told me is true. Not that I doubt for a moment that you would lie to me, but I have to be certain before I indulge you with my private information. You do understand my predicament, don't you?"

Suzanne told him that she understood his dilemma, and would wait or come by in a day or two for his confirmation. The two women shook his hand and were led out of his private office. When out of the building, Suzanne looked over to Nancy and shook her head. "No wonder these countries are considered underdeveloped. I see in the city, things are hopping, but when you get down to the nitty-gritty of the everyday running of the government, there seems to be a lot of conflict. I hope that they get in touch with all of the numbers that I provided, and in a few days we'll be getting more information from them." Nancy suggested, "Meanwhile, why don't we find out if Kevin and Tim have found any of the information that we asked them to get us. We can work on finding out some answers, even if we are over here. That's why the phone services thrive like they do." Suzanne said, "I think between the phone, internet and computers, we'll be able to get along fine. Heck, we might even be able to help Inspector Gomez without his realizing what we're doing."

The two women went back to the ship and after nibbling on a few appetizers that were provided by the chef and his crew, Suzanne and Nancy went down to their cabins and pulled out their computers. They then thought about the time difference and realized that they had to wait until morning to make the necessary phone calls.

They both woke up in a better mood than the evening before. Nancy was taking a shower and washing her hair. Thoughts of Rich's body next to her in her shower at home put a smile on her face. She thought of all the times the two of them made love and how his erection felt against her upper thigh when they left the hot, steamy shower. Their love making was great, and thinking about it made her want him all the more. It was very different when she was making love with Rich. She very rarely thought of her first husband, Peter. So many bad memories were left in place when they split up. She no longer remembered the happy times, the first experience she had when making love to Peter. She felt sorry for the way his life turned out, but realized that maybe he would appreciate a fine woman if he was lucky enough to find one and not think of himself first and foremost. So many instances occurred when she was going through her difficult times that she was thankful she had found peace and happiness with Detective Richard Colangelo.

As much as she wanted to get back home and finalize their plans, she realized that the situation at hand had to come first. There was no way in Hell that she'd leave this state of affairs in limbo. No, she realized, she had to leave her thoughts behind her and focus on the job ahead of her. Thankfully, her friend and partner would be there beside her, watching her every move. She was grateful that she met up with Suzanne. She was fortunate that besides being part owner of one of the most prestigious salons in the nation, she was also doing her duty as a citizen of the United States. She was doing the unthinkable. Not everyone was cut out for the situations that she and Suzanne got into. But in reality, she felt revitalized and happy that she was able to make a difference in people's lives. No one in Suzanne's family knew that the two women were really undercover agents and Suzanne wanted to keep it that way. Rich knew of Nancy's involvement with the government, but he knew what he had to do in order to keep Nancy's activities secret. He would never tell a soul how Nancy and Suzanne helped people without the people realizing that it was these two brave souls that went behind the scenes and did what they had to do to make the world a better place for everyone else to live in.

With those thoughts, she dried herself off and started blow drying her flaming red hair. When she was young, she hated the color of her hair. Now older and wiser, she embraced the color and realized that was who she was. Yes, the temper went with the color, but that was her personality. As she looked at herself in the mirror, she liked the person in the reflection. *'Isn't that what life is all about?'* She asked herself as she finished putting on sun block with deft and nimble hands.

She looked over to her best friend, Suzanne and realized how lucky she was to have become part of Suzanne's inner circle. They were like the sister neither of them had. Suzanne was stepping into the shower and scrubbing herself as if cleansing herself of all the bad memories that lingered. Suzanne felt ashamed of herself that with all of her caring and tenderness, Stephen was not as committed to her as she would love for him to be. For the life of her, she couldn't understand why he wouldn't divorce his wife, who really wasn't a wife at all, but only on a piece of paper. Stephen often would tell Suzanne that a paper is only good for wiping your ass. It meant nothing. What they had together was what was important. Too bad she didn't have the same feelings as he. She felt very different about commitment. She wondered about her true point of view in regards to Lawrence. She laughed out loud, hoping that Nancy didn't think she was daft in the head. Lawrence only tolerated Suzanne calling him Larry. She thought that was funny. Suzanne closed her eyes, thinking of the beautiful times that she had shared with Stephen. How her heart would pitter-patter whenever thoughts of him would invade her mind, body and soul. Now, whenever she thought of him, anger took over her feelings and resentment. She didn't want that happening, but she couldn't help her belief. Yes, her judgment might not be the same as his, but she had every right to have her opinion.

She was rinsing off the suds in her blonde hair when suddenly Larry's face appeared before her. She enjoyed his entire family. It didn't hurt that it didn't matter to him that she worked or that she was a self-made millionaire. He respected her for who she was and didn't feel funny telling her that it was she that he wanted beside him in good times and bad. She enjoyed his children, even though they were much younger than her own children. She knew that Mrs. Walsh would embrace them when she finally met them. Her parents were wonderful people and would feel the same way that they felt about their natural grandchildren. She was fortunate that she had been raised with love and not the dysfunction that she often heard about. The only dysfunction she could think of was her family made much too much food for everyone to enjoy and eat. The only time she was introduced to dysfunction was when she and Brian met, fell in love, if that's what one called love, and she found out first hand, what it was to be with a mad man. Tears ran down her face as the incidents that caused her grief and unhappiness surfaced. She was glad that water was cascading down her entire hair and body, so when she emerged from the shower, Nancy wouldn't know that she had been crying. She wanted to be happy and not have to beg someone to love her for herself. As she was shutting off the water, she made a vow to try not to think of Stephen or Lawrence for the rest of their trip. She knew that she had to concentrate on the matter at hand.

She and Nancy were on a mission and she knew that they had to find the reason that Sandy Swartz was killed. She also realized that, somehow, they had to find the pirates that took off with everyone's personal items and try to get back the boat's equipment. She realized that, by now, most of the money and jewelry and electrical gadgets were long gone, but she had to try to salvage something. That's what life was all about. She was determined to make people feel good about them-selves no matter what!!! Maybe that's why she was in the profession she was in and she and Nancy were in this other secret endeavor to make them happy. If that was what life was all about, she felt glad that she was able to be a part of helping people who needed them.

Suzanne was drying herself off and she happened to look towards Nancy. Suzanne was glad that Nancy hadn't realized that she was crying in the shower. Suzanne got dressed in her casual clothes, ready to put in a day of trying to find answers to the questions that had to be answered. "Well, Miss Nancy, are you ready to start making these important phone calls?"

"I am. I also hope that we don't miss Vivian and that she's left for work. If so, then we'll make other phone calls until someone can answer the questions that are on our mind. I think we'll have to put a phone call into the doctor's office and have to wait until he returns our call."

"That's a given," Nancy agreed. "I only hope that he doesn't wait until the end of the day to return our call because most people won't realize the time difference. We'd better leave our phones beside our bed, just in case that should be the case," Nancy said.

They each sat on their respective beds and Suzanne put through the call to Vivian. She let the phone ring and was about to hang up after the tenth ring when Vivian herself picked up the phone.

Suzanne introduced herself and spoke her condolences to her and her family. She told Vivian who she was and that made a big impression on Vivian because she had heard of the Metamorphosis Spas. After that introduction, Vivian had no qualms about telling Suzanne who her mother's oncologist was and then, without her realizing what she revealed, she gave up the name of the insurance company that had the life insurance policy for her mother, even before she was diagnosed with cancer, years ago. They spoke for a good half an hour, Suzanne listening to nostalgia about her parents and some of the happy moments that she remembered. Suzanne promised to keep in touch and would definitely make it to the memorial service that the girls planned to have for Sandy when they finally got the body back from the Philippines.

Nancy was all ears and wanted to hear everything that Suzanne learned from talking to Vivian. She looked over the notes that Suzanne jotted down and made some notes of her own when listening to Suzanne relate the details of the information that she found out. "Well, I don't think that Vivian was aware that this was a mission that I was calling about," Suzanne told Nancy.

"No, the way you sounded was very realistic and she would never have thought that you were prying information from her." Suzanne answered her friend, "I didn't want to come across as nosy, but I sincerely wanted to find out why this beautiful woman died the way she did. We'll find out the reason and then it will be up to us to either say what really happened or forever keep our mouths shut. After all, I don't want to see them not get the insurance money and have Arthur living in poverty because we had to see justice served," announced Suzanne. With that said, the women went upstairs to get more sunshine. "Another thing, Sandy and Arthur had this insurance policy for years, way before she had any cancer or any other disease. Let's see what our friend Chief Inspector Gomez has to say in their quest for finding out who the pirates are or if they've found any of the items that we described stolen at any of the pawn shops in the area," Nancy said. They then went up the narrow staircase to get some vitamin D.

CHAPTER NINETEEN

Suzanne and Nancy were sunning themselves on deck and, before they realized it, the rest of the passengers were laying down beside them soaking up the rays that were brightly shining in the beautiful clear skies. Suzanne didn't want to ignore Arthur and purposely made sure that she included him in the conversations she and Nancy were having with some of the other guests.

They allowed themselves to get sun for only a little over an hour and then told the other members of the group that they were going to go into town and just walk around, all the while they hoped that none of the other guests wanted to join them. They lucked out, as the other people wanted to stay close to the ship, hoping that they'd get word that they were free to go on their way. Nancy and Suzanne knew better, and told the other people that they would get a little something to eat and then be back shortly. Isabelle was a little upset because she knew that there was always something to see and buy in town, but Cole was adamant about her staying close by the ship and dock.

It didn't take them long to get to police headquarters. When they last spoke to Kevin and Tim, they told their friends that they had spoken to the Chief Inspector Hector Gomez and assured him that they were who they said they were. They waited until the chief was ready, and then were escorted into his office. His office was very informal and quite small. Nancy spotted the pictures of who, she assumed, were members of his family proudly displayed on his large desk. The desk took up much of the room in his small quarters.

With great pomp and ceremony, he told the women to be seated. They felt that since he spoke to Tim and Kevin, he looked at them in a different light. "Now I want you to know that I spoke to your friends in the Boston, United States of America Office and they corroborated who you are. That makes me feel more at ease. I've had my men out, day and night, searching the various bars and places that the pirates would use to fence the merchandise they had stolen. I've had my undercover agents (yes, we also have them) asking questions of their acquaintances and so far we've not gotten any feedback as to who these culprits are." With a sad face he went on. "I'm not giving up, just so you know, this matter is not taken lightly by any of us. Our tourism trade depends on this being a safe Island and I can't have anyone thinking otherwise."

Suzanne and Nancy were disappointed but didn't let on. "I'm sure it will be only a matter of time before you catch these outlaws," Nancy assured him. "This is a small Island. How far can these people go without being spotted? Unless, of course, they are regular citizens who only wear the pirate gear periodically and no one has a clue who they are. That is troublesome to say the least," Suzanne shook her head in disgust as she spoke to Chief Gomez.

"All I can tell you is that my men are doing their best and I'm sure that, in no time, word will come down through the grapevine and we'll find out who these men are." With a shrug of his head, he asked them if they'd like his secretary to bring in some coffee. Both women declined and realized that they'd have to do some snooping on their own. They thanked him for his hospitality and told Chief Gomez that they'd come back at a later date.

Walking out in the sunlight, Nancy and Suzanne put on their sunglasses, trying to keep the sunlight out of their eyes. "I think we should go to a local restaurant and see for ourselves if we can do a little prying. What do you think Nancy?"

"Sounds good to me! I'm in the mood for some good Philippine cuisine." They made their way to the recommended local restaurant in town and sat down in the brown wooden chairs with a square table separating them. After looking at the meals offered on the menu, they decided on trying something local. "You know Nancy," Suzanne smiled as she half laughed, "I think I'll get something that isn't that crazy. Maybe I'll have a chicken dish of some sort."

"You're not any fun to be with. Be outrageous and let the waiter give us some of their specialties," Nancy retorted. "Well you can call me crazy, but I've sampled some of the food that the chef on board has made up from the local gardens and farms. Let's see what the waiter has to say."

When the waiter came over (wearing a white, not so clean, apron) Suzanne realized that he must also be a part-time cook. She asked him to tell them, in English, if he could, some of their specialty dishes. When all was said and done, Suzanne decided on the Chicken Inasal...Nancy decided on having them get an appetizer and wanted Suzanne to taste the delicious Sisig. "I'll tell you now not to ask what this is made from" Nancy ordered. "But before we eat this, I know beer isn't your favorite beverage, but I'll order one for both of us." "Just tell me am I going to get sick eating this appetizer?" asked Suzanne. "No silly, would I ever do that to you?" a gleeful Nancy asked. "I don't know, sometimes you are a very sick puppy and get enjoyment out of seeing me squirm."

The waiter, who they learned was named Sunny, told them his favorite items and that's what the women ordered. The beer was served nice, frothy and cold. "Well, at least they know how to serve their beer," an enthusiastic Nancy exclaimed. She lifted her glass and made a toast. "To love, life and getting the bad guys, if they can be got," Nancy laughed as she clinked her beer bottle with Suzanne's.

Whispering, Suzanne declared that she was glad that the waiter's name wasn't Mario. "It seems that everywhere we go, the guy's name is Mario." Nancy started laughing and before she realized it her entire drink was consumed and she ordered another one for herself. Leaning her head in Suzanne's direction she whispered, but not that softly, "I'm going to tell you what Sisig is made of and when you're eating it, don't you dare tell me you don't like it," ordered Nancy. "Okay, I'm all ears."

"Well, nothing goes to waste in the Filipino food. This is pork cheeks, head and liver and it's cooked to sizzling and presented to you with all the splendor you can ask for. It might be crunchy and chewy, but it's a perfect match. Just drink your beer when you have the food in your mouth. It's served with hot sauce and Knorr seasoning. If you get sick, I'll kill you so just suck it up and enjoy." With that said Nancy lifted her glass of beer again and started laughing. "You know you are one sick person," declared Suzanne as she closed her eyes and swallowed the tasty appetizer with a large swallow of her beer. "Now, isn't this a delicious dish, and don't tell me you don't like it because I know better."

"Well, I have to admit that it isn't as bad as I thought it would be. Like when I recommend Helzel, which has stuffing in the lining of the stomach, outside the animal that is. But I have to admit, that it's delicious. So, no, I won't gag but have a little compassion," Suzanne gagged or made believe she did.

The woman both ordered the Chicken Inasal, which was grilled. The waiter started talking to the women and admitted that this was no ordinary grilled chicken. The chicken is marinated in lemongrass, calamansi, salt, pepper, and garlic and brushed with achuete oil with was some kind of seed. When the dish was presented, every part of the chicken was displayed. The paa (drumstick), pecho (breast), baticulon (gizzard), atay, (liver), pakpak (wings), and corazon (heart). "It must be eaten with a generous serving of garlic rice with some of the orange oil used to marinate the chicken and poured over the rice," the waiter declared.

Suzanne whispered to Nancy, "I'm glad that I don't have a person that I'm kissing, especially after consuming these dishes. I have had so much garlic and, I have to admit, garlic lasts forever with me." Both women laughed as they enjoyed the flavorful dish that was served to them.

For dessert, the waiter presented a Leche Flan. He said this is a popular dessert among the local people. It's an egg and milk based custard capped off with glistening caramelized sugar. Well, after enjoying a cup of tea with her tasty dessert, Suzanne admitted that she was stuffed. "And, if you want to know the truth, the food was delicious. If I didn't know what the ingredients were, I'd have gobbled each morsel with more gusto. I'm not a beer drinker, but even that was delicious," admitted Suzanne.

They stayed a little longer to see some local entertainment while the natives started coming in and stayed in the bar area. Suzanne and Nancy stayed awhile and tried starting up a conversation with some of the local people who always came in after the sun came down. "I'm lucky we waited. Although the people on board the sailing vessel will probably have sentries out looking for us," admitted Nancy. Suzanne lifted her glass of soda water and lemon and toasted her friend who made her try these new dishes and she was happy to be among the locals who patronized this establishment. Whispering, Suzanne said very softly in Nancy's ear, "Maybe if we lightly bring up the subject of the recent pirate raid and killing, we might hear something that they don't realize they are saying or betray someone's trust."

Mario had felt cooped in his house, staying in for many days. He missed the comradeship of his friends and made plans to meet them at the local restaurant and pub. When going in, he spotted two women from the ship that they had recently looted. He waited for his other friends to come, as he wanted to be sure that no one spoke of what had happened a week ago. Mario eyed his cousin, Efran, as he entered the establishment and gave him a funny nod. Efran went over to Mario and asked him why he gave him the nod. "I think Sunny and Tolemeo are also coming here. Ronnie couldn't get out of his house this evening. Something about him babysitting while his wife went to a family meeting." "Don't look now, but I want you to be aware, those two women sitting at that table, are two of the woman aboard the sailing vessel that we boarded last week. We have to be sure that not one word is spoken of that. They might have big ears and we definitely, can't say anything about what we've been up to," ordered Mario.

When all of the men were seated at the bar, they ordered their drinks and appetizers. They all made small talk, being mindful not to say a word about what they were actually doing for money. As far as the rest of the patrons were concerned, they were in the same predicament that all the local fishermen were in. There was a vast reduction in money due to the lack of fish they were allowed to have on their vessels. They heard the complaints of the other men but instead of bragging to the other men, they commiserated with them. It was an act of sheer nerve; one they realized had to be put on.

Suzanne and Nancy saw the establishment fill up with all the local patrons. They kept their ears and eyes open to anything suspicious. Nancy thought that some of the men at the bar looked familiar, but it could have been all the booze and drinks that she had consumed throughout the day. She wasn't used to drinking that amount of alcohol and realized that her observations might be distorted. She decided not to tell Suzanne of her scrutiny. "Nancy, you seem to be in your own world. What's on your mind," asked Suzanne. "It's nothing, just a feeling that I had. I've probably had too much to drink and my senses aren't as tuned in as they should be," acknowledged Nancy.

"Without considering that aspect, what do you think you see?"

"If I didn't know any better, Suzanne, I'd swear that I've seen those men sitting at the bar way over to the right-hand side. But I can't swear to it. They seem familiar and they keep looking our way."

"To be honest with you, most of the Asian people look alike and it's hard for us to make an accurate assessment of the situation. I feel that the Asian people might look at us Caucasians and feel the same way. To them, we all look alike. You know my friend, Beverly, well her youngest son happens to think that Oriental women are beautiful. He's always been attracted to them. One of his old girlfriend's family used to call Keith, the white ghost. Honest, I swear that was what his old girlfriend's family used to call him."

"That's awful," Nancy verbalized. "Well it's true. I happen to love his wife and their kids are adorable. Each one is nicer looking than the next. I really believe that the Eurasian children are beautiful specimens."

"You make them sound like some piece of meat, Suzanne. They are not specimens, but happen to be beautiful children."

"You're right, Nancy, I used the wrong terminology. But that doesn't stop you from feeling funny when you spied the individuals. You're usually right about that sort of thing," Suzanne told her friend. "Well, let's hang around for a while and see what happens," suggested Nancy. They both ordered another drink and Suzanne suggested that Nancy change her order to a coffee or tea instead of another beer. "Otherwise I'm going to have to carry you back to the ship," teased Suzanne. The waiter came over and they ordered a refill. Nancy obliged her friend and ordered a cup of coffee. "I'm surprised that they even sell coffee at this restaurant. Everyone I see has a drink," giggled Nancy as she was half bombed. "You are definitely cut off from drinking anything else except a good cup of strong coffee. I hope that they know how to make a good cup of coffee here," Suzanne told her friend.

As the men talked to each other, they kept an eye on the two women who were seated at the table a bit away from them. "I hope they don't recognize any of us," a mindful, Tolemeo whispered discreetly to his friends. "I don't think that they could. To them we all look alike." With that said they all clanked their glasses and started laughing.

The women were talking and explaining their experiences since starting the trip when the group of men sitting and some standing by the bar made a ruckus. "Boy they know how to have a good time on a men's night out" exclaimed Nancy. "They certainly do. They all seem to have wedding bands on, so that's exactly as it looks, a man's night out with their buddies," Suzanne agreed. "This seems to be a pretty busy establishment for a weeknight," Suzanne observed. "Well, there aren't too many places like this around, at least in this part of town. Oh, wait a second, near the docks there are a lot of restaurants and bars for the people who live on the ships or want to stay close by. I guess this place is more for the people who live in the village or for tourists like us," Nancy noted.

For the moment, the two women forgot the men's rowdy behavior and finished talking about their experiences on the sailing vessel. They then started a discussion about the people on their sailboat and what they thought of them. Before this night, I enjoyed the couples immensely, but never got down to the nitty gritty of their personalities. I mean they all seem like great people and we really couldn't have asked for a better lot to go on a vacation with, if given a choice. I do wish that Justin could have come, but I realize that this type of vacation wouldn't be his ideal get-away. To me, Justin would like to stay in a cosmopolitan place and wander about, visiting museums and seeing his friends. He seems to have people that he knows all over the world." The woman laughed at Suzanne's description of him.

"First of all, if he were aboard and found out that you had fallen off of the mast head, he would have fainted dead away. I can picture him now, tearing what little hair he has left on his head, going in circles and screaming," Nancy laughed at her own proclamation. The women chuckled as they pictured Justin's actions when Nancy gave her narrative of their friend.

As the men at the bar were enjoying their night out, the drinks kept coming and they felt, for the first time in a week, good about themselves. Mario was feeling no pain and said to his cousin, "Don't look now, but those women over there are, I think, from the sailing ship." Efran looked discreetly towards the table where Nancy and Suzanne sat and agreed with Mario. Their agreement went down the line and stopped at Ronnie who was now dying to find out what his friends were whispering about. When Ronnie heard what the commotion was about, his piercing brown eyes looked suspiciously at the two women who were now getting curious at what those men were looking at. Talking to his comrades Ronnie told them how lucky he was that his wife's meeting was canceled. "Now I can see for myself about the two women," he said to his friends.

"You'd think that we're a piece of meat and that they want to devour us," Suzanne spoke jokingly to Nancy. "I wouldn't be taking this matter lightly if I were you, Suzanne. This is their neck of the woods and we're strangers to most of the people in this establishment."

"If you can call this bar and restaurant an establishment," Suzanne said. "Seriously Nancy, I think you'd better drink up your coffee and let's vamoose out of here as quickly as possible." She called the waiter over and asked for the running tab and bill. They couldn't get out of there fast enough. On the way back to the dock, Nancy and Suzanne kept looking behind them, making sure that they weren't being followed by those sleazy looking guys.

Safely back in their cabin, the two women got undressed and went to their respective beds. "Seriously, Suzanne, those men scared me. At first I didn't think anything of it, and then it became obvious that they were staring at us as if we were three-headed monsters. Why do you suppose they did that?"

"First of all, I couldn't get out of there fast enough. I think that they might be the men that were the pirates that invaded our ship."

"Did you get a good look at the pirates so that you can honestly say that they were the ones?" asked a concerned Nancy.

"In all honesty, I don't think I can verify that they were the men, but why would they give us the daggers with their eyes if they weren't? We weren't coming on to them and stayed to ourselves," a distraught Suzanne said. "They're probably not used to women walking around town without a man by their side. And on top of that, going into the local place where all the locals hang out, is just asking for trouble. I think we made a mistake going there," Nancy admitted.

"In the morning, after we feel a bit better, I'd like to go back to the bar. I'll ask the bartender who those men were. A little snooping won't do us any harm."

"Those are your famous words, Suzanne, and I don't want this vacation turned into some sort of adventure that gets us involved with pirates, if you don't mind." With that said, Nancy went off to take a shower. Suzanne sat up in her bed, her hands underneath her head and kept ruminating about the pirates and then those men in the bar. The more she thought of it, the more she had herself convinced that there was no other possibility why those men would show disdain for two women who obviously weren't there to do any harm to anyone.

After getting out of the shower and dressing, Nancy commented to Suzanne that today would be a good day to call Sandy's oncologist. "Let's try to find out, and if we can, come to some sort of conclusion on this delicate matter, Nancy suggested. "With the new laws, it's almost a certainty that the office, especially her doctor, will not let any information regarding Sandy out to strangers like us. I think we'll have to find a way to get either a lawyer involved or maybe our friends Kevin and Timothy can see what they can do to get answers to our questions," Suzanne told Nancy.

"We'll have to be, very sneaky if Arthur and Sandy have or had insurance policies. I'd really like to get to talk to Arthur privately, but for some reason, he seems to be avoiding us. I don't know if it's just us or if he is avoiding most of the passengers now that Sandy came to an untimely demise," Suzanne told Nancy.

"I think that I'll try to approach Arthur while you call the doctor's office. You got the number from their daughter, didn't you?" asked Nancy. "If he doesn't want to tell me what's on his mind or start answering some questions, I don't know what to do. I'll find something, you can count on me." Nancy informed Suzanne of what she was going to do.

They went up to the middle deck where a sumptuous breakfast was prepared and cooked by Chef André. It seemed that everyone was ravenous, because there wasn't a morsel left when the meal was finished. Suzanne and Nancy started talking to the guests when they spotted Arthur, sitting by himself on the top deck sunning him-self. They ambled over and sat down beside him.

Small talk about nothing in particular began and then, after a few minutes had elapsed, Suzanne brought up how courageous Sandy was. "I have to tell you that I admire Sandy for how she never let on, even to you, that she had a reoccurrence of her cancer." Arthur didn't say much, just shook his head in agreement. Ignoring his lack of conversation, Suzanne continued as if nothing was wrong. "Sandy told me, at the beginning of our fabulous vacation, that the kids gave this trip to you for your forty-fifth wedding anniversary. Am I right?" Again, Arthur shook his head. It was as if he were to speak he would lose it and cry uncontrollably.

Suzanne would not be deterred. Nancy looked on as if she didn't believe that her friend could continue this conversation. It was as if she were talking to herself. "You, Sandy and the kids must have taken the news of her cancer very hard. That's when she first found out that she had it." She continued as if he were listening and answering her dialogue. "I don't know how I would react if I found out that I had cancer. I know that my first cousin, who by the way was my flower girl at my wedding, has fought the disease since she was a young girl in her early thirties. I also have many friends who are cancer survivors and have finished their five-year dose of Tamoxifen and are doing quite well." Continuing to talk (as if to herself) she kept up the conversation. "I have a lot of patients that had that dreaded disease and after they finished their treatments, they're fine. That was very thoughtful of your children to give you such a wonderful gift." She now waited for him to talk to her, but seriously doubted if he would give up anything of significance once he started talking and answering her back.

'She keeps droning on about poor Sandy. I would like to tell her to take a long walk off of a short pier. I'd better answer, ever so briefly, and not really tell her much. I'm sure she's talking to me to either hear her-self talk or get me to tell her about Sandy and me. Well, I won't give her the satisfaction of revealing anything of importance. Sandy would kill me from her grave if I told her what and why Sandy asked me to do what I did.'

"Yes, that was nice of the kids to do that for us. We certainly didn't expect such an expensive gift. We thought that going out to dinner was all that would be done. And to answer your questions about Sandy's condition, we all went through Hell and back when we found out she had Breast Cancer. We all helped. Even our friends pitched in when she was going through her treatments. You know, we just celebrated our forty-fifth wedding anniversary and never dreamed that the kids would do such a wonderful thing as this vacation. But God works in funny ways. I mean, if we hadn't been on this trip and didn't get confronted by those pirates, I would be with Sandy, laughing and enjoying ourselves wherever we were. But that's not what happened and now I have to face reality. When I return home, I have to start making plans for a funeral or memorial service of some kind. Life just isn't fair." With that stated Arthur got up and went to the other side of the deck, as if dismissing Suzanne.

Suzanne was dumbfounded at the way he just ended their conversation and walked away. *'Maybe he thought that I was too nosey and should mind my own business. Or else he was shaken to the core and didn't want to reveal anything that might incriminate him. After all, Nancy and I saw what we saw. We can't go to anyone with our observations. We have to find out why he did what he did.'* Nancy saw Arthur walk away and didn't know if Suzanne had found any pertinent news, but hoped that she had. When she saw that Arthur had found another spot, Nancy sat next to Suzanne and all Suzanne did was shake her head back and forth. Nancy took that as nothing of importance was said. "Well, we'll find out the truth, one way or the other, don't you worry, Suzanne, the truth always prevails."

"Yes, it does, but at whose expense?" Suzanne now realized that she had to get in contact with either her friends at the FBI or a lawyer if she wanted to see Sandy's medical records. She had to find out why Arthur did what he did and she couldn't let it go until she knew the truth. Suzanne realized that sometimes the truth isn't what a person wants to hear, and she was afraid of the answers to the many questions that were on her mind. She took the suntan lotion from Nancy and started distributing it on her body, making sure that she didn't get any more spots on her chest than she already had. Before she was in the business of beauty, she had spent many hours enjoying the sun and not using protection. Even though she went to the dermatologist to get rid of the ugly age spots, she made sure that she told her clients, even the younger ones that came in, to be mindful of the sun's rays and be careful. She knew that the younger clientele didn't heed her warnings, and she cringed each time she heard them boasting about going tanning… They didn't listen to her and would have to find out for themselves the danger of the damaging rays.

When the two friends decided that they had their fill of sunning themselves, they decided to go into town and go to the bar/restaurant that they had been to the evening before. She knew Nancy's nice demeanor, and she wanted Nancy to go to the bartender, if he was on, and ask who those men were. If he wasn't on, then they'd have to wait until the next time and then go there and ask the important questions that, hopefully, he could answer.

Going down to their room to change into clothes that were appropriate to walk into town, Suzanne told Nancy what she wanted her friend and partner to do. Nancy, at first, balked at the idea but then realized that it was a task that she was good at. "Let's go, Suzie the Sleuth. I have work to do and, sitting around like we are, will get nothing accomplished." With that said, Nancy and Suzanne made their way into town with determination. While Suzanne was walking with Nancy, she saw a little kitten wandering the streets and bent down to pet it. Automatically it brought back memories and thoughts of her two, precious cats to mind. She hoped all was well and knew that Simka and Boston would be missing her. They probably thought that she abandoned them. With that in mind she knew that she had to bring home cat toys along with the gifts to the other important people in her life.

Nancy saw the look of remorse on Suzanne's face and said: "Oh for Gosh sake, the cats are doing fine. As a matter of fact, they probably don't miss you at all!!!" Suzanne was taken aback by what Nancy said and was about to say something nasty to her when Nancy burst out laughing. "Suzanne, I'm only kidding. Can't you take a joke?"

"I don't think that's funny at all. Its mean and I didn't think that you had a mean bone in your body. What would make you say something like that?"

"I won't dignify that by even answering such a stupid question. It was a joke. I know how much you love those cats and vice versa. Get over it and lighten up," Nancy said aloud.

They got to their destination and found that the bartender was indeed there. They ordered a drink at the bar and waited until he was free. He was waiting on tables and taking care of the bar as well. They took their time ordering and after having such a wonderful breakfast on board the sailing vessel, had all they could do to consume their meal. Taking their time they were waiting patiently for him to appear, before he asked them if they wanted a refill.

Suzanne shut herself off from getting another hard drink and ordered her usual tea instead. Nancy took a refill and Suzanne looked at her as if to say, how can you drink this early in the day, but kept her thoughts to herself. Nancy was handed another glass of Malibu Rum and pineapple and then she approached the bartender. "Weren't you the gentleman who took our order last evening when we dined here?" He puffed out his chest, enjoying the woman who had noticed him the evening before. "Yes, I am. I noticed you and your friend here. Did you like the food and the way it was prepared?"

"To be honest with you, yes we did. That's why we came back again today. We've been going to lots of restaurants because we're on vacation. As a matter of fact, you probably heard about our plight with those pirates that stole all of our money. There's a rumor that one of our friends got shot by those guys." The bartender was caught by surprise by her admission of being one of the passengers. "What a shame. These pirates are giving our place a bad name. I'm telling you, it's not like this around here, honest. I'd love to find out who they are and most of the people in the village feel the same way. We're law abiding citizens and we need people like you to come and enjoy yourselves without having to worry about being accosted by these banditos."

With that said Nancy leaned over and told him about her awful experience and made up some story about having nightmares since the event took place. The bartender, who told the friends that his name was Sunny, shook his head as if to say, what an awful thing to happen and agreed with her. After a while, he took care of other patrons and then came back to them. Nancy then asked him about the cute men that were at the bar last evening. "Oh you mean Mario and his friends? They're locals, village people, and fishermen by trade. They thought that you two ladies were nice and quite the lookers, if I may be so bold and tell you what they told me." He then told Nancy that Mario and his friends grew up there, and everyone knew everyone else in town. "It's a small village and sometimes, well, most of the time, we all know what's going on behind closed doors, if you know what I mean," he said with a wink.

"I understand that the fishermen are having a hard time making a living with the way that the Chinese people and government have started clamping down on your people. They are now executing their rights in the open seas due to a stupid agreement that was made years ago!" Nancy said aloud to her new friend. After he took care of a few more people, he came back to Nancy and agreed with her on her observation and what she had heard. "It's a shame," he announced. "Men like Mario, his friends, and other fishermen are having hard times earning money at their trade. It's about the only thing that they know how to do. It's been handed down from generation to generation, and no one ever thought that money would be a problem for our fishermen. They made lots of money and now," shaking his head, "they can't live the type of life that they and their families had grown accustomed to. I don't know what they'll do. They have to come up with some other way to provide a decent wage for them and their families." He wiped the counter in front of the women as he cleared their dishes. "Can I get you anything else, like dessert? "I'll tell you what, since I like you and your friend here, I'll give you the Tables Tsokalate for free. You'll love it. It's a hot chocolate drink. Tell me what you think of it."

"Well, since you put it that way, sure, but let us pay for another dessert that you think we'll like," said Nancy.

Going back to the kitchen, Sunny was happy that he was able to serve the Leche Flan with the chocolate drink. He knew that they would enjoy it. While he was back in the kitchen, Suzanne leaned over and whispered a thank you to Nancy. "You really got him talking and I think we may have found out the reason these guys are the new age pirates.

Sunny came back with the Leche flan, that was a popular dessert among the locals. The two women enjoyed the flan that they found out was made out of an egg and milk. It was custard capped off with glistening caramelized sugar. They also enjoyed the hot chocolate drink and were happy to give Sunny a good tip for all of his knowledge and friendly service. Waving goodbye and assuring him that while they were on the island, they would be sure to come back as often as possible. "I don't know how we could have eaten all of that food without splitting our stomachs," admitted Suzanne.

"I must admit that, when it comes to getting people to talk, Nancy you're as good as I am. Well, I can't really say that, but in this case you did a great job. Thanks!!" With that said, Nancy gently shoved Suzanne as they walked back to the boat and stopped off at a few interesting shops that they found on the way back.

CHAPTER TWENTY

When the women got back to their cabin, they plopped down on their beds. They were exhausted! "I'm getting too old for all of this Suzy the Sleuth Stuff," Suzanne said aloud. "Oh, you're just tired and full from all that we've consumed." Laughing, Nancy admitted out loud that she got Sunny to talk a lot about the locals. "You know, I think we might be on to something with those pirates. Let's bring our thoughts to Chief Inspector Gomez and see what he thinks of our idea," Nancy told Suzanne.

"I think you hit the nail on the head, my friend. Let's hope that Inspector Gomez thinks that there's some validity to our idea." They spent the rest of the day relaxing on board and listening to what the others did during their day in port. Suzanne and Nancy avoided Arthur as much as possible. They realized that they would have to confront him sooner or later, and weren't in the mood to address that situation just yet.

Taking into consideration the time zone difference, Suzanne made the telephone call to the doctor's office. Suzanne remembered the doctor's name Sandy told her before she unexpectedly got murdered. "If he can't come to the phone, which I expect that he won't, then I'll bring the cell with me and, hopefully, he'll call us back. I'll just have to keep trying to get him at a convenient time," she explained to Nancy. Nancy shook her head in agreement. "I'll call up one of her daughters, Vanessa or Veronica, and find out about the insurance policy, oh so subtly. I hope that we can get this information and start sorting out all of the circumstances. Meanwhile, we'll go to the Police Department and tell Inspector Gomez about our little undercover work and hope that he doesn't take a hissy fit." Suzanne agreed with Nancy's plan of action.

As Suzanne expected, the doctor's receptionist answered the office phone and told Suzanne that she would take her name and telephone number and that the doctor would call her back. Suzanne tried explaining that she was in China and that the doctor would be charged a roaming call, so if she could tell her when a good time was, she would call him back. "I hope that she understood what I was saying because if the doctor finds that roaming charge on his bill, he'll take a hissy fit," she explained to Nancy.

"Now it's my turn to try to call one of her children and find out the name of the insurance company, and in a roundabout way, find out how much money it's worth and if it's going to be double indemnity for a murder. Don't worry Suzanne, I'll be discreet and I'll ask the questions so that the secretary won't get the idea that I'm prying, I hope."

When the phone calls were made, messages were left. They'd have to try re-calling. Meanwhile, after breakfast, they'd head over to the police station to find Inspector Gomez and tell them what they did and what they suspect. They hoped that he would work with them, providing that this theory of theirs was right. "But we can't come right out and say what we think," Nancy told Suzanne. "We'll have to do it in such a way that maybe he'll work with us in solving this horrific crime. I don't know why there's always something dreadful happening; that comes about when we get involved in something or other. I mean, this was supposed to be a leisurely trip with no crimes or events occurring that we'd get mixed up in. Now here we go again, back to the same old, same old." Suzanne shook her head in agreement.

"Being the type of people that we are, we couldn't sit back and let these atrocities happen and not do anything about it." Nancy shook her head in conformity. "Let's go upstairs and have breakfast and then we'll go into town to see Inspector Gomez," Suzanne suggested as they closed their cabin door. As always, the breakfast didn't disappoint them, and when they left the table, Suzanne made an observation. "I'm not speaking for you, but when I get back, I'm going to go on such a diet. I must have gained at least 10 or more pounds on this vacation. My clothes barely fit me anymore. Yup, I've made up my mind. I'll continue to eat anything that my heart desires while we're away, but as soon as we get home, I'll have to get serious and do some diligent weight watching."

"Oh Suzanne, you're so funny. You always look good, and to be honest with you, the added weight looks good on you."

"It's easy for you to say, you're a lot younger than I am and you can put anything in your mouth and never gain an ounce. I swear it's not fair. It's like my cat, Boston. His stomach is hanging on the floor and Simka eats like a lady and is always the same weight. I watch what I give Boston, but I bet Mrs. Walsh sneaks some food his way. He was so malnourished when we found him. Now he's very overweight. We'll both have to lose weight. After all, I have to watch my girlish figure and get into all of my clothes that I have hanging in my closet. I get this curse from my Dad's side of the family. Everyone on the Pollack side has a weight problem."

"To be honest with you, Suzanne, I never thought that you had any weight problems. You always look perfect to me."

"Thanks Nancy, but I know that I have to always watch myself with calories and exercise or else I'll balloon up like a fat little pig. I don't have the extra inches of height that you have. Like Beverly, when she was pregnant, she didn't even look like she was carrying a child until she was in her eighth or ninth month. Me, as soon as I was pregnant the waist went, and I couldn't hide the fact after the second or third month." With that said Nancy put her hand on top of Suzanne's head, shook her hair and laughed. They headed out to see Inspector Gomez.

They walked up the pier and went to the village. The police station was located at the edge of the rural community. They spotted chickens in people's yards and walking along the street as if they owned it. They saw a few dogs that looked like they could use a few pounds, and some birds nesting in the trees about them as they approached the two-story structure. The women walked up the steps and hoped that Inspector Gomez could see them without an appointment.

They asked the desk clerk if the Inspector was in and a call was made informing him that two women were there to see him. They were told to wait and he would come out in a few minutes. They sat down on the wooden chairs by the clerk's desk and waited patiently, looking around the station. It wasn't as busy as the police stations that they were used to seeing. Everyone looked relaxed. They wondered if some of the policemen were out of the station looking for the pirates that were disrupting the usually peaceful village. The pier that they were docked at was one of many that the sail boat, with its heavy rope, was tied to the thick posts during their duration to this usually quiet village.

After a few minutes, they saw the Chief Inspector's door opening and Chief Gomez came out. In back of him was another officer but they weren't introduced. The two men shook hands and then Inspector Gomez walked toward the two women. Suzanne and Nancy arose and put out their hands in greeting. He asked them if they would join him in his office. They walked behind him and not a word was spoken until the office door was closed.

Suzanne was the first to speak. "Hi again, we were wondering if you've been able to find any more information about the pirates that commandeered our boat?"

"We really are putting forth all of our efforts, but so far, we haven't gotten any substantial leads. There are plain-clothes men out in the streets going to the various shops, but again, nothing has come up. As you know, this is a small village and all of the plain police officers that go undercover are really known to everyone."

"We appreciate all of your efforts, and we wanted to let you know that we've been doing some of our own investigative work." Inspector Gomez shook his head and waved the women to continue. Suzanne told him that they went to one of the local bars last evening and thought that some of the men acted a little strange when they saw that we were there. "That's not to condemn the men, but it was odd that suddenly they looked over, saw it was us (the people from the boat that was seized) and all of a sudden they got quiet and soon left."

"I'm a pretty good artist as Nancy can verify. What I'd like to do, with you or the department is to get an artist. If you don't have one, we will have to go to a larger city, I'll be glad to do so. I can help with these pictures." Inspector Gomez rubbed his chin and you could see the wheels turning in his head. "You know, Suzanne, that's not a bad idea. Do you think that if I can make an appointment for you to sit down with the criminal artist, that you'd make yourself available?" Addressing Nancy Suzanne said: "That first artist's rendition was only my imagination, now the real fun begins."

With that said, the two women waited for the inspector to make a few phone calls and then he let out a loud sigh. "It is done! The artist will be available for the two of you tomorrow. I'll give you the directions to go to the headquarters, which is located in Manila and we'll take it from there. I can't thank you enough for your cooperation." With that said; The Inspector walked them out of his office and shook their hands. To Suzanne it reminded her of her Papa. His hands were very large and he, like Inspector Gomez, was a man of immense proportion. The day was warm, as usual, and Suzanne and Nancy took their time getting back to the dock and their ship.

The rest of the day, Suzanne and Nancy hung around the boat and dock, noting the new sailing vessels coming in to get supplies for their vacations. They looked at each other, their thoughts kept to themselves, but each knew what the other was thinking. They hoped that the pirates wouldn't be pillaging the new sailing ships like they had theirs.

Nancy and Suzanne were on deck, soaking up the rays of the sun and, enjoying the quiet when suddenly they heard a dog barking. They looked around and started laughing when they spotted the dog on one of the newer ships that had docked at the pier. Suzanne loved animals and without warning, suddenly got up and went off the boat and walked up to the new ship, which the dog was declaring his. "Hey boy, aren't you a handsome specimen?" Suzanne didn't think that the owners of the sailing ship would mind but hesitated before she boarded, wanting to befriend the dog. She was patting the dog, and playing fetch with a piece of old wood she found near him. She looked at his collar and his name was etched on the piece of metal around his neck. His name was Sidney, which she thought was strange, but figured what the Hell, names don't mean squat.

She was enjoying the playfulness of the dog when the owners spotted her frolicking with Sidney. They came on board and with a questioning eye, wondered why she was obviously on board a ship that she had no business being on. Suzanne introduced herself and explained to the people why she boarded their vessel and hoped that they weren't upset. "Your dog is adorable, and I love British Labs. He's a friendly guy and we were playing catch with this piece of wood that he obviously is used to." After the initial surprise of finding a stranger on board, they warmed up to Suzanne and invited her to sit and have a drink with them. Come to find out, they came from the same place as Lawrence and were sailing around the world. They knew Lawrence and his family and before Suzanne realized it, they were calling home and got Lawrence's phone number. Before Suzanne had time to protest, they were on the phone with Lawrence and then handed the phone to Suzanne.

Obviously these people had money, because they thought nothing of the roaming charges this phone call would cost. Once they handed the phone to her, Suzanne was surprised to hear Lawrence on the other end of the cell phone. Suzanne walked away so they couldn't hear the entire conversation. She then told Lawrence, or as she liked to call him Larry, all about the vacation and what had happened. She assured him that everything was under control and she and Nancy were going to Manila to the police station to help the police artist in drawing the pirates. She hoped that, in this way, the artist could get a better perspective on what or who they were dealing with. She didn't want to stay on the phone for much longer, cognizant of the money it was costing these nice people whom she just met. Larry assured her that price was no object to the Van Der Molens. He explained that they lived in the village and he had gone to school with the husband years ago. They both declared that it was a small world.

After they got off of the phone, Suzanne was asked to join the couple for dinner off the ship. As much as Suzanne wanted to go, she explained to them about her friend Nancy and that they had plans already made. She thanked them and told them that this wouldn't be the last time she would be in their company. She again patted Sidney and told them that he was a wonderful dog. Suzanne went back to her ship and found Nancy sitting on top of the bed in their cabin. Nancy had just gotten off of the phone with Rich and told Suzanne about their conversation. Suzanne was glad to hear that everything back home was good and then slowly lowered herself onto her bed and, before she realized it, was sound asleep.

When Suzanne awoke, their room was dark and she heard the shower being used. Nancy came out and, when she saw that Suzanne was awake, put the lights back on. She explained that she didn't want to disturb Suzanne, knowing that she was probably tired from the salt air. Suzanne had to admit that it was a great vacation before the terrible, unfortunate events happened.

"Let's go up to dinner and make plans for tomorrow," Nancy suggested. "That's a good idea." The two women went upstairs and finished a delicious meal that the chef had prepared. When they finished, they didn't need much persuasion to top the delightful meal off with a scrumptious dessert. Suzanne and Nancy took a walk through the small village. On the way back to the ship, they happened to pass the small bar that they had gone into the evening before. The women looked at each other and with a shrug of their shoulders decided to finish the night off with a drink or two.

They entered the small tavern and the table that they sat at the evening before was available so they decided to go to it. The room was on the dark side, but they got used to the dim lights. They ordered drinks and were just shooting the breeze when a man came over and asked them if he could join them. Being friendly, they both said "sure" at the same time and wondered what made this gentleman want to sit with them.

Before they realized what was happening, the man introduced himself as seeing them last night and wanted to make their acquaintance. Nancy and Suzanne were slightly embarrassed but put their hands out to formally introduce themselves. Barry, which was his name, initiated the conversation, and before long, he had the two friends laughing with his friendly manner and jokes. Then suddenly he became serious and his voice was but a mere whisper when he told them that he might have answers to some of the questions they were asking the evening before.

Suzanne looked at Nancy and with a raised eyebrow asked him what he was talking about. Suzanne knew what he was saying, but wanted to hear directly from him what was on his mind. Barry leaned over the table and told them, in no uncertain terms, that he knew some interesting people who might help them in their quest to find the pirates or the men who shot the woman and stole the merchandise that they were looking for.

Suzanne played into Barry's hand and, with a doubting suspicion, asked him directly what he was talking about. "Well, it was obvious that the reason you came into our establishment was to find out if any of the people that were here would know the men that you were looking for," Barry confided to them. "It so happens that for a few hundred dollars or so, I might be able to get you some names and some shops that have your equipment." Suzanne didn't know if this guy was the real deal or simply trying to make a few bucks for himself and laugh all the way home. But, she thought that it might be worth the money to find out if what he was saying was the truth.

"We have to leave early tomorrow for an appointment that we have in Manila, but we should be home by early evening. Let's meet here tomorrow night. I'm interested in hearing what you have to say. We'll bring the money with us. I hope that you are a man of your word and will be here to tell us what we want to hear." They shook hands and Barry went back to the bar, bringing the glass with him and finishing it before he walked out of the tavern.

The women looked at each other as if to say, 'what the Hell was that all about' and ordered another drink while enjoying the music that was being played by a trio of guitars in the corner. Before they left, they put some money into the hands of the entertainers and walked out of the bar, happier than when they arrived.

On the way back to the ship, Suzanne told Nancy that they really didn't have anything to lose. "Oh no, just our lives," a pessimistic Nancy retorted. Suzanne looked at her and said: "Please, why all the drama? This is probably a scam of some sort, but we're on vacation, and if this is what Barry wants to do, I'll play along. We really don't have anything to lose, except a couple of hundred of hard-earned dollars, that is. And, I want you to know that I feel like a spy." They both laughed as they walked toward the gangway and onto the ship. A few guests were still talking and enjoying the stars in the beautiful night sky.

Suzanne lay on her bed, hands under her head, and thought of this fellow who said his name was Barry. To her he looked and reminded her of the old time actor, Peter Lorre, and started laughing. If only he had a Sidney Greenstreet as his sidekick or fellow conspirator. She had to laugh at her thoughts. Thinking about the old shows she used to enjoy going to, put her into a heavy sleep. Suzanne dreamt about many of these movies and, with a smile on her face when she awoke, felt that somehow she was part of these plots.

After a good night's sleep, the two women showered and dressed. They went upstairs and ate a hearty breakfast that Chef André had prepared and enjoyed the varied pastries that were put on the table. Suzanne felt satisfied and was now ready to meet with the artist. On the way, Nancy questioned Suzanne on her remembering the features of these so called, pirates.

"Nancy, you don't realize that, as an artist, I have this uncanny ability to visualize and remember certain characteristics that most people would never remember." All Nancy did was look at her friend and partner who shook her head in disbelief. "You'll see when the artist is through with my rendition. Then I'll make a believer out of you!" All Nancy could say was: "Seeing, is believing!"

"But don't be surprised if you see that the rendition I'll be giving the artist isn't all that accurate. After all, we really don't want these pirates to be found and tried for a crime that they didn't commit."

They arrived at the facility and Manuel, the police artist, was waiting patiently for the two women. Suzanne asked if he'd mind if Nancy was in the room with them and he had no problem with that request. It took about three hours for the pictures to be made. When all was done, Nancy had to admit that the pictures were done with such precision that she felt that the men were standing in front of her. Manuel shook Suzanne's hand and thanked her for her cooperation. He told her that he would have copies made and that the police would place the pictures in areas where many people couldn't help but see them. He hoped that this rendition would lead to an arrest or apprehension of the criminals.

With that said Suzanne shook Manuel's hand and thanked him for his patience. As the women were walking down the steps Suzanne gave Nancy a wink and the two women leisurely caught a cab. Nancy told Suzanne that she would pay for their dinner. "I guess you were right and that's all I'm saying. Don't we have to meet with Barry tonight at that local pub?"

"You're right, Nancy, I almost forgot about it. How could I have forgotten such an important meeting?" Suzanne pushed Nancy slightly and started laughing. "How could I have forgotten such an important aspect of this crime?" Suzanne couldn't stop laughing and at that point Nancy realized that Suzanne hadn't forgotten about their significant meeting.

The women ordered their usual drinks and the bartender (who seemed to be always there) told them what they wanted before they were finished. "He must own this establishment, or else he has a great memory," Nancy exclaimed. Suzanne asked for a menu, and he recited the menu that he had memorized. Half way through their meal, Nancy told Suzanne that having such a limited menu enabled the bar to make sure that when they did serve a meal, it was good. With full stomachs, both women waited patiently for Barry to show up.

"You know, Nancy, I never told you about the trip that I took to the Amazon Jungle. On part of the trip, I visited Devil's Island, which is in French Guiana. It was where Papillon and Lieutenant Alfred Dreyfus were held prisoners. They had a hotel on that Island and I swear one of the men seated at one of the tables looked like Sydney Greenstreet. By the way, did you ever see the movie Papillon which starred Steve McQueen? When I was on the Island, I saw some of the letters that Lieutenant Dreyfus wrote home to his devoted wife and family. It was sad and interesting at the same time. The Hotel had a very dim light and a large fan was circulating the stale air. Anyway, the owner was nice enough to bring me upstairs and show me what the rooms looked like. Someday, if I wanted complete isolation from everyone (don't feel bad, even you included) then I would probably go to that Island and write my memoires or just read on the bed that sat in the middle of the small room. Do you know that they do nuclear testing there and the residents have to leave the Island at least once a week? I was surprised, but I saw unusual sights there that I've never seen elsewhere. Peacocks were roaming free and, instead of dogs and cats, the Island was overrun by what appeared to be large rats or whatever. They didn't seem to harm anything. They scurried about, living on their own. It was very interesting."

"Not to digress, but I hadn't thought that when the Maltese Falcon was made into a movie picture, I think it was made in 1931; I'm sure that you never heard of that particular movie, which by the way is a classic. It was written by Dashiell Hammett and directed by John Huston. The actors were amazing. I'm sure that you've heard of Humphrey Bogart who played Samuel Spade. Well, there was Mary Astor who played Bridgitt O'Shaughnessy in the movie. That's when I saw Sydney Greenstreet, who played Kasper Gutman and I learned to love Peter Lorre who played Joel Cairo. Now those were movies that were great! Someday, I'll have to rent it and you'll be mesmerized seeing it. It's not that I don't like the movies that are made today. I saw Beaches starring Bette Midler and Barbara Hersey and cried at the end. There are a few new features that are great. But maybe being older, I appreciate movies and things that were made back in the good old days."

"Did you know that Dolly Parton wrote, 'I'll Always Love You!!' Dolly Parton gave the song to the Colonel, the one that used to manage Elvis and he wanted to give too little money to Dolly for the writes for Elvis to sing it. Dolly said thanks but no thanks. That's how come Whitney Houston got to sing that song in '*The Bodyguard.*'" Waving her hand Suzanne stated: "Oh, I'm just a bank of incidental knowledge." Nancy was laughing when they saw Barry approaching their table. He seemed to have appeared out of nowhere.

He slipped into a seat at their table and smiled a smile that reminded Suzanne of a wicked old man. They shook their heads in recognition and waited for him to make the first move. He acknowledged the two women who were waiting for him to start the conversation. Clearing his throat, he handed Suzanne a simple piece of paper with a few names of establishments that were pawn shops known by only a few of the Islanders. Nancy discreetly handed Barry some money under the table. He didn't count it in front of them, but they knew that as soon as he left, it would be counted. In a soft voice, he told them that he saw pictures of the 'would be' pirates on poles and in stores that were all around the town. "I'm sure that I recognize some of these men and, even though they may have worn beards and mustaches as disguises, anyone with a brain would know who these men are."

Nancy asked if he recognized the men and he nodded his head in agreement. "Sure I do, but that will cost you more money" he greedily told Nancy. She lifted her shoulders to her head and motioned, with her fingers, to come forth with the names. He told her that he'd have another list made with their names tomorrow evening, same time; same place. He finished the drink that the waiter had put down in front of him, and after he realized that another drink wasn't forthcoming, moved it aside, stood up to leave and turning his head on his way out said, "I'll see you tomorrow evening."

Both women didn't say anything on the way back to the sailboat. When they arrived back in their room, with the door closed, Nancy was the first to speak. Suzanne was taking off her clothes and getting into her pajamas. "I wouldn't trust that guy as far as I could throw him. But if this list proves right, then the next list most likely will also. I thought that you made sure that the pictures of the pirates didn't look like the men that were actually the men that seized the ship. How come Barry recognizes them?" "Well, smarty pants, I made the men look real, but not enough that most people would be able to say for sure that these men were the actual pirates." "Let's see what happens. Tomorrow evening should prove interesting," Nancy verbalized.

Suzanne was on her bed, listening intently when she shook her head and said that she also agreed with Nancy. "I also wouldn't trust him but, at this point in time, we haven't another choice. Let's meet up tomorrow evening and see what happens. Meanwhile, tomorrow we'll meander to these shops and see if we can find any of the items that are on the list of stolen merchandise and jewelry." Nancy agreed, but also added that some of the items might be in the back room and not readily available to just anyone. "Then we'll make it worthwhile for whoever is running the pawn shop to go into the back and get the items that we will ask for."

"You realize that you are a cunning and deceitful person whom I admire. I hope that, in the back of your mind, you're not thinking of this as a movie part and are doing this for the excitement of it all; because if you are, you're sicker than I thought." Suzanne laughed at Nancy's words and threw a soft notebook across the room hitting her softly on the leg. "You think you know me. Just get those notions out of your mind."

With that said and done, both women cuddled under their covers and, with various thoughts in their minds, fell into a deep sleep. After thoughts of the old movies, Suzanne must have been thinking of Stephen and Larry because she woke up in a sweat with the covers in disarray. She felt confused and suddenly she felt herself in a panic attack. She quickly took two pills, that she only took when she felt anxiety coming on, and downed them with water. She looked across the aisle and saw Nancy sleeping and, most likely, dreaming of Rich because she had a visible smile affixed to her face. It took a while for Suzanne to fall back to sleep, as she couldn't get into a comfortable position and had various troubled thoughts going through her mind. She found herself remembering her first sexual encounter with Stephen after their second reunion and then another thought of what would happen if the time came for her to become intimate with Larry. She felt the sweat going down between her breasts and her heartbeat racing. She picked up a soft covered book and tried getting her mind off of her sexual fantasies, to no avail. She put the book down and let her mind drift to wherever it wanted to go. Suzanne realized that she had no control over these thoughts and emotionally felt crippled when she wasn't in control of her feelings.

Suzanne let her mind drift with thoughts of Larry. She imagined how and when they would meet. Larry's own fantasies would become a reality. She envisioned that they were on his yacht with just the sound of the waves and soft music playing in the background, their kisses growing from soft kisses to passionate and hard desires. Their clothes discarded, thrown to the floor with abandonment, his long fingers finding her soft, curvaceous body and sending her entire being into an emotional turmoil, with wanton desire. His light touch was driving her wild with desires that she hadn't thought possible. He finally found her clitoris and with agility and dexterity, touched her in such a way that she had no control over her own excitement. Before she realized it, she found herself climaxing to his touch. She moved quickly and, with no constraint, wanted to please him as much as she was being satisfied.

Suzanne envisioned herself moving as the aggressor and putting him onto his back. She slowly touched every part of him, kissing him all the while. She felt his erection and knew that he was tantalized by her boldness. She felt herself kissing his entire body, every part of him reacting to her moist lips. She then went down lower until she found his throbbing manhood. Licking it from the base of his erection to the tip of his penis, she then took him and sucked until she heard him moaning with wanton desire. Before she realized what was happening, he put her on her back and entered her and thrust his pulsing and wet penis into her womanly opening. They moved in unison, in total abandonment of their thoughts or cares. All they wanted was to feel the pent up release of their desires. After they climaxed, she lay in his arms. Her head lay on his chest, his fingers caressing her arms. Not a word was spoken...

She awoke with her womanhood completely wet. 'Well,' she thought to herself, 'now I know what a wet dream is all about.' She quickly got into the

shower and felt the warm water act as a wakeup call. When she was drying herself off, she saw Nancy slowly waking up and knew in her heart that she wouldn't tell her best friend what happened while she slept. This was to be kept to her-self. She didn't know if this would ever come to be, but something in her mind realized that she knew that what she dreamed would somehow become a reality. When it would happen was completely up to her. She realized that Larry had wanted them to be a couple for many years, but had waited patiently for Suzanne to come to her senses and make his dreams come true. Well, she admitted to herself, the time was coming and the next time they were to get together, he would be in for the surprise of his life. With a smile on her face, she told Nancy to take a shower. They had a full day ahead. Nancy wondered why Suzanne was smiling but knew better than to ask her friend. She took Suzanne's good mood in stride and complied with her wishes.

CHAPTER TWENTY ONE

Suzanne and Nancy enjoyed the morning by eating a hearty breakfast on the sailing ship with the other guests. Suzanne realized that they had to wait until evening before they could get the information from Barry. On their day's agenda, they made plans to go to the various pawn shops and, hopefully, find some of the items that were on the list. While they were walking to the designated places, they saw some of the pictures of the pirates on the various posts on the sidewalks. Suzanne had to smile because she realized that she was responsible, in part, for getting these photos out for all to see.

When they got to the first shop, they walked in, they were greeted suspiciously by the man behind the counter. Suzanne understood that he wasn't used to seeing American tourists come into his establishment. They walked up to the counter and inquired about some of the items that they memorized from the list. At first he was distrustful, but after a few moments, he grasped the situation at hand. They were customers that wanted to buy these items. Abandoning his misgivings, he brought one or two items for the women to look at. Suzanne and Nancy knew nothing about most of the equipment that was stolen, but took a chance and bought some apparatus that they felt Captain Winters would appreciate, even if he had bought other pieces to replace the stolen ones. They realized that this shop didn't have the jewelry that they were looking for and thanked the proprietor for the items that they had purchased.

They went to other shops on the list and, finally, came to one that specialized in jewelry that was displayed beautifully under the bright, glass cases. When Nancy hemmed a bit and was asking for specific pieces, the owner of the shop was apprehensive. They engaged him in conversation and, after a while, he let his guard down and went into the back where the stolen pieces were hidden. Nancy guessed that he didn't dare put them out front for policemen to confiscate and close his shop. Suzanne and Nancy bought a few of the pieces that he showed them and thanked him for his patience. On the way home, Suzanne knew that Tracy would be happy to have her jewelry back as she had received it from her husband. Suzanne also knew that she had to engage the people of the town to let their guard down and, once they felt at ease and not threatened, would tell her whose pictures, they thought, were stapled to the posts. They'd better do this fast for she knew that time was of the essence and it would be a matter of days before the ship would be discharged and let go to be on its way.

After dinner, the women went again to the local bar and once again were given the same table and drinks without saying a word to the waiter. They saw Barry enter the front bar door and waited for him to sit down beside them. He shoved the list in front of Nancy and without saying a word, took the envelope handed to him. With a wicked smirk, he thanked the women for their trust and departed without looking back.

Suzanne and Nancy finished their drinks and headed out to go back to the ship and look over the list Barry had provided. They hoped that he knew what he was doing and this wasn't a wild goose chase. "You know, Nancy, we don't know if Barry is his right name or where he lives. I'm assuming that he's telling us the truth, but all we have to go on is our instincts."

"Of course, you're right Suzanne, but we really don't have another alternative, do we?" Back in their rooms, they looked over the list provided to them and made notes beside each name. "Some of the people on board are wondering where we disappear to during the day and evening. I acted as if I didn't know what they were talking about and they let it go. I hope they abandon their questions and go about their business and leave us alone to do our own thing" Nancy said aloud. "I hope that your wishes come true and tomorrow we'll start on this list. We'll never know until we see for ourselves if his list of names is real or not." With that said, both women went upstairs to enjoy the beautiful moon and stars that were shining brightly in the night sky.

Right after her morning shower, Suzanne's phone rang. Dr. Waters' office was returning her call. She didn't want to waste his time, so she got right to the point. "Dr. Waters, I know all about the HIPPA laws." She then described the situation in which she found herself and Nancy. "I know that you can't give me the answers to my questions, but would you have to tell the FBI if they were to ask you the same information?"

"The only way that I could go against the new law is if the FBI were to give me a court order requiring me to forego the confidentiality between Mrs. Swartz and myself." This was the response that she was expecting. She thanked him and knew that the next phone call would be to her friends in the FBI, and since Manila was outside of the U.S., they would probably have to get Interpol involved. She and Nancy had worked with many of the people at Interpol, so she had no objection if this was the case. She then called the Boston office and asked to speak to Tim or Kevin.

After she explained to her friends what she suspected and what she needed done, they told her that they would get back to her or Interpol would intervene and call her. She thanked them for understanding. Now it was time to wait and see. Meanwhile a lot of footwork had to be done to gather the names that matched the pictures on the many poles and stores that were showing the pictures of the pirates.

"Before we start out this morning, I'd love to present Tracy with the jewelry that we found at the pawn shop. The look on her face will be like winning the lottery," an excited Nancy exclaimed. "Go for it girl," was all that Suzanne could say. She waited until everyone was finished with their breakfast and asked Tracy if she could see her a minute. At the bow of the sailboat, Suzanne saw Tracy's mouth open and then her jumping up and down. She then saw Tracy hug Nancy, and taking Nancy's hand, brought her to see Mike who was emerging from the deck below.

Suzanne had goose bumps when she saw the three people jumping up and down when they saw the items in Tracy's possession. After a few minutes, Nancy excused herself and went to find Suzanne who was patiently waiting on one of the bench seats on deck. Suzanne told Nancy when her friend stood before her; "I saw the reaction that Tracy and Mike had when they saw the missing pieces of jewelry. Now that makes our trip to the pawnshop worthwhile. After another cup of tea, I think we should take a walk through the town and see if we can find out who these pirates might be. You never know what we'll find."

After Suzanne was finished with her second cup of tea that seemed to renew her strength, she and Nancy strolled leisurely through the town nodding their heads to many people who now were becoming familiar with them. They stopped at the local meat market and bakery and were surprised at the nice greeting they received from the proprietors of the family-owned shops. One person with whom they were becoming acquainted told them, on the hush, hush, the names of the men, in the photos. Pointing to one of the pirates, she told Suzanne that she had known Mario since he was a little boy and knew his family as well. She pointed to Efran and explained to the women how the two men were related. "I think that I know the others as well, but not as much as I know Mario and Efran and their families."

Suzanne assured the woman who owned the bakery that Mario and Efran's families would never know how they found out about them. With information and addresses in hand, the two women walked leisurely to Mario's house. Suzanne was surprised to see that he lived in a bungalow on stilts that was above the water. A large staircase led to the front door. Suzanne was reminding herself how lucky she was that she had taken up the exercise program before they left on vacation, otherwise she would have been huffing and puffing all the way up the staircase. Nancy knocked on the door and waited for a response. They heard a woman's voice asking who was there.

Hesitantly, they saw the door open a crack and Nancy spoke to the person on the other side of it. She explained that she meant no harm and wanted to be let in so she could have a few questions answered. No, she wasn't part of the local police but this was an important issue and would she be kind enough to allow the women entrance. They saw the door opening. Suzanne extended her hand and introduced themselves to Mario's wife, Maria. When the women entered the clean, small home, Maria motioned for them to have a seat. The women realized that Maria didn't speak English fluently, but with hand motions, Suzanne felt as if she were playing 20 questions, they got their point across. They found out that Mario was out doing errands. Their children were in school and would be home later, early in the afternoon. Nancy and Suzanne didn't want the children to get any ideas, so they thanked Maria and found out approximately when Mario would be returning home.

The woman did some errands about town and when they felt that Mario would be at his residence, made their way back to the neat bungalow. Again Suzanne found herself trudging up the steep stairs and, this time when they knocked, Mario answered the door. He looked like a pleasant soul and when he motioned for them into the front foyer, they obliged. Suzanne felt she was the spokesperson and with no exaggeration, told him the dilemma that they found themselves in. It was a moral issue, one that neither, the pirates, or Suzanne and Nancy had an answer for.

Mario spoke English fluently and it was easier for them to communicate than it was when they had spoken to Maria. Nothing was left on the table. Suzanne and Nancy told Mario everything that they thought should be said and then waited for Mario to tell his side of the story. At first, he denied that he was one of the pirates. Then when it was apparent that the pictures around town revealed his true identity, he became quiet. At first the silence between the three people was hard to take. Suzanne could feel the tension in the small, neat room. After a while, Mario told them a story that Suzanne and Nancy realized was really the truth, but in story form. They listened intently as Mario revealed the reason for his and his friends' new venture. After listening to his story, which lasted well over forty-five minutes all was quiet. Suzanne and Nancy were dumfounded and didn't know what to say. After a while, Suzanne cleared her throat and suggested that they set up a meeting time and place for his friends and the two women to meet.

Suzanne and Nancy found themselves at the edge of the woods. Nancy told Suzanne that she didn't think that this was a wise place for a meeting. "You realize that no one knows that we are here. We are at their mercy. They could kill us, bury us and no one would be the wiser."

"Have some faith Nancy," Suzanne scolded. "I'm as scared as you are, but I'm a positive person. I really don't think that these men mean to do us harm. When they realize that we are friends and want to help them and not let them take blame for something for which they weren't responsible. I have faith and it wouldn't hurt for you to think the same way that I do."

"Okay, Mary Poppins, let's hope that you're right and no harm will come to us. We didn't bring any weapons to defend ourselves."

"Let's put it this way, what would weapons do when we're out numbered? It looks good on TV or the movies, but let's not fool ourselves into thinking that we're invincible," Nancy said. "We're sitting targets no matter what. So, if I had a gun, it would give us better odds, but a knife wouldn't do us any good."

"I was just thinking, we should get the heck out of here and meet at a place that is surrounded by the public. At least we'd have a better chance."

"Well, it's too late now. I think I hear the men coming down the path. Just sit tight and let's see how the conversation goes."

"Thanks Suzanne, I always listen to you and then I kick myself for doing so. I hope that this turns out all right!"

The men fell in silently behind Mario as he went to the designated meeting place. He had explained to his fellow comrades about his conversation with the two women and he suggested that they meet with them to figure out what should be done. They saw a deer with its doe wander in front of them and heard chipmunks scurrying about. The various birds and wildlife made the woods come alive. Sunny whispered, "I hope we are doing the right thing." To this, Telemeo replied, "We have nothing to lose; we can deny everything and it would be their word against ours." Ronnie nudged Telemeo and said softly, "We can always kill them and leave them in the woods. No one would find them for a long time and then we'd be free to deny any sort of guilt." Sunny heard Ronnie and told him to be quiet. "These women were honest enough to tell Mario the truth, let's hear what they have to say. After all, we might be pirates, but that is not who we really are. As for killing, I don't want to be held responsible for doing something that I didn't do. Now shut up, and let's take it one minute at a time."

The sweat was pouring down between Suzanne's breasts and on the back of her neck. She felt the tension and tried to ignore the feeling of dread that was taking over. She wished that Nancy hadn't said those awful words of doom and was now questioning herself. Was it smart to meet with these men out in the woods, with no one to help or see them? Only time would tell.

The men were a few minutes away and Suzanne felt like grabbing Nancy's hand and running, but to where, she didn't know. She felt dizzy with grief but didn't know how to quell her fear or the nauseous feeling that was sitting like a whale at the bottom of her stomach.

Before the men got to the clearing that was to be the meeting place, Tolemeo kept hearing Sunny complain and told him to shut the fuck up. "I don't want to hear any more bullshit until we hear what these two women have to say, okay?" They didn't have much further to go and after Tolemeos' outburst, everyone was quiet and walked to the intended spot.

When they reached the gathering place, Mario greeted the two women and introduced the other men to them. The men were suspicious and rightly so, thought Suzanne. They all found some broken logs and used these as places to sit. Mario didn't know how to start the meeting, so Suzanne started speaking from her heart, not caring if the men were offended or not.

"I know how difficult life can get. Believe me when I tell you that I've been there myself. All of us have burdens and even though they're different we handle each situation differently. Mario told me what happened in the fishing village and my heart goes out to all of you. I truly understand what you, your families and friends are feeling at this time. Oh sure, you are probably thinking, what does this rich American lady know about not having money to raise our families and keep them in the manner that they're used to. I don't want to bore you with the unhappy situation that I had to deal with, but I assure you that I was in the same position as you are finding yourself in. Of course, I didn't resort to stealing other people's possessions, but if I had to, I'd do something in order to protect my family. Now it seems that besides being labeled thieves, you are charged with murdering a woman in cold blood. To be labeled murderers is not fair, and Nancy and I won't let you take the blame for this act."

The men were astounded by Suzanne's words. They now got up and gathered in a circle. Suzanne couldn't understand what was being said, but assumed that they were favorable comments. She saw the men shaking their heads in agreement. "I know that I don't have the power to undo any fishing agreements that you and some other governments made years ago, but there has to be some way that these burdens that you are facing can be met. First of all, the act of murder has to be dealt with. The education and food for your families are next. But, like I said, the heinous crime is the first thing that has to be brought to the authorities, and Nancy and I are working on this situation. We have called the doctor of this woman and the insurance company and are waiting for them to get back to us. I'm asking you to give us time to work out the details and get this cleared up. I beg of you not to go out as pirates any longer. I happen to know some very rich Philippine families and they have scholarships, money and charities that abound in the United States. There is no reason why they can't set up some sort of fund, (not a charity) that can reeducate you and have you trained for another type of work. I realize that fishing has been a tradition for years, going back generations, but obviously, this industry is no longer viable to keep you or your families in good financial standing. Give Nancy and me a few more days and I will have some answers for you, I hope." They got up and made a date and time to meet again. After the men left, Nancy hugged Suzanne and told her how proud she was of her. "Don't be that happy yet, my friend. This is only the beginning. I, or should I say we, have a lot of work ahead of us to make everything that we need to know verified and then we'll both feel fulfilled. Let's get out of here before I get bitten to death by these dreadful mosquitoes and insects. You know how I hate traipsing in the woods."

"Yes, I remember the times when you used to go into Carlisle State Forest, and even though you enjoyed painting pictures from the many landscapes, you always groused about the insects and bugs." They both laughed as they headed on out.

While they were walking back to the ship, Nancy commented that she was surprised that the Pirates were not as bad as she envisioned them to be. "I really thought that they'd be tough characters, not listen to what we had to say and they'd have killed and buried us in the woods."

"Well then, why did you come with me?"

"I really don't know, but I figured where you go, so go I. Anyway, you usually are a pretty good judge of character and if Mario was a decent human being, then his friends probably were as well."

Suzanne acknowledged Nancy; "Thanks for having faith in my decision. But I have to admit that deep down I was pretty scared. Luckily, everything worked out, so far, for the best. Let's see what happens when I talk to the insurance company and the doctor and our friends at the FBI. I have a feeling that the insurance company will have us running around because that's what they're noted for." Nodding her head in agreement, Nancy went onto the dock first and led the way to what they knew would be a long night of writing notes on what had to be done.

After getting connected to Kevin from the Boston Office of the FBI, Suzanne told him their quandary and listened intently to what he had to say. After a fifteen-minute phone call, she was told that he would contact Interpol and get a name and number for them to relate their story. Kevin also told them that he'd take care of the court order by contacting a fellow that he knew that was located in the Chicago FBI, and they'd get the HIPPA laws taken care of A.S.A.P. and have it hand delivered to Dr. Waters personally. He was glad that he could help. Meanwhile Suzanne was able to get through to the insurance company, and she was lucky to have gotten the number of the insurance policy and all the information that she needed. They were busy making all the necessary calls when a sudden knock on the door interrupted their business.

They found Arthur standing there, and he waited for them to invite him in. After a few awkward minutes, the women had no other recourse but to ask him into their small quarters. Arthur told them that he knew that Nancy had spoken to two of his daughters and was upset that she made the phone calls. He thought it was none of their business. Suzanne and Nancy were speechless, but then Suzanne took over, and on the defensive, related to Arthur what she and Nancy were doing. It took a while for her to state her story, but felt it was only right to be honest with him and to get to the bottom of all of the lies that were being told. Arthur sat down on one of the empty beds and shook his head from side to side. They waited patiently for words to form, but nothing was forth coming.

After what seemed forever, Arthur took a deep breath and told the women how much he loved Sandy. It was hard for him to relate his and Sandy's feelings for one another, but it seemed that when he started he couldn't stop. He told them of their many conversations in their cabin. Darkness was a blessing, for she couldn't see the tears that were streaming down his face. Listening to him talk had Suzanne's and Nancy's eyes brimming with tears. They didn't want to get too worked up by his story because they didn't know if this was an act or the real thing.

After what seemed ages, they thanked him for his revelation and acted as if they believed what he said. When he left, and the door closed, Nancy looked over to where Suzanne was seated and asked her what she thought of the unexpected meeting. "To be honest with you Nancy, I really don't know what to think. He said all the right things, but you know as well as I do that talk is cheap. We have to speak to the doctor and the insurance agency and then maybe it will help with our decision."

"I think you're right, Suzanne. We can't become emotionally invested until we hear all of the facts. What we know, we'll keep to ourselves and then you and I will talk it over."

"Good idea, Nancy. Now let's make these important phone calls. It's about the right time."

Suzanne was told by Tim at his Boston FBI office that Kevin spoke to his friend from Chicago and gave her his personal number in Chicago. She thanked Tim and when they hung up, she called Marty Robbins, who was the FBI agent in Chicago. Marty told Suzanne what was happening and when to expect Dr.

Waters would get the subpoena from the court to release Sandy's medical records. She then called the insurance company and was again put on hold. She bit her inner lip in frustration, knowing that this would happen. After holding on for what seemed over half an hour, she hung up the cell phone and vowed that, come heck or high water, she wouldn't stand for this type of indecision tomorrow evening.

They both got into their pajamas. Their plans were to meet with the so called pirates in the early afternoon. While Suzanne was lying in bed, she again thought of the woods, all of the bugs and felt a cold chill go through her. She had a hard time falling asleep and then the two faces floated by her again. She asked herself when this would end. She knew that her dilemma wouldn't end until she made up her mind about the two men that were in her life.

Suzanne was realistic and knew that Stephen would never divorce his wife. He had many hang-ups, but he also had many great qualities. However, his crazy thoughts on what was right were driving her crazy. No, he left her no recourse but to realize that he'd never change and his *mishigus* was all his own doing. He was his own worst enemy. On the other hand, Larry was free and he was truly a *mensch*. Yes, his departed wife was lovely and he had a wonderful life with her. They were lucky to have had beautiful children and money so that they didn't have monetary issues to burden their existence. She was fortunate to realize that he was the perfect man to have if she wanted a mate. He was handsome, money was not a problem and he came from a wonderful family. Besides all of that, he wanted to make her happy. She couldn't wait until she got back home from this vacation and could see him again. She dreamt, many a time, of their lovemaking and knew that it would be a wonderful experience and pleasure. A smile appeared on her face as those thoughts filled her mind as she found her eyes closing and she would be off to face another day.

When she woke, Suzanne was surprised to see Nancy had taken her shower, and was dressed and ready to go for the day. "I didn't want to disturb you, making noise and everything that goes along with being up. You seemed very content and were smiling in your sleep. I hope that the smile had to do with dreaming about Larry." Suzanne stretched out her arms and moved her neck from side to side. "As a matter of fact, I had wonderful dreams and, yes Larry was in most of them." With that said she hopped out of bed and got into the hot shower that she craved to fully wake her up.

Yelling from the shower, hoping that Nancy would hear her, she told her best friend that she would be ready in about twenty minutes. "Why don't you go upstairs and start having breakfast and I'll meet you there."

"That's a good idea. I'll see you when you get topside." With that, Suzanne got out of the shower and put her long blonde hair into a ponytail, knowing that she wasn't going to a fashion show today. While she was putting on her dressed-for-woods clothes, she felt a chill run through her body. She tried ignoring the feeling but couldn't get the sensation to leave her thoughts. She considered all of the options that they would have to mull over with the men and tried to think on what could be believed and what evidence she had to judge those impressions. Suzanne tried ignoring these cautious signals and put on a little make up. She also brought along her bug repellent to save her from the many anticipated insect bites. Looking at herself one more time, she straightened up her spine and headed upstairs to meet up with Nancy, her new-formed friends, and go to the designated meeting place.

Both Nancy and Suzanne were full from a hearty breakfast, and after talking a bit to the people on board the Vacation of a Lifetime, they knew the time was right to head out to the encounter. She hated the feeling of not knowing what to expect, but was ready to hear anything. Nancy and Suzanne had been through the town often and were getting familiar with most of the people they saw every day. They nodded to the baker, the meat man and the many people who strolled every day for the fresh items to be put on the table for their family to enjoy. Suzanne was glad that she brought her cell phone with her and, although it was too early in the States to make any phone calls, it gave her a sense of security to carry it and have it with her.

The women were in no hurry because they knew that they were early for the meeting. Suzanne could tell that Nancy wasn't as calm as she appeared. They looked into some shop windows and admired some of the items that they seemed to have overlooked the last time that they went by these establishments. It was that or that the owners had changed the displays. "We have time to go into some of the stores, let's go and try to take our mind off of this inevitable fiasco," Nancy said.

Suzanne went along with her friend's advice, but couldn't shake the feeling of doom about to enter her every bone. Nancy poked around a bit and told the shopkeeper that she'd be back to pick up the item that she purchased at the end of the day. The bought item seemed to have put a gleam on the sales person's face. With that done, they meandered a while until they came to the clearing where the forest started. "I don't know about you Nancy, but something doesn't seem kosher, if you know what I mean. I've had this funny feeling all day and I can't seem to let it go."

"Well let's try to be up-beat and not let our nerves show" a courageous Nancy told Suzanne. "Let's listen to what these men have to say and then maybe we can come to a conclusion on what has to be done," advised Suzanne. The women walked into the dense forest, their nerves shattered as they kept brushing off the many mosquitoes that were flying about. As Nancy was batting off her enemies, she said aloud, "Do you think that there is a body of stagnant water around. That's the only reason that I can think of for this many dive bombers to keep at us?" As Suzanne was swatting off the many insects she remarked, "Even the repellent isn't doing squat in getting them to ease off."

The further they walked Suzanne thought that she heard footsteps behind her and kept looking back. "What are you so jumpy about?"

"I don't know, I thought I heard footsteps in back of us."

"It's probably your imagination Suzanne, but if not, it might be that the men are behind us and walking to the meeting as we are."

"I hope so," said a nervous Suzanne. "You're usually not this jumpy. Maybe you didn't get as much sleep as you thought," Nancy said, trying to ease the tension that she saw her friend exhibiting. "It's probably nothing. I'm letting my imagination get the best of me." With that said, they continued on in silence as Suzanne's ears were attuned to any unnatural sounds.

It seemed like hours until they got to their destination. There, they waited patiently. Suzanne looked briefly at her watch to make sure that they were on time. Meanwhile, Mario led his friends and fellow comrades deep into the woods. Mario had a lot on his mind as he remembered the words of warning that his friends had given him when they had met at his house last evening. Sunny was upset and let his comrades know, in no uncertain terms, that he didn't like depending on two women, especially foreigners. "I spoke to my friends who own some of the pawn shops in town, and come to find out that these two women bought some of the jewelry and other trinkets that we had stolen from the people who were on the sailing ship. Also, another friend of mine told me that they had gone into his place and bought some sailing equipment that just so happens to have been stolen from that vessel as well." The men were not happy with that revelation.

"Before we get too upset about these things happening, why don't we just come out and ask them why they did it. To me that makes sense," an ever-diligent Mario exclaimed. The other men carried on their conversations and reverted back to the original language, Filipina, which was spoken by the native Philippines. A lot of hand motions were made and to Mario, the men didn't seem pleased by what was happening.

Mario tried to calm his friends down and didn't let them know that Sunny's revelation didn't make him happy either. The discussion went on for hours and nothing seemed to get resolved. At the end of a long night, they decided to go

home and think about what was happening. Mario saw his friends to the door but was not happy with what he was afraid might happen to these two women who were trying to help.

That morning Mario and his fellow comrades in crime met as they were supposed to and Mario hoped that his friends had thought carefully on what was said last evening. He could tell that the women were ahead of them in the forest. His great grandfather had taught him and many of his young friends to observe the ground and, like the Indians of old he trained the boys how to track enemies and animals in the deep forest. He kept his knowledge to himself, but he was worried about these two women who didn't want to see them get arrested for a murder that they didn't commit.

CHAPTER TWENTY TWO

Suzanne and Nancy got to the designated spot and sat down on a fallen log, waiting for the men to meet them. Suzanne was quiet and couldn't get the feeling of doom out of her mind. Bad vibes kept penetrating her brain and then she thought of the stagnant body of water. She didn't know if it existed or not, and thoughts of the men killing her and Nancy and dumping their lifeless bodies into the water wouldn't leave her. She tried to quell these awful images, and with an attempt to make her mood lighthearted, brought up Nancy and Rich's impending wedding plans.

Nancy wasn't buying her friend's effort to brighten her and Suzanne's mood. "Let's not even talk about my plans. Thanks for trying to get my mind set into a different zone, but it won't work. Let's see what Mario and his friends have to say. When all of this work is done, then we can lighten our mood, and I'll tell you our tentative plans." With that said she hugged Suzanne and, with a broken stick, made a tic tack toe symbol in the dry land and jabbed Suzanne to start playing the game with her until the men came to meet them.

They heard the men talking about five minutes after the women got to the designated area. They looked at each other and didn't say a word. Soon enough, all would be said. Suzanne and Nancy stood up waiting for the men to arrive. Suzanne found it difficult to breathe. She let out a big breath when she saw them taking a turn at the large tree that was their meeting place.

Mario nodded his head in recognition and motioned for everyone to take a seat on the fallen logs that were all over the forest area. He cleared his throat and began his speech. "First of all I want to thank you," spreading his hands out as recognition to the two women seated in front of him.

"I understand where you're coming from, and I think it's brave for you to do the things that you are doing to try to help us in this predicament. But there are real concerns that we can't ignore."

With that said Sunny got up and began his diatribe. His criticism and attack, Suzanne thought, was uncalled for and when he was finished with his rant, she got up and started attacking his words.

"First of all, I want to see a raise of hands as to who agrees with what I just heard Sunny say." Suzanne waited and only saw one or two men reluctantly raise their hands. "Okay, I can understand your emotions and hostility toward us. I would if I were in your shoes. But we have to get over this feeling of mistrust and know that what Nancy and I are doing is to clear your names and make people realize that you didn't have any other recourse. I certainly don't want to see the lot of you charged for a crime that we know you didn't commit." With that said, she saw the men nod their heads in agreement. "We have made calls to the States and, within a few days, I really believe that we'll have the answers that will eliminate any question of your guilt in the murder of Mrs. Swartz. You have to bear with us and have as much patience as we are having. Let me tell you, it's hard for us to stand by and not get answers to these questions. My two friends are talking to their friends from another State and, with everyone's help, our inquiry will be answered." Nancy spoke to the group; "The problem is, it sometimes takes time to solve and get the issues clarified. But, like Suzanne said, it will be a matter of a few days and then everything will be settled. I know that we have to go to the police station and we need your co-operation in this matter. First, we have to have the proof and confront Mr. Swartz with the knowledge that we possess. Now, truthfully, I'm having conflicting issues about what is right and wrong, and I hope that when I next speak to Mr. Swartz, he'll come forward and tell us the facts. If I have integrity and I know Suzanne does and I believe that you," spreading her hands across the group, "also have this honesty. I know that it killed you to go away from the industry that you loved and had been carried from generation to generation. I can understand that. If we hear the reason behind Mr. Swartz's explanation, then we'll come back to you and then we'll have to make a big decision. Do we keep everything we learned to ourselves and let the authorities muddle in this dilemma, and do we know that what we are doing is the right thing to do. This is both a moral and ethical question that we have to go to the hearts of ourselves and think about this Catch-22."

With that said Nancy sat down and looked at the group of men that she thought weren't a bad bunch of guys and realized that they were caught up in a predicament and they knew no way out. Suzanne and Nancy got up and told the men that they would get back to Mario and tell them what they learned as soon as they found out themselves. The two women walked out, not looking back. As soon as they found that they were out of the forest, a big sigh of relief was taken. "All in all, I think that this meeting went well. What did you think Suzanne?"

"First of all I didn't know what to expect. I had a big case of the Hee Bee Jeebees, and I was having terrible thoughts before I saw and met with the guys. But I've calmed down and know that my doubts were only misconceptions and nerves. I'm still a little leery about our moral dilemma, but we'll have to do a lot of introspective thinking and I'm sure that they'll do it as well. I just hope that we all come to the same conclusion and find answers to our many questions." With that said Suzanne and Nancy went through the town and picked up the item that was waiting for Nancy at one of the shops.

Nancy had the item gift wrapped and told Suzanne that she saw the most beautiful pendant and she wanted to give it to Mrs. Walsh. Suzanne couldn't get over how thoughtful it was for Nancy to do that. After they left the shop and town, they headed back to the ship where they figured that dinner would be waiting for them.

After having a large dinner, the two women looked at each other and with a shrug of their heads said why not and indulged in the opulent dessert that the chef had prepared for his guests. Suzanne could hardly move as she made her way to the cabin to change into more comfortable clothes. She knew that she had to go on a major diet when she returned home. Of course, it would be difficult with Mrs. Walsh's cooking! When she returned, she knew that a meeting with Justin was inevitable. She'd have to warn Justin of her restriction in calories and hoped that he'd be mindful of her request. Now that she was getting a bit older, there would be no more cheating on her new life of eating sensibly. Yes, she decided, it was now or never. She'd make the new eating habits a life style and, come Hell or high water, would stick to her guns.

Suzanne was resting on her bed when she got a call from Ben (who was a friend of Tim and Kevin's at the Chicago FBI). He told them that he got a court order and that it would be hand delivered to Dr. Waters' office tomorrow. Meanwhile did they need a court order for the insurance company and policy as well? When Suzanne told him that most likely they would, he put a request down for that also. When Suzanne shut her cell, she related to Nancy what occurred. After changing yet again and taking a much-needed shower, both women fell into a deep sleep.

When they woke from a good night's sleep, they headed upstairs for a breakfast fit for a king. Nancy pushed the plate away, knowing that not a crumb was wasted. "What are we going to do about getting in touch with Dr. Waters' office?" "I guess we'll have to wait until his office is open. This difference in time will drive me crazy," an unhappy Suzanne declared.

"Let's go into Manila and see if the police have gotten any new information about the pirates. At least that will keep us busy until we can use our phones," Nancy suggested. "Good idea. Let me go downstairs and get my wallet, although I doubt if I'll buy anything else. But, one never knows. If I should find something that I like, I'll need it." Suzanne said as she headed downstairs to get to her cabin.

While she was entering the cabin, she saw Arthur getting ready to take a walk around the town. She nodded to him and was about to finish her assignment when he touched her shoulder. "Hi Suzanne, what's been happening?" asked a concerned Arthur. *'Like you really care,'* she thought to herself. "Nothing much," Suzanne casually answered. Nancy and I thought that we'd head to Manila and visit the police and see if they got any information on the pirates. Would you like to join us?"

Arthur was going stir crazy and knew that she was asking him out of, he didn't know what. "Thanks anyway, but I think I'll head into town and tag along with Tracy and Mike. When you brought them back some of the stolen items, they surmised that maybe other people's jewelry might be at other places. They got descriptions of the pieces and we'll go to the pawnshops and nosey around a bit. You never know what you'll find."

"That sounds like a good idea. I wish you guys luck." She got her wallet and closed the door behind her.

She disliked Arthur for all of the lying that he was doing and knew that she and Nancy had to find a way to get him to admit the truth and to tell them why he did it. It wasn't an ordinary killing and she was stubborn enough to find out why he shot Sandy.

The women headed into Manila and, after what seemed forever, finally arrived at the police headquarters. They waited and when the Chief of Police was finished with what he was doing, he asked Suzanne and Nancy to come into his office. He again thanked Suzanne for her help in assisting the artist to get the posters out for all to see. "It was nothing, believe me. I paint and used to teach art for many years and, if I can help you solve this crime, I'll do anything in my power to do so." Suzanne didn't tell Chief Lomibao that she had contact with the actual pirates and left his sentence open ended. She couldn't wait until this evening to speak to the insurance company and get the information from her friends to find the reason behind the shooting. Of course, the most important person in the equation was Arthur. Until he told her and Nancy what really happened and why, assumptions were all that they had to go on.

Unfortunately, the Chief of Police had no new information to give them. Suzanne and Nancy knew this, but had to do something to pass the time and this was as good a way as any other. They thanked Chief Lomibao and left to go back to the ship. Before going they decided to take advantage of some of the great restaurants in Manila for their lunch. While enjoying their meal, they spotted some people that looked familiar and decided that they were becoming regulars in and about this great city. "I, for one, will never forget this trip and I'm making a promise that I'll be coming back to this great place again," Nancy asserted.

"Well, I agree with you. This has been quite a vacation, and although it was a terrible incident that caused us to stay longer than we intended in the Philippines, I agree with you that when I get my land legs again and stay in the States a while, I'll probably come back and see the other Islands that we were supposed to go to but now have to forego. Besides, we might be coming back and wind up doing business or over-seeing the business that Mario and his friends start doing."

"I hate to bring up a sore subject, but have you decided what you're going to do about your romantic dilemma? I'm not giving you my opinion or anything, but Honey, I'd take Lawrence, if it were me. Now, I'm not making your mind up, just giving you my take on the matter!"

"Gee, thanks, Nancy, or should I call you Dear Abby. Like I don't have a mind of my own," Suzanne stated. "I'm not saying that Honey, the way that Stephen treated you, I'd have told him to go to Hell a long time ago. I won't dredge up old hats, but Lawrence has loved you forever, it seems, and it's about time that you appreciate his patience and understanding. All I'm saying is, when you come back to this delightful place, I hope it's with Lawrence."

As the two women paid the bill, Suzanne gave Nancy a little push and winked at her on the way out. "We'll see what happens and that's all I'm saying," pronounced Suzanne. "By the time we get back to the ship, the time difference will be good for us to make those phone calls."

As predicted, all was quiet when they returned to the ship. It had taken longer than they thought it would, and they thanked their lucky stars that they had eaten food in town. Suzanne knew that Chef would cook them something to eat if they asked him to, but wouldn't dream of requesting such an outrageous appeal. If they found themselves hungry at an unreasonable hour, then they would forage for food and most likely find some in the galley's large refrigerator.

They sat on their beds and started dialing the insurance company. It took a while to be connected, but, at last, they were hooked up to the right department and person. Suzanne explained the situation and was glad that the company had received the necessary papers to be able to send over the information they needed.

Wiping her brow, after the long phone call and then telling the person on the other end to fax the information to the ship, they let out a large sigh. "I'm glad that we have a fax on board. We'll make sure that we are the only people that will get this message," assured Suzanne as she spoke to Nancy in whispered tones. "Why are you whispering?" asked Nancy. "No one can hear through these walls. Even with a glass propped up against the wall, it's nearly impossible to hear a conversation next door." With a look of apprehension Nancy raised her eyebrows and told Suzanne that she already tried to listen in and couldn't. Suzanne raised her shoulders and that's all that she could do.

Turning around she faced Nancy and asked again, "You did what?" Suzanne couldn't believe that Nancy would have even thought of doing such a despicable thing. "I only did it to make sure that the people next door wouldn't hear some of our conversations," Nancy answered defensively. "Well, I hope that is the only reason why you would do such a thing." As if talking to herself, Suzanne went into the small bathroom and started removing her makeup, all the while it sounded as she were talking to herself. Nancy laughed at the way Suzanne reacted to her admitted wrongdoing, but rationalized it was for a very good reason.

When Suzanne was finished doing her nightly routine, she again sat on her bed, Indian style and started calling the insurance company for the information that she had requested. Nancy was laughing when she saw that Suzanne had put the honey wheat mask on and had not taken it off before making the call. Suzanne looked over at Nancy and then realized that she was laughing at her with her mask on. "Look, I can't stop the aging process, but I can do everything in my power to keep my skin from looking like a dried up prune."

It took Suzanne about a half an hour to get through to the right party and, when she did, she was glad that they, too, had received the correct documents to be able to fax what they were looking for to them.

The next morning, the two women got up early and made sure that they were the first people who were in the office of the Captain. "Good Morning," a cheery Suzanne greeted the Captain. "I believe some important faxes have come over and we would like to see if they've arrived."

"Well, let's take a look," Captain Winters walked toward the newest machines he bought after they were robbed of the old machinery. "I spoke to Chef André and he said he thought that some mice might have invaded the refrigerator last evening. Suzanne and Nancy looked at each other and answered in a sheepish way, "guilty as charged."

"I thought it might have been the two of you since you weren't at the dining room table last evening." He chuckled as he handed the papers to the women's outstretched hands. "Thanks," Nancy said as they headed out and went back to their cabins.

Suzanne started reading the documents and told Nancy that she'd give them to her because it all seemed to look like mumbo jumbo. Nancy could tell her, in language that she understood, what it all meant.

It took Nancy about a half an hour to an hour to read over the papers and then she told Suzanne what her interpretation of them was. "It seems that Arthur is the heir to Sandy's insurance policy. It goes to the children if they should perish together. It looks like they took out this policy years ago, before any illness appeared on the horizon in Sandy's life. "That's good, isn't it?" asked a concerned Suzanne.

"Yes, as far as I can see. But there is a clause that if something like an accident or a killing that was unforeseen happened, the recipient would be receiving double indemnity. That means that the living person would inherit double the amount of money that they originally took out on the policy." Suzanne shook her head in acknowledgement and then asked Nancy to read over the medical reports.

"This seems a little more complicated." Nancy's brows knotted together as she tried to decipher the time line and all the medical terminology that was in the reports. It took Nancy over an hour to let out a deep breath and, put the papers beside her while massaging her eyes. "This is really grueling," Nancy said out loud. "Well, I can tell you that if you keep squinting like you are, you will be getting deep lines in between your eyebrows. It's called, never mind, it's only terminology that estheticians use…. Don't squint!!!"

"Yes, Mama," Nancy acknowledged Suzanne, as her friend threw a book that was on the night table at Nancy. They both laughed.

"I'll explain all the medical terms to you after we finish having our breakfast. Then we'll discuss what our next plan of action should be," Nancy told Suzanne as she got up from her bed and waited for Suzanne to follow her up the stairs.

After eating a hearty breakfast, the friends sat down on the deck and waited for a few clouds to appear before they made an excuse to the other people why they were heading to their room.

Once the two friends got back into their cabin they sat on their individual beds and each took one of the documents that Ben had obtained for them. Suzanne stated, "Boy I'm glad that Tim and Kevin have this friend, Ben, at the Chicago FBI. Without his help, these documents would never have been sent over." They were reading intensely the documents in hand and it took a while for them to finish going over them. "If you have any questions, I'll go to the library where I happened to see a medical dictionary. I mean, how lucky to have found that particular book aboard this ship. It's crazy to think that such a book would be on board. I don't think that we'll be able to decipher the terminology and maybe we can ask Mike, without his realizing that he's giving us answers to some of the questions that we might have," Nancy said aloud to Suzanne.

Suzanne agreed to Nancy's suggestion and kept reading the medical report on Sandy's aggressive treatments. She shook her head when reading how long ago the Breast Cancer first occurred and couldn't fathom how she endured all the treatments that she had as they tried to cure this dreaded disease. She didn't realize that she was holding her breath and when she finished reading that particular part of Sandy's life, she allowed herself to take in a deep breath of fresh air.

She then returned to the medical report and was smiling, until she got to the last part of the records. Then a tear rolled down her cheek. Suzanne couldn't imagine the courage that this small woman had! After all those years of dormancy, Sandy found out that the disease had re-surfaced and it was now apparent that it wasn't only her breast but had most likely spread to other organs as well. '*No wonder Sandy was coughing towards the end of the trip,*' Suzanne thought to herself as she finished reading that Sandy didn't show up for her last appointment. It was impossible to put herself in Sandy's place, but realized how she didn't want anyone else to suffer while they saw her going through yet, another surgery and round of multiple treatments.

Suzanne put the medical report down and, with a deep sigh, didn't want to think of what was going through Sandy's mind. It was impossible not to sympathize, but she found it difficult to try to understand all of the emotions that Sandy was going through. She wondered when Sandy finally told Arthur about her medical condition. She could only speculate what her husband's thoughts were when he found out her real state of affairs.

Nancy looked over at Suzanne. When she finished reading the insurance document, she put it down beside her and waited for her partner to get enough composure to explain what the text read in layman's terms. Nancy knew that she would have to read the medical records for herself, but wanted a few minutes' breather to enable herself to organize the thoughts that were going through her mind.

After fifteen minutes had passed, Nancy asked Suzanne if she were ready to explain the terminology of the insurance papers. Suzanne looked over and shook her head. A sad expression registered on her face.

"You might as well, because after you read this medical report, I really think that you'll have a different perspective on what happened. Of course, we can only speculate about it and I doubt if Arthur will come forward and tell us the entire truth, but I want your read on the situation. I'm now ready to hear what you have to say."

Taking a deep breath, Nancy told Suzanne that when Sandy and Arthur first started their family, they realized that if either of them should die, the other would need money to keep the clan together in the manner that they were accustomed to living. Now, as they grew older, and the children had colleges to attend etc., they made sure that the insurance policy was increased. By this time, they had moved into a larger home to accommodate all of the children they had. They didn't bother to decrease the policy, realizing that costs had increased and they would need the money if they couldn't depend on the other's income. What it comes down to is that they kept the policy as an ace in the hole. There was a provision that included double indemnity if an accident should occur or if an unusual death of one or the other took place. I'm sure that Sandy remembered that part of the insurance policy when her cancer had returned. "I have to say that Sandy probably remembered and was thankful that they took the insurance out before her first bout with cancer occurred. But knowing Sandy for the short time that we did, I'm sure that she remembered the double indemnity clause. I know that all the legal terms are like a foreign language to you, and I understand the way you feel. In essence, I'm telling you that, yes, the plan had a clause that definitely would double the amount of money if one of them should perish through an act of aggression or accident. I bet that was on Sandy's mind and when the opportunity afforded itself, she thought of the idea of taking advantage of the situation."

All Suzanne could do was to take a deep sigh and close her eyes. All types of scenarios were going through her mind and she tried putting them aside. She got up and handed the medical report to Nancy. "I heard every word that you told me. Thanks for interpreting the language for me. I don't think I'll have to do the same for you when you finish reading this documented account of Sandy's trials. The dilemma we have is more than mind boggling. Should we tell the authorities the truth? Then Arthur won't get the money, or even worse, he can be held on a murder charge. Do we let those poor men, who are pirates, but really not, have to pay the penalty of murder when they didn't commit that crime? It's a serious question and one that will weigh heavily on our minds when we decide what should be told and what should be held back. I suggest that we think about this matter for a day or so, go about our business, if we can, knowing whatever decision we make, someone will get hurt. Or, maybe we can come up with a solution where no one gets harmed and we can see clearly that what we say will have a dramatic effect on everyone. Of course, there will be no dire effects on poor Sandy, except that she will be looking down on everyone with a big smile on her face. It's not going to be easy for either of us." With that said Suzanne jumped out of bed and led Nancy out of their cabin for a breath of fresh air.

The next day Suzanne asked Nancy if she would mind going over to Mario's house to speak with him about the quandary that they found themselves in. "Who knows, maybe three heads will be better than two." With that stated the women walked to the street and headed for Mario's house, not knowing what to expect.

After heading out of town, the area was more desolate and they could smell the ocean ahead. Both of them were quiet as they approached the small house on stilts. When, out of nowhere, Suzanne blurted out, "I hate this feeling of having this moral dilemma hanging over our heads;" Suzanne and Nancy walked up the long stairs. "We have an obligation to tell the truth, and right now I don't know what to do."

"I know how you're feeling. I'm experiencing the same thing that you are," Nancy said. Nancy went on to tell her friend that normally she'd feel no remorse in telling everyone what really happened. "But after reading the reports, we have to find out what transpired between Arthur and Sandy. I can put myself in Sandy's shoes, and I'd probably want my husband to kill me if I knew that he could get away with murder. I know that's a poor description, but in essence, that's what happened."

"I know, I know," Suzanne said to Nancy as they saw the high staircase ahead of them. "Let's feel Mario out before we reveal what we actually know was written down by the insurance company and what we read in the hospital and doctors' records."

With that said, both women climbed the steps up to Mario's door. They knocked and were greeted by his wife, who welcomed them into her clean but small abode. The kids were playing in the small yard that surrounded the house that was at the edge of the water. Maria offered the women a cold drink, and after the long walk, they were thankful for the wet liquid that slid easily down their throats. Suzanne had to admit that the heat was starting to get to her. She knew that, especially at the time of year they would be traveling, the weather would be hot, but she never imagined it would be unbearable.

That was one of the reasons she lived in New England. The change of seasons was always a welcome relief. Just when she got tired of a season, whether it was winter, summer, spring or fall; the next season would be upon them. She wasn't used to the constant barrage of continuous hot weather. So when Maria offered a glass of iced tea, it was a welcome treat.

Mario appeared while the women were enjoying the refreshing drinks. Small talk was being bantered and, as soon as Maria left the house to check on the children, Mario got down to business. "I spoke to the guys, and, to be honest with you, we're upset at the speculation and rumors that we're hearing around the village. Some of the guys have buddies who are on the police department and they are saying that they're going to increase the search for the pirates, especially since one of the passengers was killed by us. We know that this is not true. What are we going to do about this?"

Suzanne suddenly felt tired. She was exhausted and felt drained from all of the aggravation that she and Nancy had gone through. All she had wanted was to have a great time and enjoy the beautiful weather and be at peace with the way she felt about herself. She had wanted to try to figure out what was going to happen with the rest of her private life. She hoped that all drama would be a thing of the past, and that she and Nancy would have a great vacation. Now, with robbery and especially murder, she felt that all that had happened wouldn't take away the fatigue that she was experiencing.

Suzanne looked over at Mario and she listened to his complaints, but what he was saying sounded trite. Even though his thoughts were right, she wanted to put her hands over her ears and not hear another word. She missed home, talking to her parents and children every day, seeing all of her clients and she especially missed the daily routine of her life. Yes, things hadn't turned out the way that she had expected them to but, all in all, she'd take them compared to the way things were turning out on this vacation. When considering everything, this was a nightmare.

How could such a great vacation that the girls had given to her and Nancy, turn out to be this horrendous? Everything was fine; suddenly things seemed to unravel. Between the pirates and the unexpected death of Sandy, it was as if she were living in a terrifying dream. Suzanne looked over at Nancy as Mario was rambling on and just wanted to scream. She realized that she shouldn't be feeling the way she was, but couldn't control her emotions. Suzanne concentrated on Mario's words and tried to put herself in his place. She had to do something to make everyone satisfied, but at this point, didn't know how to accomplish this.

CHAPTER TWENTY THREE

To Suzanne, the words that Mario was speaking seemed like gibberish. She knew that it was impossible and took another sip of her iced tea. Maybe if she closed her eyes and concentrated on what he was saying, she would be able to find a solution to his quandary. Both Nancy and Mario looked over at Suzanne, and before she realized what had happened, they both rushed to her side.

When Suzanne awoke, she had a cold washcloth covering her forehead and was under a lightweight cover on a bed in a room she didn't recognize. She looked around and wondered how she got there. All sorts of scenarios went through her mind when Nancy came walking into the room. "I'm glad to see that you're awake now. Mario and I were very concerned when you collapsed. We were going to take you to the local hospital, but then realized that you had fainted so we decided to wait until you came around and ask you if you'd like medical attention. I realize that this has not been one of your most peaceful vacations and, taking that into account, stayed by your side until you came to." Taking Suzanne's hand into her own, Nancy tenderly brought Suzanne's hand onto her own chest. Her heartbeat could be felt underneath Suzanne's hypersensitive fingers. Suzanne could feel her heart steady and beating, so she wasn't worried that she had suffered a heart attack like many of her relatives had before her. "I want you to feel better and the only way that can happen is if we come to some sort of resolution."

Suzanne felt foolish with all of this unwanted attention being given her. She felt all of this interest about her health unnecessary. Although this was supposed to be a calming vacation (they had been through Hell and back from the last escapade), this South Sea Holiday was nothing like she imagined it to be. She and Nancy had to finish what they had started, and knowing what really happened to Sandy was weighing heavily on her mind. Yes, their intentions were good, but would telling the authorities about the pirates and what really happened be in anyone's best interest? Suzanne realized that both Mario and his friends were in a terrible position. Arthur and his family were also in a predicament that was hard to explain.

Suzanne closed her eyes for only a moment and both Nancy and Mario rushed to her side. "Oh for Gosh sake, can't a person close their eyes without you two panicking?" The two people beside her lowered their heads and tried to act ashamed, but Suzanne knew that they were only putting on an act and they weren't sorry in the least. It was obvious to Suzanne that she had to come up with a conclusion as no one else seemed to be capable of coming up with an answer to their dilemma.

"Can I take this wet cloth off of my forehead now?" she asked Nancy and Mario. Getting up slowly from the bed that Mario had graciously put her on, she let herself acclimate so she wouldn't feel dizzy. She often made sure that her older clients positioned themselves this way when getting up from their facials and was inwardly laughing to herself thinking that she must be getting old if she couldn't get up without this ridiculous thought of falling to the ground if she rose too quickly.

'*Okay*,' Suzanne thought to herself, '*I have to come up with an answer soon or, this fiasco that we face will only get worse! If I don't get my ass into gear, nobody is going to be happy, least of all Nancy and me.*' By the time that they got back on the boat, they had made the call to Ben who was their contact at the Chicago FBI. He assured them that he had everything that they needed under control and as soon as they got him a fax number where he could send the reports, they would see what had transpired. Suzanne then informed Nancy that they would have to go back to Mario's house in the morning and get a fax number from one of his acquaintances who owned a business. It was imperative that a fax machine be available for them to receive the information that they were waiting for. With that knowledge in order, it was just a matter of receiving the facts and sorting everything out. Suzanne and Nancy were afraid to use the ships' fax machine, less someone would figure out what they were up to.

Suzanne got into bed as all sorts of terrible thoughts kept entering her mind. What happened if Mario couldn't get a fax machine? What would happen if all the material that she needed turned out to be useless? With all of these thoughts going through her brain, her common sense seemed to be on overload. Besides those terrible dreams, Stephen's and Lawrence's faces appeared in the scenarios and, when morning time came, Suzanne looked and felt as tired as when she went to sleep the evening before.

While waking, Nancy looked over at her friend and couldn't believe the dark circles that Suzanne had under her eyes. "What the Hell happened to you? You look like you didn't sleep a wink the entire night!"

"Don't get me started. I'll go into a hot shower, and hopefully, it will revive the energy that seems to have seeped out of me. I'll be fine afterwards."

"I hope so because, truthfully, you look awful!"

"Thanks, Nancy, I really needed that encouragement."

By the time Nancy had finished her shower and was dressed, Suzanne didn't look as bad as she felt. Putting the palm of her hand up to ward off any bad comments from Nancy, Suzanne told Nancy that she'd meet her upstairs at the breakfast table. Suzanne slammed the door to their cabin and tried to get a better attitude so the other guests wouldn't think anything was wrong.

She greeted the other members of the party. They had no idea on how bad Suzanne was feeling from the terrible night sleep (or lack thereof) that kept her awake for most of the hours of darkness. It was bad enough, she thought, that she dreamt about the awful situation that she found her and Nancy in, but on top of that, to have visions of Stephen's and Lawrence's faces before her like visions from the deep beyond, it was getting on her nerves, to say the least.

The other people had no idea of Suzanne's inner feelings, and when Nancy joined them, she dared not look into her best friend's eyes. They both ate heartily. No one realized the mental anguish that was eating their stomachs, minds and spirits. After they ate a hearty breakfast, they apologized for their having to leave and made some excuse for their abrupt departure.

They found themselves once more at Mario's house. When he greeted them at his front door, a large smile was plastered on his face. "My wife's first cousin has a store in the city and, if we hurry, we can use his fax to get the necessary information. I already called him and he gave us the clearance to use it whenever we need it."

It took them awhile to get to Manila from the small seaside resort town where Mario resided. If anyone were to see the three people walking purposely on the street, they would never have thought that their minds were going in a million directions. Mario was worried that he and his friends would be condemned for murder and never see their families other than from behind iron bars. His friends, who had put their trust in his hands, would never forgive him if he didn't prove their innocence. That weighed heavily on his mind as he walked beside the two women whom he had put his trust in. He hoped that his instincts were right and they would prove that his reliance on them was the correct thing to do.

The store was just opening and the first customers were entering when they opened the large, brass doors to the establishment. Suzanne was impressed by its enormity. She was astonished when she realized that all of this business came about from one family's vision and determination. She was overwhelmed when she saw all the merchandise on display. It reminded her of some of the large department stores that were in New York and Beverly Hills. The store was at least five to six stories in height. She hurriedly looked at some of the merchandise and was impressed at what she saw. Besides having the latest in fashion for men, women and children, the furniture department, where the offices were located, had a vast selection of merchandise.

Suzanne made a mental note that she would come back here and get something to remember this trip. Although it wasn't one of the most relaxing vacations she and Nancy had taken, it certainly was one of the most interesting. With that in mind, she quickly kept in step with Nancy and Mario as they made their way to the offices in the back of the store.

The woman that greeted them was a very dedicated secretary, and Suzanne liked her immediately. She made them their favorite coffees and waited for them to finish their business. Suzanne looked quickly over the medical reports from Sandy's hospital records and then quickly glanced over the insurance policy. She didn't understand all the wording and hoped that Nancy could decipher the legal documentation once they were in their cabin and could take their time in reading the documents.

They headed out, thanking Mario for the use of his cousin's place of business, and hurriedly went back to the ship to read over and interpret the language in the insurance document and the medical records. Once back in the cabin, they went to their respective beds. Each woman had a document in her possession. Suzanne made a mental note to go back to that store if they had time to do so. She saw an outfit out of the corner of her eye that she hadn't seen anywhere and couldn't wait to try it on and possibly buy it.

After looking at the documents for over an hour, Suzanne let out a sigh of exasperation. "Okay, I've read this mumbo jumbo for a while now, and I still really don't understand what they are saying. Here, you look at it and tell me what it says." Nancy read the insurance policy for about a half an hour and then went on to explain to Suzanne that the policy would pay the surviving spouse. In case of both deaths, the children would equally share the benefits. There was over a million dollars in cash and that didn't look good for Arthur. "If he had put on an act, it sure worked because the two of them couldn't have looked more in love," Nancy expounded.

"Yes, I have to admit that they looked like two kids still in love with each other. I can't imagine being in love for that long a time and not show some sort of irritation with my mate," admitted Suzanne. "Maybe it's meant to be that I'm not married and settled down with one person."

"Fiddlesticks, it's just that Stephen wasn't the one for you. Now get your mind off of yourself and let's read on."

After handing Sandy's medical records back to Nancy, Suzanne waited for her analysis. "You are so good with this type of thing," declared Suzanne. "I guess we all have our specialties." Putting her hand onto her chin she thought awhile and said, "Oh yes, I guess my good qualities are making people happy, writing, great smile and I can't make up my mind on who to make love to." With that said, Nancy threw over the copy of the insurance policy and started laughing. "You know you're crazy, but I still love you."

Becoming serious again, Nancy went on to explain the money aspect of the insurance policy to Suzanne and then, when she assumed Suzanne understood her explanation, she asked if she was ready to hear about Sandy's medical reports. "Yes, hit me with your best shot, because we have a lot of people who are relying on us for the truth, whatever it is. It's going to be us who will be saddled with the moral issues if there are any discrepancies."

"I know what you mean, Suzanne. This is going to be a hard subject to discuss. Someone is going to be hurt, one way or the other." With that said Nancy sat quietly for a while and then told Suzanne that she'd been thinking a lot about the problem and thought she might have come up with a solution.

Suzanne suddenly sat up in her bed and looked over at her best friend. With a scowl on her face, said, "Okay, hit me with your best shot. Gee, somehow it sounded better when I played the record."

"Are you talking about that song that Pat Benatar sang on her second album Crimes of Passion?" Jumping out of bed, Nancy held onto a pretend microphone and started singing the song that she knew by heart because she loved Pat Benatar. Suzanne pulled the covers of her blanket over her head and started yelling, "I give up; I give up"!!!

"I bet you thought that I was too young to remember Pat Benatar, but I used to love her singing," she told Suzanne as she finished the song and sat back down on her bed. "Seriously, I didn't know that you liked Pat Benatar. I remember that my daughter, Hope, enjoyed singing her songs all day long. She could imitate that singer as though it was actually her singing." "Well then, the next time we all get together, Hope and I will just have to get up and start singing her songs," declared Nancy. "Oh no, another Madaline and Dorothy in the making," cried Suzanne.

"Now let's get serious," Nancy said. "This is how I interpreted the wording of the insurance policy." She told Suzanne her rendition of it and then said to her friend, "Let's go to Arthur's room and sit down with him and lay everything we know on the line." Suzanne questioned Nancy's rationale, and she was hesitant for a moment. "What happens if he gets angry and goes off the deep-end? There's no telling what might happen if he loses his temper." Nancy stood up, pulling Suzanne off of the bed and said, "There's no way to know until we confront him with our knowledge. Now, come on, and let's hear what he has to say for himself."

"Before we go, explain to me about the medical portion of Sandy's illness. Then I'll be prepared to confront Arthur and know what we're up against."

"That sounds reasonable," Nancy admitted.

Suzanne sat down on the bed for the umpteenth time and listened intently to what Nancy told her. "We have to start by telling him what we saw. That's a must. Now I want you to ask me any questions that you have regarding the medical record."

"To tell you the truth, I think I understand what I read. Sandy had Breast Cancer; and got the necessary treatments for it. Then she was on 20 mg of Tamoxifen for five years. She's been cancer free, but psychologically, it did a number on her. From what I gather, it also was a very stressful time for her family as well. The chemo and radiation therapy took a toll on her body, and her entire family and friends pitched in when she was too weak to drive herself for her treatments. It looks like her oncologist did the necessary procedures and then the Radiologist and the other doctors took over, with her doctor keeping an eye on her entire ordeal."

"Then about four months ago, Sandy started coughing and the cough got increasingly worse. She went back to her regular MD and he, in turn, told her to have x-rays. When he did the entire body scan realized that the cancer had returned to other areas of her body, mainly her lungs. Am I reading this correctly?" Suzanne asked Nancy.

"Yes, unfortunately you are."

"Now please don't interrupt my dialogue."

"After she got the results of the body scan, she then went to her oncologist again, and this time, he wanted to begin treatments for her Lung Cancer. What I'm reading is that she just walked out of his office and did not make another appointment with him or anyone else that I can see. If what I'm reading is right, then she ignored his input and wanted to live life and not burden Arthur or her family with yet another round of surgery's or treatments. You know, poo, poo, I hope I never have to be burdened with that decision, but I can honestly understand her mind set," a disturbed Suzanne announced. "I mean, here she went through Hell and back and now, after all these years of being cancer free, she finds out that it's come back. Hello!!! I can understand her rationalization or how she must have felt when the doctor told her that her cancer returned."

"I'm not saying that this is what I would do, but I can put myself in her position and understand why she wanted to ignore what she knew was the truth. Here her family and friends did everything for her and Arthur and now she would have to burden them again. I wonder if she confided to Arthur or another person who was close to her. Maybe she waited until they were on the cruise and then told Arthur what was happening to her body. I could see that she was getting weaker and she looked rather pale. Even though we were in the sunshine for many days, she still looked sickly to me."

Nancy sat back, her pillow at the base of her spine and thought for a while. "You know Suzanne, what you said makes sense to me. We'll never know what really happened, but all the evidence points to just what you said. Let's go to Arthur now, before he goes away for the day and confront him."

"Before we go, I have to tell you that, before we left, I was rather upset at what happened in my family. You know that I'm an only child and my father's brothers only had one child apiece also. Wendy, my flower girl at my wedding to Brian, was much younger than I was. Wendy had lymphoma years ago, when she was a young girl. It came on suddenly. Anyway, she got that attended to and had the operation and the doctor told her not to have another child after she went through her radiation treatment. Well, she didn't listen to him, not wanting to have just one child as she was an only child. Anyway, she went ahead and had another child, a little boy, (who isn't so little anymore) and has become a very handsome young man. Anyway, she didn't feel well and went to her oncologist again and found out that she developed lymphoma of her thyroid gland. This was a first, and she actually made the journal of medicine. Anyway she thought she had it licked. A few years ago, she developed Lung Cancer. To make a long story short, she had one lung removed and thought that was the end of it. Then about a year later cancer came back and started destroying her second lung. She never gave up. She was a fighter... Unfortunately the cancer won. Her eldest daughter married and she wouldn't let the couple move up the date or change it. They tried talking to her, but she made up her mind and no one could change it. She was a very religious girl and maybe she felt that it was God's will. Of course, everyone was upset, especially her immediate family, but her daughter got married to a wonderful guy and the entire family will remember her."

"I often remember her when she was little, and I still have pictures of her being my flower girl at my wedding. There are many stories that I could tell you about Wendy and my other cousin Stuart. The many Jewish Holidays we shared when my father's parents would have a large group of people over and their house was only a bungalow. They didn't care. Everyone sat at one long table that extended from the dining room into the front of the living room. There was an abundance of food and, believe me, no one went home feeling empty. My cousins would be there also. Everyone was welcome. There are many issues that I normally keep to myself, as I don't want to burden anyone. You have been like a sister to me, and God only knows I would never have survived, if it hadn't been for you, Dorothy or Mrs. Walsh. But believe me, I have a number of concerns that come into my mind and I keep them buried within myself. I don't want to be a burden to anyone and, if I feel a need to let off some steam and bring up a subject that I have conflicts with, you'll be one of the first to know."

"But I'll wait for another day and time to tell you more stories. All I'm saying is, I can put myself into Sandy's situation and understand her feelings." With that said, Suzanne got up and took Nancy's hand and they headed for Arthur's cabin.

Nancy took hold of Suzanne's hand and stopped her. "Gee, I thought that we were so close. How come you never told me this was happening to your first cousin?"

"Maybe if I'd have mentioned it to you, it would have become a reality and, to be honest with you, I didn't want to think about it because then I would know that it was true. I'll say one more thing. When it was getting closer to her death, she wouldn't let anyone visit her or talk to anyone. She had a hard time breathing and talking on the phone. There were so many things that I wanted to say to her, but I feel that there was never any closure between us." Nancy saw the tears building up in Suzanne's eyes and saw that she was getting so emotional that it was hard for her to talk. "Okay, let's forget about Wendy and get this job done with Arthur." Nancy tried making light of the situation, but there was nothing light about what they were about to confront.

Arthur heard the knock at his door and thought it might have been the cabin boy asking a question. When he opened the door and saw Suzanne and Nancy, he wasn't happy. He had tried avoiding them as much as possible and now was the moment that he had dreaded. He told them to enter and asked what they wanted. Nancy started the conversation by asking him if he had time to talk. "Well, I was going to go to the palace to see if they had any openings for a guard, but I guess that can wait." *'Always the kidder,'* Nancy thought to herself. "Where are my manners? Come, I know these cabins aren't spacious but I think there's room for the three of us to sit." Motioning them to sit on the chairs in the small room, he sat on the bed. "How can I be of service to you ladies?" With that opening Nancy cleared her throat and told him that she and Suzanne saw the incident that happened outside of his cabin with Sandy when the pirates attacked their ship. Arthur couldn't deny the fact, and with all the hemming and hawing that he tried, there was no denying the truth. He was speechless.

Suzanne felt it was up to her to start and finish this discussion. "Look, Arthur, as hard as it is for you to go back home without Sandy, we're having an awful time knowing that we saw what really happened." Suzanne tried looking directly at Arthur but he was avoiding looking into her eyes. "I want to hear what really happened and why you did what you did. We saw the way the two of you were when you were together. All the play-acting in the world couldn't have matched what was between you. There was charisma and love and there is no denying that." Arthur laughed to himself. *'I guess I am a great actor. I missed my profession.'* "We didn't tell anyone on board, but sometimes we work with the FBI. Now I know that you're asking yourself, how can people be part-time FBI agents? I don't want to get into the story now, but believe me when I tell you that we're the real deal. I can call up my friends now and have them confirm what I just told you, but I don't think that will be necessary, will it? We had them fax over your insurance policy and Sandy's medical records."

"I know that there are privacy issues in place, but believe me when the FBI orders something sent from the court, nothing is private anymore." Arthur stared at the two women like they had two heads. Then they saw the tears come to his eyes, and he lost all of his composure. All he could do was shake his head in disbelief.

"I told Sandy that I couldn't do it. I didn't know that she was sick until she finally told me she was. I lay here at night, and all sorts of questions that I want to ask her are in my head, but she doesn't answer." A laugh escaped him and then he said, "If I hear from her now, then I know that I've lost it." Suzanne often spoke to her grandparents and didn't make fun of his feelings; she believed in speaking to the dead and often times heard their answers. She avoided his diatribe and continued. "Anyway," Arthur continued. "At first I was upset at the way she handled everything, but then I listened to her explanation, and I never thought that was what she planned to do. I honestly think, before the pirates came aboard, that she wanted to wait until we were home and then she wanted me to give her small amounts of poison so no one would be the wiser. Then she told me that she would lie awake at night thinking of different ways that she could die so that I could get double indemnity. I thought that she was going a little crazy. When we were on this trip, she would go to the various religious places and stay and pray for hours. I would watch her and wonder, but never would I deny her. I didn't know how sick she was until I finally got mad one day and asked her why she wanted to go to the different religious places when there were so many other places to visit and things to do. That's when she calmly told me that the cancer had returned and she didn't want our family and friends to have to go through the entire process again. She honestly thought that it was God's will. She told me many times how she was thankful that she had me for her husband and that the kids, even though some of them have problems of their own, were her pride and joy. She couldn't have asked for a better life."

"The opportunity presented itself, and before we could discuss anything, she saw the pirates and got the weapon and shoved it in my hands and demanded that I shoot her." Suzanne saw his reactions and heard what he was saying. Suddenly Arthur started shaking his head and quivering and his entire body started convulsing. She could see heavy sobs racking his body. He put his head between his hands that were leaning on his knees and kept shaking his head. "What was I to do? Everything happened so fast!! Sandy was always the leader in our household. She told me to jump, and I'd ask her how high." He wasn't joking; Suzanne and Nancy could see that.

Suzanne and Nancy let him cry. They went over to him, trying to console this man who was obviously in such agony and turmoil. Suzanne touched his head softly while Nancy patted his back and they both let him cry his heart out. When Arthur was visibly better, Suzanne sat down and told Arthur that his story was heart wrenching and they would leave him alone and discuss what they would do.

The women went back to their cabin without saying a word. When the door was closed they lay down on their beds and were alone in their own thoughts.

"Well, that was quiet a story," Nancy said. "Yes, my heart goes out to everyone associated with Sandy and Arthur. I don't know how he can live with himself after what he did. It's bad enough that you learn that your wife is ill, but then when she tells you that she doesn't want to burden anyone else and that she wants you to kill her for the insurance money, well that would be hard for anyone who was truly in love with their spouse," admitted Suzanne. "When I wished death on Brian, and believe me, there was many a time, I truly, deep down, wasn't sad that he died. I know that I shouldn't say such an awful thing, especially when you had feelings for him in the end. But just think, you'd never have met Rich, and that's what I describe as a mench!"

Nancy didn't say a word and let her friend and partner ramble on, realizing that in her mind she was justifying Arthur's actions. Nancy left Suzanne alone for a while. When she felt enough time had elapsed, she sat up in her bed and told Suzanne that they had a lot to talk about.

Instead of going upstairs with the other people on the ship, they decided that they didn't need food, and it was more important to finalize or at least talk about what they now knew and what they would have to do about Marco and his friends. "Well," Suzanne finally said, "I guess there are a lot of predicaments that we have to figure out. First of all, I can understand how Arthur is feeling, and at the same time, I realize that Mario and his friends, who everyone thinks are pirates are in one Hell of a mess." Suzanne shook her head and told Nancy that she hoped that they could come to a good conclusion for all.

"I've been racking my brain with different scenarios, and I honestly don't think that Mario and his friends will be able to avoid punishment if they are found to be the pirates. Now, they have nothing to worry about if everyone keeps his mouth shut and the authorities don't find out who the pirates are. We have to try to convince Mario and his gang of men that they can't keep up this pirating business. There has to be something that they can do in order to make the same kind of income that they were used to bringing in." Nancy was quiet for a while and then abruptly stood up and told Suzanne that she had an answer for Mario and his friends. "Now we know that these guys aren't stupid. They have good heads on their shoulders. What if I were to give them some starter money to set up an import and export business of their own. There are many crafts that are unique to the Philippines and the outskirts of town. We both have connections all over the world and we do have influence with some big businesses that would like to carry some exclusive items that no one else carries."

Suzanne piped in that Lawrence has stores everywhere, and she was sure that he wouldn't mind carrying some items that were different. With that in mind, they got a pen and pencil in hand and made notes that they could present to the men. After a few hours, Suzanne suggested that they call Mario and make an appointment for him and his friends to meet at Mario's house and let them make the decision about the idea to set up a corporation and start being productive individuals and not have to resort to thievery to make a living. "After all, let's not kid ourselves, Suzanne. I have plenty of money and it keeps accumulating interest in the bank that, at this point, the percentages for anything is a laugh. I'd be making more money if I invest it with these guys and set up another business." Suzanne laughed at her friend and said; "Okay, so I'm just another investment to you, hey?" She poked Nancy in the ribs and a large smile appeared on her face. After being quiet for a while Suzanne told her partner in crime: "You realize, Nancy, that whatever happens, it will be Arthur's word against ours." With that said she was quiet and didn't have anything else to say.

Nancy let Suzanne stew for a while and then said, "You know that we have a different arrangement, and no, you aren't another investment to me. My goodness, Suzanne, we're sisters, at least I consider us so."

"I know, I'm just teasing you." They called Mario at his house and set up a time for he and his friends to meet.

The night was clear as the two women walked to Mario's. The moon lit up the sky enabling them to see clearly. Suzanne pointed to the bright stars and admitted to Nancy that she was not astronomically astute but pointed to the North Star. She then told Nancy that she heard it was really called Polaris. "This isn't the brightest star in the universe, but I've never been good with the stars and such. I know how to recognize the big dipper, but that's about all."

"Well my dear, you have attributes that are incredible in other ways so don't worry about that sort of thing."

"Thanks Nancy, I mean it. Even though I graduated from high school with great marks and was on the National Honor Society, I don't profess to know everything." They both laughed as they tried to avoid a mangy cat that was being chased by a small dog.

CHAPTER TWENTY FOUR

Suzanne and Nancy finally arrived at Mario's house on stilts and climbed up the steps leading to the small but meticulous living room. Suzanne observed the blend of different provincial pieces, obviously used, but orderly and clean. Beside the sofa, there were several dissimilar chairs, unlike she'd ever seen before. Maria, Mario's wife, took the children to her Mom's house in order for Mario to have the privacy that he asked for. When everyone had arrived, they sat around the table and waited for Nancy to speak.

"Hi guys," Nancy said as she addressed the men seated in the small room. The windows were opened and the breeze felt good as it came through the house, which allowed the cool night air into the stuffy room. "I'm glad that you could make it this evening and I think that you'll be interested in what Suzanne and I have come up with as a solution to your problem." There was a definite buzz from the men as they wondered what this long legged, red head had to say. "As you know, or maybe aren't aware of, is that Suzanne and I are business women back in the States. I'm not bragging, but we've been very successful in our line of work, and it helped a bit that I was left a lot of money by my parents when they died unexpectedly in an airplane crash. I won't go into the gory details, but let me assure you that what we propose for you will allow you all to start anew and provide the type of living or maybe more than you were used to making." Nancy let her words make an impact on these men who didn't look like business men in the least. After all, all they knew was how to fish as that's what they were trained to do by their fathers and their father's before them.

Being schooled abroad had its attributes. When Nancy realized that even though these men understood English (it was taught in the schools and used by The Government in the Philippines) she wondered if it would be easier communicating with them in their native tongue. Most of the Philippine people communicated in English, but some of the old-school people still spoke in one of the eight major dialects. She wasn't schooled that well in Togalog, which is one of the main languages spoken. She listened to the men and realized, with a sigh of relief, that they were speaking English among themselves. They wanted Mario to be the group spokesperson and gestured for him to speak. "Miss Nancy, we don't really understand what you are trying to tell us. Could you let us know and advise us on what you're asking us to do?" Nancy was taken aback by his speech.

"Well, Suzanne and I are saying that we know what happened to you and why you decided to become New Age Pirates. We realize that you are really fishermen by trade and that's all you know how to do. What we're saying is that we're willing to teach you a new profession, and I have enough money to be able to back you up in the business that we will teach you. It's going to be very different than what you know how to do, but I know that you are all smart men and with a little bit of help from us, we can teach you how to open up a different type of business that will give you the kind of money that you're used to making, and possibly more."

The men listened intently as Nancy spoke and then crouched together as they talked among themselves. They were very animated and, after ten minutes went by they sat down, crossed their arms in front of themselves and nodded their heads to listen to more of what she had to say.

"First of all, Suzanne and I want to thank you for listening to what we are proposing. We know that you despise what you were forced to do. You're not pirates and this is not what you want to do to provide for your families. As for being wanted, on top of burglary, you are now wanted for murder, which, by the way, we know that you didn't commit. Suzanne gave the police some pictures. She was, and still is an artist and helped the crime lab with drawing characters of men that didn't resemble you in the least. So as far as the police are concerned, they are looking for men that have no similarities to you. We honestly don't think that anyone would recognize you from the posters that are up all over town. The only way that you will be captured is if one of you or your family members has a big mouth and tells another person, even in confidence, that one of you are the pirates the police are seeking. I advise you to make sure that your families don't say a word to anyone, and I'm not joking. Don't forget that the people that you used as fences might inadvertently talk to the police and cannot be held accountable for what they tell the police, especially if there is reward money to be had. You have to realize that they might be more deadly than any of your family members. If we can be assured that this doesn't take place, then Suzanne and I will teach you how to become importers and exporters."

"Each man has a different ability and we will use these accordingly. We'll find out what you're best suited for in this business and teach you how to work that particular part of the company. One of you might be great with numbers and will make a great accountant for the corporation. One of you might have a great eye for something unusual that people will want to buy. It could be food, which I admit might be hard to deliver fresh, or some sort of craft that isn't in the usual aisles of the gift shops. One of you might be great at getting a large industrial area ready to take on large boxes and be in charge of inventory. There are many jobs that have to be done in order to make it a viable large production, commercial business."

Nancy was looking at the individual men and their faces, hoping to get a vibe about what they were thinking. Without saying another word, the men again hovered amongst themselves and Mario stood up after conversing with his friends. "Miss Nancy, if what I'm hearing you tell us is what I think I'm hearing, it's like a dream come true. Are you telling us that you'll give us money and teach us a business like we see in the big city? When we read magazines, usually in the barbershop, these people are rich citizens. Is that what you're saying to us?"

Suzanne stood up and said, "I'll speak for Nancy and tell you yes, that's exactly what Nancy is telling you. I won't go into detail about what happened to me, but when I met Nancy, it was like a dream come true for me. I wasn't rich, was going into a profession that I had no knowledge about, I just had common sense. I had the desire and wanted to help people. My family needed me and depended on me to live, just as your families depend on you to make a good living for them. It's no different than it was for me."

Nancy and Suzanne stayed many hours grilling the men on their likes, what they enjoyed doing (besides fishing) and got a good idea of what they might be good at. The women were exhausted by the time they were ready to call it a night. The men insisted on walking them home to their sailboat. God forbid something should happen to these two women who were salvations to them. They couldn't believe that the Gods were looking down on them, and after all their prayers they were finally going to get their answer. Mario couldn't wait to tell Maria. The other men walked briskly to their homes, their excitement held tightly within themselves. They made arrangements with the women to meet the very next morning, but before they were to meet up with Nancy and Suzanne, they would go to church and thank God for all of their good fortune.

Suzanne and Nancy were glad to see the reaction that the men showed. "Well one down and one to go," Nancy said to Suzanne as she opened the door to the cabin. "By that, do you mean that the men are all settled? Now it's up to us to grill them more and find out their strong points and get them headed in the right direction."

Suzanne and Nancy were too excited to fall asleep. They took out pens and started writing down areas that were needed for the company that they would start. On one side of the paper they wrote down the business application that was needed. Say, for instance, a bookkeeper and accounting executive. Then the other areas that would need to be filled to start the business and have it become a viable operation. On the other side of the paper, they wrote down the names of the men. "I hope that by seeing that there's another way of life besides pirating, they will dig down deep into their knowledge banks. Even if they have to go back to school for a while and learn some necessary tools for the particular field that interests them, that will be the easy part," assured Suzanne as she finished writing on the pad of paper.

"In the morning, after thinking what we offered them as a way out of their predicament, we'll help them in what has to be done," Nancy said to Suzanne as she headed for the bathroom, getting ready for bed.

"Nancy, are you asleep or can I talk to you for a while?" asked Suzanne. Suzanne could see the moon shining through the small window in the room. The stars were illuminating the sky, reminding her of the beautiful evenings that she spent in Bermuda with Stephen. She tried quelling any other thoughts other than what had to be accomplished but found it difficult to get her feelings out of her mind. "Yes, my eyes are closed, but I have so many things going through my psyche that I can't mentally shut down. So tell me what's on your mind."

Suzanne started listing a multitude of thoughts that pertained to the men with whom they were going to work with. "It will be difficult to start a new business venture for them, but it isn't impossible! I know I'm probably going a bit too fast. I'm mentioning these opinions as feelings that I have on one hand and then, on the other hand, I'm thinking of all the work that is ahead of us with these men. Then I jump to all the things that have to be done with Arthur and the insurance company. What has to be done in order for us to maintain our own sanity? We have to make sure that our actions are going to be the right ones, and we're not doing anything irrational because of our emotions. Are we too close to the situation at hand? Will we be able to live with ourselves knowing what really happened? All these questions are going through my head. I don't know if I can sleep with all of these thoughts swirling and making me crazy. I can't seem to unwind and have a peaceful night's sleep."

Nancy sat up in her bed and went over to Suzanne's bed, and while patting her arm, talked soothingly to her partner. "I know what you're going through and feeling. Believe me I understand your dilemma. We somehow have to go through with what we started and ask God for help. I'm not one of religious convictions, but in this case, I really believe that God will show us the way and what happens, will happen for the best. Maybe your beliefs are starting to rub off on me, who knows? But try to breathe deeply and start thinking of good things that have happened in your life. When we wake up in the morning, we should feel renewed, not tired. I assure you that unless you think good thoughts and are kept up all evening long, you will be tired and cranky when you finally wake in the morning. So my dear, try to get rid of these emotions that are running through your head and relax. That is an order. It's going to be difficult to get that to happen, but try." With Nancy's help Suzanne started unwinding and the pent up feelings she was having were starting to get undone. Before she realized what happened, Suzanne closed her eyes and slept the sleep of wellness and thoughts of a better time and place took over her sleep.

They left the sailboat after breakfast and made their way back to Mario's house. Suzanne looked rested and was ready to take on the world. Nancy, on the other hand looked tired and when Suzanne looked over at her friend, she realized that Nancy had probably taken on the burden that Suzanne was able to shed. They trudged up the stairs and knocked loudly. Mario opened the door gesturing them in. The other men were seated, waiting for the women to advise them on what procedures had to be done first and foremost. The meeting lasted for over two hours and by the end of the session, the men had a good idea on what kind of business they would like. Nancy suggested that Tolemeo go back for a few courses on accounting in order to help his cousin, Ronnie, with the bookkeeping part of the corporation. Mario and Efran would take business courses at the university while learning how to operate an import and export firm. They decided that Sunny, who had a lot of interesting friends and acquaintances, would find the right type of items that could be used as the base of the company. His vast networking would pay off for all of the men in the long run. The women would go into the city with the men, and besides hiring a lawyer for their upcoming business, set the corporation in motion by filing a business name for their upcoming conglomerate.

The process for hiring the lawyer was not as easy as it seemed! They visited many a firm until the women finally found a law office, a large office that her lawyer friend recommended that lived in Manila, that wasn't too big to handle the proposed new business. With that set in motion, they left the men back at Mario's house and made their way back to the ship after a tiring and long day.

Nancy received a message from Rich saying that he needed a date for their arrival because he had a surprise waiting for her when she returned home. With that she called Rich but he wouldn't let the cat out of the bag. He insisted that she would be very happy when she finally got this vacation over. She and Suzanne were both mentally and physically exhausted and they personally wanted this vacation to end. Although it was supposed to be a real vacation it had turned out to be far more than they expected it to be. The other couples were delighted with the extended time but Suzanne surmised that Tracy and Mike had a time limit to their vacation. The other couples didn't say much, so Suzanne and Nancy thought that they didn't mind the extra days on board the vessel. They realized that Arthur was upset, as he should be, and knew that their part of the mission wouldn't be complete until the insurance issue was behind them.

Nancy listened to her answering machine and, after figuring out the time difference, had to wait to call Rich. Meanwhile, she kept thinking what the surprise could be waiting for her when she returned. It was as if she were on pins and needles with the excitement and all the thoughts of what it could be. Suzanne tried calming her friend down, but to no avail. "I love him so much and he is always so thoughtful, it's killing me not to know what he has planned."

"Well, it's not helping matters with you racking your brains out imagining what he has planned. You're going to have to wait and find out once we return home," Suzanne told Nancy. "I know he's a tight-mouthed person and he won't give anything away if he puts his mind to it. But it's killing me not knowing what he's going to tell me."

"Let's put it this way," suggested Suzanne. "It's not going to do either of us any good you frying your brain out trying to figure what he has in store for you, so let's put your mind to better things, like figuring out what we have to do about Arthur."

"I know what you are saying is right, but I'll call him when the time is good. I know he won't say anything to give away his secret, but it doesn't hurt to try."

That evening waiting for the time zone to get better so it wouldn't be in the middle of the night when Nancy called Rich, Suzanne was figuring out what she had to do in order to find out what really happened with Arthur and Sandy. When Arthur told the two women what happened to Sandy, at first Suzanne felt terrible. Then, the more she thought about what he said she felt she had to make sure that he was telling her the truth. She lay in bed that evening, trying to sort out the various scenarios in her mind, knowing that Nancy had Rich's secret on her mind. It was as if she were working alone. She looked across the aisle and could tell that Nancy's mind wasn't on what had to be done. She got out of her bed and went and retrieved the medical report, going over what it said one more time.

Everything that Arthur said was verified in the paper in front of her. She didn't know how to find out if there was anything else that could be relevant. While Nancy was in la, la land, thinking of Rich, Suzanne was being practical and had different methods in mind to try to talk to Arthur, even if she had to talk to him by herself. She couldn't blame Nancy for her happiness because she remembered when she felt the same way when she was going out with Stephen. Now that the romance seemed to be over, she tried quelling her doubts about Lawrence, knowing that this mystery had to be sorted out. When she returned home, then she would put her mind to sorting out her romantic situation. Now was not the time to be thinking about either man when she felt Arthur's situation had to be solved. Suzanne tried closing her eyes to sleep, but it eluded her. As much as she didn't want to think of her love life, or lack thereof, she couldn't help but think about the two men who were causing her sleep deprivation.

Lawrence's face was before her, and she imagined what it would be like holding his beautiful bronzed body in her arms. She knew that he was well built and she could tell what his body looked like underneath his suits. Besides, she saw him in his bathing suit when they were on Beverly's and Louis' boat years ago. If anything, the years had been good to him. He made sure that he worked out (he made time for this every day). That's something she had to start doing for herself.

After her and Nancy's recovery from their many operations and rehab she made herself go to the gym. But now she realized that was just as necessary to continue working out. Besides making her feel better and have more energy, she wanted to look in the mirror and like what she saw. At this point, whenever she passed a mirror on the way to the shower she avoided looking at herself. She realized that self-confidence was important in every aspect of what a person does. After all, what if she started getting intimate with Lawrence? It's not like she was a woman of the world with all sorts of lovers waiting for her. She only had Brian and Stephen. Of course, she read a lot of romance novels, but doubted that those happenings were real. From what some of her clients told her, she surmised that they very well could be. *'Well, I'd better start brushing up on my skills if I'm to satisfy Larry.'* Suzanne forced herself out of bed and while Nancy was sleeping, she found a spot in between their beds and started doing some crunches and her body only allowed three pushups before she called it an evening.

She realized that she needed to work on stamina if she wanted to make herself presentable and not be self-conscious if and when she made love to Larry. Before she fell asleep, she put Aquaphor on her lips to ensure that they would be nice, soft and pliable, just in case any kissing happened. Now she really wanted to figure out what could be done in this case that was taking huge amounts of time and effort out of their everyday lives. With those thoughts, she closed her eyes and, after a few minutes of thinking of the men in her life, a smile was on her face when she felt slumber upon her.

Nancy and Suzanne awoke to a glorious, sunny day. There was hardly a breeze, even on the coast where the boat was anchored. "It's going to be another scorcher," Nancy announced to Suzanne as she scantily attired herself for the upcoming day. "I can remember when I was a young girl and I was buying bathing suits for the season. I brought in a two-piece bathing suit to the fitting room and, when I looked in the mirror, I froze. I put my own hands and arms across my body and hurriedly took off the offending suit. I don't think, even when I was thin, that I wore a two-piece bathing suit." Nancy laughed at her friend and told her to get over her inferiority complex. "Let's go out today and buy one for you." Suzanne was astonished and made up some excuse why they couldn't go shopping during the day. With that said, the two women sat down for another great breakfast and then knew that pretty soon they would have to confront Arthur again and try to get to the bottom of this life insurance business.

Suzanne kept making excuses during the day, to put off meeting Arthur and dealing with the situation at hand. Finally, after a few hours passed, Suzanne knew that she had to have another face-to-face with Arthur. "Okay, I've hemmed and hawed all day and I'm taking a deep breath and I'm composing myself for what has to be done. Come upstairs with me and let's get this over with," Suzanne explained to Nancy.

Nancy dutifully went up the stairs to the main deck as Suzanne led the way. She looked over the entire deck and didn't see him anywhere. Finally, when she was about to give up, she spotted Arthur sitting by himself, in a corner, with some straw in his hands. He was obviously trying to whittle the time away and it looked like he was attempting to make a matt to bring back home for one of his grandchildren.

Suzanne and Nancy asked Arthur, "Mind if we sit with you?" Arthur seemed to have no recourse, so he gestured for them to join him. Taking in another deep breath, Suzanne started talking about nothing important and then out of nowhere, she told Arthur that she had to have a serious discussion with him. Arthur shrugged his shoulders and put his hand out as if to say, the floor is all yours.

"I know that we've spoken before about the terrible thing that we saw and we believe what you told us. The question before you and everyone, especially the people who will be the judge or God or whoever, is have you told us the truth? How do we know that Sandy handed you the rifle and demanded that you shoot her. You told us that a few nights before this catastrophe Sandy told you that her cancer had returned. We saw your reaction when we last spoke, and we do believe what you say. But does this mean that the courts are going to blame the pirates for this murder? Will this enable you to get double the money once the claim is made?"

"You know, Suzanne, I've been grieving so much that I didn't even think of the consequences. That isn't to say that Sandy didn't think of what would happen. She was the brains in our marriage. Sure, I made the money and worked hard, while Sandy raised the kids. But she and I both realized that she could have gone on to college and become an executive. She was smart, and even though she was quiet, she had brains besides beauty."

"Nancy and I looked over the entire insurance policy and there is a section there for an accidental death claim. Could you please tell us about the policy and when you bought it and why you did?" They saw Arthur inhale deeply; his hands were shaking. With a laugh, Arthur told the women how they bought the insurance policy and why. "We were young kids who had to get married, but we knew that we loved each other deeply. As it turned out, we had five children. We made a pact that I would go back to school and she, in turn, would take care of the child at the time. As it turned out, Sandy stayed home, taking care of all five kids, and now I'm glad that she did. We worked our butts off and then we would talk while the kids were asleep and we had our alone time."

"I hope that I'm not boring you with these trite matters, but to me, our life together was very happy. Although we struggled financially, the love that we had for each other got us through many a tough time. One day we received a phone call from an insurance agent and made an appointment to see him when the kids were settled down and asleep. It turned out, in later years that this man became a broker and eventually owned his own insurance company that sold all types of insurance and worked with many different companies. Please excuse the rambling."

"That's all right, continue your dialogue and take your time. It seems that we have plenty of time." Suzanne was serious about this matter and wanted an accurate account of all that happened. What better way than to ask Arthur himself? Suzanne and Nancy both thought that he was an honest man and he wasn't putting on an act of remorse. He was truly sad that he lost his best friend, companion, lover and wife.

"We were young when we had our children. We knew that we didn't have a lot of money. Food alone was costing us a fortune for our brood. But somehow we managed to stay afloat and we were able to save some money. I worked two jobs to keep us one step away from the poor house." Arthur laughed at his try at humor but realized that this reminiscing was helping him. "After listening to Mr. Long's spiel, we told him that we'd talk it over and let him know what our decision would be. You see, we were young, just starting our family and we realized that if we were to take out an insurance policy, it would be wiser and cost us less money the younger we were. It was Sandy's insistence that we take out the accidental death clause in a rider. After all, if something happened to either of us, we needed money to keep us afloat and we realized that the survivor would have to go back to work in order to maintain our way of life."

While listening to Arthur talk, Suzanne remembered when she and Brian had taken out an insurance policy when they were first married and were starting their family. It all made sense to Suzanne. After taking a little break, Arthur continued, as if talking to him-self he said, "Who would have thought that this accidental death clause would have to be used? Most people never think that way, unless of course, you have a plan that would be nasty. But I guess there are people like that in this world. That's why the jails are filled to capacity in most States."

"Anyway, getting back to our situation, it's hard for me to remember to think and say me since Sandy and I were a couple, to have to say I again. Sandy encouraged me to take out the accidental death rider. To be honest with you, we haven't thought of the insurance policy in years. When Sandy became ill the first time, she brought up the insurance. I guess it didn't matter if she got ill years later, because we were young when we purchased the policy and, at that point in your life, a person doesn't think of illness. She told me that the insurance company would give us the money and all sorts of things must have gone through her mind. She told me that we'd have to get a burial plot and she wanted us to go and pick out the coffins to be buried in. I, of course, didn't want to hear about it, but she insisted that we had to make plans because she didn't know how life would turn out. I was the complacent one and went along with her. She was sick and I didn't want to give her a cause for any more emotional upset. So we bought a family plot. I was making a lot of money, for us that is, and since we could pay it out monthly, I figured it wouldn't hurt. The same went for the casket."

"I imagine that Sandy was thinking a lot about the policy and all, especially when she found out that the cancer had returned. It wasn't confirmed, but she knew how she felt and realized that something wasn't right. In all the times we were together she didn't tell me her feelings. It wasn't until we were aboard this sailing ship that she confided to me what was happening. First of all, I was upset that she didn't want to help herself but, in essence, she was thinking of the family and friends that helped out when she had her first bout with cancer. I thought that something was funny when she became more devout and wanted to visit all of the shrines on this trip. I didn't put two and two together until she confided in me what was wrong. Of course, I was devastated, but she wouldn't let me be morose about anything. She insisted that we continue this trip and wanted me to remember our happy times and that's why she insisted on making an album of us enjoying our time together." The tears were now flowing freely down his face, and he wiped the wet moisture with the back of his hand.

"I guess when the pirates came aboard, Sandy must have remembered about the accidental death rider because she was determined that this is what she wanted for me. We had a $500,000 life insurance policy on each of us. When this sudden turn of events happened, she had a look on her that was gritty. She was firm and unwavering when she shoved the rifle into my hands and yelled at me to shoot her. I thought that she had lost her mind, but then I remembered, like it was yesterday, the many talks we had about the insurance. Funny what comes to mind when you least expect it."

Suzanne and Nancy saw Arthur shaking his head, as if someone else was saying what he was saying. He realized what he was telling us, but all of the emotions were full force, not letting him out of its grip. "Before I could think, I heard her shouting to me and yelling to pull the trigger." Arthur shook his head as in disbelief. "I don't care about the money; all I want is to be able to hold Sandy again and whisper sweet nothings in her ears and love her." He put his face into his hands and cried like a baby. Suzanne and Nancy felt sorry that they made him recant his story to them.

They thanked him for his honesty and walked away, making sure that he was all right being left on his own. "Do you think we should go back and walk him to his cabin?" Nancy asked Suzanne. "No, I think he needs this alone time to get himself together and if he wants us, he knows our cabin number."

Suzanne and Nancy got ready for dinner, and for the first time in many years, Suzanne wasn't hungry. The idea of food made her nauseous. She and Nancy knew the truth, and in her mind, asked herself if what she thought was right. While taking a hot shower, she couldn't get Arthur's words out of her head. Not saying anything and allowing the phony pirates take the blame for murdering an innocent victim, while Arthur was able to collect the insurance money, especially with the accidental death rider, seemed wrong. Could Suzanne live with that decision? She and Nancy had a lot of thinking and talking to do. She realized that Arthur wouldn't deny that the pirates killed Sandy, because he was still letting her rule his thinking. After all, that is what she wanted him to do and get the money she thought they deserved. She asked herself if she were in Sandy's position, would she be able to have her loved one live with the guilt. Maybe it wasn't guilt to her way of thinking. Suzanne would never know what Sandy's thoughts were.

The two women were dressed up for dinner when a knock was heard on their door. Arthur was standing in front of the cabin and asked to come in. "Of course, how rude of me," Nancy uttered as she motioned for him to take a seat. "I want to thank you for letting me speak what was on my mind. Saying all of those words made me realize that, no matter what happens, Sandy will be happy that I listened to her and now she can rest in peace knowing that I will be taken care of. That's not to say that I won't distribute the money to the kids. They need the money more than I do. Thanks again, ladies, for letting me say what had to be said. Now you know what I've been feeling all along and I think that Sandy would want me to retire and just settle down being with the kids and be there for them."

The three people walked up the stairs, knowing in their hearts that what they knew would be kept among them-selves. No one would be the wiser.

CHAPTER TWENTY FIVE

Suzanne and Nancy were busy packing. They were glad that the police were able to tell Captain Winter that the ship was cleared and they could start back to their base port. Suzanne felt relief when the all clear was given and now she and Nancy would get back to their homes, family, friends and business. Nancy was happy that she would be going home and once again seeing Rich and making plans for their up-coming nuptials. The last time she spoke to Rich, he mentioned a surprise and she was anticipating it with baited breath. Nancy couldn't imagine what it was, but she was looking forward to seeing him and finding out what he had on his devious mind.

Suzanne was in the cabin, calling home to tell Mrs. Walsh and the children of their arrival. She was certain that the other couples on board were sharing the same feelings as hers. It was a great vacation, considering all the unpleasantness that happened, but all in all, it was one vacation she would always remember. Suzanne couldn't wait to show the many pictures from their various destinations, and she couldn't wait to see the reaction when she presented the many gifts that she bought along the way for her family and friends.

Lying in bed, Nancy and Suzanne discussed the unfortunate happenings, but decided that all's well that ends well. Suzanne remarked that she hated being devious. She realized that with their new endeavors, the would-be-pirates and their families would benefit from all the new beginnings. Nancy was not one to dilly dally and was already getting her lawyers in place to start the new corporation for the men. She also had to get them ready to take classes so they'd have the knowledge that they would need to make this a profitable enterprise.

When eating their meals, every couple showed the other vacationers all the various merchandise that they were bringing home. The pictures that they showed each other were spectacular, and Tracy was trying not to tell her own little secret, but realized that it was hard to keep her mouth shut. Without true confirmation from a doctor, Tracy struggled to keep her secret to herself, but finally one evening she blurted out her suspicion. Mike was so proud he thought that his insides would burst with pride. "If there were a time in our lives when this surprise package was supposed to happen, it couldn't have been at a better time in our lives." He was going back to his position, and he knew that he would be voted among his peers to become a partner. This was a given, as sure as Mike was a true Yankees fan, even though he loved the N.Y. Mets as well. He didn't care because he enjoyed watching both teams, one American League the other the National league. He realized that this new baby would be loved, and this would be the beginning of their family. He hoped that his love of baseball would be carried on with his offspring.

Tracy tried telling Mike not to tell a soul. One evening, after dinner, Mike blurted out his reason for being entirely happy. "I come from a large family, and I want you to be the first to know that we consider you part of our extended family. That's why you'll be as proud as we are that we will now be a family of three." Everyone was happy and toasted to the happiness of the young couple. Of course, Tracy would toast with a glass of sparkling water and lemon, but that was fine with her.

Nancy and Suzanne had contacted the crew of their airplane, and they were waiting for the happy sailors to land. The gifts that they received were unexpected and admired. At Logan, Nancy and Suzanne were getting into their individual cars. "Thanks for making this one of the most memorable, if not the most emotional trips, that we've been on," Suzanne said to Nancy. Suzanne couldn't help but mention their trip to Japan and Beppo and told Nancy that, even though they had gone through a lot both emotionally and physically, that trip was different in many ways. Suzanne would remember this trip always, especially when another corporation was coming into being. She was happy that they were getting back to what most would consider normal lives. Suzanne knew that this wasn't the case with Nancy and her, but, with all things considered, she was glad that she was able to see sights that she normally wouldn't have ever imagined possible.

While Suzanne was driving home, thoughts of Arthur and Sandy appeared before her. The other couples were in her mind as well as she thought of the good times. Sure, she had to admit that she would never forget her frightening experience of almost drowning and how she was miraculously saved. Then she realized that she made wonderful friends that she could always count on. It was a sad ending for Sandy and Arthur, but she hoped that Arthur would be able to bounce back and live a life without Sandy. She knew, or thought she knew, what a wonderful couple they were and hoped that he would get over his mourning.

Nancy was driving home on Route 128, going to her house, knowing that she'd have a lot of airing out to do. When she made the turn to her street, she saw that some of the windows were opened. She wondered what that was about. When she entered her supposedly empty house, she was surprised to see Rich standing there with a shit eating grin that she hadn't seen before. "Surprise, Honey," he yelled. She ran into his arms and they kissed each other long and hard. Suddenly Nancy realized that standing a few feet away was Mr. Yahuhito, his hands hiding the smile that was evident on his face.

"I was able to get transferred to Boston and I took it upon myself to make the move. I hope that you're not disappointed."

"Are you kidding," a giddy Nancy remarked. I'm so happy I'm pinching myself from hoping that this is not some cruel joke or dream."

They all went into the kitchen after Nancy and Rich brought in the luggage that she had taken with her. "Before I do another thing, there are some things that I brought back that I think you'll enjoy. You too, Mr. Yahuhito; come join us for some great tea."

"Nancy, you shouldn't be waiting on us, you just returned home from vacation. Let us do that for you," Rich adamantly told his fiancée. "It's nice of you to think that way, but Honey, this entire trip I've been waited on hand and foot. The two of you sit down, and let me wait on you. Don't get too used to it, but for now, it will be my pleasure."

As they sat down to sip their tea and eat some pastries that Rich had brought home from the bakery in town, Nancy got out the presents that she brought back for the two men. She was surprised about Mr. Yahuhito, but was also pleased that he had decided to join Rich in his new home. Rich had Mr. Yahuhito move into the maids' quarters, assuring everyone that they would have the desired privacy required if they were to live together in harmony.

Rich loved all the new presents, clothes and accessories that Nancy had brought back from her latest vacation. Nancy then told the two men of all the happenings while the ship sailed along the South China Seas. Rich shook his head in amazement when Nancy went into detail about the awful experiences that they encountered. "I can't believe that you're sitting here, calm as can be, relating all the terrible incidents that you and Suzanne experienced. I'm surprised that you stayed aboard the vessel when you could have easily come home." "I guess it's our stubbornness that made us see this vacation to its end. Yes, we could have called it quits and, in most circumstances, other people would have ended the vacation then. But, we endured. The people that we met became like family to us. Each couple was wonderful, and maybe that's why we stayed aboard. In the end it all worked out. Let me tell you what we did for those men that used to be fishermen."

Nancy went on to tell Rich and Mr. Yashuhito, (who were spellbound at her stories,) about the new age pirates. "It wasn't as if they were really pirates." She went on to explain how they no longer could make their living fishing in the seas where they were brought up. "So to make a long story short, we are now proud partners of a new corporation in the import and export business." Rich kept shaking his head in amazement. "Leave it to you to take advantage of a bad situation and turn it around to your benefit." He hugged her tightly and listened intently as she showed him the pictures of the various countries and places that they visited. After a couple of hours, they all were exhausted and went to the upstairs bedrooms to call it a night.

Rich was glad that Nancy was home, and he could share the bed with his true love. After they both showered, he showed her how happy he truly was. Nancy loved the way Rich's lips felt and couldn't get enough of his body beside her. He slowly caressed her body, and she was glad that she didn't bother putting on a nightgown after her shower. He took her breast in his mouth and sucked her erect nipples, taking one, then the other and then he slowly licked her breasts until she moaned with delight. He went further down her body, his tongue not wavering until his fingers found her wetness in between her long and lovely legs. He heard Nancy moaning with anticipation, as his erection was hard and long. His pre-come was evident as her hands caressed him and she erupted, her climax evident with her cries of delight. He entered her quickly, their rhythm, like dancing to an exotic record, was fast, then slow and finally he couldn't hold his emotions any longer and moved quickly spewing his liquid into her.

"I'm glad that we're able to enjoy each other in every possible way," Nancy said as she played with the dark, wavy hair on his chest. "You have just enough hair on your upper body. It is perfect for me to enjoy moving my hands through it." Rich laughed at her remark and told her that he was glad that she didn't have any body hair that was unsightly and the hair that was in between her legs was just enough for him to enjoy. "At least I know that you are a true red head and that your color doesn't come out of a bottle."

"You're such a smart ass!! Nancy asked Rich, "How do you know that I don't color my hair down below?"

"Let's say I'm a man of knowledge, and I'd know if you weren't a true redhead," declared Rich as he tenderly rubbed her arms putting them both into Morpheus.

The next morning Nancy couldn't wait to call Suzanne and tell her about the surprise that greeted her when she returned home. Suzanne was thrilled for Nancy and then told Nancy of her experience when she drove into the garage. "First of all a big sign was hanging from the front of the house welcoming me home. Then Simka and Boston both ran to me and wouldn't let me out of their sight. Usually they would ignore me until I got the message that they weren't happy that I left them. But I guess because I was away for such a long time, they dispensed with their usual display of temperament and showed me that they were happy to see me back where I belonged. I then called the girls and told them that

I would meet them tomorrow evening. I'll bring them the presents that I bought for them. I think they'll like my taste. Mrs. Walsh was thrilled with her new clothes and items. Let's face it, at her age, what can a person give to someone who has everything she needs? My parents will be at Hope's house, and then I can disperse all the gifts and presents at once."

After Suzanne got off the phone, she called Justin and Madaline and sat on the phone a long time, getting a date and time for them to meet. She'd surprise the two unsuspecting people with some gifts they weren't expecting. When she called the shop the next morning, she found out her schedule and couldn't wait to show the Boston Estheticians their unexpected presents.

With that all done, Suzanne was ready to start unpacking and have leisurely time until the following day when clients were booked. She made a note to call her friends from the cruise to find out how their homecomings turned out. Meanwhile, she made sure that all of the vacation pictures were in order for her to show everyone. She was glad that she and Nancy hadn't called it quits after she almost drowned. She endured and was glad that things turned out even better than expected.

Renée and Paul Murphy made it home and were happy that they were able to get there without any special fanfare. Paul opened the kitchen door and a large smile appeared on his face. On top of their counter was a huge trophy with a blue ribbon adorning the award winning gold car!! Renée and Paul started yelling and smiling. "I can't believe that Corey came in first place. Sam, his dad, must have been so proud of him," Paul screamed at his wife who was already half way out the back door.

"Let's go next door and find out all about it. I bet they're still up, it isn't that late in the evening," Renée declared. They rang the back door bell, and when Sam opened the door, Paul and Renée pushed through like linebackers at a Patriots game. The entire family came into the kitchen, and they were all talking at once. Paul, the one who usually took charge, held up his hands and yelled "quiet!" They all obeyed. "First of all, I can't tell you what a nice surprise we had when we opened our door and found the trophy on display on the kitchen counter." Taking a kitchen stool out, Paul sat down and declared, "Tell us all about the event and I don't want anything left out."

After hearing all the details, they all decided to go into the living room and hear about Paul and Renée's experiences on their vacation. Paul and Renée didn't want to go into a lengthily explanation of the problems on board, but in the end, Renée went next door and brought with her the camera with all the pictures that they took. She also brought with her the gifts that they selected for their favorite neighbors.

"All in all, we can honestly say that we had a ball. You can tell from these pictures that we didn't miss anything at the various places that we toured. We made wonderful friends, and I hope that we keep in touch with all of them. When you spend over a month living in the same small space, you can't help but get to know everyone." The two decided that they wouldn't tell their friends or colleagues about the pirates or the killing on board the ship. This upsetting detail they would keep to themselves. They knew that their acquaintances would want to hear the happy times and didn't want to know of any unhappy situations that occurred when they went away on their vacation of a lifetime.

Their neighbors and closest friends were thrilled to look at the pictures and were doubly happy at the various presents brought back from countries and places that most of them wouldn't have the opportunity to visit. When it came time to leave, Paul told Sam that Corey deserved the trophy and should display it for all to see. "After all, it's not every day that a young man can win a prestigious medal and plaque such as this." He handed the trophy back to young Corey and told them that they were exhausted and would have no trouble getting to sleep. With hearty good byes, they left and entered their own home, glad for the peace and quiet.

Finally in their own bed, they snuggled together, happy for the experiences that they had, but most of all, for being healthy to enjoy all of the various encounters that most people weren't able to experience. Renée snuggled closer to Paul, and before they could make love, they knew that after a good night's sleep and rest, they had nothing to do but to please each other in ways that only two people in love could do.

Tracy and Mike Razzaboni were able to make it home in time to call their parents and family and let them know that they were back from their vacation. They didn't want to inform the relatives of their happy news until Tracy had the doctor confirm that she was pregnant. After all, she wanted to be able to tell them of the impending date of their new addition to the family. They talked on the phone for what seemed hours. After promising to send the pictures of the vacation to the various computers, they hung up the phone and scrounged the kitchen for something to eat. They realized that they should have stopped at a restaurant on the way home but were very anxious to get back to their normal routines.

After spotting some cans of soup, they heated them up and found some crackers to put into the hot liquid. "You know, after enjoying Chef Andrés elaborate meals, this is about the next best thing that we've ever had." They laughed at Mike's remark. They left the suitcases at the front foyer and headed upstairs for some much-needed rest. They would take the next day off and separate the clothes to be washed and all the packages for the various co-workers. "I don't know about you, but I'm exhausted," remarked Tracy as she fell on her bed and within four minutes was sound asleep.

Mike looked lovingly at his wife, who was as beautiful as she was the day he met her. He was thankful that she was carrying his child who would only add more beauty to their wonderful life. He put his hands under his head and silently thanked God for all the blessings bestowed upon him. With that thought in mind, he drifted off to sleep.

Joe and Sam entered their apartment and were thankful that there weren't a lot of steps leading to the door. They left the suitcases inside the door and plopped down on the comfortable sofa in the living room. "I have to say that this was the best vacation that I can ever remember taking. Of course, on a lot of vacations, I was so plastered that I don't remember what happened." Joe giggled with excitement as he took and kissed Sam's hand. "You are definitely nuts," uttered Sam as he watched Joe out of the corner of his eye. He thought to himself that tomorrow he'd call Lisa and make arrangements to meet up with her and his three sons to show them some pictures and give them the gifts that he brought home. He knew that his sons would be excited to receive the presents, but Lisa was another story. As much as she tried acting like nothing bothered her, he knew her well enough by now that she was still embarrassed that he left her for a man. He called his parents and sisters to tell them that he arrived safely and sat down and put on the television while Joe called his family. They both had enough sense to go out to eat. Tomorrow they'd do the food shopping to make sure that there was enough to eat at the apartment.

After a leisurely evening, they decided to call it a night. They snuggled together, and before they realized what was happening Joe got horny and started making advances to Sam. Sam got all hot and bothered and was on top of Joe before he realized what he was doing. Sam started kissing Joe's ears and his neck, all the while, he felt his erection getting larger and larger. He entered Joe before he realized what was happening. The sweat was pouring down Sam's neck as he moved quickly, and he could feel his warm liquid oozing out of his partners body. He fell in exhaustion and lovingly moved to his side while Sam lovingly patted his partner's arm, inducing them both into a sound night's sleep.

The next morning Sam called his ex and made arrangements as to when he could come over to give the boys their gifts. Lisa would be surprised when he presented her with one also. When he arrived at the house, the boys were jumping up and down with excitement as they opened the various souvenirs with appropriate elations. They were happy as pigs in shit. Lisa didn't want to embarrass either of them, so she quickly opened her present and thanked Sam.

He showed them the pictures, eliminating the ones that showed both Joe and Sam together enjoying their time away. When it came time to leave, he looked adoringly at his boys, knowing that they were being brought up with a loving mother and people who gave them enough love to give them the right mindset in a home that was divided by divorce. Joe and Sam were just that, a happy couple that didn't let the smallness of people's minds bother them. The ugliness of small-minded people would not spoil the love that the men felt from all of their family and friends.

Cole and Isabelle had a long way to travel to finally arrive home. They decided to stop by the local pub for some fish and chips and a few drinks while they talked to their mates and told them of the terrific holiday they had. The only presents that they brought back were for their neighbor, who drove and picked them up from the airport. Other than that, Isabelle had bought things for herself, Cole and their home. Isabelle didn't forget about the baby pram set she bought at one of the stalls. After waving and saying cheerio to their fellow mates and making a date to see them soon, they were on their way to their small, but neat cottage. After kicking off their shoes, they sat down, exhausted from the long flight and all of the harrowing experiences that they encountered on what was supposed to be a fun-filled vacation. Although they did enjoy themselves, Isabelle was going to ring Edward, their holiday agent, and give him a piece of her mind when she told him of all the terrible things that happened on their holiday.

When morning arrived, she called on the telly and told Edward all about the incidents and harrowing experiences they encountered. Edward felt awful, but didn't know what he could do to make up for their frightful occurrences. He'd make it up to them the next time they were to go on holiday, he promised. She hung up the telly, and with a huge sigh, took down the messages left to her by her service that answered their phones when no one was around. She numbered them in order of importance, and like always, was back doing the business that she knew and loved.

Suzanne met Nancy at the office ready for another full day of pleasing clients and looking over the books that her daughters left for her to examine. She thought of all the wonderful places that she and Nancy had been and was happy that they had made friends with people who she normally would have never met. Nancy informed Suzanne of Rich's surprise and was happy for her friend and business partner. She called Mrs. Walsh and asked her when would be a good time for them to entertain and make a delicious meal for Nancy, Rich and of course Mr. Yashuhito. Suzanne knew not to make any set time for a lunch break, knowing that most of her clients were determined to have their appointments with Suzanne and only Suzanne. She asked herself what would happen if something really bad had occurred and she couldn't take care of these people any more. *'I guess that, like anything else, they'd adjust and get used to someone new.'* With that thought, she suddenly became morose and depressed. She then admonished herself for having those thoughts and tried to have a positive attitude for the rest of the day.

When she arrived home, Suzanne purposely stayed up late to make sure that she called Madaline and could talk to her for a while. When she got Madaline on the telephone, she told her of all the experiences that she and Nancy had, leaving out the more disturbing incidents. When saying goodbye to her friend, she knew that she had to make a date to see Justin and give him the small items that she knew he'd like. In the morning, she called Justin and made arrangements to go to his condo and bring pictures and the gifts she bought for him. After having a long day at work, she walked into her house and immediately was greeted by Simka and Boston. The two cats weaved in between her legs, not allowing a safe passage to the kitchen where Mrs. Walsh had a nice hot dinner waiting for her.

The next weekend, after a long and busy week, she decided to drive out to Nancy and Rich's place to get some needed relaxation. It seemed as if she never was on a vacation and needed a vacation from this one. Mr. Yashuhito answered the door, and with a big smile, greeted her and ushered her into the large foyer. Nancy and Rich formally introduced the two people in their lives who were so important to them. After drinking some nice tea, they all settled down and talked of their experiences on the Vacation of a Lifetime. They went over some pictures they had taken and Nancy showed off the new pieces that she bought overseas and showed Suzanne where she strategically placed them. To Rich, it didn't matter where she put them, as long as his Nancy was safe and secure at home with him.

Suzanne walked along the beach after a lunch made by Mr. Yashuhito. She laughed to herself knowing that Mrs. Walsh could show Mr. Yashuhito some easy meals to prepare and make it seem like it took forever. Suzanne would have to talk to Mrs. Walsh, but she knew that her surrogate mom would be glad to show off for this nice older gentleman.

Suzanne wondered if she should call Arthur and find out how he was doing. When she came back from her walk along the beach (that had the birds scurrying about) she sat down and asked Nancy her opinion on what she should do. Nancy deliberated for a while and then answered her friend. "We should call most of the people who were on the ship and ask them how they are. After all, we consider them our friends, and it's only fitting to find out how they're doing now that they're back to their regular routines. Okay, since tomorrow is Sunday, that's a great time to call them."

Rich and Nancy made Suzanne sleep over their house, considering that they had many bedrooms to spare. Suzanne didn't like driving in the dark, so they didn't have much persuading to do. She called Mrs. Walsh, making sure that her housekeeper wouldn't worry if she didn't come home. She felt that she was like a teenager, having to report in to her parents. With a laugh she got herself ready for bed, borrowing some night clothes from Nancy. She was glad that Nancy was a partner in the spa because she had all the products necessary for her bedtime routine. She lay awake, trying to fall asleep but had a hard time doing so. Thoughts were milling around in her head, first of Stephen and then of Lawrence. She punched her pillow, feeling like a teenager, torn between two loves. She remembered the time she first met Stephen while she was in Bermuda, on a well-deserved vacation. She got all tingly thinking of their love making and tried putting the thoughts out of her mind. Then suddenly Lawrence's face was before her, and although she never as much as kissed him, she imagined how sexy and soft his mouth would be. '*This is ridiculous,*' she thought as more images of Lawrence came to mind. He had a gorgeous body and imagined her hands caressing his every crevice. She also thought of his hands on all of her womanly parts, causing her to stir uncomfortably in a bed that she wasn't used to. She got up and quietly went down stairs, looking for a magazine to read so she would not have those wanton thoughts disrupting her. She found a book in the library that she hadn't read and brought it upstairs with her.

The next morning, she made everyone her famous French toast and put heavy garnishes around the toasty concoction. She was glad that Nancy had bought all of the fruit that was necessary. Nancy also had the cinnamon and confectioners' sugar to sprinkle on top of her magnificent breakfast. She let Mr. Yashuhito observe her making their breakfast and realized that he was memorizing all that she did. A smile crossed her face at his eagerness to learn. Meanwhile, Nancy was communicating with Mario and his faithful men, keeping tabs on their grades and what they were learning in order to have their company be as good as possible. Nancy was very generous in sending money to the men and their families until the corporation was opened for business.

When the dishes were cleared and everything put back, Nancy and Suzanne decided to make the phone calls to their new friends. Renée and Paul were happy to hear from Suzanne and Nancy and couldn't wait to tell them about the trophy and blue ribbon that their next-door neighbor had won. Of course, Paul bragged about his part in making the racer that won. They talked for a while and then told the lovely couple that they would get back to them and they would meet for a nice dinner at the Capitol Grille on Boylston Street in Boston. After they hung up the phone and finding out that Renée and Paul had gone to the medical building to give the workers their presents and show them some pictures that they had taken, the two couples knew that their friendship wouldn't be a fleeting one.

It was time to get in touch with Tracy and Mike. When Tracy answered the phone, they knew that she and Mike were well and spent about another fifteen minutes talking about what was happening. They found the due date and made notes to continue their friendship, making sure that they'd be around for the delightful event.

When they called Joe and Sam, they heard a lot of noise in the background. Telling the two men that they would call back at a better time, Joe assured them that there was nothing wrong. "It's only Sam's kids playing on the computer and making one Hell of a mess. But really, they're here usually every weekend, and I take it in stride. That's why we enjoyed our vacation so much. There were no kids to worry about and we could go about on our own time with not a care in the world." Suzanne told Joe that she had a spa in downtown Newburyport and when she knew her schedule there, she'd call and they could meet for lunch or dinner. With that thought, they said their goodbyes and would definitely get together in the next month or so.

They decided not to call Cole and Isabelle, realizing that they really didn't have anything in common with the lovely couple. Nancy and Suzanne would remember them fondly. Sometime in the future they would call, and for the heck of it, find out how they were doing.

They tried calling Arthur, but no one answered the telephone. They waited awhile and tried again but still no one answered the phone. "Let me find out if I can contact one of their children. Maybe he's visiting with them. I think I have one or two of the kids' numbers in my telephone book at home. When I get back to Stoney Brooke, I'll call you. In a few days, we'll get in contact with Arthur, I'm sure."

Suzanne went home and that evening wrote down the numbers of some of Arthur's children. When she left work that evening, she called one of his daughters and after hearing a busy signal tried again. Thinking to her-self that the best thing she paid for was for call waiting, and if someone was on the phone, the telephone would beep letting her know that someone was trying to get in touch with her. She called Nancy informing her of what was happening. Suzanne let an hour go by and then tried calling again. This time a young girl answered the phone and put her mother on the line.

"Hi Veronica, this is Suzanne Morse. You might not remember me, but maybe your Dad told you about me and Nancy and the vacation that your parents took. First of all, I want to tell you how sorry I am about your Mom, and I'm sending my condolences to you."

"We received your card in the mail, and thank you for your sympathy. I wish that I had some good news to tell you, but at this point, all of my sisters and brother are at a loss for words," said Veronica.

"What do you mean by a loss for words?" Suzanne asked. "You know that my parent's trip was paid for by us kids. We decided that instead of waiting till their fiftieth anniversary, we'd give them a forty-fifth anniversary present instead of making a big party like everyone else. You probably know that my Mom had a terrible bout with cancer, and we thought that she was completely cured of the disease. We used to take care of her and make sure we drove her for her radiation and chemo appointments. There was always something fresh and hot waiting for my Dad because my Mom would be in no shape to cook after her treatments."

Suzanne felt a chill over her entire body, but didn't let that disturb her. "Go on Honey, tell me what's wrong." Well, apparently you know that when my parents were young and just married, they took out an insurance policy in the amount of $50,000. In the meantime, their family expanded, but they paid their premium on a regular basis, not giving it another thought. As the years went by and the kids came, my parents never let on that anything was wrong with their marriage. But one never knows what goes on behind closed doors. My poor Mom didn't even know that my Dad was cheating on her, for years I suppose, until after she died. Boy did he change!!"

"Wait a second, back up a bit," Suzanne told Veronica nicely. "What do you mean by cheating on her? When they were on vacation with us, they seemed like the most happily married couple I've ever seen." Suzanne didn't want to tell her that she and Nancy had contacted the insurance company and found out about the rider for paying double if the person that died because of an accident.

CHAPTER TWENTY SIX

Suzanne's head was spinning and she felt perspiration flowing down her armpits. *'Could this be true?'* "Let's back up a minute, okay? The last time that my partner and I saw your dad, he was in a horrible state and couldn't wait to get home to be with you kids. Nancy, my business partner, and I had many a long talk with Arthur, and we saw the unhappiness and all the pent-up sadness that he had when your Mom was shot by the pirates. From what I'm hearing you're telling me that this was all an act?"

Suzanne wanted to throw up. She and Nancy knew the truth, and because of their putting themselves in Arthur's position, purposely lied to the authorities. What she was hearing was not what she thought she'd be listening to. She saw the tears roll down his face, they saw and felt his hurt when Sandy shoved the gun into his hands and demanded that he shoot and kill her. "Tell me Veronica, do you know how long this affair, that you say your father has been having, has been going on?"

"Apparently, my Mom was oblivious to my Dad having an affair. She was so wrapped up in us kids and our lives. Then, when she got sick, it all went downhill. When my Dad said he was working late and couldn't make it home in time for dinner, we didn't think anything of it. We just thought that he couldn't and wouldn't face the fact that my Mom was ill with cancer. I honestly don't know how many girlfriends he had over the years, but it seems this chippy he's been seeing has been around for over ten years. She's a real douse, that one. It seems when the insurance company gave him over a million dollars, (because of the accumulation of interest), he and this babe went away, far away, and it doesn't look like they'll be back anytime soon." Suzanne could hear the bitterness in her voice. As she talked, Suzanne wondered if her other siblings felt the same way and supposed that they did.

Suzanne felt as if she was going to faint. She had to get off of the phone and call Nancy as soon as possible. This couldn't be real. It couldn't be happening. Through the years, she'd made a point of being honest and getting the bad people to pay their dues. Now suddenly, she and Nancy were the culprits in this awful drama. They knew that the pirates hadn't really killed Sandy but let them take the blame for it. It was fine with them because Suzanne had made sure that

the pictures that she helped the police artist draw and put all over the town didn't resemble the men in any way. She had to get in touch with Nancy and see what could be done.

Suzanne dialed Nancy's home telephone number and Mr. Yashuhito answered. Trying not to sound any alarm, she asked nicely if she could please speak to Nancy. After a few minutes Nancy answered.

SOMEWHERE IN THE CARIBBEAN

The beautiful couple was under the canopy that was built especially for privacy. They would bask in the sun, and after a while, would go into the warm Caribbean water, frolicking and enjoying the beautiful weather. They would slither away under the canopy made of white linen with decorated, colorful pillows adorning the sandy floor. There was a bottle of wine and tall wine glasses to be used when they felt parched from the hot sun.

Arthur and Emily had waited for a respectable amount of time to whisk away from friends and family and finally, after many years, enjoy only each other's company.

When Arthur and Sandy's children had given them that present as a forty-fifth wedding anniversary gift, Arthur had no knowledge of what was going to happen. With the addition of their brood of children, Arthur felt pushed away from the family. Many times his co-workers would go out for a long lunch or an early dinner and he'd never been a part of their carousing. After their fourth child came along, he found himself going to the bars for a drink before he would have to leave for home. When he did get to the house, he'd find the house in disarray while Sandy was either bathing the children or trying to put them to bed. It was up to Arthur to make himself something for dinner. Once in a while, a plate would be left for him to put into the microwave oven to heat.

Arthur often felt out of place in his own home. He didn't feel wanted or needed except for the money that he provided for his growing family. It was a co-worker that asked him to join him at the local pub downtown for a few drinks before he headed home. Arthur told himself why not, no one even knows when I'm home. He found himself going out to the various bars more frequently. At first he ignored the women who tried to cozy up to him and then, finally, his reserve left and he sought out the various sluts who thought it was cool to go out with a married man. His first affair lasted a year or so and then, when the woman became serious, he dumped her. This happened for six years and then he met up with Emily.

Emily was different than the other women who he usually attracted. Her figure was exceptional, especially when she wore those low cut sweaters that showed her beautiful cleavage. Her long legs showed her well-toned muscles when her micro miniskirts would be shoved up exposing her lace under-ware and her beautiful soft, well-formed buttocks. As soon as he saw her, he noticed that he had the largest erection in years. He thought to himself that he would love to get into that piece of ass.

He hated going home but did so out of duty. When Sandy became ill, he felt obligated to be the faithful husband and supportive father that he thought he should be. He would come home and find Sandy completely spent from the various treatments she was undergoing. He consciously didn't see Emily for a while, but she called him at work and set up a time and place to meet. After that meeting, he was lost. He would get a reservation for a hotel room in the middle of the day, going without lunch just to be in her arms and make mad, passionate love. Arthur was out of control and completely lost when she went down on him for the first time. He never had a woman take him completely as she did. He would often empty his semen in her mouth, then watching her swallow it, the thought drove him crazy. She never had children so her cunt was tight as a drum. He would pump her until they both were left spent.

Emily never once mentioned him divorcing or getting rid of Sandy and his family. He often thought of those things himself but was not going to upset the apple cart if Emily didn't ask him to. Their affair was going on for over ten years when the children surprised Sandy and him with their anniversary gift. He told Emily about it and felt terrible taking Sandy away with him when he really wanted to be with her.

Then without him having to do a thing, he found himself in a terrible situation for which there was no rhyme or reason. Sandy admitted to him that her cancer had returned. At that point, he couldn't get out of the marriage. It would make him look like a terrible piece of shit. At first she didn't tell him, but when he started getting curious as to why she went to all those shrines on the trip, she then admitted that the cancer had come back and she didn't want to put him, family or friends through any more trouble than they already had. He felt guilty and awful at the same time. He found himself thinking of Emily on their trip and feelings of remorse would overwhelm him.

Arthur popped open the champagne, filling the fluted glasses to capacity. They made a toast to each other with their tall goblets. The glasses clinked, causing the bubbles to spill over the top. Their laugh was contagious as the lovebirds were kissing and hugging. Suddenly, without any warning, he ripped off the top of her two-piece bathing suit and fondled her voluptuous breast with his hands. Her head was spinning, but not enough. She ripped his suit from his body and lifted her bottom to expose her nudity. Without any warning he was on top of her, their bodies in perfect rhythm. After they were spent they lay in each other's arms, not caring who or what passed their den of iniquity.

He felt Emily dozing off and a smile was on Arthur's face. He thought to himself that if there were an award for a professional actor, he would certainly win. He didn't do anything on purpose, but had to admit that he took advantage of a situation that came up. When Sandy and he first took out their health insurance policy, he did so thinking that he'd go first since they were almost the same age. Men in his family usually died at a fairly early age. Then, when she first developed cancer, he thought of the money that he would get. It wouldn't cost $50,000 for a plot and a casket. He'd have all that money to do what he wanted. When Sandy shoved the rifle into his hands and told him to shoot, he automatically did as she told him to do. He was in a cloud, not realizing what he had done. When his senses returned, he realized that not only would he be getting all that money, but remembered the rider that they signed so many years ago that gave him double for a wrongful death or an accident.

It wasn't until Suzanne and Nancy questioned him that he realized that those two nosey women were the only people who saw him shoot Sandy. When they confronted him, he had no recourse but to put on the greatest performance of his life. He had to admit that his acting was wonderful. No one under those circumstances could perform like he did. No, he literally got away with murder and Suzanne and Nancy couldn't admit or prove that what they saw really happened. He was laughing all the way to the bank!!!

They finished putting their bathing suits back on and headed for the glorious suite that they rented for a month. Arthur had secured his money in an offshore bank that was noted for its discretion. The authorities couldn't find it because he filed a phony corporation and put his money into that account. He had received the name of a man who made counterfeit documents that he and Emily could use forever, if it were up to him. As far as the children were concerned, they had their own lives to worry about, and he did his part in raising them. He didn't let his conscience get in the way. He and Emily would have a grand time, the money would make money and they would be living the life of Riley. When the couple got back to their spacious room, they again went on top of the bed and lying side by side enjoyed the peace and contentment that they felt they deserved. Before getting dressed for a delicious dinner at one of the local restaurants, Arthur proposed a toast. He filled the large fluted wineglass again with a rich tasting wine and entwined their arms, drinking out of each other's goblet. He proposed a toast: "Here's to a wonderful storybook ending. I hope that our lives will be filled with peace, happiness and contentment for years to come. I love you, Emily. Thank you for making me the happiest man in history!" Emily could feel her face flush with excitement.

When she first met Arthur, he wasn't the same man that he was today. As the years passed, she found him to be exciting and wanted him in every way possible. Now her dreams were becoming a reality, and as far as she was concerned, there would be no way that their ideal life would ever end. She looked forward to their nomadic lifestyle and loved being with this man who never ceased to amaze her. Yes, she realized that they would always have assumed names, but that was a price that she was willing to pay. Emily looked over at Arthur and saw the man that she loved with the two filled glasses in his hands. They proposed a toast to each other: "To life, love, happiness, living a care-free life that we both deserve and want. May we never be found out, and if it means being on the run for the rest of our lives, so be it. I wouldn't change this life style for anything!" a happy Arthur decreed. "I only wish us happiness, to be in love forever and always be each other's best friend and lover. To you, my darling, may our lives be blessed and truly happy!" They clanked their glasses and drank the liquid till there was no more to be consumed. They tossed the empty glasses into the fireplace at the end of the room and high fived each other.

The couple couldn't wait until they were seated at a fancy restaurant and then enjoy another day of fun filled, sunny weather. Emily was happy as could be and was truly in love with Arthur. She didn't care if she had to live this nomadic life style forever.

STONEY BROOKE

"Nancy, are you by yourself or are there other people around?" Suzanne asked. "Suzanne why are you asking me such a stupid question; Rich is in the next room, and Mr. Yashuhito is in the kitchen cleaning up. What's your problem?"

Suzanne then admitted, "Well, my dear, I think we're in big-time trouble!" Suzanne then went on to tell Nancy everything that Veronica told her. "We've been had, and I feel like a real schmuck."

Nancy told Suzanne to cool down and take a deep breath. "Are you sure that Veronica is telling you the entire truth?"

"I wouldn't put my hand on a Bible, but from what she said, yeah, I think we've been out foxed."

"No one has heard from Arthur since he cashed in the insurance policy and now he can't be found. He's nowhere. He's one cool character, I'll tell you that."

"Well, he's a rich cool character," Nancy piped in.

"What are we going to do?" asked Suzanne. "It seems that we are accessories to murder and lies. The entire melodrama is a lie."

Suzanne was not one to cry easily but found herself crying into the telephone. "We've been had and not by a professional."

"Suzanne, there has to be something that can be done. Think, for God sake, think."

"I'm thinking and all I can think about is that our asses are in a lot of trouble. We'll have to contact the insurance agency. Maybe they have a person who can track down this money that doesn't rightly belong to Arthur. Can you think of another way of handling this situation?"

"My head is spinning this minute and I'm sitting down. Do you realize that we lied to the authorities, and we could do real time if this is found out," Nancy shouted into the phone. "We need a person, like one of us, who can think with a clear head."

Suzanne was thinking while standing in the kitchen. Mrs. Walsh was still upstairs and no one else was in the house to see or hear what she was saying. "I think I'm going to faint. But before I do, I'm going into my bedroom, lie down and come up with some sort of solution. Don't leave your house until you hear from me, okay?"

"Where the Hell do you think I'll go to? I have the goose bumps all over my body and I'm hyperventilating. Wait, my anxieties are kicking in. I have red, swollen bumps emerging on my body. Oh God, this is awful. I'll be going upstairs, soak in a bathtub and put on medicine to contain the swelling of these welts. I can't believe that we've been fooled, especially by an amateur." Nancy said aloud, "Call me when you think of something and while I'm in the tub my mind will also be working overtime."

With that said, Suzanne hung up the phone and was thinking her best alternative method of madness. She realized that there was an insurance fraud agency and that they looked into illegal matters. With that in mind she got out of bed and returned with her telephone book.

Picking up the telephone she called the two people who she trusted as much as Nancy. She looked into her telephone book and dialed the Boston FBI number. When someone picked up at the other end of the phone, she asked for either Tim Cassidy or Kevin Halloran. She was told to wait. When Tim answered the telephone, he asked who was speaking. All Suzanne could manage to say was, "Would you please have Kevin get on the other line and no one else? This is Suzanne Morse." When Kevin picked up the other line, all Suzanne could manage to say was, "Gentlemen, I think there might be a problem!!!"